THE DIVINE COURAGE TRILOGY BOOK 1

DEFENDER

C.C. URIE

For Kayden

TRIGGER WARNINGS
WARNING: SPOILERS

- Larken is in multiple aircraft accidents and has severe PTSD because of it
- Larken is emotionally abused by her mother and older brother, and her father is an alcoholic
- A war takes place throughout this Trilogy and there is blood, shootings, stabbings, and other injuries
- One character is a narcissistic abuser who becomes obsessed with his victim and has lustful thoughts about her, makes several innuendos, and tries to stalk her which may be upsetting to some readers
- This Trilogy deals with adult themes like abandonment, self-worth, relationships, and other complicated emotions

"Arise, shine, for your light has come, and the glory of the Lord
rises upon you." -Isaiah 60:1 (NIV)

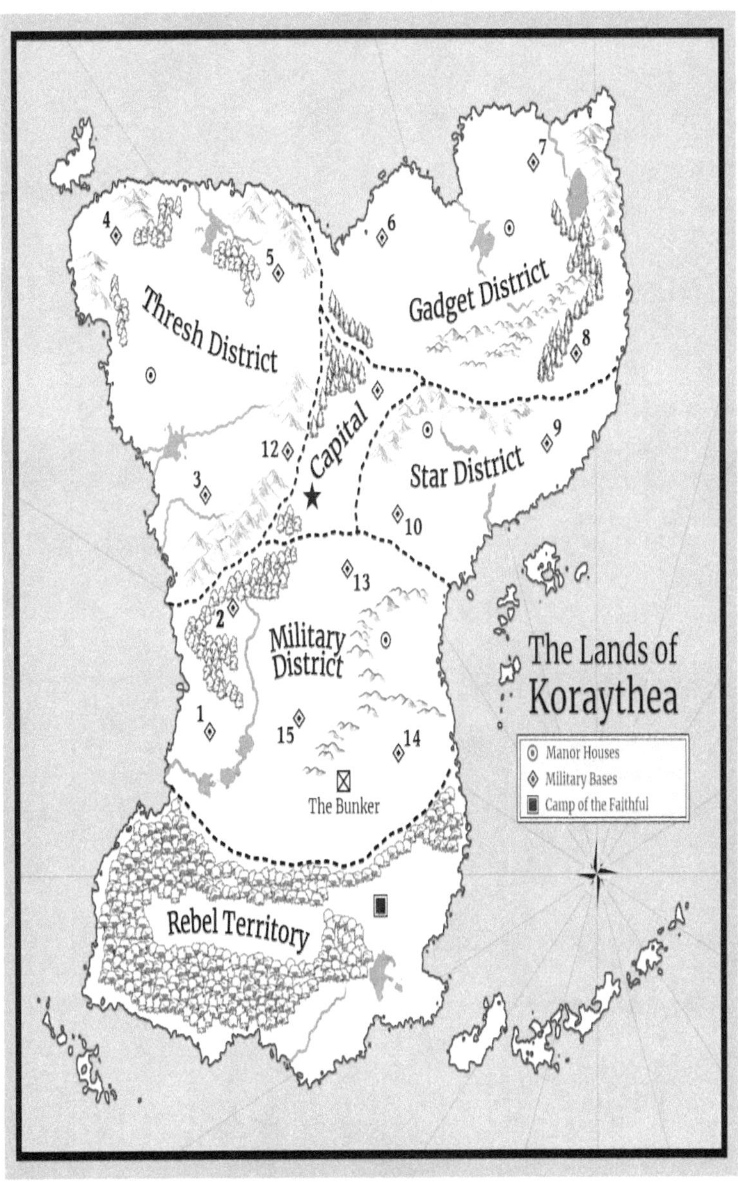

Thresh District
Gadget District
Capital
Star District
Military District
The Bunker
Rebel Territory
The Lands of
Koraythea
Manor Houses
Military Bases
Camp of the Faithful

CHAPTER 1

Larken woke up knowing that it wasn't going to be a good day. She had tossed and turned all night, either nightmares or worry keeping her up. It felt like she had only just slipped into a dreamless sleep when all the lights in her room turned on and the shower started running.

She groaned and buried herself into her bed, using one of her many pillows to cover her face. Her soft sheets caressed the bare parts of her skin, soothing her. Larken wondered what they would do if she just didn't show up. Would they continue as if nothing had happened? Probably not, seeing as she was the main event.

The mattress was firm enough to support her back but soft enough that she sunk in slightly. The pillow muffled the sound of the running water and encased her in blackness. She had just started drifting off again when all her blankets were pulled off of her. Larken sat up, snarling.

"Keep your fangs to yourself, darling," Cam said. The tight black pants he wore looked ridiculous with the off-white designer V-neck that probably cost a small fortune. His shirt pulled tight over his muscular torso, which Larken had always thought was more cosmetically altered than not. With his butterscotch hair and strong jaw, he didn't look like a man nearing his mid-forties, and the women that flocked to him seemed to appreciate his muscular build and dust-colored eyes.

Cameron Brady had once been a renowned stylist. Everyone had wanted him, or, rather, they had wanted his eye for beauty. Net dramas, modeling agencies, the rich and wealthy, anyone that could afford him. He was famous for being able to take the ugly and undesirable and make them stylish. But then there was the incident—a secret affair with a model half his age and the drunken brawl with her father—and then no one wanted to be associated with him. The perfect man for styling the black sheep of the Military District.

"You had better hurry up; your mother won't be happy if you're late."

Larken wanted to tell him exactly what she thought of her mother, but she kept her mouth shut. She purposely ignored the camera that kept an eye on her room. The last thing she needed was a weaselly surveillance guy to tell her mother what she had said and risk the day getting worse. She reluctantly got off the bed, making sure her nightgown didn't bunch up around her hips, and headed for the shower.

"Atta girl," Cam said, and then smacked her backside as she walked past.

Not for the first time, she imagined what it would be like to punch him in the face. She would never see him again after today, so maybe there was still a chance to make her fantasy a reality.

Larken shut the door to her bathroom and locked it. It only took Cam walking in on her in the shower one time to turn locking the door into a compulsion. She stripped off her white cotton nightgown and stepped into the tiled shower. Water sprayed out of jets on the walls and ceiling, creating a mist that shrouded her in a sticky warmth. The blue-green tiles made her think of the ocean, and she wondered if she would ever get a chance to see it before she died.

Hot water pelted her skin, undoing all of the knots in her back and relaxing her. This was going to be one of the things that she would miss. Her shower, and the animals. She had already said goodbye to her horse, Buttercup, and the pack of wolf-hybrids that guarded the grounds. The thought of their wagging tails and lolling tongues burned her eyes. Larken would miss her late-night rides and the way the hybrids would tackle her in their pursuit to find whatever goodies she had hidden away in her pockets.

Pushing the images away, Larken started soaping up her hair. The scent of warm apples filled her mind, leaving room for little else, as she roughly scrubbed her scalp. When she was younger, Larken fantasized about cutting all of her hair off. She thought that, by ridding herself of her wheat-colored locks, she might somehow fit in. That she might somehow *belong* to the family that didn't want her. But when she brought the idea up to Liam, her older brother, he just laughed and told her that the only thing cutting her hair would do was make her uglier than she already was.

A knock sounded at the door, and she could tell by the sound that Cam was annoyed, but she didn't care. Larken stayed under the hot water for a moment longer, wanting to prolong the inevitable for as long as she could. She held her face under the spray, forcing her lungs to their limit. Even when the subtle pounding in her head told her that it was time to breathe, she didn't pull away.

"Larken, you have exactly one minute before I get the guard outside to break down this door."

She pulled her head from the water, her face tight from the heat, and gasped. She rubbed the water from her eyes and face. Turning the shower off, she grabbed a towel and began to dry off. She ran a hand through the condensation on the mirror and looked at the face that greeted her. She hated everything about the woman she saw. Larken had often speculated she was the product of an affair because her teal eyes and blonde hair didn't match either of her parents.

There was another knock and Larken scowled at herself. "I'm coming!"

"Thirty seconds!"

"Cam, if you knock down this door—"

"Your clothes are here, get a move on!" he interrupted.

"I'm brushing my teeth! Just give me a minute!" she called as she turned the faucet on. She wrapped her towel around her body and then loaded up her toothbrush.

The scrubbing sound warred with the running water. She lost herself in the repetitive motion of brushing her teeth. Dipping her head to the stream, she let the icy liquid fill her mouth, relishing in the cool burn. She spit and dropped the toothbrush on the counter.

Body still damp, Larken dropped the towel and pulled on her cotton robe. She picked up the towel again and began rubbing her head with it, trying to dry her hair, and left the bathroom. Cam stood by her closet, arms crossed and foot tapping. He had never liked her, and she had always made sure he knew her feelings were mutual.

"We haven't got all day, you know."

"Because it takes me five hours to get ready," she mumbled.

"Yes, we all know that if it were up to you, you would simply roll out of bed and continue with your day. *Like an animal.*"

"Better an *animal* than a man whose only skill is applying lipstick," she shot back.

Cam only allowed them a moment to glare at each other before he called for the rest of his team. He went into her large closet, muttering about how he wouldn't miss her. Before she could let him know that she wouldn't miss him either, she was pulled into the chair in front of her large vanity. Hands began tugging at her hair and fingers were smearing lotion onto her face. She kept her eyes and mouth closed, not trusting the hands that were invading her personal space. A blow dryer had been turned on, and the back of her head was blasted with heat. Larken chanced cracking an eye and saw that the team had split up, two moving to the closet where Cam was, and the other two staying behind to work on her. Larken's communicator started buzzing on her nightstand. It was either a news story about today or a message from Vallen or Wardell.

She watched the device moving around from the vibrations, and then asked, "Is this really necessary? I mean, I won't be able to look like this after today…I don't think."

The petite woman who pored over the makeup turned with a gasp. "Of course it's necessary! You should always try to look your best."

The woman turned back and lifted a compact with something bright pink to Larken's face. Shaking her head, she put it back and started looking for a different color. Larken took in her slim frame and realized that she hadn't met this woman before. With her big green eyes, pale blonde hair, and manicured nails, she was obviously from the Star District.

Cam walked over and said, "Green and brown are her best colors, Vivian."

"Oh, right!" she beamed at Cam.

Cam gave her a subtle wink that Larken noticed. She rolled her eyes. So, this was the woman Cam was now sleeping with. Larken had heard talk that he had found a new play-thing on his last visit to the Star District. It looked like the gossip was true. She shivered despite the heat from the blow dryer; this woman wasn't much older than her. She never understood how her parents could stomach having him around. Trogar Hale was the Military District's Luminary, the head of the District. As such, the Hale family should be the example of how to follow Maxim. But, Larken wondered if her family truly believed that, and keeping people like Cam around made her question her family's faith even more. As for herself, she tried to live like Vallen's example, but why would she matter to someone so great, when she didn't even matter to her family?

Larken was brought back to herself when the blonde tried to put lipstick on her. She pulled her head back and glared. "I don't wear lipstick."

"Well, why not? It would look good on you."

Cam answered for her before Larken could speak. "She bites her lips when she's on camera, gets it all over her teeth." He glared at her and then added, "An awful habit, really."

Larken glared back as whoever was behind her started curling her hair. She fought the urge to suck in her bottom lip, not wanting to give them the satisfaction of knowing that they were all causing her stress, much like being filmed did. The woman began humming an off-key version of one of the newer hits that Larken hated. Larken clenched her jaw and forced herself to breathe through her annoyance. She might not know what would happen to her after today, but at least she would be on her own.

The curling iron grazed her neck, burning her skin. Larken hissed and barked, "Hey, watch it!"

Her communicator started buzzing again, and Larken knew at once that it was Vallen. If it had been her younger brother, he would have waited for a reply. Her instructor wasn't quite as patient. Vallen Maxwell was a Lieutenant that had been given the rank of General, along with an early retirement, when he had gone out on a top-secret mission with five other men and had been the only one who returned. Since then, he had become Larken's instructor. Her father had insisted that he be the one to train her, much to the annoyance of her mother. And even though Vallen was no-nonsense and probably more stubborn than she was, she loved him like a father, and she would miss him terribly when she left.

Once her makeup and hair were done, Larken was ushered to the closet. She didn't get a good look at her face, and she hoped that she didn't look stupid. Cam watched her like a bird of prey, waiting for her to accidentally rub her eye or something, like she couldn't help but ruin his hard work. She just sighed and asked, "Where is it?"

Cam gestured to a garment bag. Larken unzipped it and felt her mouth drop, horrified.

"I'm not wearing this! This isn't even the uniform!"

"It is for today. Hurry up and get it on."

"I'm not changing with everyone in here."

Cam let out a sound that was half a sigh, half an exaggerated groan. When he realized she wouldn't budge, he started ushering everyone out of her closet. She locked the door after it closed and began loosening her robe. Her closet and her bathroom were the only places in her room that didn't have cameras, and for obvious reasons, she had insisted on the locks.

She started to get dressed, a blush starting at her chest and working its way up her face. This was mortifying. She was supposed to have been issued a uniform, not an edgy outfit that could be found in a fashion show. After pulling on her black shirt, Larken shimmied into tight, dark grey pants that squeezed her calves. Her hips were almost too wide for them, and she had to suck in her stomach to button them. Looking in the mirror, she blushed even hotter. The outfit fit her almost too perfectly. The pants showed off her curves, while the shirt looked more like it was a wrapping instead of an article of clothing. Starting at her left shoulder, fabric loosely stretched down to her right hip, and the fabric on her right shoulder loosely stretched down to her left one. It gapped at the sides under her arms and cut deeply down her front and back.

Her cleavage was on full display, and she wondered if she could pin the shirt before she had to leave. If she could get to her communicator, maybe she could send a picture of the offending material to Vallen, and he could find something else for her. She was used to being in the spotlight, but she had never worn anything this daring before.

The doorknob rattled, and when Cam couldn't get in, he knocked on the door. "Larken, let me in."

"Cam, please don't make me wear this," she pleaded.

"Let me in and we can fix it," he said, sounding strangely kind.

Tears pricked her eyes and she unlocked the door. She didn't want anyone to see her like this, especially a grown man that she had often caught staring at her for longer than necessary. But, what else could she do?

The door opened, and he looked down at her. His eyes lingered in certain places for too long, but he sighed and asked, "Vivian, darling, can you please bring me some pins?"

Larken breathed, relieved that she wouldn't have to go out like this. She pinched the fabric at her chest closed, but Cam smacked her hand away. "Don't wrinkle it."

"Sorry."

Vivian brought a little box full of pins, and Cam gently pushed

Larken deeper into the closet. He had her stand in front of the mirror and stood behind her. Peering over her shoulder, he tugged at the back of the shirt until her front looked more covered. He started pinning, saying, "Your back will be more exposed like this, but I'm assuming that you're okay with that?"

She nodded, grateful that he was somehow making it work. Larken was once again reminded that, even though she thought he was a creep, he was the best at what he did.

An impatient pounding sounded at the door to her room, and she heard it open with a, "I'm sorry, Miss Hale is—"

"I don't care," Vallen's deep voice interrupted.

Larken smiled, knowing that he had pushed his way into her room. He appeared in the doorway to her closet a moment later. The worn black jacket and white shirt he wore were as familiar to her as the weapons he had trained her to use. His eyes roamed over her, narrowing. He stood there for a moment while Cam continued pinning, and then he said, "That isn't standard uniform."

Cam accidentally stabbed Larken with a pin; at least, she thought it was an accident. Either way, she jumped and sucked in a breath.

"Hold still," Cam growled.

"I've been trying to get a hold of you," Vallen said, eyes watching Cam's hands intently.

"I haven't been allowed to look at my communicator."

"Your interview time has changed."

Cam stilled and rounded on Vallen. "To when?"

"Five minutes."

Cam looked at the back of her shirt and said, "It'll have to do. Get your shoes on."

Larken scanned the closet, looking for boots, but only found a pair of impossibly high black pumps. Her eyes widened, and she turned to Cam, but he was already barking orders and pushing his way past Vallen. She stared down at the heels, wondering how she was supposed to walk in them when Cam yelled at her to get a move on.

She marched forward and braced herself by placing a hand on the wall. Crouching, she slipped one on and tentatively tested her balance. Her left ankle wobbled, the heel not sitting right on the carpeted floor. Pushing through it, she reached for the other heel and lifted her right foot. There was a split second of stillness before her ankle rolled painfully and almost snapped. She reached for the wall with her other hand to catch herself, but Vallen appeared behind her, holding her waist and steadying her.

"Those aren't military-issue either."

"Thanks for the help," she said, standing on wobbly legs. He helped her put on her sword belt, and then she clutched his elbow until she was out of her room and on the tiled floor.

"Wait here, I'll get your communicator."

Vallen disappeared back into her room, leaving Larken to stand in the hall and stare at the place where she grew up. Never again would she see the sand-colored carpet or the white walls. Her bed was still a rumpled mess, the pale blue sheets on the ground where Cam had left them. Vallen came back and handed Larken her communicator. They began walking as she looked through her missed messages, news stories that focused on her, and a count-down that was no longer relevant. She cleared the alarm that she had set to go off in one hour and forty-three minutes and started coughing as she breathed in a mouthful of hairspray.

Vallen started yelling at Cam and his team, using his hand to try and clear the fog that was making him cough as well. Vivian started dabbing at Larken's face, making little fixes. She stopped when Vallen said, "You won't need to make her eye pretty if you pop it out."

What Larken had hoped would be a quiet walk to remember the good things about her life had been rushed and stressful. She had no time to think or even breathe. The only thing she could do was put one foot in front of the other and try not to fall over. Her ankles and feet protested the heels, and she wondered again why they couldn't just give her a proper uniform.

"Do you really need to wear that? It's garish," Cam scoffed, indicating her belt.

"You would rather I leave with nothing to defend myself?" Larken asked, trailing her fingers along the worn leather. The holsters were empty; she would be issued new guns, but she refused to leave her sword behind. A stunning weapon made up of glass, crystal, and carbon, with a silver hilt. It had been a gift from Vallen on her sixteenth birthday. The only one she had received.

Before she knew it, she was past the pearly white entrance hall, through the courtyard, and up on the platform that her mother and father used for interviews. Cameras flashed and people were cheering. She couldn't find her family in the crowd, but she knew that they were there…somewhere. Larken wondered if she would be able to say goodbye to Wardell before she was made to leave. He might not be the perfect brother, but at least he accepted her existence. Then again, maybe a child of six couldn't fully understand what was happening today.

"Miss Hale," a woman from the crowd asked, pulling Larken's attention back, "how do you feel?"

"Proud. It is an honor to serve my District and my country." Larken gave the answer that she was told to give the night before when they practiced.

"How is this different from any other TONES Festivals you have experienced in the past?" another woman called.

The TONES, Transition Of Newly Employed Soldiers, Festival was celebrated every year. A full week where anyone who wanted to volunteer to fight could submit their admission form and take up the cause. Larken could remember watching interviews and news specials covering TONES Festivals when she was little. As part of the Hale family, she had been expected to understand everything there was about the military and how it functioned. Every year, the four Luminaries, as well as the Magnate, were required to make a donation of some sort to fight the resistance. In the years before, the Military District had donated arii or the plans for a new weapon that could be used. This year, the Star District donated a large sum of arii, the Thresher District agreed to keep supplying food to the various bases across Koraythea, and the Gadget District donated new communicators and gun attachments. And this year, the Military District decided to donate her.

Larken stared blankly at the woman from Star District with lavender-colored hair who had asked the question. "This TONES Festival is different because today I am enlisting. I will be heading out to the frontlines after this interview."

The reporters started fighting each other for her attention.

"Are you scared?"

"What will your uniform look like?"

"What division will you be in?"

"One at a time, please," she said. "No, I'm not scared. My uniform will be standard issue, and I'm not sure where I will be placed yet. But, I will proudly go wherever they have need of me."

The voices and the lights were becoming too much, and the questions were getting further and further from the point. When someone asked about who would do her hair when she was at the base, she looked at Vallen with pleading eyes. He stepped forward and said, "That will be all. Miss Hale has an aircraft to catch."

The crowd erupted into disappointed groans, wanting her to stay longer. But she couldn't get away fast enough. Their small group pushed through the crowd, Cam's team helping keep the reporters at bay. They reached the Vixon 720, a shiny black and gray luxury four-seater aircraft shaped kind of like a trilobite, and Vallen opened the door for her.

She turned to the beauticians and stylists that had tormented her for the last six years and said, "Goodbye."

Cam, aware of the cameras on them, pulled her in for a hug, almost as if they had grown close in their time together. She stiffened and let him have his moment in the spotlight. She could see the headlines: *Heartbroken Cameron Brady Says Goodbye To The Military District Sweetheart.*

When she thought the hug went on for long enough, Larken tried to pull back. Cam just smirked at her while still holding her at arms-length and said, "Too bad we never got to see if you hated me in bed too."

Larked glared, hauled her arm back, and punched him in the face. Her fingers hurt, but it was nothing compared to the glee she felt over his wails of pain. Blood was already staining the front of his designer shirt, and he clutched at his nose with both hands. Vivian screamed and looked like she was going to faint. The reporters went wild, trying to push their way to the aircraft and ask more questions. Larken only smirked and got into the aircraft. Her new life was waiting.

CHAPTER 2

"What?" Larken grumbled over the buzzing of her communicator.

Vallen just continued to glare at her.

"He deserved it," she said, defensively.

"I have no doubt that he did."

"So, what's the problem then?"

"That temper of yours is going to get you into trouble in your new life."

"If the men at base don't proposition me, then we won't have an issue."

Vallen just continued glaring.

A particularly violent vibration shook Larken's communicator. She looked down to see a headline about an interview her brother had given just moments before. Opening the link, Liam's face filled her screen. He had their mother's light brown eyes, and their father's dark brown hair and jawline. Liam looked like everyone else in the Military District; the only difference was that he had been born a Luminary's son.

"And what do you think happened, Mr. Hale?"

Her brother scoffed and answered, *"I think that she can't go anywhere without trying to be the center of attention. This TONES Festival isn't just about her. She—"*

Larken closed the interview, ashamed at the tears that burned her eyes. She shouldn't care what he thought, what any of them thought. But she did. She wanted her father to be proud of her, her mother to look at her with kind eyes, and for her brothers to love her. She wanted to be more than just a donation to the cause.

"Larken," Vallen growled.

"I'm fine!" she hissed, wincing at the pathetic way her voice cracked.

Vallen sighed and pushed up from his seat across from her. He resettled himself on the one next to her and pulled her close. Larken tried to fight the tears that threatened to fall, but in the end, she couldn't. The only family that she had ever known was holding her, and she didn't even know if she would see him again.

"They're just a bunch of fools."

"Are they?" she looked up, searching his dark eyes.

He grunted, the sentimentality of the moment obviously making him uncomfortable.

Larken sniffed back her tears and pulled out her communicator to check her eyes. Vallen collected himself as she wiped away the runny makeup. When her instructor didn't move back to his seat, she paused and looked up at him. He looked at her intensely, but no malice shone in his eyes. She waited for him to look away, but he never did.

Her forehead wrinkled as she asked, "Can I help you?"

"You have a smart mouth."

"Thanks?" She went back to fixing her makeup, but his eyes were still on her. She looked up again and asked, *"What?"*

"You are going to meet a lot of new people. I want you to remember what I taught you."

"Punch first and ask questions later?"

Vallen didn't look impressed. "No."

"Give them two sentences instead of one before deciding if they are an enemy or an ally."

He nodded.

"What sort of people am I going to meet?"

Vallen just sat there, jaw set and arms crossed. She wasn't going to get any more out of him. Sighing, she asked, "Well, can you at least tell me why I should be worried about meeting enemies on the frontlines? Isn't that why I'm going?"

He looked at her for so long that she thought he might not answer. But he muttered, "Who said anything about the frontlines?"

She felt her eyes grow, and she knew that that was the last he would speak before they reached their destination. This Vixon belonged to her parents, and she would be surprised if it wasn't bugged. Who knew who could be listening in? Vallen was smarter than to give away all of his secrets, but what exactly did he know? Larken tried to distract herself with her communicator, but her mind was spinning.

What did he mean? Will I have to look out for double agents? Her stomach fell. *Will there be men there working for my mother? And what will happen to him for warning me?*

Larken shook her head and started playing some music on her communicator. Happy and jumpy melodies spilled from the device, and her head was soon bobbing along. Shadric Barlow's tenor voice filled the cabin, and his sweet words of summer love and kisses in the rain had her smiling. It was when she started humming that Vallen cleared his throat. Larken turned the volume up. He looked out the window and she almost missed the tick in his jaw that told her he was fighting a smile. Almost.

"Aren't you a little old to still be listening to that?"

"I will never outgrow my love for Shadric Barlow. If I did, it wouldn't be true love," Larken said dreamily. She had first heard him sing when she was thirteen, and she had been in love with his voice ever since, much to the annoyance of Vallen.

Vallen grunted and Larken laughed. She let herself get lost in the music and stared out the window. The world zoomed past underneath them, and Larken didn't want to miss a second of it. She had never been allowed to leave the grounds of the Military Manor before, unless it was for a gala or some other District function that she needed to play the part of the beloved daughter for. The land that flew by underneath them was beautiful. Well, the subdivisions and buildings weren't, but the ponds and sparse plant life were. They were traveling to the very edge of the District, to the border between the colonized world and the wilderness. Larken had been four when the rebellion had started and a rebel force called the Faithfuls had broken away and escaped past the border. That was also when Vallen had come into her life.

She had never been brave enough to ask him about that mission. He had always been open and honest with her, even telling her the things she didn't want to hear. Her instructor never kept anything from her that he thought she needed to know. But, even though she was afraid to ask about that particular mission, she didn't think Vallen would tell her about it. His features always went dark when the rebellion was brought up in front of him, and she often wondered if it was because he had lost his whole squad, or if it had to do with something else. And now, she was about to see everything he had firsthand.

Her stomach clenched, and as if in answer, the Vixon bounced. Larken grabbed the black leather seat, her knuckles going white. The Vixon dipped again. Vallen pressed a button on the wall and the intercom sparked to life. "Get it together!" he barked. "We have a nervous flyer back here."

A masculine voice that cracked from the technology answered, "Sorry, General Maxwell. We're experiencing a little turbulence. Everything should be fine in a moment." His voice didn't sound much older than Larken's, and she forced herself to remember that he wouldn't be General Vallen Maxwell's pilot if he hadn't passed all the proper flying tests.

Vallen released the button and pressed another. A compartment opened, revealing two whisky glasses, but instead of the dark gold liquid, they were full of water. He grabbed one and handed it to her. The Vixon jolted again, and a little bit of the liquid sloshed over the side.

"Careful," he said.

Larken grabbed the glass and sipped at the icy contents. Her stomach started to settle, but then there was another bump. Larken tightened her hand on the glass just as her music started cutting in and out. She looked up at Vallen with wide eyes just as the intercom sparked back to life.

"General Maxwell, sir, I think there might be something wrong. The controls—"

But they never heard what was wrong with the controls, because something rammed into the side of the Vixon, making Larken scream and drop the glass. It thudded softly on the carpeted floor, the water was instantly absorbed, and all that remained aside from the wet spot were the chunks of ice. She scrambled for her communicator, but the screen kept glitching between her music, recent news stories, her messages, and the last episode of the net drama she had watched.

"*Vallen?*" she half-cried, half-moaned in her worry.

He just pushed her back into her seat and started pulling out the contents underneath. First, he pulled on what looked like a backpack, but she recognized it as a survival bag. Her palms were so sweaty that she dropped her communicator. She grabbed it, but as she did, the Vixon started to dip. This time though, it didn't pull back up. Larken looked out the window, horrified but unable to help herself. Black smoke followed them as they dropped.

"Looks like they took out one of the engines," Vallen said. Larken felt like she was going to be sick. She must have looked it too, because Vallen narrowed his eyes at her before saying, "Bite your tongue or something; we don't have time for that."

Doing as he ordered, she bit down hard enough to feel pain, but not so hard that she might accidentally bite her tongue off if they were to jolt again. She looked back out the window, then chided herself for doing so. Watching her death approach wasn't going to help the situation. She reached for her harness, but Vallen grabbed her wrist and shook his head.

"At this point, it would be more dangerous. I might not be able to get you out when we crash."

When.

There was no if. Only when.

Maxim, help us!

Her stomach flipped like it did on an elevator as the speed of their descent picked up. Sweat collected at her temple and the back of her neck burned. Larken grabbed at her wrist, but at finding no hair tie, her eyes welled with tears. A calloused hand cupped her face and forced her to look up.

"Hey, I'm here."

His hand felt so warm, just like his dark eyes. Larken's eyes roamed over his soft features. She wasn't used to seeing him without any frown lines and was once again reminded of how handsome he was, even at the age of forty-one. He had only ever looked this way once before that she could remember. Larken had followed him to his rooms, not wanting to be around her family. It wasn't uncommon for her to do that, but that time had been different. There had been a picture out on the coffee table of his sitting room. She had looked at it to find a man with skin the color of ebony with his arm around a petite blonde woman, and a baby Vallen. He had answered her when she had asked about it, like he always did. That day had been the tenth anniversary of their death. He had the same expression on his face then as he did now.

"We'll get through this."

She nodded, and he pulled her close again. No sooner did she close her eyes, than they hit. Her teeth knocked together painfully, but Vallen was as unmovable as a boulder in a strong current. The Vixon slid through the earth; the sound of crunching metal had her wincing and tightening her hand on the lapels of his jacket. When they stopped moving, a sob escaped her, and she shook as Vallen rubbed his hand up and down her back.

The door, that was now more above them than across from them, opened on squeaky hinges. The pilot, a boy who couldn't be more than sixteen, looked in. He had a dimple on his left cheek and a small spattering of freckles. His hair was close-cropped and the same shade of dirt brown as his eyes. "Everyone alright?"

Larken started laughing hysterically. Her hands were still shaking badly, and both the pilot and Vallen had to help her out. The boy's hands were soft as they gripped hers and pulled her out. Vallen had grabbed her waist and lifted her. Larken's whole body felt slow, like something inside of her was broken. Neither the boy nor Vallen seemed fazed by the crash, but then again, they had both probably been in more than one before.

The pilot kept up a steady stream of chatter, trying his best to keep things jovial. He pointed south and said, "We still have about a hundred or so miles to go, but we passed a subdivision not too long ago. We should be able to call for help there and—"

The sound of a gunshot broke the air, and the boy jolted forward slightly. His mouth parted, and blood trickled from the corner of it. Larken screamed as he fell, his blood quickly pooling on the dirt. The bullet had hit him between the shoulder blades, just under his neck, turning his light blue uniform dark crimson.

"Get your shoes off now," Vallen growled.

Larken kicked off her heels and had barely righted herself before catching the two guns Vallen tossed to her. Normally, she would prefer her sword. But what good would that do her when they were being shot at? He took off towards the subdivision they had passed, and she followed. Every stick and rock that she stepped on cut into her feet, but she kept running. They passed a few news drones laying on the ground, the ones that often followed her family's aircraft and hovers, trying to find a story. One of them was close enough that she could see the screen opposite of the lens glitching like her communicator had. For a split second, she wondered how much of the crash the thing had been able to capture before it hit the dead spot and fell to the ground. Larken had a new worry. Had their crash been reported, or had the Vixon glitched so badly that it had been unable to send a distress call?

Larken looked over her shoulder often, terrified that she would be shot at next. Vallen was just ahead of her, and she couldn't catch up, no matter how fast she ran. She looked over her shoulder again and then collided with something. The smell of cloves and sandalwood told her that it was Vallen. She peeked around his broad frame to find a group of eight men heading toward them.

Every single one of them wore a military-grade black helmet and had the vizors down, covering their faces. They started firing their guns at them, and Vallen turned and pushed her. She tripped over her feet but was able to get control over her body. Her instructor was now her shield, never faltering behind her. Occasionally he would fire off a shot of his own, but he was more concerned with getting her back to the destroyed Vixon. His cry had her almost tripping as she turned back.

"Keep moving!" he shouted, now limping. Blood glistened in the afternoon sunlight on his left thigh, making the fabric of his dark pants look glossy.

"Vallen!"

"I said keep moving!" He pushed her. "Get as far from here as possible."

"Please don't leave me!"

"Just keep running, Larken. I won't be far behind."

His lie almost had her knocking him over and running into the fight herself, but the look in his eyes had her nodding. She sped up, his silent plea choking her. There was more gunfire and she wanted to look back. In fact, she almost did, but something whizzed by her face. The men who had been hiding out and shot the pilot were running towards them now. Three men before her, the remaining men behind her. Larken didn't know what to do. She was afraid that no matter which way she decided to run, there would be someone waiting for her. The Vixon was at least bulletproof, so it was probably the safest place to hide.

Making up her mind, Larken started running in a zig-zag, dodging bullets on her way back to the destroyed Vixon. She just prayed that it was Vallen who would tell her the coast was clear, and not one of the masked men telling her of his death. She was almost there when a sound like a roaring engine caught her attention. She looked up, and out of the sky hurtled a military-grade aircraft. A door was open and three men, wearing the same helmets as the men attacking them, were firing guns at the men on the ground.

Larken stopped and turned, following the aircraft with her whole body as it flew over her. They were making quick work of the attackers and gave Larken the chance to help her instructor. She rushed to Vallen's side. He had been shot again in the right shoulder, and she drew his left arm up over her shoulders. He leaned heavily on her, his teeth gritted in pain.

"I *hate* being shot."

"I can imagine," she panted, still watching the aircraft.

Once the last man was down, the aircraft began its descent and was soon idling about fifty feet from them. Vallen stuck his hand out in front of him and started touching his palm, one finger at a time.

"Everything seems to be working at least," Larken said.

He grunted. The three men jumped out of the aircraft and started running towards them. They were wearing dark grey uniform pants with black T-shirts that stretched over their chests and arms. Larken wondered if they just didn't have enough time to get into their tactical gear, or if they simply didn't think that they needed it. One of the men had a gun in each hand, another had an ancient-looking shotgun, and the tallest had a later model tech-gun that fired continuous rounds that could be altered to explode when the bullets hit. The men reached them before they closed half the distance.

Two of the men were about the same size, and they were both a little taller than Vallen. The man with the two handguns looked closer to her height. He put his guns away and opened his vizor, revealing a dark blond beard and hard green eyes that made Larken think of ice. The man with the shotgun opened his vizor as well. He had dark brown eyes that danced like he was laughing at a joke only he knew. They matched his lanky build somehow, and so did his stubbly jaw. The man with the tech-gun kept his vizor down, and Larken was left to guess at what he looked like. He reminded her of a mountain, huge and muscular, and she wondered how he would fare in a spar with Vallen.

"Lookie here, boys! Seems we found ourselves a little, lost bird!" the lanky one said with a thick drawl.

The shorter one rolled his eyes before walking up to help Vallen. Vallen just waved him away, not leaving Larken's side.

The muscly one reached up and touched the side of his helmet before saying, "General Maxwell and Miss Hale are in custody."

His voice was like gravel, harsh and smoky. It gave Larken goosebumps and she hoped that Vallen thought her shiver was from the aftershocks of everything that had just happened and not from hearing this man's voice. She had to look away from the stranger, so she distracted herself by trying to get a good look at Vallen's wounds. He bled freely, but he insisted he didn't need any more help than what Larken could give him. She was the only one he allowed close to him. The five of them made their way to the aircraft, the three men taking up their weapons and scanning the area as they did.

The aircraft wasn't shiny or sleek like the newer models, but clunky, steel grey, and looked like it could carry about fifteen people. The men turned to try and help Vallen into the aircraft, but before he made any other movements, he asked, "What song does the brown bird sing?"

The muscly one with the gravelly voice answered, "The one that Maxim taught her."

Larken didn't know what they were talking about, but the answer seemed good enough for Vallen. He allowed Larken to help him forward and then tried to hoist himself up into the aircraft on his own. One glare from Larken had him accepting help from the men. The muscly one and the shorter one were both up in the aircraft, and they helped pull Vallen in. The shorter one and Vallen disappeared into the cabin, and the other turned and pulled off his helmet.

Wait, she thought, still confused about the question, *am I the bird?*

As if to answer her question, the lanky man cooed, "Little Bird, where are your shoes?"

Larken looked down at her feet. They were dark from the dirt and bleeding in spots. She winced and answered, "Over by the Vixon."

"I'll get 'em," he said and started running off in that direction.

Grabbing onto the first thing she could reach, Larken started trying to pull herself into the aircraft. As she looked for something else to grab onto, a hand was thrust in her face.

"Thanks," she said, grabbing it and looking up.

Her breath caught in her chest as she was greeted with a pair of hard hazel eyes. They flashed between brown, gold, and green, making her think of a thunderstorm. His jaw was set, clean-shaven, and it looked like it had been carved from stone instead of bone and flesh. His nose was a little crooked like it had been broken before and left to heal on its own. Normally, medics could fix something like that easily, but it made him look real and not polished like a Star. He was the most beautiful thing she had ever seen. He was also frowning at her.

Larken felt suddenly embarrassed, but she wasn't sure why. Was it because she looked like a mess? Or that she was most likely the reason he had to come all the way out here to rescue them? Whatever the reason, she couldn't look him in the eye as he helped her up. After he let go of her, he started messing with a pack that had been strapped to the ceiling. She clenched and unclenched her fist, trying to forget the warmth of his calloused hand.

Looking around, she found Vallen settled on a bench and that the man with the beard had pulled out a medical kit. He opened it, but Vallen pushed his hands away. She rolled her eyes and took a better look at the cabin. Nothing, in particular, stood out to her, even though she had never been in a military aircraft before. The benches had individual seats in them, lipping to form the outline of a person's thighs. There was a completely flat one that Vallen now occupied, his leg stretched out and the cloth of his pants torn away from the bullet wound. The windows were large, and more than one full-sized man could easily scout the area from the air. Everything was grey, white, and orange and smelled like cheap cleaning products.

The aircraft dipped a little, and Larken lurched for the nearest unmovable object. Vallen, even though he was currently focused on examining his injuries, growled, "We just crashed out of the sky. Please refrain from shaking the aircraft."

The lanky man who had caused the dip when he had leaped into the aircraft apologized sheepishly, giving Vallen a small bow of his head. He took off his helmet and grinned at Larken as he tossed it into a bin that had been latched to the floor. Having a better look at his face, she noticed that it was thin and boyish, and his hair was dark and messy. He walked up and handed Larken her shoes, saying, "I can see why you ditched them. Not the best for dodgin' bullets."

She knew that he was trying to be friendly, but she couldn't bring herself to smile at him. Her nerves were still fried, and the adrenaline had started to leave her body.

"Loxly's the name. Loxly Beau."

"L-Larken Hale," she stuttered as her hands started shaking again.

The brooding giant walked past her, his chest rubbing against her arm in the small space, and sat in the cockpit. "Loxly, you coming? Or are you going to keep flirting instead?"

Larken blushed from her roots to her toes, and with her free hand, she grabbed her arm where he had brushed against her. Loxly just grinned even wider and gave her a slight bow. "I'd love to stay and talk, Little Bird, but I'm our ride home." He winked and jumped into the pilot's seat.

Realizing that these three were the only men here, Larken wondered who had been flying when they were shooting their assailants. She must have been wondering out loud, because Loxly hit the dash affectionately and said, "This baby's got auto-landin'. Gives me the chance to play sharpshooter."

Her knees wobbled and she looked for a place to sit. She wanted

to stay out of Vallen's way and let the green-eyed man help him, but he obviously had other ideas. He barked her name and told her to *come here*. When she had situated herself on the bench across from him, he said, "Let me see."

"Vallen, they aren't that bad. I mean, you're the one who got shot. Can't you just focus on yourself for a minute?"

"No."

She sighed, knowing that he wouldn't drop it, and lifted her right foot. He rested it on his good knee and tore open an antibacterial wipe. Vallen got to work, telling her with his eyes to *suck it up* whenever she hissed in pain. After he smeared the bottom of her foot with an ointment and wrapped it, he motioned with his fingers for her other one.

"This can't be good for your shoulder, you know."

"It went through, doesn't even hurt that bad anymore."

"What does today put you at? *Um, ow!*"

"Nineteen," he said, not sounding the least bit sorry as he pulled a giant splinter from her heel.

"That means I'm still in the lead at zero."

Vallen looked up then, his eyes deadly serious. "And it better stay that way."

His words rattled her, but she still gave him a playful salute.

"I'm serious, Larken."

She sobered. "I know." Larken looked around the aircraft. At the medical supplies, the guns, the miscellaneous pieces of tactical gear, and said, "I just don't know if I will be able to keep that promise anymore."

CHAPTER 3

When Captain Soren Deckard woke up that morning, he had expected it to be a normal TONES Festival day. He had expected to see starving children dropped off so their families could receive compensation for their *donations*. Or teary-eyed teens saying goodbye to their parents or younger siblings. Maybe even a proud adult or two that were excited to be volunteering to fight the rebellion. He did *not* expect to go flying out into the middle of nowhere to rescue the newest member of his squad.

He had watched the whole thing happen. Loxly and Hinlee had been bickering about her hair, like they often did. She liked to keep it short, something about it not getting in the way, and Loxly insisted that guys liked girls with long hair.

She had retorted with a, "Brecker likes me just fine, thanks."

Brecker, in turn, glared at the woman who had him wrapped around her finger. "I do *not* want to be in the middle of this."

A news station was on in the background, muted but still filling the common room with aerial views of the Military District Manor. Images of the white marble columns, sprawling gardens, and training fields filled the large screen. Soren had been to the place only twice, and each time was to receive a change in title. When he had been promoted to Major, and then a few months ago when he had been promoted to Captain. The screen went back and forth between live videos of the excited crowd and a reporter with lavender hair. Soren didn't really care about the reporter or the Manor, but he did care about getting a good look at the Military District's Sweetheart. The Hale family had been paraded on television, visited the frontlines for morale, were *literally* everywhere. But, Soren couldn't remember for the life of him what little Miss Larken Hale looked like.

Hinlee laughed at something Loxly said, and she snuggled into Brecker's side. He was quiet but looked at Hinlee like her laugh was the most magical sound in the world. Levi threw darts at a dartboard that he had stuck a picture of a black silhouette on. He had just landed one where the figure's right eye should have been. If Soren was stupid, he would have thought that the man had missed. But he wasn't stupid; Levi had an accuracy that could put even the most seasoned soldier to shame.

A flash of wheat-colored something caught his eye, and he suddenly felt annoyed. The elusive Miss Hale was now on the screen; her hair held loose curls that just barely brushed her shoulders, and makeup colored her face. She looked more like a doll than a soldier. A pretty doll, he'd give her that, but a doll nonetheless. And dolls didn't fight in wars. They played dress-up and lounged around all day, watching as the world went on around them.

Disappointment burned his blood and Soren turned back to Loxly and Hinlee's conversation. They were now discussing guns. Hinlee was a fan of automatics, while Loxly liked his ancient shotgun that his grandfather had given him when he had left the farm.

Levi's rough laugh caught Soren's attention, and he looked over at his Second in Command. He watched the television, and Soren looked as well. He saw the District's Sweetheart smirking as she climbed into a glossy black aircraft, while a man, who was obviously from Stars, clutched at his nose as it bled profusely.

"What happened?"

Without looking at him, Levi answered, "Looks like the princess has one heck of a right hook."

"Oh yeah!" Loxly said. "Wasn't she trained by General Maxwell?"

"Is that why she decided to enlist?" Hinlee asked.

"My arii is on her family getting rid of her," Levi said.

"That's a little harsh," Hinlee chastised.

"It's probably the truth." Levi shrugged. "I know what it looks like to not be wanted. And trust me, she isn't wanted there. None of her family were there to see her off."

Hinlee hummed and then asked, "What do you think, Decks?"

"I don't care either way, just as long as she does what she's told."

"Lady and gentlemen," Loxly drawled, "our favorite stick in the mud, Captain Sourpuss."

Both Hinlee and Brecker laughed.

The conversation went on, Brecker eventually getting up to play darts with Levi. Loxly had pulled out his shotgun and started cleaning it. Hinlee filed her nails, the scratching sound grating Soren's nerves. He thought about going for a quick workout before their new squad member arrived, but Hinlee gasped and pointed at the television. "Quick, someone unmute it!"

Soren looked up and watched as the luxury aircraft that the girl and General Maxwell had just gotten into not even an hour ago fell from the sky. A plume of black smoke trailed behind it, and then it collided with the earth. The screen pixelated, showing flashes of the closely approaching ground before going completely black. The television then switched to a woman in her thirties with hair so pale it looked silver.

Her mouth formed soundless words, and Loxly unmuted the television in time to hear her say, "*—no idea how the crash happened. All we can reveal at this time is that there were technical difficulties with the drones, and we are left to assume the aircraft experienced the same problems. As for the engine,*" the screen changed to show a slow-motion review of the footage, "*we can clearly see a missile-type projectile hit the left rear engine. We have no word on if there are any survivors,*" *or if the Faithfuls are the ones responsible for the crash."* The screen switched back to the reporter. *"As of now, the Hale family has not released any comments, understandably so."* The reporter then went on talking about the TONES Festival and how Miss Hale was involved.

Soren was already in motion before his communicator started wailing, indicating that there had been an emergency. "Levi, Loxly, you're with me."

"Yes, sir!" they said together, suddenly serious.

The three of them gathered up their weapons and rushed to the aircraft designated for their squad, an Arsene 890 that could hold up to twelve people. Loxly wasted no time hopping into the pilot's seat and giving the engine life. The beast fired up and was out of the hangar and on its way to the crash site in less than a minute. But the Miss Hale from the interview looked to be a far cry from the one they had found.

Now, watching their reflections in the mirror that sat in the middle of the dash, Soren could see General Maxwell waving away Levi's help, and the girl sitting across from him. Her hair still held somewhat of a curl, but her eyes were red-rimmed and mascara stained her cheeks. He wondered if it had been the crash that had her crying, or if she had already been in hysterics before they were hit. If the aircraft had indeed glitched, they would have had trouble staying airborne. But, then again, maybe it was watching her instructor get shot that had caused her to cry. Soren watched as the General cleaned her bare feet and bandaged them up. It reminded him of a story that his mother had told him long ago, back before she had traded him to the military for arii, about a man that worshiped Maxim cleaning the feet of a dirty beggar.

He watched as General Maxwell coaxed smiles from the girl, despite his clear discomfort. Soren wondered what the two had been through to create such a bond between them. They acted more like father and daughter than teacher and pupil. General Maxwell reached up and cupped her cheek, causing her chin to wobble slightly.

"Kinda weird, ain't it?" Loxly asked.

"What do you mean?"

"He's supposed to be the scariest guy out there, but she doesn't seem to be afraid of him."

"No, but why would she be? He's been employed at the Manor for the past sixteen years. She's probably just used to him."

Loxly shook his head. "It's still a little weird."

Soren just grunted and went back to watching her.

"You keep starin' at her, and I might have to consider you competition."

Ignoring him, Soren asked, "You like her?"

"You don't?"

"No. Now, shut up and pay attention."

Loxly laughed and then started pretending to panic. "Oh no, Cap, there's a huge cloud in front of us! I don't think we're gonna make it!"

Soren just growled low in his throat. That had Loxly laughing again, and then he started up a conversation, one that only he was a part of. Soren would occasionally nod his agreement, but he would be lying if he said his attention wasn't on the girl. She eventually fell asleep, and strands of her wheat-colored hair stuck to the condensation on the window. General Maxwell, a man that Soren had always admired, stood shakily and awkwardly seated himself next to her. He shrugged off his black jacket and covered her with it. She snuggled in close to him after he wrapped his arm around her. The sight of it did something weird to Soren's chest, but he couldn't look away from her reflection. Her shaking had stopped, and her lips parted as her body fully gave in to its exhaustion.

Levi murmured something too quiet for him to hear, but he heard General Maxwell say, "She hates flying, to begin with, but she's tough. She'll get through it."

Levi's voice hummed again, and General Maxwell answered, "I'm fine, I've been through worse."

"Are you even listenin' to me?" Loxly asked.

"You said something about upgrading your shotgun, but you never end up doing it."

Loxly raised an eyebrow at him. "Lucky guess."

Soren grunted.

"Here's an idea, how 'bout you take over, and I can stare at the pretty girl?"

His glare had Loxly laughing. He didn't want Loxly to get the wrong impression, so he said, "What Levi said earlier is bothering me. I'm just trying to figure it out."

"What? That the Vendor should do away with the pickled herring? I don't think it's that bad. I don't like it myself, but I don't think they should completely do away with it."

Soren sighed.

"Look, Cap, not everyone willin'ly volunteers like me. She has her own story and she'll tell us about it when she's ready. You need to give her the same amount of time as you did Levi and the rest of us."

Loxly had a point. Soren couldn't rush her, as much as he wanted to. He thought back to her interview. She hadn't looked excited or happy; her teal eyes had been flat. And the only time she came close to smiling was after she punched that Star guy. No, she definitely wasn't here by choice. So, what was it?

Soon, Loxly was calling out, "Harnesses on! We'll be dockin' in five!"

Soren watched as General Maxwell shook awake a rough-looking Miss Hale. Levi took his seat and buckled himself in, not sparing the other two a glance. Loxly started flipping switches and humming an off-key tune that was often played at tabernacle. He grabbed the little radio and held a button on the side as he said, "Squad 19, comin' in hot."

A crackly voice responded, "Roger that, Squad 19. What aircraft will be docking?"

"Arsene 890."

"Cleared for landing."

Loxly dropped the radio and the cord recoiled into the dash, locking the radio into place with a little *click*. "Hold on to your boots, folks, we're goin' in."

The Arsene dropped smoothly until they were level with the hangar. Loxly flew in and landed flawlessly. A small jolt shook the aircraft when it touched the ground and had the girl jumping, but General Maxwell was quick to squeeze her shoulder. Soren decided that he agreed with Loxly; it was weird watching the fiercest man that had ever gone through the military doting on the girl as if she were a puppy.

Levi was the first up and had the door open in seconds. Soren was up next, and he hopped out of the Arsene as the District Sweetheart helped General Maxwell to his feet. Together, the four of them were able to help him out of the aircraft. Somehow, Loxly and Levi ended up flanking the General, leaving Soren to help the girl down.

She stood in the doorway, heels in one hand, and the blood-stained jacket gripped closed with the other. Her eyes focused on anything that wasn't him, and she said, "I can do it myself."

Her voice was a sweet soprano that sounded like melted butter and birdsong. Fitting, since her name was Larken. He just shook his head and said, "Princess, if you try and jump out of that aircraft, you're gonna hurt your feet even more."

Her big doe eyes landed on him and narrowed, making them look more green than blue at the moment. *"I said I could do it."*

Soren just grunted and reached up, grabbing her hips, not giving her a choice. He tried to ignore the way her curves felt underneath his hands as he pulled her from the Arsene, but the warmth of her skin could be felt through her tight pants, and it did something weird to his stomach. He set her down, none too gently, and ignored her wince as he slapped the button that closed the door. He only watched long enough to see that it started lowering before turning back to the girl. "If it hurt that bad," he said snidely, "imagine landing on them after falling five feet."

He left her huffing by the Arsene and caught up with the other three. Loxly laughed good-naturedly, and General Maxwell threatened to break him in half. Soren knew that if anyone was capable of that feat, it would be the General. The girl caught up to them, hanging back a little. She hadn't made a sound, and Soren didn't dare look over his shoulder at her, but he knew that she was there. He couldn't even hear her breathing, but what else could he expect from someone who had been raised by General Vallen Maxwell?

Levi reached out and pulled the door to the hanger open, and they were accosted with shouts and camera flashes. The girl fell back, and he looked over at her. She curled in on herself slightly and looked like she wanted to run the other way. Was she afraid of the limelight? Or was she embarrassed at how she looked? Soren looked out and saw Brecker and Hinlee trying in vain to push the crowd back while live feed of their struggles played across a few of the televisions in the background. Some members of other squads tried to help as well, but most of them just stood there, waiting to get a good look at the Daughter of the Military for themselves.

A bubbly Star with cotton-candy-colored hair bounced forward and pushed past Soren. She waltzed up to the girl and exclaimed, "Oh, dear! Just look at you!"

"Who are you?" she asked.

"I'm Cindy, your new stylist!"

"Where's Cam?"

Cindy's smile faltered a touch. "They thought that, given the circumstances, it might be better to switch things up a bit. I'll be working with you for the next few months and see how things go from there."

All color left the girl's face. "*Months?*"

"Yup!" Cindy took a step back. "Now, let me get a look at you. Well, there isn't really anything we can do about your appearance. But, then again, it might be better to send you out as you are. *Tug a couple heartstrings,*" she said with a wink.

"Wait, what? Send me out where?"

"You need to let the world know that you're alive and well, Miss Hale."

"But I'm not well. I was in a crash and my friend has been shot. *Twice!* We need to see a medic."

"All in good time," Cindy said, waving her hand in the air like she was capable of brushing her new charge's problems away. "We can all go to the medic when you're finished. Then, we can talk about your new look."

The girl's eyes narrowed. "What's wrong with the way I look?"

"Oh, um, nothing," the stylist muttered, her eyes roaming over the girl, contradicting her statement. "We can talk about all of that later. But *now*, we need to get you out there."

"But I don't want—"

Cindy just threw her head back and laughed as she grabbed the girl's elbow. "Don't be silly, of course you do. Every girl likes getting attention."

"That's not even a little bit true," she argued, as she was pushed out into the sea of reporters.

CHAPTER 4

Larken stumbled, and the insane Star's grip loosened some. She tried to tug her arm back, but the grip tightened again. There was something off about the stylist. She seemed happy and bubbly, but she also seemed like she could secretly be a serial killer.

Cindy positioned her in front of the reporters and backed away. Larken looked at the faces of the reporters, and she recognized a few from earlier that day. Various soldiers tried to push the mass of reporters and cameras back, while others stood along the wall watching her. Larken's first impression was already ruined and her cheeks burned. She wouldn't be able to start over after all. She would always be *The Daughter Of The Military.*

"What happened to the aircraft?" a voice called.

"Were you injured?"

"Who designed the shoes you're holding?"

Questions bombarded her so quickly that she didn't get a chance to answer. She felt like a cornered animal, and she looked for anywhere that she could hide. Vallen's jacket hung heavily on her shoulders, and she pulled it tighter around herself. Larken had made up her mind to retreat and hide behind Vallen when she heard someone calling out her name. She looked around; everyone called her name, wanting her attention, but that voice, in particular, sounded familiar. A blond head bobbed through the crowd and pushed against the mass of people. The soldiers didn't hold him back and separated for him to pass through.

Dominic Braves stood before her, grinning. "You're alright!"

Larken looked up at Liam's closest friend. He looked handsome in his navy and gold Captain's uniform, his dark blond hair combed to one side. His smile showed off his dimples, and his chocolate brown eyes sparkled. Dominic was a well-renowned Star, as well as a high-ranking member of the military. He had taken up his father's career and looked just like his mother, who had starred in many net dramas in her youth. And now he was looking at her with something a little more than friendly concern.

"I saw the whole thing. I was worried."

"Dominic, what are you doing here?"

"I'm here to see you, obviously." He winked. "I had business in the area, and I thought I would stop by and offer to show you around. But then I saw the crash on the news. I was so worried, Lark." He reached up and cupped her cheek as he said the last bit, his eyes looking genuinely concerned.

The reporters went into a frenzy and the flashes increased.

"Miss Hale," one man shouted, "are you in a relationship with Captain Braves?"

"Does your brother know you are seeing his best friend?" a woman called.

"Captain Braves, what happened to the brunette you were seen with last week?" another woman asked.

Larken remembered that story, and the image of Dominic sticking his tongue down the brunette's throat at a cafe surfaced in the front of her mind. She pulled her head back just enough that he let go. Something seemed off; he was her brother's best friend, and her brother hated her. She didn't have much experience in the area of friends, but didn't friends usually hate the same people? And what was with the nickname?

"I'm fine."

"I tried messaging you, but you didn't answer," he said, unfazed by the distance she had put between them.

"My communicator was destroyed in the crash."

"We'll have to get you a new one then." He grabbed her shoes and placed her hand in the crook of his elbow. "Come on, let's get you to a medic."

"I'm fine, seriously. It's Vallen—"

"Just let someone look at you, please? For me?"

The way he looked at her kept her quiet and she followed, too shocked to do anything else. Dominic wasn't a good person, and he was an irredeemable womanizer. So why was he suddenly being so nice to her? It wasn't because her brother asked him to check in on her. So, what was really going on?

Larken looked over her shoulder and found Vallen glaring holes into the back of Dominic's head. She was surprised that the Star couldn't feel it. Cindy looked a little lost, obviously wanting her to stay and give an interview, but not wanting to go against Dominic. The crowd quickly swallowed them, and two more people joined their little group. A woman a little taller than her with short red-brown hair that was styled similarly to Dominic's, and another big man that looked to be the same size as Vallen. The man had a clean-shaven face with brown hair and eyes, which were common in the Military District, and he kept stealing glances at the woman as if to make sure she was okay. Larken's lips twitched a little at that.

Dominic kept up a steady stream of conversation, explaining various things that they passed, but she wasn't paying attention. Larken was more concerned with Vallen and how he fared. She had somehow fallen asleep on the way here, so she didn't really know how he was doing. Did they manage to stop his bleeding? Had there been any pain serum in their medical kit?

"You aren't listening to a word I'm saying, are you?" Dominic murmured in her ear.

"Sorry," Larken looked up at him, only to find that his face was very close to hers, "I'm worried about Vallen."

Dominic's features softened from their usually playful

demeanor. "I understand, he's important to you and he's hurt. I know how you feel."

"What do you mean?"

"Someone important to me is hurt too."

Larken looked away. *He can't be implying what I think he is, right?*

"Only, she doesn't care that she's injured. What do you think I should do?"

Heat crept up her neck as she said, "I really don't know."

Dominic sighed. "I don't either."

Someone cleared their throat behind them. Larken looked and found that the others were closer than she had thought. The big muscly guy glared at Dominic.

"Is there a *problem*, Captain Deckard?" Dominic huffed.

"Maybe you should focus on getting to the medic instead of running your mouth, Captain Braves."

Dominic laughed. "Of course, getting to the medic is of the utmost importance." His eyes fell to Larken's as he said, "We need to make sure that General Maxwell and Miss Hale are in top physical condition."

Larken's mouth fell open and she dropped her face in embarrassment. She blushed hotly, and her throat felt tight. Never before had someone so openly flirted with her. Well, someone who wasn't one of her father's drunken peers, anyway.

Dominic was thankfully silent the rest of the way to the medic. They passed men and women, some running and barking orders, others taking their time. Each television they passed either showed flashes of her crash or rows of slow-moving text, giving what she could only assume were orders. Occasionally there were sirens or a voice asking various people to report somewhere over the intercom.

Larken could feel the panic rising inside her and she tore her hand away from Dominic's elbow as soon as they entered the door with a little red cross painted on the glass. Her fingers tightened on Vallen's jacket, and she pretended that, if she squeezed it closed hard enough, she would turn invisible. The door shut behind them and the two men set Vallen on a chair, his dark skin unusually pale.

She couldn't see any bleeding, but the tendons in his throat stuck out in pain.

Larken's eyes drifted over the people who had crowded into the little waiting room with them. They landed on the muscly guy, Captain Deckard, only to find his eyes narrowed into a glare. He was also frowning, and she started to think that was just how he would look at her.

"Well, that was annoying."

Larken blushed again, only this time, she didn't back down. She set her shoulders and said, "Like I can pick and choose when they show up."

"Just keep your head down and keep us out of it."

"Right, because I asked to get shot out of the sky!"

"*Larken*," Vallen warned.

She crossed her arms and looked at Vallen. His eyes were telling her to shut up, but she wanted to keep fighting. Her whole body felt too tight, like it might explode. She needed an outlet, and if this gorgeous soldier was volunteering…

Vallen said her name again, leaving no room for argument. She sat next to him with a huff, dropping his jacket into his lap as she did so. She had just sat back and crossed her legs when a medic rushed out, pushing a stretcher. Loxly and the bearded guy helped Vallen onto it, and Dominic took his empty seat. She tried to stand, wanting to follow them into the back, but Dominic grabbed her elbow. "You promised to let someone look at you."

"But—"

"He is in very capable hands. *Please*, Lark."

The door swung on its well-oiled hinges behind them once before another medic came out. She had dark green hair pulled up into two buns and was chewing gum. Her nose had an emerald stud in it, and she wore makeup in shades of dark green that made her copper eyes stand out. She blew a bubble and it popped across her lips, the bright pink drastic against her dark lipstick. Crossing her arms, she popped her hip to the side and looked Larken up and down. Then she said, "My cousin had to fix Cameron Brady's nose. Well done."

Larken couldn't help the smirk that twitched her lips. "He deserved it."

"Of course he did, the man's an animal." She nodded with her head to the door that still swung in and out slightly. "Come on back, we'll take a look at your feet."

Larken stood and Dominic stood with her, still holding her shoes. The medic looked at him and asked, "Are you her Captain?"

"Well, no, but—"

"I am," Captain Deckard interrupted.

"Then *you* are welcome to come back."

The broody Captain stayed put, and Larken was completely fine with that. She followed the medic back, and she released a pent-up breath when they were in a private room. Larken hopped up onto an exam table and let her head drop into her hands. She pressed her temples, trying to fight off the headache that threatened her.

"Rough day?" the medic asked.

"You could say that."

Larken looked up and the medic blew another bubble. It popped as she pulled a tray and a dermis gun out of a cupboard. "Let's take a look at those feet, shall we?"

Larken held up her right foot and let the medic get to work. They were quiet while she unwrapped Larken's foot, but then the medic said, "Name's Jodi."

"Larken."

Jodi looked up, a smile tugging at her dark lips. "Kinda figured your name wasn't actually *The Military Heiress*."

Larken laughed, unable to hold her emotions back any longer. She was just glad that she was laughing instead of blubbering like an idiot. Jodi looked her foot over and hummed. "Whoever patched you up knew what they were doing."

"It was Vallen."

"Cool. I've only ever heard stories about him ripping people in half with his bare hands. I guess it makes sense that he would know how to properly care for a wound."

"So, do you think I'll be able to walk again?"

"Probably not."

"Well, that sucks."

The two laughed. Jodi grabbed the dermis gun and got to work on her foot. "This is gonna get rid of your callouses, but you should be fine after four or five workouts. Maybe two, with the quality of mats we have. Any questions?"

"I'm fine as long as you aren't giving me a bone graft."

"*We still have time,*" Jodi said in a sing-song voice, getting to work on her left foot. "Besides, I wouldn't think you would be too eager to get back out there. I like my men big and scary, but even that's a bit much."

Larken just sighed, the bottoms of her feet burning as her skin was replaced.

When Jodi finished, she took a stylus out of the breast pocket of her coat and ran it along the middle of Larken's foot. "You feel that?"

"Yup."

"What about that?" she asked after doing the same thing to the other.

"Mmhmm."

"Then I pronounce you ready to wear those ridiculous shoes that I'm assuming were yours."

"That is *literally* the best news I've heard all day," Larken deadpanned.

"Of course it is. And, hey, if those guys get annoying, you can just take them off and stab 'em with them."

"There's a thought. Self-defense heels."

"Protection Pumps," Jodi supplied.

The two laughed and Larken hopped off of the table and followed Jodi out into the waiting room. Dominic stood as she entered, and the short-haired woman smiled at her, but everyone else continued with what they were doing. She turned to thank Jodi, and she winked, saying, "Don't have too much fun."

She left and Larken turned to Dominic. "Any word on Vallen?"

"They want to keep him overnight. He said he would visit you before he heads out tomorrow."

She nodded and then turned to Loxly and the guy with the beard. "Thank you, guys, for helping him."

"No thanks needed, Little Bird," Loxly drawled as he stood. "I'm hungry, who's up for dinner?"

"Oh, no," the woman said, "it's your night to treat. Don't think you can weasel your way out of it."

"Spiteful witch."

"Gunslinging hick."

The two were grinning at each other despite the insults.

"Okay, okay, come on. My treat," Loxly said.

Everyone stood and started leaving. The woman stopped halfway out the door, the man who had been on her heels the whole time stopping behind her as well, and looked at her. "You comin', Larken?"

"Me?"

She laughed. "Who else?"

"Yeah, sure. I'd love to join you!"

"Okay, but you don't have to be so polite about it." She winked. "We'll be just out here."

"Okay."

The two left, leaving Larken and Dominic alone. Dominic wasted no time dropping her shoes into a chair and pulling her into a hug. She didn't know what to do, so she just stood there.

"I messaged your family. They're happy you're safe."

"Hey, Dominic?" she asked, her face pressed against the soft cotton of his uniform. The smell of blueberries clung to the fabric, and she found it comforting despite herself.

"Yeah?"

"Can we agree not to lie to each other?"

He didn't say anything for a while, but then said, "Okay."

"And no more talk about my family."

"Got it." He pulled away. "Well, it would seem that you have dinner plans and I have some things that I need to get done, but let's plan on lunch tomorrow. Sound good?"

"Sure?"

"Perfect." He leaned in and kissed her cheek. "I'll see you then."

Larken watched him leave, her hand going up to her cheek. Even after the door shut behind him, she could still feel his lips there.

What is Dominic planning? And why do I feel like I am at the beginning of a very long and cruel joke?

CHAPTER 5

Soren was the most patient man he knew. He could take the unruliest, clumsiest, and the most disrespectful child and train them to be a fierce soldier over years of hard work. Throughout his life, Soren had trained his body, teaching himself the proper way to hold a gun, the right way to throw a dagger, and how not to break his fingers when he punched someone. He had even waited for every single one of the misfits in his squad to open up and trust him. So, why was he slowly going insane the longer the Hale girl was in the examination room?

Braves grated his nerves, telling Hinlee how he had always harbored secret feelings for Larken and how the crash made him realize that he better get his act together. Soren's jaw clenched as he listened to the moron, who had been handed his title, drone on and on. He talked about his life in Stars, and how he hoped to someday share it with her.

When Larken had come back out, Soren rolled his eyes as Braves stood. They talked about General Maxwell, and Hinlee had bullied Loxly into taking his turn with paying for dinner. Soren was the first one out of the room, unsure why he felt so irritated. The rest of the squad followed, and Loxly asked, "How about pasta?"

"I want steak," Levi said.

"I don't have enough tokens for steak."

"And why not? A sharpshooter like you should be rolling in them."

"Not everyone is lucky enough to find a sponsor, green-eyes."

"And it's not Levi's fault he's so pretty," Hinlee chided.

Levi glared at her and she giggled. She looked around and asked, "What do you think is taking Larken so long?"

"Maybe Captain Manicure wanted to kiss her goodbye," Brecker suggested.

Soren's jaw popped from clenching it so hard, and somehow, he knew that he would have to fill out a mountain of transfer refusals in the morning. Braves didn't even live on base; he shouldn't get to have the team he wanted. She was now a soldier, not somebody to parade around at a dinner party. If he had wanted her, he should have let her know when he had the chance. And Soren just somehow knew that Braves would be making a lot more random appearances around base.

The door opened and Braves walked out, looking sickly smug about something. He nodded his head and said, "Captain Deckard."

Soren just stood there with his arms crossed, not bothering to acknowledge him. The girl walked out a moment later, a slight blush still on her cheeks, and Soren wondered for a moment if the creep had tried to kiss her. Well, he would just have to let her know that this wasn't *that* kind of team. The squad came first, relationships were second. They couldn't go out into a fight if one of them was more concerned with what was happening back at base. They couldn't go out at all if they didn't trust each other.

Hinlee wasted no time sidling up next to her and asking, "What took you so long?"

"Oh," her cheeks got a bit pinker, "he just wanted to make plans for lunch tomorrow. I think that's when he is going to get me my new communicator. I'm not really sure."

"You're not?"

"No, he's my brother's friend, not mine. I'm honestly not sure what he's up to."

Hinlee had a way of drawing out more than people typically wanted to share. And judging by the shade of red creeping up the girl's neck, she had just shared more than she intended.

In an obvious attempt to change the subject, she asked, "You said something about dinner?"

"Oh, yes! Dinner. Every week the five of us, well, six now, get together and one of us either pays or cooks," Hinlee explained, smiling.

"Why?"

"Because," Loxly lowered his voice and suppressed his accent the best he could, "it's a great way to bond. And a bonded squad is a winning squad."

"Decks does *not* sound like that," Hinlee said through her laughter.

"He would never say something that stupid either," added Levi.

"You keep bein' mean to me, and you can buy your own dinners."

"How does that work?" the girl asked.

"What? Dinner?" Loxly mused. "Well, it's an evenin' meal that people eat—"

"That's not what she meant, stupid," Hinlee interrupted. She looked at the girl and said, "We rotate through the squad. The new cycle will start with Soren, since he's the Captain and was the first member of Squad 19, and then end with Loxly. He's the newest member."

"When did you join?" she asked.

Loxly just rolled his eyes. "The same day as these other three idiots. I was just the last one to the sign-up sheet."

"That would mean that you're next," Hinlee said, "but since you don't have any tokens and won't even be active for another four days, we can just skip you this time."

"And what do you eat? I thought that there was just the cafeteria."

"There is," answered Hinlee, "but there are a few places on the edge of base. Soldiers can't afford to eat there all the time, but there are special places to take visiting family members. That's where we go. Unless it's Levi's night. He's the only one who can really cook."

The six of them walked on, talking and deciding where they all wanted to go. The Hale girl surprisingly didn't have much of an opinion. Soren would have thought that she would be the most opinionated of all of them, but she just kept quiet, only asking questions about things one of them mentioned that she didn't understand. She looked haggard and like she could fall over and sleep on the ground. But, even with her disheveled appearance, everyone they passed looked at her. The women either sneered or giggled, whereas the men they passed took their time smirking and looking their fill. A few were even brave enough to look over their shoulders at what he could only assume was her backend, making Soren want to gouge out their eyes.

The group decided on the little oriental place they frequented. When the girl asked what kind of food they had, Loxly grinned and said, "Just wait, you're gonna love it!"

They entered the rundown building, and the bright green walls with gold dragons greeted them. A squeal of excitement startled the girl, and a little ball of energy hurtled and collided with Loxly. He scooped the child up and spun her in the air as giggles poured out of her mouth. She wrapped her little arms around his neck, and he planted a loud kiss on her fat cheek. Balancing the child on his hip, Loxly said, "Little Bird, this is Chin Jing. Jing, this is—"

Jing interrupted him and exclaimed "Larken Hale!"

Loxly, Hinlee, and Brecker all laughed. The Military Sweetheart just smiled, her eyes looking uncomfortable. But pushing through it, she said, "What a pretty name, Chin Jing. What does it mean?"

Jing beamed. "It means precious crystal!"

"And how old are you?"

"Five!"

"Wow, you're practically a lady."

Jing just leaned into Loxly's ear and whispered none too quietly, *"I like her!"*

Loxly laughed. "I do too, squirt. Where's your dad? We're hungry."

"Papa!" Jing shouted, making Loxly jerk his head back.

Chin Wong, the young widower who owned the place, popped his head up to look at them through the service window. Something sizzled in the kitchen, and he spoke loudly to be heard over the sound. "Loxly, good to see you. The usual?"

"We'll need a menu tonight, Mr. Chin."

"What for? You have it memorized."

"*Larken Hale* is here, Papa!" Jing yelled, unable to contain her excitement anymore.

"Who's that?"

The Hale girl took everyone by surprise by throwing her head back and laughing. Jing started laughing too, wanting to be a part of whatever was so funny. The girl grabbed at her sides as her laugh turned to an unladylike wheeze. When she composed herself, she wiped away a tear and said, "I'm no one. Just a soldier. But I would like a menu, please."

"Fine, fine," Mr. Chin said, waving a ladle through the service window. "Just take a seat, I'm almost done."

The group squeezed their way into the booth they usually sat at. Somehow, Soren ended up in the middle with Levi on his right, blocking his way out, and the girl at his left. She smelled like aircraft fuel and smoke, and he wondered how he didn't notice it before. Hinlee sat on her other side, with Brecker between her and Loxly. Jing bounced excitedly on Loxly's lap. She jabbered until her father came out with a see-through tablet and shooed his daughter back to the kitchen, telling her that her own dinner was ready.

Mr. Chin made small-talk with Loxly while Hinlee helped their newest squad member decide what to get, scrolling through the pictures and descriptions of the different meals. When all of their orders were placed, Mr. Chin disappeared into the kitchen, taking the menu with him. Sounds soon filled the air, bringing with it the smell of cooked meat and vegetables.

Turning to her new friend, Hinlee asked, "So, is it just me, or is Mr. Chin—"

"Totally handsome?" she finished. "Very net drama worthy."

Hinlee turned to Brecker. "See? I told you."

"I have no comment," Brecker said.

The girl pulled Hinlee's attention back to her by asking, "What are tokens?"

"It's what we use instead of arii. Each week we get a certain amount of tokens based on our rank, squad number, and successful missions, and we get bonuses if we do something that makes us stand out."

"Like breakin' a record, or beatin' a Caption or higher-up in a spar, things like that," Loxly said.

"You could also get a sponsor," Brecker added.

"Which shouldn't be a problem for you," Hinlee said with a wink.

"A sponsor?"

"Yeah, you know," Loxly leaned in, putting his elbows on the table, "a Star or someone with a lot of arii can make a monthly donation that is converted into tokens."

"And you can have more than one?"

"Your boyfriend has the record set at ninety," Levi grumbled.

Color flooded her cheeks. "He is *not* my boyfriend!"

"Whatever."

"No, not whatever," she said, looking Levi dead in the eyes. She still blushed, but her words were hard. "If you, as a man, aren't held accountable for every girl who thinks you're attractive, then I expect to be treated with the same sort of respect. The only difference between you and me is that the only people who see your pictures are the ones you choose to share them with."

Levi looked away, cowed. Loxly whistled and Hinlee cheered, "You tell 'em, girl!"

The Hale girl glared at Soren, obviously not finished. "Everyone gets a new start here, and I refuse to be the exception."

He felt his left eyebrow raise, but before he could say anything,

Mr. Chin rushed out of the kitchen and dumped hot plates in front of them. The savory smell of chicken, beef, and sauces filled the air. Loxly prayed, as he was the one paying, and they all dug in.

Soren kept his eye on the girl. She still looked upset, but her hunger won in the end. She used her fork and stabbed a piece of chicken that was covered in a red-gold sauce. Bringing it to her lips, she took a little nibble and then promptly stuffed the whole thing in her mouth. She stabbed a piece of carrot next. Soren couldn't help but notice that she left her broccoli untouched.

Loxly had started up a new conversation, unable to be quiet for long. He started asking about the life of the Military Heiress, no question too farfetched. He asked about what other foods she had never had, places she had gone, and what Stars she had met. Hinlee asked questions too, but hers were mostly about fashion.

"And do you have to wear heels like that *all* the time?" Hinlee wondered.

"No, not always. Usually, I'm training or hanging out with Vallen, so I just go barefoot. But it's a different story if there's a chance that I might get my picture taken," the girl answered

"And what was that like?" Brecker asked. "Training with General Maxwell?"

"Well, I can tell you that if Cam hadn't insisted on me getting treated with my own personal dermis gun, I would be covered in scars. But," she added, "he has his fair share from me too."

At some point, the dishes were cleared away and Loxly was forced to pull out his communicator. He messed around on the screen, and something in Mr. Chin's pocket chimed. Mr. Chin just nodded his head and told them to enjoy their evening. Jing peeked her head out from around the kitchen door, a bit of sauce on her chin, and called, "Bye-bye Loxly!"

He blew her a kiss and she giggled.

"You're good with kids," the girl said.

"Of course he is," interrupted Hinlee. "He still is one."

Hinlee and Loxly bickered the whole way back to the common room. Soren had hoped that the girl would pay attention so that no one would have to show her around in the morning, but it would seem that the day's events and a belly full of food were just too much for her. Soren watched her ankles wobble dangerously in her heels, and she stumbled more than once. Her shirt hung loosely on her right shoulder, a pin in the back barely clinging to the fabric.

When they reached the common room, Hinlee locked elbows with her and pulled her down the hall to either her new room or the showers. She could take care of the girl for the rest of the night. In the morning, he would look to see whose schedule was open first thing. They could show her around and be done with it. He walked to his room, already exhausted thinking about tomorrow. He couldn't get his boots off and fall onto his bed soon enough.

CHAPTER 6

Larken hadn't wanted to shower again, but the woman, Hinlee, had pointed out that she should if she didn't want her pillow to smell like fuel. And now, as she stretched and buried her face in it, she was glad she had. Larken closed her eyes and just started drifting back off when a loud knock sounded at her door, with a rude, *"Get up."*

That voice.

That obnoxious voice.

Larken hated that it was equal parts grating and knee-weakening. She sat up, looking at the door, and made the ugliest face that she could. She hoped that being woken up by men who annoyed her didn't become the norm.

Larken stretched, her right shoulder popping as she did. She groaned at the sudden pain and rubbed the tight muscle until it dissipated. Her body felt a little sore, reminding her of the crash the day before, but it was dull enough that she could trick herself into thinking Vallen had just pushed her a little harder in a workout.

Looking around her room, she slumped. Everything was a light and colorless tan, like a slab of clay that had hardened in the sun. The walls were bare, and the floor felt cold against her feet. She would have to invest in a rug or something, and a better mattress.

Standing, she looked for anything that resembled the little metal vat that Hinlee had pulled clothes out of for her the night before. The makeshift pajamas she wore were Brecker's. Hinlee had offered some of her own, but she had the build of a young boy. When Larken had held up one of Hinlee's shirts to her chest, the soldier had just laughed and led her to Brecker's room. Brecker, she had found out, was in a relationship with Hinlee. Which made sense, because he had stared at her throughout their entire meal the night before.

There was another knock, but Larken ignored it, still looking for the iron latch. She looked over each wall, unable to find it. Every other minute, another annoyed knock sounded at the door. When she had reached Captain Soren Deckard's breaking point, he pounded on the door and barked, "Cadet Hale!"

Annoyed as well, she marched up to the door and pulled it open. He glared, his eyes flashing gold, and she glared back. "What is taking you so long?"

"I was fixing my makeup." She crossed her arms. "What do you think? I can't find that stupid clothes vat."

As if suddenly realizing her lack of clothing, his eyes dropped to the oversized shirt that hung off her left shoulder and the pair of boxers that hugged her hips. His eyes shot back up, and he pushed his way into her room. He refused to look at her as he scanned her room. He sighed and moved to her bed. Grabbing the frame, he pulled it to the opposite wall, revealing the vat.

"They should already have your measurements. Hurry up," he said, then stormed out of her room.

Larken gave a mock salute and muttered, "Aye, aye, Captain!"

She opened the vat and found a black tank top and a pair of grey pants that fit much more comfortably than the ones she had worn the previous day. Even though there weren't any more knocks, Larken could feel Soren staring at her door. Pulling the top down her torso, she huffed at the hint of cleavage that showed. She pulled her shirt up but knew that there was no helping it. Shrugging, she grabbed the socks and boots that were still waiting for her in the vat.

The boots pinched a little, but it was nothing that wouldn't stretch in time. Hopping up after giving the last knot a rough tug, she opened the door.

Soren stood there, his arms crossed and a murderous scowl on his face. Larken crossed her own arms and let herself fall against her doorframe. Unable to resist poking the bear, Larken asked, "Got a brush?"

"No."

"But how will I ever fix my hair?"

"Deal with it," he said, pushing off the wall and starting down the hallway.

Larken followed and, noticing that Hinlee's door was open, snagged an old and worn hair tie that she saw on her nightstand. She would buy Hinlee new ones to replace the one she took, if she wanted. Although, she didn't think Hinlee would mind since her hair was too short to put up. Grabbing her snarled mane, Larken threw it up into a haphazard bun on the top of her head while asking, "You draw the short straw or somethin'?"

"Our dorm usually always has someone here. Your schedule will be broken up to accommodate gym time, combat training, first aid, time at the shooting range, basic mechanical work, specialized weapon training, meals, and one hour of recreational time. The squad members rotate time spent in the dorm, that way if there is an emergency, there will be someone to notify the rest of the squad. I was the first dorm shift today."

"How unfortunate," Larken teased.

Soren grunted and continued on his way. She had to jog a little to keep up with his long strides. When he stopped, she almost collided with him but decided that bumping into the wall would be better.

They were standing in front of what looked like a giant communicator that took up a section of the wall. The outer casing of the thing was a bright green that played off nicely against the aged yellow of the walls. Soren tapped the screen, and it went from a dormant black to a white screen that glowed blue. Larken noticed six names, with *Soren Deckard* at the top of the list and *Larken Hale* at the bottom.

"This is the Vendor," Soren said, tapping her name. "This is where you will place all of your orders. Food, toiletries, weapon repairs, anything you need. You are responsible for all the meals that you don't get at the cafeteria."

"What do you guys do?"

"We all eat in the cafeteria when we can. Like Hinlee said last night, Levi is really the only one who can cook well," he answered, hitting a little tab that looked like a picnic basket. "This is the food tab. In it, you will find everything that can be delivered to the base. You may have to acclimate your diet some."

"Shouldn't be too hard," Larken mused, more interested in the image of a bright yellow and pink apple just under Soren's right hand. The memory of the tart flavor had her mouth watering, and she wanted some breakfast.

Soren only grunted like he didn't believe her and continued. Pushing a little curved arrow, he went back to the home screen and hit a tab in the shape of a toothbrush. "Here, you will find all your toiletries. Again, you are only able to order what can be delivered to base."

"Oh dear, what will I do without my diamond and gold-infused eyeshadow?"

Soren tapped the back button harder than she thought he needed to, and she snorted. Ignoring her, he said, "The T-shirt is for clothes repairs or special laundry orders; otherwise just stick your dirty clothes in the chute in your room. And the sword is for your weapons. Food is delivered on Mondays and Thursdays. Everything else is delivered on Fridays. Care packages, letters, and things like that are delivered on Sundays. Any questions?"

"Yeah, how do the tokens fit into the box?"

Soren stared at her blankly for a full minute before saying, "Maybe Loxly can help you figure it out since you two seem to think the same way."

Larken laughed, impressed that he was able to get an actual jab in instead of just a grunt. When she regained control of her voice, she asked, "Seriously though, how does it work? Is it like a credit line or...?"

"You will receive a pin number to go with your military account. When you are ready to make a purchase, you will enter it for verification and it will automatically take the tokens from your account."

"Nifty."

"Sure," Soren said, clearing the screen and starting back down the hall.

"When will I be able to order new stuff?"

"By the end of the day, I imagine."

"But I thought Hinlee said that I wouldn't be active for another four days? Well, three now, I guess."

"Well then, I guess you better get friendly with your squadmates and see if anyone will lend you some tokens."

"Okay," she said, "but what about other things?"

"What do you mean?"

"Like, how would I go about purchasing a rug?"

"A rug?" he scoffed.

"Hey, it's not my fault I don't have big macho toes like you do. Those floors are cold."

His jaw ticked just like Vallen's did when he was fighting a smile. Larken decided that making Captain Killjoy smile would be her goal for the day.

"There is an option under each tab on the Vendor for special requests. It's probably under there. But Hinlee would probably know more about that than me."

"So, you don't know?"

"*No*, I don't care."

They entered the comfy-looking room she had walked through last night before hopping into the shower. Larken didn't really pay it any notice since she was trying hard not to collapse from exhaustion. But looking at it now, she saw that there were three crimson couches surrounding a coffee table, facing a giant television. Everything was made up of worn wood and warm red paint. There was a billiards table, a dartboard, and a table off to the side that was large enough to seat six people. Off in one of the far corners, she could see the makings of a kitchen. Larken knew that this was the common room without having to be told. Everything about the place looked warm and inviting, and she wanted to sit on one of the couches just to see how far she would sink in. A faint smell of sweat filled the room, but it mostly smelled like fresh water. It was the same smell as stepping out of an aircraft at a lake and taking that first deep breath of summer. And even though she stood next to a grumbly military Captain, Larken felt more at home here than she ever had at the Manor.

"This is the common room. You can hang out here in your free time, or in your room, it doesn't matter to us. The remote is first-come first-serve, as is the stereo. Keep in mind that this is a public area and should be treated as such."

"No chillin' in my undies, got it."

Instead of a laugh, Soren choked and looked away. The tips of his ears went pink, and Larken had to bite her tongue to keep from laughing. Soren went to one of the couches and sat down. Larken followed and tried to get a good look at the tablet that sat on the coffee table. He picked it up and stuffed it in her hands. "You will be able to get a map on your new communicator. Someone will show you how to access it later, but for today, you can use this."

They spent the next hour discussing the map and the certain areas she needed to familiarize herself with as soon as possible. Soren's communicator chimed every now and then, but he ignored it, giving her his full attention. Larken would have thought that the attention was nice until she remembered that the only reason he was giving it to her was because he thought that she was incapable of figuring it all out on her own.

"So, do you have any questions?" he asked.

"For the meals, you said you all eat in the cafeteria. Do you get the food and bring it back here?"

"No."

"But I thought that there had to be someone here at all times?"

"There has to be someone here to alert the squad if they are needed in the field. But we are all together in the cafeteria, so no one needs to be here. Not that we're going to be called out anytime soon. You have to get your certifications first."

"So why not schedule everything else the same so everyone is together all the time?"

"Because we would probably kill each other," he said with a straight face.

"Oh."

"Everyone excels at something. Hinlee is a great mechanic, Loxly is the best sharpshooter we have and a great pilot to boot, and Levi is the designated field-medic. They all go through the normal routines, but they also spend more time in the fields they are best at. So, you might only get six hours in the shooting range a week, but Loxly will get anywhere between twelve and eighteen. Your schedule differs from week to week, depending on what the program writes for you."

"And you?"

"Me?"

"You're a Captain, so what do your schedules look like?"

"My time is divided up among everything equally. I also have the least amount of free time."

"So, there's a chance that my schedule might look like that too?"

Soren laughed at that, but it was more malicious than jovial. "Not likely."

"Why not?" she asked. The lack of food in her belly and her irritation were a bad combination, and she felt her temper rising.

"Look, Princess, I get that you were raised to believe that you were the best at everything, but—"

"First of all," she barked, a fire shooting through her veins, "I never said I was the best. I just asked if there was a chance. I know I'm not the best, but Vallen never handed me anything either. I had to fight for every single one of my victories, and I would be more than happy to knock you onto your pompous backside to prove it to you."

Soren glared daggers at her, his hazel eyes flashing gold.

"Second, my name is Larken. Not *Princess*, or *Sweetheart*, or *Heiress*. Larken. And the next time you try to belittle me for the family that I was *born* into, I won't think twice about breaking your nose."

The two glared at each other, breathing heavily for a moment, when someone broke the tension by clearing their throat. They both turned and found Hinlee and Loxly standing awkwardly in the doorway.

"What?" Soren barked.

"I'm here for my dorm shift," Hinlee said.

"And I was asked to escort Miss Hale to lunch," Loxly drawled.

Larken wanted to rage and tell him that he could escort himself somewhere unpleasant, but it wasn't Loxly who had upset her, and she didn't know the way to wherever Dominic was wanting to meet. So, she stood and said, "Thank you, Loxly."

She ignored Soren as she walked past him, and she ignored the fact that his knees brushed her left leg as she did so. Hinlee gave her a small smile but then glared at Soren when she thought Larken had looked away.

At least someone is on my side.

CHAPTER 7

The two walked in silence for a long while, Larken still fuming and not paying attention to where they were going while she tried to drown out the chaotic sounds of Base 14 around her. It wasn't until Loxly had to pull her away from colliding with someone that she let out a breath and forced herself to cool off. She was still huffing when Loxly asked, "You wanna talk about it?"

"Yes. No. *I don't know.*" She started rubbing at her right temple and groaned. Dropping her hand, she huffed, "It's always like this. I shouldn't be so upset."

"I get it," he said, stuffing his hands into his pockets. "You wanted a fresh start, and you didn't get the one you were expectin'. It's okay to be upset about it."

"It's not though. I know better than to let it get to me. I just don't know why *he* upsets me so much."

Loxly sighed. "He's just like that. When Levi joined, the two were constantly throwin' punches."

"Really?"

"Well," Loxly pulled a hand free and rubbed the back of his neck, a sheepish look crossing his face, "that's what I was told. I wasn't actually here when Levi joined. I came three years after him.

But, I'd be lyin' if I said I didn't try to break Soren's nose my first week here."

"Did he deserve it?"

"That's not the point. The point is, he just has the kind of personality that rubs people the wrong way, but he isn't so bad when you get to know him."

For some reason, Larken was reminded of the hybrids that roamed the Manor grounds. No one wanted to go near them because they were afraid of getting their throats torn out. But they were the only ones that she found peace with apart from Buttercup or Vallen. Could it be that Soren was just like them? Deadly and abrasive, but also loving and loyal? None of the squad members seemed to have a problem with referring to him without his title, and they all seemed to care for him deeply. Even Levi, who seemed a bit standoffish. Maybe she was the one who needed to show him that he could trust her, and not the other way around.

"Feel free to tell me to mind my own business," Loxly said.

"No." Larken looked up into his dark eyes. "No, I'm glad you said something. I'm just letting it sink in, is all."

"So, you aren't goin' to put in for a transfer?"

"I can do that?"

"Well, you could, but you'd break my heart, Little Bird."

Larken laughed. Loxly was sweet, and she knew that she had found a good friend. The two talked and joked the rest of the way to the designated lunch spot, Larken feeling much better. When they reached it, she almost kept walking. It looked like a cafeteria, but on closer inspection, she noticed it was much fancier. When Loxly hung back, Larken stopped walking, waiting for him to go in.

"That's the Dining Hall," he said. "I can't go in there. I'm not a Captain, and I'm not authorized. But you go on ahead. I'll set a timer for an hour and head back this way. But take your time, Little Bird, I don't mind waitin'."

"And if I decide to stay with you?"

"Well, I'm sure we would turn a couple heads, but I'm okay with it if you are," he said with a wink.

Larken laughed, still feeling a little nervous. She didn't want to go in, but she also needed a communicator.

"Don't worry, I'll be waitin' right here," Loxly promised.

Taking a deep breath, she squared her shoulders and nodded. "Right here?" she asked, pointing to where she was standing.

"Right here," he confirmed.

"Okay then, wish me luck."

"Good luck. Oh, and don't order the clams."

"Wasn't planning on it," she called over her shoulder.

The Dining Hall turned out to be a long room with tables of various sizes that were covered in white tablecloths. Miniature crystal goblets served as the drinking glasses, and the windows stretched from the floor to the ceiling. Everything was bright white, and the decorations were made of wrought iron, twisted in elegant knots and stars. It was like a fancy restaurant in the middle of the base. High-ranking officers of various ages were sitting at the tables with their colleagues or a pretty girl. Every so often, Larken saw a woman in uniform, but they weren't nearly as common. When she reached the middle of the hall, she paused and looked back, wondering if she might have missed him. When she couldn't find Dominic, she stopped a passing waiter and asked, "Is Captain Braves here?"

Before the gangly youth could answer, she heard the Star's familiar voice call, "Larken, over here!"

She smiled at the waiter and said, "Never mind."

Larken made her way to the table set for two, very aware of how out of the way it was. That uneasy nervousness attacked her stomach again, and she fought the urge to grimace at him. Dominic remained standing until she reached the table, and then he moved to pull her chair out for her. As she sat, she couldn't help but notice the whiff he took of her hair. "I hope this is okay. I wanted to make your transition a little easier and thought the Dining Hall would have more food that you were used to."

"I'm fine with anything," she said as he pulled away and took his seat. "I didn't usually eat with the family."

Dominic laughed as if she had just told him a joke. She raised an eyebrow and he sobered. "Wait, you're serious?"

"Why would I lie about something like that?"

"No, that's not what I meant. I mean, I know you're not Liam's and Cornella's favorite person, but surely you get along with Wardell and Trogar?"

"Well, Wardell isn't so bad, but he isn't old enough to know better. And my father is so drunk that he usually can't tell if I'm there or not."

"Sorry, Lark, I didn't know."

She just shrugged. "Why would you? It's not like we were close growing up."

He reached across the table and grabbed her hand, and Larken reluctantly met his brown eyes. "But I was there, I should have noticed. I should have said something."

Having taken after Vallen, Larken suddenly found herself itching all over, the tenderness of the moment almost too much for her. Raising her right shoulder to her chin, she pulled her hand free and Dominic let her. Larken decided to distract herself with the menu that rested in front of her, but she couldn't really see what it said. What did Dominic mean? Was he playing with her? Or was he sincere?

The gangly youth that she had stopped only minutes before was suddenly at their table, listing off the day's specials. Dominic ordered what sounded like a very expensive bottle of champagne and a medium-well steak. Panicking, Larken scrolled to the seafood section. Everything was fancy and she didn't recognize anything. But all fish tasted the same, right?

"And for you Miss?"

"I'll take a glass of water and the halibut."

"Very good. I'll be back with everything shortly."

The waiter left, taking the menus with him, and Dominic smiled at her for longer than she felt comfortable with. She was used to being the center of attention wherever she went, but this was all new. Larken wasn't the one that handsome men talked to. She was the black sheep, the pariah, not the girl who got the fairytale ending.

When Dominic realized that she wanted to get up and leave, he grinned and said, "I've got something for you."

"You do?" Her throat felt dry, and she wondered where the waiter was with her water.

He just laughed and placed a white box with a red bow on the table. He slid it to her and said, "Open it."

Larken's hand shook as she reached for the box. She pulled it the rest of the way and took the lid off. Placing it down so as to not crush the bow, she looked at the contents and smiled.

Larken picked up the communicator that she had forgotten about in her discomfort and tapped the screen. It lit up as Dominic said, "It's the latest model. I don't think Liam even has this yet."

She played around on the device for a few seconds; all of her music was gone and she only had one contact. Unable to keep from teasing him, she asked, "And who exactly is *Captain Debonair?*"

"I think I'll let you figure that one out on your own." Dominic winked.

Larken wanted to keep playing on her communicator and try to figure out how to get all of her stuff back, but the food arrived. The waiter placed her fish in front of her, and then Dominic's steak in front of him. Then, he put down her water and pulled the cork from the champagne. He poured two glasses and then left the bottle at the table.

Dominic raised his glass to her and said, "To new and unexpected friendships."

Larken clinked her glass against his and refrained from saying that she thought he might have more than friendship on his mind. She brought the glass to her lips, the bubbles tickling her nose. Taking the smallest sip she could, she set down the glass, forcing herself not to cough. She took a large bite of fish to cover it up and quickly gulped down some water. Larken hated alcohol, and she hated the man it turned her father into. She never drank it if she could help it, and Dominic would have to be satisfied with the small sip she did take.

The two fell into pleasant conversation, Dominic taking the lead and Larken nodding along and adding her thoughts every now and then. When they were finished, the waiter returned and asked about dessert. Dominic looked like he wanted to order something, but Larken was ready to leave so she shook her head no. It was nearing 2:00, and she was anxious to see Vallen. The waiter left again, Dominic having already had his tokens removed from his account.

"Would you like me to walk you back to your dorm?"

"No, I promised I would meet back up with Loxly. He can take me to see Vallen."

"Are you sure?" Dominic asked, looking more like a sad puppy than a Captain.

"Yup." She stood and dropped the white cloth napkin onto the table. "Thanks for lunch, Dominic."

"Of course, anytime."

She turned to leave, but he grabbed her hand.

"We'll do this again, right?"

"I don't know my schedule, but I'm sure we can work something out."

He smiled and brought her hand up to his lips. They were warm and burned her skin. "I'll count the seconds," he said and let her go.

Larken almost tripped on her way out of the Dining Hall, and then almost ran into two different servers. When she was out of the Dining Hall, she let loose the shiver that had been building up through the meal. Her whole body shuddered, and she even shook her head. A laugh caught her attention and she froze, body rigid.

"You eat the clams?"

"Of course not!"

Loxly walked up to her and laughed again. "Then what?" He leaned in, suddenly skeptical. "He didn't kiss you again, did he?"

"What? *No!*" It was only half a lie. Dominic kissed her, but not in the way that Loxly meant.

"Good, because I'm gonna be the first one you kiss," he teased.

"I'll tell you what, I'll kiss you when you realize that we would make a terrible couple."

"That doesn't sound very appealin'."

"It wasn't supposed to." She winked, and it was her turn to laugh.

"So where to now, Miss Hale?"

"The medic?"

"Sure, follow me."

Loxly put his hand on her lower back and guided her down the hall. He removed it after a few seconds and tried to tease her about how glamorous she made the uniform look, but she suddenly felt nervous. She didn't know what to expect from Vallen. He had been shot, twice, because of her. He hadn't seemed upset on the aircraft, or even when he had been taken away, but now he had had almost twenty-four hours to think about what happened.

Is he mad at me? Is he—

Loxly grabbed her right hand, saving her thumbnail from her teeth. She let him and surprisingly found comfort in the action. Larken looked up at him, and he winked. "Just don't squeeze too hard. I need my fingers to shoot and would prefer you not to shatter them."

Larken smiled weakly and went back to staring at her feet. Somehow, her free thumb found its way to her mouth.

Loxly interrupted her anxious thoughts by saying, "I heard that when General Maxwell was stranded in the wilderness, he strangled a bear with his hands."

That had Larken chuckling a little. "He told me that he came across a cub in a trap, and then he freed it. The mother *allowed* him to live."

"That story isn't anywhere near as excitin'."

"Sorry to disappoint you, but he's a pretty boring guy. He acts more like an old man than a war hero."

Loxly laughed. "How do you mean?"

"His knee, the one that wasn't shot, tells him when it's going to rain. He's in bed every night by 8:00. *And* his favorite thing to do is remind me of everything he had accomplished by the time he was my age."

Loxly sniggered, his eyes twinkling.

"In fact, he was probably the one who started the rumor about the bear in the first place."

"Maybe he could help me with some rumors of my own then," he said. "I could use a sponsor or two."

"You don't have a sponsor?"

"Levi is the only one in Squad 19 that does, and he just has the one."

"And you guys all think I'll get more than that?"

Loxly squeezed her hand and said, "We have a pool goin'. I put you at over a hundred."

Larken pulled her hand back and stopped walking. "What?"

"I have the most faith in you. Levi only thinks you'll get thirty or so."

Her mind spun. "You guys are placing bets on my popularity? *That's so humiliating.*"

"Relax, Little Bird, we don't mean any harm. It's all good fun. Besides," he said, walking again, "I was plannin' on taking you out when I won."

"And how much do you think you're going to win exactly?"

"Fifty tokens to play."

"*I can't believe this,*" Larken groaned, covering her face.

"Well, you better get used to it. Everyone in Squad 19 is made fun of for somethin'. Hinlee's too nice, Brecker's a push-over, Levi's pretty, and Soren's the livin' embodiment of a pet rock."

"Because of his stony exterior?"

Loxly's lips twitched. "Because he's no fun."

Unable to help the small smile that twisted her lips, she asked, "And you?"

"You can't tell?"

"No, not really."

"I'm a dumb hick."

"Oh." Larken paused and then asked, "Does it upset you that they make fun of where you're from?"

"Nah. I know they don't mean it. And they all make time to see my old man when he visits. In fact, I'm a little flattered that the only thing they could come up with was the way I talk."

"I suppose that's true."

"It is. They're all great, you'll see. Just give it time," he said, pulling open the same door with the red cross they went through the day before.

Larken had been so distracted that she hadn't noticed where they were. She wasn't ready to face Vallen yet, and she started wringing her fingers. Loxly just walked into the waiting room and pushed his way into the back. He held the door for her and motioned with his head for her to follow him. She did, and the familiar smell of antiseptic hit her as they made their way to Vallen's room. When they reached it, Loxly knocked and a familiar voice told them to, *"Come in."*

The two entered the room, finding an aggravated Vallen sitting on the examination table and a bored Jodi looking at his shoulder.

"Raise your arm," she said.

Vallen did, and there was the unmistakable sound of popping gum as he moved his arm.

"And make a fist."

"I did all of this yesterday," he grumbled.

"And I'm making you do it again, *so deal with it,*" she said, clipping the last few words.

Larken barked a laugh and Vallen glared at her, making her laugh harder.

"Any tingling?" Jodi asked.

"No."

"Then you're all set. The grafts will be sore for a couple days. I can write you a script for something, but a big tough guy like you probably doesn't need it."

He just grunted.

Jodi turned and rolled her eyes at Larken. She had styled her hair in two fancy braids that hung past her breasts. "You here to pick him up?"

"I am. He give you any trouble?"

"Mr. Macho-Soldier over here has been complaining *nonstop*."

"Well, at least we know that he still has his wits."

"Watch it," Vallen warned.

"Does he need anything?" Larken asked.

"Nope. My boss made the decision to keep him overnight so he would actually get the recommended ten hours of bed rest. He's free to go out and live his best life," she said with an unenthusiastic celebratory finger twirl.

"Beating the snot out of me in the gym *is* his best life."

"Oh," Jodi deadpanned, "how unfortunate for him then."

Vallen grumbled about head-strong women with no respect for their elders while he stood and shrugged into his, now clean, jacket. All of his clothes were clean as well, but they still held the holes from the bullets, and his pants were still torn where he ripped the fabric to examine his wound. Larken wanted to offer to fix them, but she knew that he didn't have the time. He was already almost a whole day late from reporting back to her mother. That, and she didn't have any of her things. She wasn't the best seamstress, but Vallen had never seemed to mind when she would mend his things before.

He walked up to her and said, "Glad you get along. Medic Brocklin will be taking over for Medic Lattic."

"Who's Medic Lattic?" Jodi inquired at the same time Loxly asked, "Takin' over for what?"

"I didn't use the same medic as my family, I used Vallen's," Larken said.

"And that would be why I never heard of him." Jodi blew a bubble. Her makeup wasn't quite as dark today, but there was still quite a contrast between her lipstick and the bright pink of the gum.

"*Takin' over for what?*" Loxly asked again.

"Larken gets injections for her shoulder," Vallen answered.

"Why?"

Vallen gave Larken a look, and she sighed. "When I was sixteen, I was being stupid and I hurt it really bad. I cracked my shoulder blade, and it messed up my whole back. I get pain treatments, muscle relaxers, and adjustments every other week."

Thankfully, Loxly didn't push for the whole story, and she was glad. It had not been a proud moment for her. She had gotten hurt because she tried to prove that she was ready for something Vallen had told her she wasn't. If she had listened, she would be fine now. But this was something she was going to have to live with for the rest of her life.

"Lucky for us that we're best friends now," Jodi said.

"How did you get stuck with being my caretaker?" Larken asked. Vallen couldn't have known that Jodi was the one who fixed her up. He had been in this room the whole time.

"Medic Krugly was originally going to do it," Jodi said, "but he also made the mistake of talking about how cute your butt was in front of this guy." She motioned to Vallen with her head. "He asked me when I started his discharge exam."

"Wait, when did he see me?" Larken asked, the name not sounding the least bit familiar.

"He was the one who brought General Maxwell back here yesterday," Loxly answered, prickling.

Larken couldn't remember for the life of her what the guy looked like. She had been so worried for Vallen that she hadn't even looked at the medic. Jodi just righted herself and said, "Better get used to guys looking at your new squad member, buddy. She's got a great butt, and guys are gonna talk about it."

Vallen frowned, and Loxly blushed severely. Larken just laughed, deciding that she really liked Jodi. The four made their way out of the room, and Jodi gave Larken a nod before saying, "See you Friday."

Larken nodded back, and then followed Loxly and Vallen out. It didn't take Vallen long to turn to her and say, "I thought I said I would come find you."

"Sorry," Larken said, looking at the callouses on her left hand and shrugging slightly. "I sort of used you as an excuse."

"An excuse for what?" Vallen crossed his arms and raised an eyebrow at her. He had a day's worth of growth on his face and head.

"To get out of having dessert with Dominic," she muttered grumpily.

"You better be talking about cake and not—"

"*I am!*" she interrupted, her cheeks going hot as Loxly started coughing. "He took me to lunch and gave me a new communicator."

"Let me see it."

Larken handed the communicator over willingly. Vallen started taking the device apart. He looked for hidden cameras, poisoned needles, and everything in between. When he was satisfied, he put it back together and started tapping at it quickly. He snorted in his throat and muttered, "And I expected to find incriminating pictures of Braves on here."

Her cheeks heated again. She hadn't even thought of that, but it sounded exactly like something Dominic would do. Well, the Dominic she watched her brother spend time with. When Shadric Barlow's latest hit started blaring from the device, she jumped and threw her arms around her instructor. Larken placed a very loud kiss on his cheek and he pushed her off, his jaw ticking like it often did when she showed him any affection. Vallen had restored all of her music and the few photos and contacts she had. He couldn't figure out how to load where she had left off in the net drama she was in the middle of, but that was an easy enough fix.

"I'll leave you to it," Loxly said. "I have to get to the shootin' range."

"I'll be checking in soon, Cadet Beau," Vallen replied.

Loxly's back stiffened, and he saluted his superior.

When Loxly's footsteps could no longer be heard, Vallen gave Larken her communicator back. On the screen was a series of green, blue, pink, and red lines. There was also a blinking pale yellow light, that she assumed was supposed to be her. "You know how to use that?"

"Is this the map?"

A nod.

"No, Captain Deckard told me that someone would teach me how to use it later."

"It's later," Vallen said, his voice the clipped tone he used whenever he taught her a new maneuver. "The green lines will take you to a medic, the pink is every hall in this building, and the red is what you will follow in case of an emergency and you need to evacuate."

"And the blue?"

"I set the places you will frequent the most with your favorite color."

She smiled but didn't let him see it. Larken was well aware of the rumors about him that continued to spread through the country like wildfire. Loxly wasn't the first to ask about the bear, but he was the first she had been honest with. Vallen was the biggest, scariest guy out there, but she liked this version of him the best. The one who worried about her and how she might be taken advantage of. The one who remembered her favorite color, her favorite foods, and her birthday. Her throat suddenly felt tight, and she cleared it.

"Take us back to your dorm," he ordered.

Larken looked at the map and started following the line she thought led to the dorm, the little yellow light moving as she did. It didn't matter if she chose the right line to follow or not; Vallen would walk silently with her until she figured out how to use the map and find the dorm on her own. He wouldn't judge her or be upset with how long it took—he only cared about the result. He had been the same way whenever he taught her something new, and they would only move on when she had it perfect.

Together they made their way back to her dorm. Vallen was silent and scowled whenever they passed someone he felt stared at her for too long. Eventually, they reached the dorm, having only gotten turned around once. When they entered the common room,

Vallen glanced over everything and said, "You'd think in sixteen years, someone would change something."

"You were in Squad 19?"

"This was Squad 12 territory long before it belonged to Squad 19."

"I guess you're gonna tell me that you were in the room at the end of the hall next."

"Do I really need to?"

Larken just shook her head, pursing her lips to hide a smile. She supposed she should have been more surprised that she was in his old dorm, but she wasn't. Vallen had spent eleven years here; he would know this place as well as his rooms at the Manor.

Without saying a word, she led the way to her new room, Vallen close on her heels. He would know everything that happened here. What she ordered, personal information about her squad members, and how long she ran the water for a shower. And she knew that if there was even the slightest deviation in her patterns, he would be here before she could tell him what was wrong. Although, she didn't foresee herself taking a long hot shower at the end of a bad day. Hinlee had let her use ten tokens for ten minutes the night before. She had just finished rinsing her hair when the water had shut itself off.

Larken opened the door and Vallen pushed his way in. He was quiet for a moment and then said, "You'll need a new mattress fitted for your frame."

Rolling her right shoulder at the mention of her new mattress, she murmured, "I know."

"Although, it might be easier to get a new frame altogether."

"Maybe."

"Is there anything you want me to send over when I get back?"

Larken pushed off the doorframe and stopped by her desk, running her fingers along the cold silver hilt of her sword. She murmured, "I have everything important to me right here."

Vallen made a gruff sound deep in his throat that caused her to look up at him. This was it, this was *really* it. This was goodbye.

"Listen," Vallen rasped, "I won't be here to break any legs, so you're gonna have to do it yourself to show you're not to be messed with. Understood?"

Larken nodded, throat tight and eyes burning.

"This isn't the end, Larken. This is your new beginning. I will always be one call away."

A tear slipped out of her eye, and she tried to sniff it back. She brushed it away roughly with her palm as it ran down her cheek. Vallen made another gruff noise and walked up to her. She sobbed into his shirt when he pulled her close and nearly broke her in half. His warm hand rubbed her back, and he murmured into her ear, "You don't let anyone tell you who you are. You go out there with your head high and show them that you aren't someone who can be hidden away. You go out there and prove that you were born for this."

She could only nod into his chest. Larken couldn't breathe, let alone speak.

Vallen kissed her temple and said, "I'll visit soon. If anything even the slightest bit unusual happens, you let me know immediately."

In one last desperate attempt to keep him close, she threw her arms around his neck and in a broken voice whispered, "I love you, Vallen."

Vallen grunted and pulled back. His eyes were red and glossy, but there were no tear streaks on his cheeks. He straightened his jacket, thought a moment, and then took it off and tossed it onto her bed. "Pull yourself together, cadet."

Larken sniffed wetly.

"I expect you to send that back to me when you get your own. And make sure you get a few more blankets; this room gets cold at night."

Larken nodded again. He never said it, she didn't know if he was even capable of saying those words again after everything he had lost, but she knew that he meant them. With a final nod, Vallen left her standing in her room and closed the door on his way out.

She pulled herself together, knowing that crying would only make her look weak. When her puffy eyes were the only evidence left of her tears, a soft knock sounded at the door.

"Yeah?" she choked out.

The door opened, and she turned to find Hinlee with an expression Larken had never witnessed in person before. There was a moment of uncomfortable silence, and Larken thought Hinlee might ask if she wanted to talk about it. Instead, she asked, "Want some chocolate ice cream?"

CHAPTER 8

The forty or so soldiers in the gym cheered again as the girl, *Larken*, knocked her sixteenth opponent to the ground. Her hair had been pulled back into two intricate braids that started at her forehead and ended at her shoulders. Her wheat-colored hair looked brown from sweat, and she had flyaway curls at her temples. Sweat ran down her face and arms, soaking the tank top she wore on her sides, back, and chest. She was giving it her all, earning the respect of everyone watching her as she did.

Even Soren had to admit that she was incredibly skilled. She looked more like she was dancing than fighting. Every sweep of her leg, every punch that she threw, it was perfection. He could see the training of the man he had idolized since birth in her movements. The training videos he had spent so much of his life studying, and she was the living embodiment of them. Soren should have been jealous, but instead, he was just as speechless as the rest of them. And it was impossible to tear his eyes away.

A line of men had started just outside the worn red mats, but Soren wasn't sure if they wanted to test her skill or just get close to her. Both options annoyed him, if he was being honest. She had been activated that morning, and Soren had already filled out transfer refusal forms for sixty-two out of the one hundred squads at this base. And he had been assured that there were base transfer forms on their way to him as well. Not to mention all of the sponsors he had to approve for her that morning; she had filled up all two hundred slots in less than twenty minutes. Meaning that Loxly had won the bet, forcing Soren to deposit the two hundred tokens into the sharpshooter's account. Loxly had then bragged, very loudly to the whole of the cafeteria at breakfast, that he was taking her out.

Another victim was pushed down to the mat and everyone cheered again. Soren saw a few of the female soldiers filming her with their communicators. He would have to ask her how she felt about it. Soren was pretty sure she wouldn't care since she was beating up men almost twice her size, but he didn't want those videos floating around if they made her uncomfortable. There were also quite a few soldiers transferring tokens to their friends, obviously thinking that their squad members could take down *The Military Sweetheart.*

The next guy had a cocky grin on his face as he strutted up to her, and something about him rubbed Soren the wrong way. He looked her up and down, not stopping until he was right in front of her. Leaning in close, he said something only Larken could hear. She jolted back like he had slapped her, then punched him in the face before taking his legs out from under him. A guy started shouting over the jeers and laughter and tried pushing his way through the mass. Soren only sighed and uncrossed his arms. The poor sod writhed on the mats, bleeding everywhere, and Larken looked like she was ready to stomp on his face. The man's Squad Captain, Captain Seamus Fletcher of Squad 15, ran out onto the mat, still shouting at her over the noise. Soren pushed off the wall, annoyed she was already starting trouble.

Here we go…

When he got close enough to decipher Fletcher's words from the crowd, he heard him shouting, "—my Second in Command!"

"I don't care who he is!" Larken shouted back. "Anyone who

talks to me like that is gonna get punched in the face! You should be happy that a broken nose was all he got!"

"Okay, that's enough!" Soren barked, standing behind his newest cadet and crossing his arms.

Fletcher turned on him and shouted, "Did you see what she did?!" He pointed at his Second like Soren hadn't just witnessed what happened.

"Of course I saw it."

"Then you know that she—"

"I know that out of the seventeen other matches, none of them ended in a bloody mess."

Fletcher balled the hand that he was using to point at his Second and looked ready to punch him. Soren just grabbed Larken's sweaty elbow and pulled her out of the gym. A chorus of *boos* and *spoilsports* followed them. Soren pulled her all the way back to the dorm, Larken trying to yank her arm free the entire time. People stared, already pointing and whispering behind their hands. Soren's blood heated more and more with each step.

When he pushed the door to the common room closed behind them, he tossed her in front of him and barked, "What did I tell you about drawing attention to this squad?"

"It wasn't my fault!" Her cheeks were a warm red and her chest heaved with her labored breathing. Even a disheveled mess, she was still gorgeous, and that somehow irritated him even more.

Levi sat in his usual spot on the middle couch, pretending to read a book. He would have been more convincing if his eyes hadn't stopped moving when they had barged into the dorm.

"So, you weren't the one who punched him?"

Levi gave up the pretense and looked over at Larken, eyebrow raised in mild interest.

"He shouldn't have said what he did!"

"And what did he say?" Soren asked, wondering for the first time what exactly could have upset her like that.

"Something that would have made Vallen cut out his tongue before killing him."

"Well, you should have handled it better."

"I handled it the way I saw fit! If you don't like it, then transfer me!" she shouted and then stormed off to her room.

Soren felt like ripping his hair out or punching a wall. He wasn't sure which sounded better yet. But, instead of doing either of those, he let himself drop onto the couch adjacent to Levi's.

"Something exciting happen while I was sitting here?"

Soren stuck his fingers into his hair. "She punched out Fletcher's Second in Command."

"I know him. Brecker knows him better."

"What do you mean?" Soren's tone was still aggravated.

"I mean," Levi said, clearing the screen of the clear tablet and setting it on the coffee table, "the guy is a piece of trash and has one of the foulest mouths I've ever heard. He's always getting in trouble and written up for harassment. He's also the reason that Brecker was written up, and that him and Hinlee are even together."

Suddenly, Soren remembered and sighed deeply. "That was him, wasn't it?"

Hinlee had been so upset, not knowing whom she could talk to about what had happened. She didn't want the men that she had come to love to think that she was unable of taking care of herself. But she also didn't want that guy to think he could talk to her like that. Hinlee had decided to handle the situation herself, and Brecker happened to be in the same gym as them. Brecker had the guy down only a minute after opening his mouth. They announced their relationship the next day.

"You should apologize," Levi muttered, picking up his book again.

"I thought you didn't like her."

Levi cleared his throat gruffly. "I don't."

"Right," Soren said, standing.

Soren wasn't a fan of crow, but he would eat it this once. He made his way down the hall to Larken's room. He counted as he did, trying to cool down before he talked to her. He would apologize, but he would also tell her that that kind of behavior was no longer acceptable. He wasn't General Maxwell, and Soren would not coddle her as he had. Soren stopped in front of her door and raised his hand to knock. His knuckles were about to hit the wood when he heard it. Pressing his ear to the door, Soren listened as Larken tried in vain to suppress her tears.

Dinner that night was uncomfortable at best. Not only had Loxly made good on his promise to Larken, but he decided to treat everyone to a steak dinner as well. Loxly was the only one dumb enough, and kind enough, to blow two hundred tokens on his friends. The hole-in-the-wall place they were at was referred to as The Grill and had been decorated with tables carved from pine with chairs to match. Everything was smooth, polished, and bright. The tables held white placemats, and a fishbowl sat in the middle of each one with little floating candles and pale pink flower petals in the water. The whole place always reminded Soren more of a summer cabin than a grill.

Everyone around the table was unusually quiet. Loxly tried to get a conversation started a few times but had to resort to murmured comments with Brecker. The news about what happened in the gym had spread through the base like an electric fire, and everyone had chosen a side. Hinlee had shouted anyone out who tried to tear down Larken in front of her. Even now, she was glaring at Soren like *he* was the one responsible for the whole event.

The food had arrived without ceremony, and Loxly said a quick prayer before telling everyone to dig in. Larken just stared at the piece of meat on her plate, and Soren felt suddenly uncomfortable. He wanted to pull at his shirt collar, to get up and leave, anything but sit there and wonder at the irony of the situation. What was she thinking? What was she feeling?

"You're supposed to eat it, not stare at it," Loxly said around a mouthful of food.

"I know."

"Then what's wrong?" he demanded, voicing the question that everyone else was too afraid to ask.

"I didn't mean to cause you guys trouble today." She didn't look up at any of them.

"That idiot is a pig, Larken," Hinlee said. "Don't even give it a second thought."

"I know that, but this is still going to happen a lot. I know that me being here isn't easy for anyone, as nice as you all have been about it."

Hinlee glared at Soren again. He glared right back.

"That's why I put in an official request to have half my sponsors transferred to squad sponsors."

"Can you do that?" Brecker asked.

Larken shrugged. "Vallen said I could. And he already approved it."

"So, what does that mean?" Hinlee asked.

"It means," Larken said, finally looking up from her steak, "that everyone is getting a new mattress, better weapon care, new furniture and appliances for the common room, anything we want."

"So, we can get a coffee maker?" Loxly asked, his hand already shaking slightly, thinking about his next fix.

"If that's what you want." She looked back down at her steak. "If Captain Deckard approves it, that is."

"Oh, please, Dad, can I?" Loxly asked, his hands clasped in front of him in a pleading gesture.

"Only if you promise to share with your brothers and sisters," he deadpanned.

Loxly punched the air in triumph, then said, "Little Bird, you're the best!"

Everyone at the table seemed to perk up and attacked their meals with gusto. Everyone, that is, but Larken. She still picked at her very red, unseasoned piece of meat. Each time she sliced through it, Soren wondered if she could have used a butter knife instead, it looked so tender. But she had ordered the cheapest cut out of everyone. And Soren wondered again at what was going through her mind.

Then her words caught up to him. It wasn't so much that she already had a negative reputation. It was that she had been reduced to tears and had to call General Maxwell on her first day. She was supposed to be starting over, beginning a new life like everyone else who enlisted. And already, she had been forced to call home. What had that conversation been like? Did she tell him what that guy had said to her? Was General Maxwell already moving to have him dishonorably discharged? Or was he planning on cutting out the guy's tongue like Larken had said he would?

There was still so much he didn't understand about her. And, as the meal went on, Soren reluctantly found himself wanting to. He wanted to understand her, he wanted her to feel like she could come to him with her problems like Levi and the others did. After all, that's what made him such a great Captain. It's what made them a great team. Only, Larken didn't feel that way. He had made her think that the only way to earn forgiveness was to give half her earnings to the squad to use on better beds and a dishwasher that didn't sound like it was trying to summon demons whenever it was started. It would seem he had a lot more to apologize for than just his harsh words.

When they had finished dinner, Loxly paid and Hinlee told Brecker how she was going to decorate her new room. She often asked Larken's advice, but then stopped with a gasp. "Wait? Does this mean that I don't have to pay for hot water anymore?"

"Nope, you can take as much time in the shower as you want," Larken answered.

"That sounds *amazing*."

"Don't get too ahead of yourself," Brecker warned quietly. "It will still be at least twenty-four hours before she gets her first deposit. I don't see how the squad fund will be any different."

"I have a question," Levi mused. "Won't your open slots fill up again if you're donating half your sponsors?"

"They will eventually," Larken answered. "But Vallen made it so anyone else who applies after I've hit my limit will have to donate to the squad as a whole, unless I choose to put their arii elsewhere, like weapon research or something."

"Well, I can't say I'm upset about getting a new fridge," Levi said, now done with the conversation.

The group stood and slowly made their way back to the dorm. Soren knew that he would have to make his move soon, otherwise, he was bound to lose Larken behind a locked door for the rest of the night. He gently grabbed her elbow and forced her to the back of the group with him. Her skin felt soft and warm, now that it wasn't covered in a chilled sweat.

She looked up at him, asking what he wanted with her teal eyes.

"I need to apologize. For today, and for how I've been treating you. I want you to know that you can trust me to be a good Captain. I will stand by you and the choices you make from now on, and I don't blame you for what happened today. And it isn't fair that I rose to Hinlee's defense when it happened to her and was annoyed with you."

Larken was quiet, and he thought she would continue to ignore him for the rest of the night. But instead, she looked up at him and said, "I forgive you. As for the other stuff, Vallen wouldn't have let me into your squad if he didn't think you could be trusted."

She rushed to catch back up with Hinlee, who locked elbows with her. Hinlee looked over her shoulder at him and whispered something in Larken's ear. No doubt asking her if he had said something rude. Which he hadn't, this time. And he was left to wonder again at what kind of woman Larken Hale was. She ordered cheap food, donated half of all her future tokens for the better of the squad, forgave him easily, and cried behind closed doors. Her actions didn't scream Military Heiress, and she seemed more lonely than anything else. It would seem that crow would now be a frequent meal for him, and that made Soren want to kick something.

CHAPTER 9

Larken's alarm went off and she groaned. Her eyes felt like they had sand in them, and she was in desperate need of water. She hated crying, and she hated that that pervert had gotten the better of her. Not only was she embarrassed, but she was ashamed of how she had shouted at Soren. He had apologized, but she was still a little worried that he would take her up on her offer and transfer her.

She had barely shut herself away in her room the day before when her communicator started going off. Accepting the video call from Vallen, she burst into tears before he could even ask what had happened. Larken had placed her hand over her mouth, trying to keep control over her emotions, but seeing his face, knowing that he was nearly two hundred miles away, was just too much. He had waited for her, not once breaking the silence, just looking at her with those dark eyes of his. Aside from Vallen, not many people had ever seen her cry, and she planned to keep it that way.

Larken sat up, her shoulder stiff. She needed a hot shower to loosen the muscle, but the alarm on her communicator went off again, telling her that there wasn't enough time. She didn't know how she was going to make it another three nights on that mattress.

Larken rolled her shoulder and a sharp pinch had her holding her breath.

A knock sounded at her door, and from the other side, Loxly called, "You up, Little Bird?"

She couldn't answer; she could barely see past the tears blurring her eyes.

"Little Bird?"

Larken forced her breath out of her mouth and sucked in more air.

"I'm coming in," Loxly said before tentatively pushing the door open a crack. It was flung open the rest of the way when he saw her, and he rushed in. Kneeling in front of her, he asked, "What can I do? Do we need to go to the medic?"

Larken just grabbed his shoulder and forced him back a little. Leaning forward, she grabbed her right shoulder and pulled down. The loud *pop* brought sweet relief with it, and she shuddered a sigh.

"Are you okay?" Loxly asked, moving his hands to touch her, but then thinking better of it. His brown eyes were worried, reminding her of the hybrid puppies back at the Manor. He obviously wanted to comfort her but didn't want to hurt her.

"I'm fine, just slept on it wrong."

"You sure we don't need to go to the medic?"

"Positive." Loxly didn't look convinced, so she added, "I'll take a hot washcloth though."

"On it!" He bounced up and left the room. It might not be the hot shower that she was hoping for, but it would help. She would just have to get up earlier from now on.

Larken used Loxly's absence to quickly get dressed, the grey pants and black tank top the same style as the day before. She dumped her pajamas into the laundry chute and was lacing up her boots when Loxly knocked on her door again.

"Come in."

Loxly walked in and handed her the rag. Larken pushed off the straps that rested atop her right shoulder and pressed the rag there.

The rag burned a little, her skin cool from the temperature of the room, and goosebumps erupted across her flesh.

Trying to lighten the mood, Loxly raised an eyebrow and asked, "You change your mind and decide to tell me what you did to it?"

"Nope!" she said cheerily and stood up. Three rivulets ran from the rag down her shoulder blade and were caught by her shirt and bra strap. Already annoyed by the wet elastic, she tossed the rag into the laundry chute. Turning to Loxly, she beamed and asked, "So, what are we doing today?"

"I'm gonna give you a set of wings, Little Bird," he answered with equal excitement.

The happy-go-lucky feeling that she had only moments ago vanished and was replaced with a sinking unease that had her wanting to crawl back into bed. "Umm, no thank you."

Loxly threw his head back and laughed. "I figured that's how you would feel, but the best way to get over your fear of ridin' is to get back on the horse."

"Are you sure we can't just ride actual horses instead?"

"Now, Larken, have you ever heard of a bird that couldn't fly?"

"Penguins."

Loxly laughed lamely and rubbed the back of his neck. "I guess I set myself up for that one."

"Yes, you did."

"No matter," he said, grabbing her elbow and leading her out of her room. "You still need to learn to pilot your own aircraft."

"I *really* hate flying."

Stopping in the common room, Loxly turned to face her. Reaching up and tentatively cupping her cheek, he looked into her eyes. "Can you trust me?"

Can I?

Was she even capable of trust after what her family had put her through? But she trusted Vallen, and he was the one who picked this squad for her. She might not know Loxly as well as she knew Vallen, but if he trusted Squad 19 to take care of her, who was she to disagree with him?

"Yes," she finally answered.

"Good, because you haven't experienced flyin' until you get into an aircraft with me." Loxly gestured at himself with his thumbs.

The two of them left the dorm, and Larken teased, "If I didn't know you any better, Cadet Beau, I would say you were trying to get me alone."

"Who says I'm not?" he tossed back with a wink.

Both laughing, they made their way to the same hangar that Larken had been in only days before. She hoped with her whole heart that she wasn't expected to learn on that beast of an aircraft that had picked her and Vallen up. But when they walked through the door, instead of taking a right where a large group of soldiers were headed, Loxly led her to the left, away from the aircraft. Breathing a sigh of relief, Larken was able to laugh when Loxly poked her in the side and asked, "You didn't think I was gonna let you practice on my baby, did you?"

"I won't lie, I was afraid you were."

"Nope, your first time will be in the Pumpkin."

"The what?"

Loxly pointed, and three aircraft down, Larken saw something bright orange and shaped like a potato. She immediately understood where the name came from.

"It's that color because if we're in a horrible crash and our radios don't work, it'll be easy to find."

The fear of crashing clawed its way back up Larken's throat, and she stopped walking.

Loxly turned, realizing his mistake, and quickly said, "Not that we're gonna crash. Don't forget, I'll be the co-pilot and will be able to correct any mistakes you might make."

"*Not helping*," she groaned and turned away from him, closing her eyes as she did so.

Placing a hand on her stomach, she mentally ran through the very first maneuver that Vallen had ever taught her. She did that every time she was about to have a panic attack, but this time, it wasn't working. Focusing on her footwork and her breathing, she ran through it again and again in her mind. After the fifth time, her breathing leveled out and she was able to open her eyes.

Turning back to Loxly, she squared her shoulders and nodded. "Ready."

"Great!" he said, but the excitement didn't quite reach his eyes. He was still worried about her, but he was right; the only way to get through it was to get through it.

"After you," she said.

Loxly turned and held an orange wristband she hadn't noticed to a scanner. The two-seater aircraft beeped three times before the scanner flashed green, and a *click* sounded as the two doors unlatched. Loxly pushed the one he was next to up and held his hand out for her. "It's a bit of a jump."

"Everything always is for me," she said jokingly, accepting his help and launching herself into the pilot's seat. She secured her harness and pressed the button that would latch the aircraft door closed.

Loxly jogged around the front of the aircraft and hopped into his seat. He hit the button and secured his harness as the door closed. Pulling the strap to tighten it around his small waist, he turned to her and said, "Ready when you are."

Larken wanted to say she would never be ready, but she swallowed the comment and nodded. She put her hands on what she assumed was the steering wheel. It looked like an old wagon wheel, but with the top and the bottom cut off. Looking over the controls, she felt her hands tighten.

"Do you have any idea what you're doin'?"

"Not a clue," she said without looking up.

Loxly laughed and unbuckled himself. Scooting to the edge of his seat, he leaned over and said, "Here."

Larken watched as he pointed to a red button, saying, "This one starts and stops the engine."

She hit it and the aircraft fired up, making her stomach flip.

"This one," he pointed to a green button this time, "fires up the levitator."

Larken hit that one as well. The aircraft jumped a little and started floating in the air. This was really happening; they were really going to let her try and fly this thing. She had never been more afraid for someone else's well-being than she was for Loxly's in that moment.

"Push up on the wheel to go forward, down to go back. Do you see that switch to the left?"

Larken looked and found a little silver switch sticking straight out. "Yeah."

"Flip it up and push the wheel up when you want to ascend. Push it down when you need to descend."

"And this one?" Larken asked, pointing at a matching switch to the right that was pointing all the way down.

Loxly flipped it up, and the space in the hangar around them lit up. "It's the lights. Middle for dim, up for bright." He turned the lights off, buckled himself back in, and said, "Let's go."

"Wait, that's it?"

Loxly gave her that crooked smile of his and said, "This is a very basic model. Dependin' on how you do today, I will either graduate you to somethin' bigger or keep you at the basic med-craft level."

"What do you fly?"

"Everythin'. Now, quit stallin'."

Larken grumbled and started to slowly push the steering wheel up. The aircraft jerked more than she was expecting, and she screamed. Loxly just laughed and then told her to keep going. Trying again, she pushed the wheel up and got them moving. She kept the pace very slow, and she became annoyed when she saw Loxly's knee bouncing out of the corner of her eye.

"Take a left up here." Loxly pointed as he spoke. Larken turned the wheel a little, her fingers still clutching it tightly enough that her knuckles were white. Loxly grabbed the radio that was on the dash to his right and said, "Requestin' flight for the Pumpkin."

A woman's staticky voice responded, "Squad and flyer?"

"Squad 19, flyer Hale."

"Cleared for takeoff. Happy flying, Beau."

"Thanks, Shelly." Loxly set the radio back in its holder and started drumming his fingers on the dash.

"Do all the dispatchers know your voice, or is Shelly just special?" Larken teased.

"Aww, you jealous, Little Bird? Don't be, you should know by now I've only got eyes for you."

Larken barked a laugh, but her response was shut off by the door to the hangar opening. She gasped, and Loxly beamed at her. She had missed the view the last time, too afraid to look and still half-asleep. But now...now she could see the blue sky and the rolling hills. It was like a painting, and she wished she could sit there and stare at the view the rest of the day. Instead, Loxly cleared his throat, and she was forced to move.

A small, high-pitched sound emitted from the back of her throat without her permission as she pushed the aircraft out over the ledge and into the sky. Off in the distance, soldiers could be seen running through a training field, androids chasing after them. Loxly didn't say anything, but she could hear the silent laughter rolling off of him in waves. Slowly, they moved, and still, his knee kept bouncing. She was about to open her mouth to tell him to knock it off, when he said, "We're in the way. You need to move faster in case a larger aircraft needs to get in."

Larken pushed up on the steering wheel a little more and they sped up the tiniest bit.

"More."

Larken pushed a little more.

"More."

Again, she pushed a little more.

"*More.*"

Irritated, she pushed the steering wheel as high as it would go. She hit the back of the seat with the force of the movement. Loxly grabbed onto the dash and hit the roof, whooping loudly. When she could no longer see the hangar door, she stopped, and her body jolted forward. Her hands were shaking, and she put them on her cheeks, trying to steady herself.

"That was great!"

Larken dropped her hands to her lap, turned on him, and hollered, "That was not great! I want to go back!"

His wide grin fell when he looked at her, and he pulled one of her shaking hands free. "Hey, you can do this."

But the truth was, she couldn't. Larken couldn't remember ever being so afraid in her life. She closed her eyes, not daring to look out the window. Instead, she felt herself leaping, her fingers just brushing the handles she was supposed to grab, and then falling. Her shoulder throbbed and then the feeling changed, her stomach flipping like it did when they were catapulting to the ground.

Strong hands gripped her face, forcing her to open her eyes. "Larken, breathe."

She gasped a breath, black spots dancing in front of her eyes as she did so. When had she stopped breathing? Was it before or after she had started falling? No, she wasn't falling, she was safe with Loxly. He was here; he was keeping her safe.

After getting her breathing under control, Loxly raised a dark eyebrow and asked, "Are you ready to try again, or do we really need to go back?"

"I—" She looked down, her face hot. "I don't like heights."

"I've noticed. But I've also noticed that you don't like special treatment. So, do you want to try again?"

She didn't look up, she couldn't, because then he would see it in her eyes. She wanted to go back. She wanted to have this one exception, this one time where she didn't have to be treated like everyone else. But that wasn't who she was.

"Let's try somethin' else," Loxly said, letting go of her. She looked to see him reaching up to a little latch in the middle of the roof. Pulling it open, he flipped the switch in it, and the buttons on his side of the dash lit up as the ones on hers dimmed. Closing the latch, he pushed on his steering wheel and they set off again. She clasped her hands tightly in her lap and he said, "I'm gonna take you to my favorite spot."

She said nothing, just staring at her white knuckles, willing her hands to stay still.

Raising his voice, he mocked, *"Why, Cadet Beau, you wouldn't be tryin' to take me to a secluded area so you can have your way with me, would you?"*

Snapping his fingers, he said, "Aww shucks, looks like you caught me."

"Cadet Beau, you're so handsome and kind, you don't need to resort to trickery. I would have—"

Larken couldn't hold it in anymore and laughed. She laughed so hard that she was snorting and wheezing and crying. "I *do not* sound like that!" she gasped.

Loxly laughed as well, saying, "Got you out of that funk though, didn't I?"

"Sure, okay."

"Hey, I helped."

She looked at him and smiled. "You always help, Loxly. I'm lucky to have you as a friend."

He sighed and muttered, "Again with the friend thing."

She snorted and braved a glance out of the window. "Where are we going anyway?"

"I told you, my favorite spot."

"And where is that?"

"Well, I could give you the coordinates, but I don't think they'd mean much to you."

Larken rolled her eyes. "Fine, I'll wait."

Loxly's lips twitched, and Larken looked out the window. She refused to let her gaze fall past the clouds and eventually closed her eyes. Occasionally there was a loud beep or two short ones, but she trusted that Loxly knew what he was doing. It wasn't long before Loxly murmured, "We're here."

Larken opened her eyes and gasped. All around them was blue sky and flat earth. Grass stretched under them like an ocean, and the wind blowing through the greenery made the grass look like there were actual waves rolling through it. But it was the sky that kept calling her back. The blue looked so bright and soft, it reminded her of a blanket that Vallen kept in his sitting room for when she got cold. The sun sat high and was reflected in the clouds, turning them a soft yellow instead of white. Looking at it, a warmth spread across her chest, comforting her, making her feel like she was seeing the sky for the very first time. They started descending and Larken found herself straining to keep the sky in her line of sight.

When they were a good ten feet above the ground or so, Loxly turned to her. "Do you remember the dings that went off on our way here?"

"Yes."

"What did you notice about them?"

She thought and then answered, "After the long one, we dropped, and after the two short ones, we went higher."

"Cadet Larken Hale, you have passed and are cleared to fly med-crafts. Now," he turned and messed with something on the far right of the dashboard, "since this is a replica of a med-craft, it also has the same functions." He punctuated his words by slapping a yellow button she hadn't noticed before. There was a loud noise, and then the windshield started descending into the aircraft as the roof folded until it was closed away somewhere inside the back. Looking at her, Loxly's lips split into a wicked grin. "Ready?"

Stomach tensing, she asked "Ready for wha—"

Loxly pushed the steering wheel all the way up, and they shot off. Larken screamed, gripping her harness to make sure she was still latched in. Tears streamed from her eyes, but Larken wasn't sure if they were from the wind or fear. Loxly was hollering and whooping loudly, obviously in his element. Her hair whipped around her face; one strand kept finding itself stuck to the corner of her mouth no matter how many times she pulled it away. At this speed, the grass looked even more like the sea, and she wanted to reach out and run her fingers along the surface. A longing so strong filled her, and she wondered how she could be homesick for some-where she had never been before.

Loxly maneuvered the aircraft flawlessly, and when she got her fill of the landscape below them, she looked back up to the sky. If she had been able to take a good breath, the sight would have stolen it from her. The sky and the clouds above raced past her as if pushed by the wind. Her wild hair, the sting of the wind, her tears— they all faded away at the sight and she felt her lips part on their own.

"Do you feel it?" Loxly hollered over the wind.

"Yes," she murmured, surprising herself. But she could. Her stomach, instead of being a tight ball of nerves, felt light. Her heart beat easily, and she felt a smile touch her lips. When her hand moved up to try and touch the expanse of blue, she didn't stop it.

Loxly raised the aircraft, humoring her and making her belly flip. Instead of screaming, she laughed. Sticking both hands in the air, Larken kept laughing as Loxly let loose and seemed to go even faster than they were before. Larken wondered how she never realized that flying could be like this. Because that's what this was. She was *flying*, and nothing else mattered in that moment. Her only concern was going higher and faster, and how much longer she had before it was over.

When Loxly eventually slowed down, she beamed at him. She didn't know what to say, or how to thank him for what he had given her. Larken was still afraid of heights, and she probably would be for the rest of her life, but she had this moment, and that was enough for her.

"Well, Little Bird, it looks like we found your wings."

Larken just sighed and leaned back into her seat, smiling.

CHAPTER 10

Larken's hair was a snarled mess, and she looked a little wobbly on her legs, but that smile could lift anyone's spirits. Too bad Soren wasn't in the mood to have his spirits lifted. Her laugh echoed in the hangar, and the melodic sound grated on his nerves. Pushing himself up from the wall, he approached them, stuffing his hands in his pockets so they wouldn't see his fists. When Loxly noticed him, he grinned and asked, "What's up, Soren?"

"You're late," he growled.

"Not that late."

"Cadet Hale was supposed to report to med-training three hours ago. What were you doing?"

"Oh, you know," Loxly slung his arm around her shoulders, "we went out to my secret spot and had some fun."

He grunted when Larken elbowed him in the side. Her cheeks went pink and she dropped her gaze to the ground. She mumbled something that sounded like, *"I'm going to go clean up,"* and left.

It wasn't until after she pulled out her communicator and disappeared around the corner that Soren turned on his friend. "What were you doing?"

Loxly reached up and rubbed the back of his neck. "Well, we

managed to get out of the hangar before everythin' went wrong. That crash did her no favors. She started freakin' out and had a panic attack. I took her to that field and flew her around until she got comfortable, and then had her try again. She passed the basic test, but I don't think she'll be able to handle anythin' more advanced." Loxly dropped his hand and looked at him with those eyes that reminded Soren more of an injured puppy than a grown man. "Sorry, Soren, but when General Maxwell called me this mornin' and said keep her out there until she passed, I assumed that her schedule had been cleared. I didn't mean to get you into hot water."

"What?"

"General Maxwell—"

"No, I know, I just—" General Maxwell had called Loxly? Was he really that worried about Larken? If he had known to call and that she would try to come back, then why hadn't Soren been contacted about a schedule change? He pinched the bridge of his nose.

"Just, what?"

"Why wasn't I told about the change in her schedule?"

"Dunno, Cap, but I'd try to figure it out before it happens again." Loxly clapped him on the shoulder. "I'm headin' back to the dorm. I told Hinlee that if I was back before 11:00, I would take over for her so she could surprise Brecker in the gym. Let me know if you need anythin'."

Soren nodded and stood there a moment longer, trying to figure out what was happening. Not getting anywhere with his thoughts, he walked over to the Arsene, passed it, and headed to the mini Vendor that hung on the wall behind it. Hitting the screen, Soren tapped the word REPAIR at the top, and then ENGINE, just trying to see if his feeble theory was correct. He would cancel the order, but as he waited for the next screen to load, he had an uneasy feeling. When it pulled up and he saw the words WHO IS ORDERING REPAIR?, he looked down the list. Larken's name wasn't there.

Smacking the wall next to the Vendor with an open palm, Soren ignored the sting and cleared the screen. He pulled out his communicator and pulled up the personal files on his squad. Clicking Larken's name, he pulled up her profile. But, instead of all the information that he had clearly read just the day before, the words blurred together with a giant CLASSIFIED in the middle of each page.

Jamming his communicator into his pocket, Soren left the hangar and stormed to the administration office. He ignored everyone and everything on his way, even more furious than he was while waiting for Loxly and Larken to come back. This whole thing was a mess, and he thought he knew who was at the bottom of it all.

Finally reaching the office, Soren pushed his way in, startling the wide-eyed secretary that sat behind the desk. A tablet sat on her desk, giving the latest stats about his fellow Captains that were currently out in the field. She was small, smaller than Larken, and built more like Hinlee. She hid behind an oversized sweater and a pair of glasses that looked too big for her face. She tried her best to compose herself and ask how she could help him, but his glare had her shutting up as he walked back to the office he needed. Without even knocking, he walked through the fourth door on the right and slammed it behind him. Crossing his arms, he glared at the Head of Base 14.

Connie Dayton looked up at him and sighed. She wasn't much older than him, only ten years or so. Her dark brown hair had been pulled back into a tight bun and her shirt cut low, leaving nothing to the imagination. She just shook her head and asked, "Really, Deckard?"

"Did Braves stop in for a visit this morning?"

She blushed clear down to her chest. "Last night, if you must know. I take it you found out about the suspended file?"

"I refused that transfer, as well as all the others."

"And *I* placed it under consideration. Braves has had trouble keeping squad members. They're either not serious enough or are discharged for injuries."

"They aren't serious enough because they're too busy chasing tail instead of honing their skill. And since when are *recurring headaches* a reason to be honorably discharged? They aren't even smart enough to use the term migraine in the media, or apparently know that there are treatments for those now."

"*That is enough*, Captain." She stood and walked around her desk. She wore a navy blazer with a matching skirt that cut off mid-thigh, and her hot pink heels looked like something Larken's stylist would pick out. "I understand that you have grown used to having her in your squad, but you need to realize that not everything is about Squad 19 all of the time. There are other squads in more need of what Larken can offer them than yours. You'll just simply have to wait until I make my decision. That is all."

"But—"

Her brown eyes narrowed to a glare. "I said, that was all. See yourself out."

Turning before he could say something stupid that would earn him a write-up, Soren stomped out of the office. He kept going and ignored the secretary when she called, "Have a nice day!"

Slamming the door shut behind him, he turned and punched the wall. How had he messed things up so badly this quickly? Forcing some of the hot air from his lungs, Soren tried to calm down. A voice behind him had him riled up again and ready to hit something with a little more flesh.

"Lose something?"

Turning slowly, Soren glared at Braves. A smarter man would have cowered, but Braves wasn't smart. His arms were crossed, and he leaned lazily against the wall a little ways down the hall. Pushing off, he made his way to Soren, smiling easily.

"Don't mess with me, Braves, I'm not in the mood."

"Who's messing with you? Not me. I was just doing what Miss Hale wanted."

"Really? Because when we talked about it, she said that you weren't even friends. It was right after I mentioned that you couldn't be bothered to be here most days."

Pink touched Braves's cheeks and his eyes hardened. "What we are or are not is none of your concern, Deckard, so why do you care? You don't even like her," he sneered, ignoring the jab about his work ethic.

"We have reached an understanding over the last week we have gotten to know each other, unlike you, who has known Larken her whole life and only cares now that she is out of reach." Soren balled his fist and did everything he could to keep it at his side.

Braves smirked. "We'll just see about that." He huffed a cold laugh and then made his way down the hall, disappearing into the crowd.

Soren counted to five, struggling to keep himself from running after Braves and breaking his face. Instead, he walked the other way and took the long route back to the dorm. He counted each step he took, clenched and relaxed his fists, whatever he could to try and steady his heartbeat. Soren was livid, and he had every right to be. Not only had Braves tried to take Larken, but he had also tried to take Loxly and Levi before she had even joined. He had always gotten in Soren's way, and Soren could never do anything about it before. But now he had General Maxwell on his side, and that gave Soren a sick sort of satisfaction. He might not think the world of Larken, but Hinlee and Loxly were already attached to her. So as far as Soren was concerned, she was now part of the family.

Soren pushed into the dorm and Larken's laugh was cut short. She sat on the couch, blonde hair now brushed and smoothed back into a ponytail, and she wore that oversized jacket she had taken to wearing whenever she felt too exposed emotionally. A sandwich stuffed with lettuce was halfway to her mouth, and Loxly crunched on something noisily across from her. Soren walked over to her and she hastily set down her sandwich, wiped her mouth off on her sleeve, and brushed her hands off on her pants.

Soren wanted to make a comment about how someone who had been raised in the Manor shouldn't have such poor table manners, but he just stuck out his hand and said, "Communicator."

She pulled it out and said, "I tried messaging you, but it didn't work. Sorry about—"

He snatched it from her hands and pulled up General Maxwell's information. He saw that under his name, he was also registered as an emergency contact, and he had also been labeled as her father. Smart, since anyone calling her dad would be routed to him. But Soren would be lying if he said the sight of those six letters didn't tug at something in him. Not jealousy, he hadn't even known his own father before his mom gave him up, but pity that she couldn't rely on hers.

He hit the call button and it barely rang once before General Maxwell answered. His deep voice was crisp and to the point when he asked, "What is it?"

"General Maxwell, this is Captain Deckard. We have a problem," Soren said while walking away. There was no reason for Larken to hear what was happening; it would only make it seem like she was getting passed around to different squads. He would explain everything when the problem had been resolved.

"Does this have anything to do with her being reported missing for training today?"

"Yes, sir." Soren kicked the door to his room closed behind him, but it bounced and remained slightly parted. Sitting on his bed, he said, "I received the same report, then went to the hangar to wait for her return from her flying exam. Only after coming back did I learn that you contacted Cadet Beau this morning."

"I figured you didn't receive my request. What happened?"

"Larken is in transit, sir. Captain Braves put in for her despite my refusal. He went to go see Connie Dayton last night, and now all of her information is locked."

"I'll take care of it. Just keep her in the dorm until I get this sorted out. The last thing we need is her trying to use her PIN somewhere and have it not working on top of everything else that's been happening." Soren heard him sigh on the other side of the communicator, and in a much softer voice, he asked, "How did her exam go?"

Soren was taken aback but answered, "She had a panic attack in the air, but Cadet Beau was able to talk her down and get her to take the exam. She's been cleared for med-crafts, but he doesn't think she will be able to handle anything more advanced."

"Good, good. Let me talk to her. She's probably eavesdropping close by."

Soren stood and opened his door. Sure enough, Larken jumped back, her cheeks going pink. He held out her device and said, "It's for you."

Bringing it to her ear, she demanded, "What's going on?"

Soren could hear the low mummers of General Maxwell's voice, but nothing else. As he spoke, her face fell and she walked to her room and shut herself away. Soren shut the door to his bedroom and walked out to the common room; he would like to talk to her about what was happening, even though General Maxwell was probably explaining everything to her.

Loxly had his ankle resting on his knee, an arm thrown over the back of the couch, and was guzzling down some water. Soren sat in the spot just to the right of where Larken had been and looked at his friend.

"You work it all out?" Loxly asked, leaning forward to set his glass on the table. His plate had a few crumbs on it, but Larken's still held most of her sandwich. "Shaved chicken breast," Loxly supplied. "It was pretty good."

"And when did you learn the word *shaved* could be applied to poultry?"

"When Larken made it for me."

There were so many jabs he could have made, most of which related to Larken being named after poultry herself. Instead, he said, "Braves went over my head to try and have her transferred last night. As soon as she was placed in transit, I couldn't access her file or any of the messages sent through the system relating to her."

"But," Loxly dropped his leg and leaned forward, "we're keepin' her, right?"

"Of course we are." Loxly's eyebrows shot up to his hairline, so

Soren added, "I would never hear the end of it from you and Hinlee if we didn't."

"*Uh-huh*," Loxly said, leaning back into the couch again.

Soren was about to tell him to shut up when they heard Larken's door open and shut. She rounded the corner into the common room, that jacket zipped all the way up. The collar was pulled up under her ears, and Soren was sure that if it had a hood, she would have that pulled up as well. Her eyes were rimmed in pink, but she didn't appear to have cried. She just sat back down where she had been before and pulled her knees to her chest. "I guess I know why my message didn't go through." She dumped her communicator in Soren's lap and said, "Vallen says I need your private extension in case something like this happens again."

Soren added his number to the device and sent himself General Maxwell's information. His own communicator chimed in his pocket, letting him know that the message went through. When he finished, he handed it back to her. Larken took her communicator, shoved it into the jacket pocket, and then pulled her hands up into the sleeves. The three of them were quiet for a while before she said, "If you wanted to transfer me, I would understand. It's not like I'm an easy person to be around."

"You think it will be easier with another squad?" Soren asked before Loxly could say something sappy and stupid. "You'll be treated the same somewhere else as you are here. You might as well be around people who like you."

She looked at him, her teal eyes saying something he didn't understand.

"Besides, are you really going to take away Loxly's coffee machine before he gets a chance to try it?"

"*Maker*, coffee *maker*. Get it right."

Larken smiled, looking so very tired. Soren looked away and said, "Why don't you go relax?"

"Are you actually being nice to me?" she asked, half-surprised, half-teasing.

"No, you just look like crap."

"Just what every girl wants to hear. No wonder they're all banging on our door to get the chance to speak to you," she said as she stood.

Loxly barked a laugh, and Soren couldn't suppress the smirk that touched his lips. Maybe the two of them would get along better than he had originally thought.

CHAPTER 11

Larken ignored the call on her communicator, just like she had been ignoring all the messages as well. They had all been the same, saying that he had only wanted the best for her and that he hadn't meant to upset her. But Dominic didn't understand why she was upset. It wasn't that he was trying to control her, she was used to that. It was that he created another rift in the squad. Her communicator started buzzing again, and she ignored it once more.

"You need to take that?" Hinlee asked, the part she was breaking down for Larken still in her hands.

"No, sorry," Larken said, turning the vibration and sound off and sticking it in her pocket.

"*Like I was saying,*" Hinlee pointed at a white spot on the piece of rubber hose, "this part is no good because it's going to bubble soon. Fix that and then you fix the problem."

"Which was a clicking sound at takeoff?"

Hinlee sighed and set the part down. "No, it's not. But that's okay. At least you're pretty."

"*Hey!*" Larken gasped and then threw a crumpled piece of paper at her.

She laughed and said, "Unfortunately, I don't think I can clear you for mechanical work. But you're good at lots of other things, so don't feel too bad."

Larken sighed and dropped onto a stool. "I haven't even been active four days, and I've already been in a fight, gotten someone kicked out, almost failed my flying exam, and failed my mechanical one."

"You also have an oil smudge on your cheek, but I wasn't going to say anything and make you feel bad."

Larken only laughed dejectedly and said, *"Thanks."*

"What do you have after this?"

"Gym time with Brecker."

"Aww, super jealous."

"What does Brecker do?" Larken asked. "Soren said that everyone in the team excels at something, but he didn't mention him."

"Brecker is the one who goes out into the field and assesses the situation before we all get off the aircraft. So, he spends most of his time in the gym."

"And I'm sure you have no problems with that."

"No, I can't say I have any issues with the results of his hard work." Hinlee waggled her eyebrows, making Larken laugh.

"How long have you been together?"

A dreamy smile lit up her face as she said, "Three years."

"And he's the one?"

"Most definitely. I can't wait for the day this war is over and he drags me to the tabernacle."

"Does it scare you that he's the one who goes and makes sure that everything is safe?"

"It does, but I know Maxim has a plan for us, so I try not to let it worry me."

"I wish I could be more like that."

"What? Not worry?"

"Know that Maxim has a plan for me. My whole life, I've felt a little lost. It's better here, but I don't know. I'm probably not making any sense."

"No, I get it. Your whole life you've been told what to do and how to do it. You've always had to think about how your actions affected your family and not yourself. I would probably feel a little lost too." She looked at Larken kindly and added, "As for the trusting thing, I think you need to listen to others less and Him more. He will tell you what path to take."

Larken held Hinlee's gaze until her skin started to itch. A communicator on the table started buzzing, and Hinlee pulled off one of her grease-stained gloves before picking it up. "It's Brecker. He wants to know where you are."

"Shoot!" Larken pulled out her communicator and saw that her alarm to remind her to start heading for the gym went off ten minutes ago. "I turned everything off so we wouldn't have to listen to it."

"I'll tell him you're on your way, don't worry."

"See you tonight!" Larken called over her shoulder as she rushed out of the garage.

She passed various aircraft or other more archaic modes of transportation in various states of repair. There were some aircraft suspended in the air on hoists, while others were completely dismantled with a small group of people around them, watching as the machine was put back together. The place reeked of fuel and oil, despite the open garage doors that everything came and went through, and Larken was glad when she pushed out into the hallway.

She looked at her communicator, but she didn't see a missed message from Brecker. Though he also knew that she had been with Hinlee, so she didn't really blame him for messaging her instead. Larken had everyone's personal number now and no longer messaged through the Squad Communication System. After what had happened the previous day, she didn't trust the SCS anymore.

Larken kept her eyes on her communicator, following the map, and a third eye up so she didn't run into someone. Not that it would matter; she was so small that the men she passed probably wouldn't even feel it. Larken had pulled her hair back into a ponytail that morning, knowing that she would spend the afternoon working out, but now she wished she had something to hide behind. Larken felt like everyone was staring at her, and she wanted to scrub her skin until she didn't feel their gazes anymore.

Turning down a hall she almost missed, she heard someone calling her name. Stopping, she shuddered when she recognized whose voice it was. Larken didn't know if she wanted to turn and yell at him or try and hide. But Dominic's warm fingers were already grabbing her elbow before she could decide.

"Lark, hey, please talk to me." His voice was soft and sweet, like melting butter.

Knowing she shouldn't, Larken turned to face him as an alert sounded for Squad 25 to report for duty. His normally styled hair was mussed like he had constantly been running his fingers through it, and he had dark bags under his chocolate eyes. He even looked slightly pale. She didn't hold back and said, "You look awful."

He smiled softly and pulled something from his pocket. "And you look like you've had an interesting afternoon."

The thing from his pocket turned out to be a white handkerchief, and he brought it to her left cheek. Larken had forgotten that Hinlee said she had an oil smudge there. Her face heated as he got closer and started rubbing her cheek. She could see his individual eyelashes, and for some reason, they were captivating. Then she remembered the last time they were this close, he had kissed her. Larken had to fight not to jerk her head back until he pulled away.

"There you go."

She brought her palm up to the spot that he had wiped at. "Thanks, that probably explains why I felt like people have been staring at me since I left the garage."

"They were more likely staring at you because you are a beautiful woman." Then he muttered, "*As much as I hate it.*"

"You hate that people think I'm beautiful?"

"I hate that other men stare at you."

"Oh," Larken said, too stunned to say anything else. She didn't know why, but every time she thought she was used to how forward he was around her, he would say things like that.

His face went serious, and he cupped the cheek he had just cleaned. "Lark, I'm so sorry. I didn't mean to go behind your back, and it wasn't my intention to upset you. I just wanted what was best for you. I swear it."

"What's best for me, Dominic, is having a squad and a Captain that live on base with me that I can grow close to. This is my first chance at a real family, and you doing that, you trying to have me transferred, keeps putting a strain on that."

"I didn't know, I thought—"

"You thought, but you never asked. I'm tired of never being asked what I think or how I feel, Dominic. I don't want to live like that anymore."

"Then I'll drop it. I will let it go and never bring it up again. I should have asked what you wanted, I'm sorry."

"Thank you."

"I promise, I'll always ask you before I do anything in the future." His smile turned sly. "Unless I kiss you, of course. There is nothing more unromantic than asking a pretty girl if you can kiss her."

Face hot, Larken turned and said, "Just make sure that girl wants to be kissed before you do it. Otherwise, it's harassment."

Dominic laughed and stepped up to her side to keep up with her. "So where are you going now?"

"To the gym. I have a date with Brecker."

"Do you think Hinlee will mind?"

"Don't worry, she knows." Larken stopped and looked up at him. "How did you know they were dating?"

"Everyone knows that they're dating. They're the lovebirds of Squad 19."

"Oh," Larken murmured and continued to the gym. His answer had merit, but she couldn't shake the feeling that he wasn't telling the whole truth.

They reached the gym, and Larken turned and raised her hand to wave goodbye, but Dominic pulled her into a hug. He smelled like fresh linen and blueberries. His hands splayed across her back, holding her to him tightly. Her cheek was pressed to his uniform, and she hoped that there wasn't any more oil on her face that would stain it.

"I really am sorry."

"I know," she whispered. Larken let herself wonder for a moment what would happen if she actually believed him. Would he prove to her how sorry he was? Would he keep his promise of always thinking of her first? No, probably not. Dominic was too selfish for that. He was friends with her brother after all, and that told her all she needed to know.

He pulled away and tilted her face up to look at him. His fingers were warm on her chin and he asked, "Will you stop ignoring my messages now?"

"Possibly."

"Then I will try to remain optimistic. I hope you have a good workout."

"Thanks. I hope you have a good whatever it is that you're doing today."

"Well, I will now." He winked and then brushed her cheek with his thumb. "I'll message you later about lunch sometime."

"Okay."

He dropped his hand and then started backing away. Larken didn't know why, but she didn't want to go into the gym until she saw him leave. Was she worried that he would follow her in? Or was it something else?

Why do I do this to myself?

Shaking her head, she turned and walked in. The gym was huge, with high ceilings and mats that stretched out across the floor. The deep blue mats made it look more like artificial water with the occasional red landmass. Men and women trained with each other and against basic level practice droids, nothing like the ones Vallen had her use. There were doors that she could only assume led to different areas to work out since everyone on the mats was practicing combat.

Brecker was in the middle of the floor, sparring with a practice droid. He didn't use any weapons, just his fists. When she reached him, he punched the thing in the chin and grabbed its head. Then, after breaking its neck, he asked, "Hinlee said you were on your way; what took so long?"

"Dominic caught me in the hallway."

Brecker scowled and rolled his eyes. It was worlds different from his usually soft expression, and she worried that he might be upset with her instead of Dominic. Seeming not to notice her unease, he asked, "Your legs run as well as your mouth?"

"Um, yes?"

"Good, let's go." He turned and started walking to the doors that she assumed led to the tracks.

Together, they went in and then set off. Larken kept up with him stride for stride, the burn in her legs reminding her of what she was capable of. She was strong, her body was a weapon, and she could do anything. Her shoulder throbbed, reminding her that that wasn't true, but she ignored it. In this moment, she was pure power. All she had to do was put one foot in front of the other, nothing else. She only wished that she had some music.

CHAPTER 12

T he alarm went off and startled Larken so badly that she bolted upright. Placing her hand on her heart, she tried to remember why it was beating so fast. She closed her eyes, and the sensation of falling had her eyes flying open once more. Larken shook herself, forcing herself to breathe. "Just a dream," she whispered, grabbing her shoulder. "It was just a dream."

Jumping out of bed, she grabbed her communicator and turned off the alarm. Larken saw that she already had a message from Dominic wondering when she had an opening in her schedule. She honestly didn't know. Apart from her day of flying, her schedule had been so packed that she found herself nodding off in the cafeteria or whenever she sat down. Her new life was less physically demanding, but all the new places and people were starting to catch up with her.

Pulling off her pajamas, she put on her uniform and angrily adjusted her left bra strap. The material it was made of had given her a rash. She wondered if there was a way to use her tokens to order different ones, but she didn't know who to ask. Maybe she would ask Hinlee. Larken knew she couldn't ask the person who showed her how to work the Vendor; she wouldn't even be able to get the words out. Shuddering, she decided that she would mess around with it on her dorm shift. And if she couldn't figure it out, she would just ask Vallen.

Stretching her right arm, Larken was careful not to move her shoulder the wrong way. She was scheduled to see Jodi first thing tomorrow morning; she just needed to get through the rest of the day and one more night. Larken had tried looking at the Vendor to see what was available mattress-wise, but Vallen had told her on Monday not to worry about it and that it had been taken care of.

Larken was excited to see what she was getting, having never received many gifts growing up. The others were excited about their purchases as well. Loxly had been going on nonstop about his coffee maker, and Hinlee had ordered a few new things for her's and Brecker's rooms. Levi picked out what new appliances they needed for their kitchen, and Soren was very tight-lipped about what he ordered, if he had even ordered anything at all.

Yawning, Larken left her room and made her way to the kitchen. She grabbed a mug and started fishing around in the drawers. When she didn't find what she was looking for, Larken started opening the cupboards. It wasn't until she opened the sixth one that she was startled by a voice asking, "Looking for poison? You know, you aren't treating tonight, even though I think you should. You have enough tokens. Though, I can't say I'm not glad you won't have a chance to spike my dinner."

"For your information," Larken said, ignoring Soren and reaching for another cupboard, "I'm looking for tea."

"Don't have any, we're coffee people."

She felt Soren's warmth as he walked up next to her, crossing his arms and leaning against the counter to watch her. "You mean Loxly is a coffee person."

"Same difference. You can ask Levi, but I wouldn't get my hopes up." Larken looked up at him, but he leaned forward, trying to keep his eyes on her back. "What happened to your shoulder?"

Blushing, she faced him full-on, not letting him get a better look. "I hurt it a few years ago, you know that. Don't ask stupid questions."

"It's all red. It wasn't like that yesterday," he said, pushing off from the counter and looming over her.

"And how would you know what it looked like yesterday? Do you have a thing for shoulders or something?" She took a step back.

"Fine, I'm guessing. What's wrong with your shoulder?" He took a step as well. *"The left one."*

"Slept on it wrong." She took another step and her back hit the wall.

"Looks serious." He took a step, and then put a hand on the wall, caging her in. "Do you need me to escort you to the medic?"

"No."

"What's wrong with your shoulder, Larken?"

His face was only a few inches away from her and his eyes flashed green. He was so close and so handsome, Larken couldn't think, so she panicked. Instead of calmly explaining the situation, she opened her mouth and yelled, "My military-issue bra is giving me a rash!"

He coughed, his face going red, and Larken pushed around him and fled. Soren didn't try to stop her, and she doubted she would be able to look him in the eye for the rest of her life. She didn't need tea, she didn't need her sword, she just needed to be away from Soren. Leaving the dorm, Larken ran until she reached the separate building designated for medic training, passing reporting soldiers and full squads in their tactical gear. One pull on the door told her that it was locked. Larken kicked the wall, fell against it, and slid to the ground. Crossing her arms atop her knees, Larken buried her face and groaned.

It had to be my bra. It had to be a rash.

Larken groaned again.

Minutes ticked by, and still, her embarrassment didn't ebb. The scene kept replaying in her mind, getting worse each time. Why was she so flustered? It's not like she was the only one who had ever worn a bra before. And hadn't she teased him about underwear only a few days ago? So, why was now different? Maybe it was the way that sleep still clung to his eyes. Maybe it was the way he spoke, the very sound of that gravely voice that always made her knees a little weak. Or maybe, it was because he had been so close to her. The only other man that had ever been that close to her had been Dominic, and he had kissed her then. Could that be it?

But they didn't have that kind of relationship. They barely got along on the best days. So, why would she think that? Unless…

Do I want Captain Soren Deckard to kiss me?

A new wave of embarrassment washed over her, and she whined in the back of her throat.

"Rough day?" Her head snapped up, and she found Levi standing in front of her. "Sorry to tell you, it isn't even noon yet."

"*I know*," she groaned, dropping her head again.

"Well, sitting there isn't going to make it any better. Get up."

Reluctantly, Larken unfolded herself and stood, accepting the pack that Levi dumped into her arms. She fumbled to get her grip on it while he unlocked the door. Pulling it open, Levi looked over his shoulder and raised an eyebrow, silently asking her if she was coming.

Darting around him, she scurried into the building and waited for Levi to follow her. Even though the doors were made of glass and there were large windows everywhere, she still waited for him to turn the lights on before she moved. The whole place reeked of iodine and bleach and was made up of big white walls and open spaces. Larken looked at everything, feeling like her presence tainted the cleanliness of the place.

The two of them kept moving, Levi not looking back once to see if she was still following him. Turning down one hall, the smell of iodine turned to chlorine, and Larken sighed at the welcomed change. "You guys go swimming on your breaks?"

"It's for physical therapy," Levi grunted.

They took another turn and entered a room the same size as the gym she had just trained with Brecker in. The white walls and the large windows were the same, but this time, instead of that awful tan and grey speckled tile that paved the halls, the floors were covered in pale blue and green mats. It had a soothing effect, and she wondered if it was more for the medics or the patients. There were also little benches, like the ones she laid on for her corrections, placed randomly around the room.

Levi grabbed the pack out of her hands and headed to the back right bench, the one closest to the windows. She followed, trying to discreetly scratch her shoulder with the strap of her tank top. Dumping the pack on the ground, Levi motioned for her to sit on the bench. Her cheeks heated and she asked, "Did he tell you?"

"The only sign that grump gave that anything happened between the two of you was that he blushed enough for Hinlee to notice when Loxly asked about you at breakfast."

"Then how—"

"I was still in the dorm. I was actually getting out of the shower when I heard you shouting about your unfortunate predicament."

Larken swallowed and looked away from him. Her face felt hot again, and she wanted nothing more than to disappear.

"Do I need to examine you over there? Or are you going to be mature about this and come have a seat?"

Not really having much of a choice, Larken took a begrudging step forward, and then another until she was able to lower herself onto the bench. She watched as Levi unzipped the pack and pulled out a set of gloves and a medic kit. Pushing the straps off her left shoulder, she exposed as much of the rash as she could. Levi worked silently, looking at it and then fishing around in the kit.

"So…?" Larken asked.

"I'm afraid there is no easy way to say this. We're going to have to amputate."

"Wait, what? Are you serious?" Larken's pulse skyrocketed. *What's wrong with my shoulder?*

Smirking, Levi uncapped a tube of ointment and said, "No. It's contact dermatitis. It happens to a lot of the new recruits, nothing to be embarrassed about." He started rubbing the ointment onto her shoulder. "Shouting about it for your whole squad to hear though…"

"You're not going to let that go, are you?"

"I wasn't the one yelling about my bra."

Larken sighed and pulled her straps back up. The itching faded quickly, but her face was still warm.

"Talk to Hinlee about it; the same thing happened to her. She'll be able to help you out."

"Thanks."

"Okay, exam time."

"Right, what do I need to do?"

"I'm going to dictate scenarios, and you'll tell me the correct way to respond. If you pass, then you'll move on to practicing with the androids."

"Sounds good to me."

Levi sat on the bench next to her and hunched forward, resting his elbows on his knees. He scratched at his beard and then looked at her. "You're on the field and the soldier next to you is shot in the leg. What do you do?"

"What do I have on me?"

His lips twitched. "You have a belt, your gun, a small medic-pack with only the basics, and a communicator."

"I would call for help, give my location and the type of injury, and use my belt as a tourniquet. Then I would disinfect the wound, slap a bandage on it to keep out infection, and move on."

"Good. Next question."

CHAPTER 13

Larken yawned broadly, and Soren thought she deserved it. Stifling his own yawn, he felt a new wave of annoyance wash over him. Not only had their dinner run late the night before, but a dorm-wide alarm sounded two hours before any of them had to wake up for *mandatory renovations*. Why he had to be up when he didn't order anything for his room, Soren had no idea, but here he was.

With an hour until the cafeteria opened, all six of them were in Soren's personal gym that he had been given with his title of Captain. It was nothing big, just one of ten small gyms given to exceptional Captains, but the six of them could work out together comfortably. Brecker and Hinlee were running around the track that hugged the wall, and Loxly stretched. Levi sat on the only bench in the room, hunched over with his head hanging down slightly, and Soren suspected that he was asleep. Soren had just finished his own stretches and was debating between running or fighting with an android. But Larken, she flawlessly moved through a series of techniques, keeping an android that had to be a medium level or higher at bay, while yawning every few seconds. She didn't even look awake and somehow didn't miss a single step.

The smell of coffee told Soren who was now hovering over his shoulder, even before Loxly opened his mouth to speak. Soren, not in the mood for whatever *observation* Loxly felt compelled to share with him, asked, "How do you expect to hide on the battlefield or in enemy territory when you always smell like stale coffee beans?"

"Good morning to you too, Cap."

Soren grunted, his attempt to dissuade Loxly from speaking not working.

"She's somethin', ain't she?"

"If by *something*, you mean a pain in the neck, then yes."

"So, you haven't noticed how she barely has her eyes open and is still winnin'?"

Soren didn't say anything, and he hated that his silence was as much of an answer as if he had said yes.

"What time do you think she was up trainin' before she joined? She seems like she's used to this."

"Why don't you go ask her?" Soren asked, hoping that Loxly would pick up on him wanting this conversation to be over.

"You know, I thought about it. But then I was worried that if I startle her when she's like this, she might accidentally kill me."

"Right, *accidentally*."

"For your information, Cap, she thinks I'm sweet."

"Well, that makes one of us," Soren said, admittedly a little more intrigued about Larken's old training schedule.

Walking past the spot where his glaive rested against the wall, the rod only a slightly tarnished silver with a carbon-infused crystal blade, Soren went to the weapon rack that Squad 19 stashed their extra weapons on and grabbed his sword. The brass felt cold against his hand as he gave it a few practice swings. Soren stood ready, waiting for the right moment to act. He watched as Larken yawned again, not even breaking a sweat. Either she was a lot more skilled than he thought she was, or she had the android on a level that was too low for her. And since her previous teacher was famed for his brutality and fighting skills, Soren guessed it was the latter.

He smiled.

Looks like you're in for a rude awakening.

She pivoted her foot slightly and Soren was on the move. Larken raised her blade and turned, about to deal the fatal blow. Soren quickly flipped the off switch on the android and pushed it out of the way, just in time to catch her blade with his. Her eyes shot open and he smirked at her. He watched as her eyes turned more blue than green, and a wicked smirk of her own twisted her lips.

Before Soren could even gain his footing, Larken spun out and was back with another blow aimed at his left knee. Soren blocked it and decided to go on the defensive until she wore herself out. He caught three more of her blows before she grinned and said, "Big mistake."

Doubling her efforts, somehow Soren went from blocking to having his right foot pulled out from under him. His backside hit the gym mat with a *thud*, and everyone stopped moving. No one said anything as he looked up into her eyes and raised an eyebrow.

"Did you really think that you were the first person to try tiring me out?"

"How many times did it take you to learn to cheat like that?"

Larken threw her head back and laughed. "Vallen calls it cheating too." She smiled and offered him a hand. He knocked it away gently and stood on his own. "It took me a year to realize that Vallen was letting me tire myself out. He told me before we started every day that I needed to use my head and not just blindly attack. When I realized what he was doing, it took me another year to get the maneuver perfect. And I built up my endurance during that time, so, if your ploy had worked, we would have been here for a long time."

Soren could only smirk.

Who is Larken Hale? And what goes on in that head of hers?

A squeal sounded in the gym, and Hinlee bounded up to her. Grabbing her elbow and pulling her towards Brecker, she said, "You *have* to show me!"

A hint of pink touched Larken's cheeks, and she looked over at him with wide eyes. Looking back at Hinlee, she muttered, "Oh, um, I've never taught anyone anything before. I can try to do it slowly, but I—"

"Don't worry about it. Soren will be able to see it, then he can teach us all." Larken still looked a little reluctant, so Hinlee added, "We're at war, Larken. Do you really not want your friends to know how to take down men like General Maxwell?"

That was the end to Larken's protests and she sighed, still looking more embarrassed than Soren thought she should.

The rest of the day hadn't gone any smoother. Breakfast had been awkward, what with everyone staring at them and speculating about all the delivery drones and the commotion of the renovations. Then, it was Soren's turn to give Larken an exam and approve her for whatever weapons she wanted to use for her specialty training. She chose everything, unsurprisingly. He pushed her harder than what was required for the examination, but he wanted to pay her back for the little stunt she had pulled that morning.

Lunch had been the same as breakfast, but this time, some of their fellow soldiers were brave enough to walk up to them and ask Larken about her *special deliveries*. Loxly, of course, would tell everyone about the new coffee maker that he ordered, and Hinlee jumped to Larken's defense as well, explaining how she ordered a few new things for her room. Brecker and Levi only admitted to making purchases when Hinlee kicked them under the table.

But it was after lunch that things had really started going downhill. They had their first group session scheduled, and it had not gone well. First, the tactical gear that Larken had been given didn't fit. So, they were late to the field because they had to wait for the adjustments to be made. Then, Larken had looked ill and shook from the time they boarded the Arsene until they reached the correct altitude. Loxly had then kicked Soren out of his copilot seat and given it to Larken. The shaking had eventually stopped, and she didn't look quite as green, but Soren still felt annoyed that he had to trade his comfy seat for the hard bench that he had to share with Levi.

Once they landed, they had to wait because some of the practice droids had some kind of virus that one of the base technicians was going crazy trying to figure out. When they were given the okay, they jumped from the aircraft, but they had to hang back to help Larken. She was so short that, if she were to jump from the Arsene unassisted, she would roll an ankle, or worse.

When they had devised their plan of attack, they set out, and Hinlee immediately stepped into a rabbit hole and twisted her foot. Brecker had pushed through and finished scouting for them, but then remained by her side for the rest of the time, changing out ice packs to help with the swelling. Levi joined the fray, but he quickly ran out of ammunition, choosing to carry medical supplies over weaponry, as had been decided before they started. Soren had been fighting with an android and used his glaive to cut what would have been the carotid artery had the android been human, only to look over and see Loxly fumbling on the ground. A mist had set in, telling them that it would soon rain, and Loxly was having a hard time trying to find the ammo he had dropped in the tall grass.

Larken was far ahead of them, taking out each android that she came across. It had been decided that she would take point in the formation, but she hadn't realized that the rest of her squad had fallen behind. She was quickly overtaken by the sheer numbers of androids that came out of the woods and surrounding areas.

And now, they all sat silently at dinner, not looking up or talking to each other. Hinlee would move every so often, and then wince when she did. She was out of commission for the next three days, with plenty of bed rest and an uncomfortable-looking splint, to top everything off. Soren scooped up his last bite of stew, not even registering the taste as he swallowed. They were supposed to be one of the best squads, if not *the* best, but today they were a far cry from it.

Soren's communicator chimed in his pocket and he pulled it out. Reading the message, he said, "We can go back to the dorm now."

Loxly pushed up from the table and sighed, *"Finally."* He helped

Brecker get Hinlee to her feet and added, "I'm so ready to fall into bed."

"You and me both." Hinlee agreed. "Although, I was looking forward to trying out that new shower head I ordered. It's supposed to massage the knots out of your back, but," she looked at her foot, "I guess it'll have to wait."

"I could always try it and tell you if it works or not," Loxly suggested.

"Fat chance. You keep to your own stall, don't go contaminating ours."

"Well, we'll just see what Larken has to—"

"If you wanted a new shower head, you should have talked to Brecker and ordered one," Larken interrupted.

"Oh, come on! I'd let you use mine!"

"And I would be the one stuck cleaning all the hair from the drain," Brecker muttered.

They all bickered good-naturedly on the way back to the dorm. Even Levi threw out an insult or two. Soren was just ready to collapse onto his bed. He felt like a failure as a soldier and as a Captain. Soren also worried that the day's events would reach General Maxwell. This was not the kind of impression he wanted to make. He wanted to show General Maxwell that he had made the right decision in picking Squad 19 for Larken. But, after the day they had, he wouldn't be surprised if General Maxwell transferred Larken somewhere else. Not to Braves's squad, but somewhere.

A flash of blonde appeared in the corner of Soren's eye, and he grimaced as he looked down at her. Larken smiled softly and met his gaze. "The first time I sparred with Vallen, he broke my nose. Today was a lot more fun than trying to stop the bleeding and waiting for the medic."

Before he could say anything, she hurried forward and jabbed a laughing Loxly in the side with her elbow. He reached out an arm, wrapped it over her shoulders, and pulled her close. He could then be heard asking her what flavor of coffee he should try first. Soren smiled a little, remembering that she preferred tea. His eyes fell to her left shoulder, noticing for the first time that the little red bumps were now almost gone.

When they reached the dorm, Levi held the door to the common room open for Brecker and Hinlee. Loxly then caught it, and Larken didn't even have to duck to walk in under his arm. Soren closed the door just as Hinlee was situated on the couch, and she sighed as she leaned into Brecker's side. Levi was already in the kitchen, preparing a cold compress for her, but Soren suspected that he also wanted to get a good look at the new appliances he ordered. Loxly soon joined him and gasped at the sight of his new machine.

The thing was the same size as the old fridge and could apparently make any kind of specialty drink. Loxly started messing around with it, and soon the smell of fresh coffee filled the air as he asked if anyone wanted anything.

Loxly sat next to Larken with a steaming blue mug, and she narrowed her eyes at it. "How much did that thing cost?"

"Can you really put a price on true love?" he asked in return.

"It was over three thousand tokens," Hinlee said. "I was talking to him when he placed the order."

Loxly took a noisy sip and sighed. "Tokens well spent, I assure you."

"Does it make tea?" Larken asked as she pulled out a buzzing communicator.

"Why would it make tea? It's a *coffee* maker. Why do I have to keep explainin' this to all of you? It's a maker," Loxly looked up to Soren, "not a machine, and the thing this maker makes is *coffee*," he said, looking back to Larken. "Does everyone understand now?"

"Yes, Professor Beau," Levi mocked as he gently set the compress on Hinlee's ankle. She jumped slightly at the cold but then relaxed as Levi took the seat next to Soren.

Loxly gave some retort, but Soren missed it, too busy watching the way Larken rolled her eyes and typed out a message. Not even a second later, her communicator buzzed again. She went on like that for a few minutes, not noticing that she was being watched. Soren thought he knew who was messaging her, and it irritated him. She looked too tense to be messaging General Maxwell, and no one in the common room had their communicators out.

Hinlee dozed against Brecker, who talked to Levi about the new dishwasher. Loxly added his thoughts every now and then but was mostly only concerned with his coffee. It didn't take long before he leaned over and looked at Larken's communicator.

"Who's *Captain Debonair?*"

Larken scoffed. "Like you can't guess."

She started typing another message and Loxly snorted, causing a faint smile to play at her lips. The communicator buzzed again, and three seconds later, Loxly was gipping his side and laughing. "Poor boy doesn't know what he's gettin' into, does he?"

Larken typed out another message. "Nope."

"I'll remember to keep him in my prayers." Loxly laughed and then took another swig of his coffee.

"Prayers or not, he isn't going to get what he wants."

"Which is?" Soren asked, his scowl firmly in place.

Larken turned red. "*Cake,* obviously."

Loxly snorted into his cup so hard that he started choking. Larken glared at him, and Soren could feel the unspoken words passing between them. He wasn't sure which annoyed him more, the fact that Braves was still bothering Larken or that Loxly and her were close enough now to have silent conversations. Deciding to put an end to it before he said something in his sleep-deprived aggravation, Soren stood and made his way to his room. The first thing he noticed was the smell. Then he remembered that Hinlee had taken the time to order them all new mattresses and new sheets.

Well, I guess that answers my question from this morning.

Soren pushed away the annoyance that surged at the new furniture smell and started readying himself for bed. When he dropped onto his bed, he couldn't say that he hated the feel of the soft pillowcase against his cheek or the way that he sunk into the bed pleasantly instead of maneuvering around the uncomfortable bar that ran down the middle of his old bed frame. Soren barely had time to breathe before he was fast asleep.

CHAPTER 14

"Wait, so you've never been to service before?" Hinlee asked. "I've seen services, I've just never been to a public one." Larken was in her usual spot, sandwiched between Hinlee and Loxly. Soren walked behind them with Levi, his now usual spot as well. "We have a preacher at the Manor, but he never really made a lot of sense, and I think he only talked about what my mother wanted him to. I asked him about it a few times when I was younger, when what he said went against what Vallen taught me, and he could never give me a straight answer. So, I normally just watched net sermons or talked to Vallen."

"You're missin' out, Little Bird."

"There's going to be singing, right?" She sounded excited.

"And a band," Loxly added. "I don't mean to brag, but I've been told I have the voice of—"

"A dog with a stomach flu?" Hinlee interjected.

Larken turned her head to the mechanic and started laughing, her damp waves moving with her. Soren had listened to Hinlee gushing over Larken's hair that morning before they left the dorm and ask why she didn't wake her up when the stylist was there. Larken had explained that she thought Vallen fired Cindy and she had just braided her hair when she got out of the shower the night before, adding that she used to do her hair that way whenever Vallen would take her out somewhere nice.

Soren wasn't sure how he felt about this side of Larken that he was just now seeing for the first time. The one who dressed up the best she could in uniform for tabernacle and was excited to experience something new. He also wasn't sure how he felt about this new version of General Maxwell that he had been learning about. He had always looked up to him because he was a good soldier and a man of faith. Soren had never, in all of his years, ever considered the fact that he also played the role of caring father.

When they reached the tabernacle, they all eased their way in, greeting the other soldiers that wished them a *good morning* or a passing *hello*. The familiar and comforting sight of the worn wooden pews and stage greeted them. The windows were skinny but tall and let in the yellow light of the sun that had the tabernacle looking hazy and warm.

They made their way to the designated Squad 19 pew. Hinlee's limp was a little more pronounced now that she had to try and maneuver around pews as well as other people. Brecker was there whenever she stumbled and was more than willing to help her to her seat. Soren's heart warmed at the sight. Even when no one was looking, they were still so kind and loving to each other.

They all squeezed into the pew, Soren in an end seat, and Levi in the other closest to the wall. Somehow, Larken ended up in the only seat next to Soren, with Loxly on her other side. The rag-tag group of musicians walked onto the stage and picked up their instruments. Everyone stood, leaving Larken in her seat until she realized what was happening. Quickly standing, she teetered a little and reached out, gripping the pew in front of her to regain her balance.

The singer began talking about the good weather and how he was looking forward to the visitor's day coming up next month, and Soren noticed a strange smell. No, strange wasn't the right word. *Different.* He breathed deeply, trying to figure out what it was, and Larken looked up at him with wide eyes.

"What?" she whispered

"Do you smell that?"

Her cheeks went pink. "Does it smell bad?"

Soren sniffed again, and the strong smell of summer danced under his nose. It was a little salty and the scent of citrus almost covered it. He was reminded of the sea and pink fruit. Larken reached up and pulled on a strand of her wheat-colored hair, and that's when he realized where the smell was coming from. He raised an eyebrow at her, silently asking for an explanation.

"The new shampoo I ordered came yesterday. I had to guess at what I wanted since I couldn't open it and smell it when I picked it out. Is it bad?"

"What's it supposed to be?"

"Grapefruit and orange blossom."

Before Soren could help himself, he leaned in and got a whiff of her hair. He could smell the grapefruit now that he knew what it was, and he could smell the hint of water that still clung to her strands. A calm washed over him, and he didn't want to pull away when he did. Looking up at the stage, he muttered, "It's fine."

He didn't look at her for the rest of the service. Not when she laughed at the preacher's jokes, not when she leaned over to ask Loxly a question about what the preacher was saying, and especially not when she sang. He had never heard a voice quite like hers, and she somehow knew all the words to the songs they were singing. Many people turned to look at them, but she was lost in her own little world, like she was communicating with Maxim in a foreign language that she could only understand.

When the service had ended, they waited for the tabernacle to clear out a little before trying to make their way to the cafeteria. But when Soren stood, he noticed that the normally empty pew reserved for Squad 22 had what looked like a blond idiot sitting there. Soren sat back down and grabbed Larken by her elbow, pulling her back to the pew as well. Leaning in, he was momentarily lost in her big doe eyes that looked more blue at that moment, but managed to ask, "You wanna see your friend today?"

"My—?" she looked over at Loxly confused, and then turned back. "What?"

He just raised an eyebrow, waiting for her to understand. She narrowed her eyes at him, trying to figure out what he meant, and then they widened. Shaking her head, she whispered, "Not really. He tried to make lunch plans for today, but—"

Soren didn't let her finish; he just leaned forward and met Levi's eyes, which wasn't that hard since the other members of the squad were all watching him and Larken anyway. He nodded and they slowly started creeping out of the pew the other way. Soren kept his hands on Larken's shoulders, and Brecker and Loxly flanked him, helping him hide her. They walked like that all the way to the cafeteria.

Once they had their food and were sitting at their usual table, Loxly turned to Larken and said, "Let's talk about those pipes."

"What pipes?"

"*Your* pipes. How long you been singin' like that?"

Hinlee turned on her too. "Oh my gosh, yes! You sounded amazing!"

Larken's eyes went wide and color crept up her throat. "Oh, um, all my life?"

"Want me to introduce you to String?" Loxly offered.

"Who?"

"String. Not sure what his real name is, only ever met him the one time. But he plays the guitar, that really moody one in the corner this mornin'," Loxly said around a mouthful of food. "He's in charge of music for this base. I could introduce you and you could—"

Face pink, Larken interrupted, "That's not necessary. It's one thing singing in the back of the tabernacle or when I'm with Vallen; it's another getting up in front of people and actually doing it."

Loxly shrugged and then started talking about a new upgrade that he learned about for his gun. To the sharpshooter's credit, it was a different upgrade than the one he was going on about the week before, but Soren didn't keep up with the conversation, still bothered by the way Larken had shrunk back into the pew when she learned Braves was there. Instead, he looked to Larken, who pulled apart her roast beef with her fork, and asked, "How often does he message you?"

"Too much," she grumbled, not needing him to say who he meant. She stabbed a hunk of potato and stuffed it in her mouth, opting for the diced baked potatoes instead of mashed. "It's not that I hate him or anything, I just feel weird around him."

"How so?"

"Like…" she finished chewing and swallowed. "I feel like I have to act like the person he thinks I am instead of *who* I am. He calls me Lark all the time and always says that he's glad we're friends. But I always feel like Liam's younger sister instead of me."

Soren looked deep into her eyes and asked seriously, "Would it help if I called you Lark too?"

Her hand shot out and she smacked him playfully in the bicep, rolling her eyes as she did so. "*HAHA*, very funny."

Soren couldn't help the snort that worked its way out of his throat and turned back to his food. "Sorry…Lark."

Instead of yelling, she giggled, and he chuckled as well. Loxly looked up and gasped, "Cap! Are you actually laughin'? I didn't think you knew how!"

Soren scooped up a bit of his mashed potatoes, pulled his spoon back, and hit Loxly square in the chest.

"My Sunday best!" Loxly exclaimed while grabbing a napkin.

"Sorry, Cadet, hand slipped."

"Yeah-huh, just you wait till we go gunnin'. I'll get you back."

"Gunning?" Larken asked. "Like, in the arenas with the paint?"

Loxly dipped a clean napkin into his water and then brought it to his shirt. "We're too fancy for paint. When we hit a limb, your gear locks up and you can't use it anymore. So, if I shot you in the leg, your gear would lock and you would have to limp if you decided to keep goin'."

"That still sounds really fun!" She had dropped her fork and leaned onto the table, hanging on to Loxly's every word.

"I'll take you some time," he said with a wink.

"Really?! You mean it?"

Loxly clearly hadn't expected her level of sheer excitement, and he blushed slightly as he stuttered out, "Y-yeah, sure, Little Bird. Whenever you want."

"How cute!" Hinlee crooned.

Loxly blushed harder and shot her a glare, only making her laugh.

Grinning, Larken took another bite of food. Soren watched her chew for a moment, then asked, "You've never been?"

Her smile faltered a little and she said softly, "You need friends to be able to go. And what's the point of going out to do it with Vallen when we used real weapons at home?" She tilted her head and rubbed her jaw against her shoulder, and Soren wondered if she was wishing she had that black jacket.

"We'll take you, Larken, don't worry about it," Hinlee assured, giving her a side hug. Larken's smile was back, and it lasted through the rest of the meal, the walk back to the dorm, and even when they were all hanging out in the common room.

They decided to play cards that afternoon, and Larken was surprisingly good at it. She was as cut-throat in the game as she was in her fighting. Soren could only assume that General Maxwell never went easy on her in anything. Loxly was griping about all the points she had dumped on him in the last round when a knock sounded at the door. Levi got up, leaving Soren's side and disappearing somewhere behind him.

It wasn't long after the door opened when they heard a familiar voice say, "Care package delivery."

Larken dropped the cards she had been shuffling, shot up out of her seat, and bolted across the room before any of them had time to blink. General Maxwell barely had time to dump the care packages into Levi's hands before he caught Larken and spun her around, a soft smile on his face. When he set her down, he tousled her hair. "Hey, runt, how you doin'?"

Larken just laughed and pulled him into the common room. She told him all about that morning, what the service was like, the music, her excitement over going gunning, everything. General Maxwell listened to what she had to say, not interrupting her once. Levi handed out the little care packages that Rich, Loxly's father, sent everyone every week. Hinlee tore into hers, opening the chocolate that she and Rich both loved, and stuffed a piece into her mouth before offering one to Brecker.

When Larken had finished talking, General Maxwell asked her about her exams and what she had been cleared for. He already knew about her basic aircraft license and probably knew about all the other ones too, but she still told him about how she failed her mechanic exam and passed all the others with top marks. She then went on to tell him about their first outing, and General Maxwell actually laughed, making him look so much different from the fierce warrior that was all anyone saw.

"My first time out, my buddy shot himself in the foot on accident. We had all received new guns that day, and we learned that they were a lot more sensitive than what we were used to. But, getting over-powered by thirty androids?" He looked at his former pupil. "Larken, that's unacceptable."

She blushed. "Well, actually, it was really misty out, and I slipped on the wet grass. Then I was at gunpoint before I knew what was happening."

General Maxwell's jaw twitched. "That's still no excuse."

"I'll make sure they only send us out when it's sunny from now on," she said, her face just as impassive.

General Maxwell smiled slightly. Then he stood and said, "I was only cleared for five hours. I have to head back."

Larken's face fell, but she didn't protest. She just stood and followed him to the door.

"You find a sweater yet?" he asked her.

"I'm still choosing between an orange one and a bright pink one."

He pulled her into his arms, grumbling, "You hate both those colors." Then he whispered something in her ear, kissed her temple, and left.

Larken stood there, staring at the closed door for a moment, then announced that she was getting in the shower. Soren watched her disappear around the corner and had a funny feeling that she would be too vulnerable to spend any more time with them for the rest of the day.

CHAPTER 15

Larken sighed, scrolling through the Vendor. She had already added a few things to her basket, but she still felt like she was missing something. The Vendor only seemed to have raw ingredients, but having never ordered any before, she didn't know the quality. Her turn for dinner was coming up, and she wanted everything to be perfect. Larken should have ordered food the previous week to play around with the ingredients, but she hadn't thought about it. Vallen never minded her cooking, but he also wasn't very picky about what he ate. It was the soldier in him.

It had been almost a month, and Larken had adjusted to her new life well. Her schedule was now pretty regular, and she spent most of her time training with Soren, Brecker, or Levi. It had been no surprise to her that she excelled at the things Vallen had ingrained in her since the first day he arrived. She had gone to lunch with Dominic twice since that first time, and each time he was a little less unbearable. They were now to the point that she would even message him back most of the time rather than ignore him. But her favorite parts had been the services at the tabernacle, what she learned there, and how her relationship with Maxim had grown. She looked forward to each Sunday, and then to the little packages that Vallen would send her that held little notes or some form of sweet that she liked.

Her room had been fixed up as well. The dorm around her had gone through several changes over the past few Fridays. Hinlee kept finding things for her and Brecker, so there were always packages for them. Levi started replacing things around the kitchen, the latest of which had been a new microwave. The meal he had cooked for them the other week was *divine*, and Loxly had fought her for the leftovers. Which was why Larken was so nervous to cook for everyone. She didn't want to look like an idiot and accidentally make everyone sick.

Soren ended up ordering a new television and making a few minor changes to the common room. Couches were brought in with the last Friday delivery, and even though they were new and amazingly comfortable, they were still the same shade of crimson as the previous ones. Hinlee had done up the shower stall that the two of them shared and, at the request of Loxly, fixed up his and Brecker's as well. Larken had also seen a new shower head getting installed in the stall Levi and Soren shared, but not much else where Soren was concerned.

Hinlee had also helped the boys make whatever changes they wanted to their rooms. She had already ordered them all new beds and sheets, but she helped them pick out other furniture that matched their new additions. Hinlee had offered to help Larken as well, but she liked what Vallen had chosen for her. She had a new wooden bed frame that was stained the same shade as dark chocolate and a midnight blue comforter and sheets to cover her new mattress. She could still remember the moment of relief that first night she had laid on it.

A blue rug that was the same color as her bedding took up the majority of her floor, and her desk had been replaced with what she had thought was a dresser. Soren had come to her room to remind her of their training session when he saw it and teased her about the shoes that were undoubtedly in it. Wondering what the drawers were filled with herself, Vallen hinting that the dresser would be full when he had surprised her, she pulled open a drawer only to find a new gun. The dresser turned out to be a weapons case, full of the newest models of guns and the highest quality crystal blades to match her sword. She had only laughed at the grimace on Soren's face as he left.

But her favorite things were the pictures that Vallen had sent. The clear tablets had been fused to the wall or sat on the weapons case. There was one of her on her sixteenth birthday opening her sword. Another of her looking dreamy-eyed at a hologram of Shadric Barlow that Vallen had taken himself. She could still remember how he had teased and heckled her into posing for the picture in the first place, saying that everyone needed a picture of them and their *true love*. Quite a few were of them sparring, but her favorite one was the one where Vallen had her in a headlock and she had pretended to choke to death. It was the last one that had been taken of them together before she left, and she often found herself staring at it.

Larken sighed, not knowing what she was forgetting. She wanted to order more pictures, but she didn't know where she could find them, so she had to resort to sending the pictures she wanted to Vallen and waiting for them to arrive. She rested her hand against the frame of the Vendor and started clicking her index nail against it as she thought. It wasn't until Loxly appeared over her shoulder that she remembered, the impossibly strong smell of the black dark roast he sipped at reminding her.

"Whatcha doin'?"

"Honestly, Loxly, why did you get that thing if you only drink your coffee black?"

"I have a refined pallet." He took a noisy sip. "You gonna answer my question?"

"I'm just getting a few things for myself."

"*Like?*" he drew the word out and took another drink.

"*Like*," Larken said, drawing the word out like he had, "some tea—"

Loxly interrupted her, placing his hand over the top of his mug and saying, "Shhh, don't listen to that uncultured monster."

"*And,*" Larken continued, as if he hadn't cut her off, "a few things to try for next week."

"Next week?"

"For my meal."

"Shoot, I forgot about that. I guess I better come up with a place for tonight."

"You haven't planned anything yet?"

"Nope!" he took another swig of coffee. "I went twice last month, I don't think I should have to go again."

"You chose to do that."

"Well, I guess we can go see the Chins. Haven't seen my girl in a while."

"How did you get to know her so well anyway?" Larken asked, tapping her basket and checking out after adding some jasmine tea to it.

"She thought I looked funny, and she thought I talked even funnier."

"Well, she obviously loves you now."

"Sure does. I'm just waiting for you to come 'round."

He took another drink as she scoffed, "Unless you turn into Shadric Barlow, I'm not interested."

"I would disagree, but *he has the dreamiest eyes,*" he teased. Larken smacked him, making him laugh as he tried not to spill his coffee. Then he said, "Wait, why would you be gettin' stuff for next week?"

"Why do you think?"

"I thought we would be goin' back to The Grill. I was gonna order the fanciest cut on the menu."

"Well," Larken turned, and her communicator buzzed, alerting her of her recent transaction, "I hate to disappoint you, but you thought wrong."

"I didn't think little birds knew how to cook."

"Been cooking for me and Vallen for the last thirteen years."

The two headed back to the common room. Larken liked it when her dorm shift lined up with Loxly's rec time. He was her best friend here, and she liked being able to hang out with him and catch up. "Do you like it?"

"What, cooking? It's not my favorite, but I don't hate it."

"Then why do it?"

"I may not *love* cooking, but I am a fan of eating."

Larken dropped onto one of the couches and pulled Vallen's jacket off the back of it. She wrapped it around her arms and folded her legs up under her. Loxly took his place on the opposite couch as he asked, "They didn't feed you?"

"I had the choice to eat with my family. But that would also mean that I would have to spend time with them."

"Wasn't there anyone you liked?"

"I liked my dad when he wasn't drinking. My little brother, Wardell, was okay too. But he wants to grow up to be like Liam, so he was only nice to me when it was just the two of us." Felling too vulnerable, Larken stuck her arms into the jacket sleeves and zipped it up. She should have returned it by now, but she couldn't bring herself to part with it yet. "What about you? What's your family like?"

Loxly put his empty mug on the table and leaned back, his hands cupping the back of his head. The smile that covered his face hurt Larken a little. "It's just me and Dad. My mom left when I was little, so I don't remember her. But my dad is the best there is. He inherited Grand-Dad's farm and still runs it by himself. But he's always here every visitor's day."

"That sounds wonderful," Larken said sadly. "I'm a little jealous, actually."

"You shouldn't be." His smile fell, and he looked more serious than she had ever seen him. "You don't have to be blood to be family."

She nodded, not looking at him.

"I'm serious, Larken. You have General Maxwell and us. You're not alone."

"I know, I guess I just miss the way it used to be with my dad."

"I understand. I miss my dad too."

"What made you decide to join the military?" she asked, voicing the question that had been in the back of her mind since meeting him.

"I tried to make it big in the city. I wanted to go to school to become a gunsmith. But after three weeks of not eating, I decided somethin' needed to change."

"How old were you?"

"Seventeen."

Three years younger than her, and the others were even younger than that when they joined. A sick feeling twisted Larken's stomach. They were really all each other had, and she had come and disrupted everything.

Seeming to sense the dark turn her thoughts had taken, Loxly asked, "So, what are you gonna make?"

"I haven't decided yet. Chicken, maybe."

"You know, you're less likely to kill us with undercooked beef, right?"

The sound Larken made was something between a scoff and a laugh. She threw one of the pillows on the couch at him and he laughed. "Shut up!"

"Just sayin'."

"I seem to recall a few chicken sandwiches that I've made for myself mysteriously go missing."

"That chicken was already cooked before they packaged it and sent it here."

Larken opened her mouth to reply, but Hinlee and Brecker walked into the common room just then. They were holding hands and Hinlee was smiling. The sight warmed Larken and she once again found herself fighting off jealousy.

Brecker kissed Hinlee's cheek and said, "I'm gonna go shower before dinner."

"Take your time, we won't go anywhere without you."

Brecker untangled his fingers from hers and made for the bathroom. He stopped and looked at Larken, saying, "She used to tell me not to use up all the hot water. I think you saved our relationship."

Larken laughed. "I'm glad I could help."

Brecker left and Hinlee dropped onto the couch next to her. She put her feet up on the table and rested her head on Larken's shoulder, sighing contentedly.

Levi walked in a few minutes later, and Soren a few minutes after that. Soren dropped onto the free couch, and Levi excused himself to shower as well. Loxly and Hinlee harassed each other and Larken laughed whenever Hinlee said something particularly scathing.

Larken's communicator buzzed and she pulled it from the jacket pocket she had stuffed it in. A new message blinked up at her, and she also saw a notification with a link to a news story on Liam. She was about to click the link when a new message appeared from Vallen. She clicked that instead.

Don't watch the interview.

She typed out a quick, *Why not?*

When there was no immediate answer, she decided to look at the other message. She sighed when she saw the name Captain Debonair.

I promise I didn't do it.

"Do what?" Hinlee whispered.

Larken made a noise in her throat, indicating she didn't know.

Dominic messaged again.

Everything he said was a lie.

"Everything who said?" Hinlee sat up a little straighter, no longer resting her head on Larken's shoulder.

"Liam." A sinking feeling pulled at her stomach thinking about what could have happened that involved both Dominic and her brother.

"What would he have said?"

"Only one way to find out," Larken muttered, clicking the link to the news story.

Once again Liam's face filled her screen, but this time it went back and forth between him and a reporter with sunflower yellow hair in a tastefully frilly dress the same color.

"I'm honestly surprised that he hasn't tried something before now," Liam said. He wore a soft periwinkle-colored suit with a cream-colored shirt and dark brown shoes. His hair was brushed to the side, and he looked so much like their father in that moment.

"And what do you mean by that?" The woman's voice sounded nasally and annoying.

"I mean that Dominic is the type of guy that would try to get with your sister because she's your sister. And Larken is the type of girl that would want to be with a guy like that. Anything to keep herself in the spotlight."

Larken wanted to turn her volume down or close the interview altogether, but it was like watching two aircraft collide in mid-air. She couldn't stop it, she couldn't turn it down, and she couldn't look away.

"Your sister hasn't been seen with a man in, well, ever. What do you think makes her relationship with Captain Dominic Braves different?"

"It's different because now that she's been hidden away at that Maxim forsaken base, people aren't talking about her anymore. I wouldn't be the least bit surprised if there was a little back-scratching going on."

Larken's hands shook slightly.

"Well," the reporter continued, *"we know that Captain Braves isn't a stranger to the media."* The screen cut to a picture of Dominic and a woman, with pink hair so pale that it almost looked silver, passionately kissing. *"This photograph was submitted to us anonymously this morning. If he was indeed in a relationship with Miss Hale, and they are still together after the surfacing of this photo, that would put Captain Braves in his longest public relationship to date. Tell me, Mr. Hale, are you surprised at your friend's actions?"*

"Not at all. Everyone knows what kind of person Dominic is. I'm not friends with him because he's a good boyfriend, I'm friends with him because he has a nose for the races."

Larken blushed. Of course Liam would ignore her mortification and talk about those stupid hoverbike races instead.

The camera was on the reporter again. *"We have attempted to contact Captain Braves, but we were unable to get his side of the story. And as Miss Hale is busy fighting, we were unable to contact her as well. As for their relationship, we can only wonder how things will play out. Fortunately for us, though, we won't have to wonder long at how singer-songwriter Amy Beth Porter was able to land the leading role in the upcoming net drama—"*

Hinlee gently grabbed Larken's communicator and closed the news story. Larken's hands were still raised as if she held the device. She didn't look away or blink, fearing that any eye movement would turn the humiliated burning into something more. Levi and Brecker chose then to, awkwardly, walk into the common room.

"How 'bout we order in tonight?" Loxly asked.

Larken bowed her head, letting her hair fall into her face. She wanted to crawl into bed and never come back out.

I should have listened to Vallen. I should have never opened the stupid link.

But she had, and everyone heard exactly what her bother thought of her.

"Good idea, Lox," Hinlee said. "Do you need me to go with you to pick it up?"

"No, I think Soren and I can handle it."

"Okay, just get me my usual then."

"Same," Levi added.

"Sure," Loxly said as he and Soren stood. "Brecker?"

Brecker nodded.

"We'll be back soon," Loxly said, and then shut the door behind him and the Captain.

An hour later, Larken was picking at her food. It smelled delicious, but she had no appetite. She had recovered her communicator from

Hinlee and had placed a permanent block on any news stories or articles relating to Liam. Dominic had sent her many more messages that she had ignored, and Vallen still hadn't replied to the one she had sent him. But he was probably doing damage control and couldn't break away to talk at the moment.

Everyone acted like nothing happened. They were all talking about their days and what they had enjoyed about their training. Larken only half paid attention, wanting to hide away. She felt too exposed, too raw, and she *hated* it. It was a back and forth of trying to ignore everyone around her versus listening to what the others were saying to try and ignore what had happened. Now, she was currently trying to forget her embarrassment and listened to Loxly as he shared a story about how he bumbled through his required first-aid that morning.

"It wasn't until I felt a pinch in my thigh that I realized that I had even lost my needle."

"Serves you right for trying to flirt your way through your training," Hinlee said around a mouthful of beef.

"I like blondes," Loxly sighed, "but the practice droid *isn't* my type."

"Lack of personality?" Hinlee asked, faux sympathy coloring her words.

"Always complainin'." Loxly raised his voice and mocked, *"That needle doesn't go there. That's not where my pulse is. Stop compressing my lung."*

Everyone laughed, and even Larken's lips twitched. She never could be upset for long when Loxly was around. He was like Vallen in that regard. The two were polar opposites, but they both understood her and knew what she needed.

A knock at the dorm door cut through the laughter, and Hinlee said, "I'll get it."

Everyone went back to eating as she got up to open the door. Even Larken stabbed a piece of her chicken and made to bring it to her lips, before pausing when she heard a familiar voice ask, "Can I talk to Larken?"

Larken dropped her fork into her paper container and lifted the collar of Vallen's jacket in an attempt to hide herself.

"She's not here," was Hinlee's reply. Brecker stood and was at Hinlee's side in four steps.

"I can see her, she's right there."

"She said Larken isn't here," came Brecker's deep voice.

"This is *ridiculous.*"

"Bye now," Hinlee said, and Larken assumed that she tried to shut the door in Dominic's face.

"Come on, look, I just want to talk!" Dominic sounded desperate. "Lark, please, just hear me out!"

Larken felt like she might be sick, but she knew that Dominic wouldn't leave her alone until she faced him. After all, he had resorted to cornering her in a hallway the last time he had upset her and she had ignored him. She stood and felt Soren's hard eyes on her as she did. Refusing to meet them, Larken walked to the door. She wrapped her arms around herself, wishing that it was Vallen holding her instead of his jacket.

Hinlee whispered loud enough for Dominic to hear, *"You don't have to talk to him, you know."*

"I know," she croaked and walked out into the hallway.

Dominic started pacing, sticking his hand into his hair, and breathed heavily. When he had finally decided on the right words, he turned to her and said, "I didn't do any of that. That picture was taken over *three* years ago."

"I know."

Her words caught him off guard, and he asked. "Wait, you do?"

"Yeah. Her name was Machelle, right? She was the racer that got you and Liam season passes that one time."

"Yeah, that's her." He shook his head. "If you weren't upset with me, then why were you ignoring me?"

"I'm mad at Liam. I'm mad that I let my curiosity over your message win out over Vallen's advice. And I'm mad that everything you do now will turn into a story about me as well. That's why I was ignoring you."

"Larken, I—"

"I just need a break, Dominic. I need a chance to figure out who I am away from the Hale family. I need to focus on me and *not* what the reporters are saying about me. I'm having a hard enough time here, in case you haven't heard."

"I heard that you cut off a guy's hand for grabbing you." His lips twitched. "But I somehow don't think that's accurate."

"I broke his nose and he was discharged," she said, rubbing her right temple. "But that's not the point. *The point* is that I need to be Larken for a little bit. Not Miss Hale, Daughter of the Military. You understand?"

Dominic let his head fall back, and he sighed deeply through parted lips. He closed his eyes and stood like that for a long while. When he looked at her again, his brown eyes were hurt, but he cupped her cheek and said, "Whatever you need. I will do *whatever* it is you need, Lark."

"Thanks," she mumbled. "Look, I gotta get back. I'm supposed to be bonding with my squad right now."

"Sure. I'll check in with you tomorrow." He smiled and then added, "You don't have to answer, but I'll message you. Just in case."

He leaned in and kissed her cheek like he always did now when he told her goodbye. Larken closed her eyes, wanting to hide the emotion she knew he would be able to see there. When he pulled away, she turned and quickly slipped back into the common room. She shut the door and leaned against it, letting her head rest there. No one said anything, and no one said anything when she walked past them and then locked herself in her room for the rest of the night.

CHAPTER 16

Larken grunted as sweat dripped down her face. There weren't many people in the gym this soon after breakfast, and it was relatively quiet. Soren should have been running his own drills with his glaive, but he couldn't pull his eyes away from her. It would appear that neither could anyone else.

All of the practice droids were on standby, waiting for their human partners to give them a command, but they were all watching as Larken took on three herself, just like he was. And, judging by the way the androids attacked her, they were turned all the way up to the max difficulty. She shouted, swinging her sword over her head. The longer the fight went on, the more careless she became. Soren's stomach twisted as he watched her punish herself.

The emotion that rolled off of her was thick enough that every breath he took tasted like shame and rage. Not only had Brecker risen to her defense the night before, but Loxly had been ready to spring across the room at a moment's notice. Soren also didn't miss the way Levi's fist balled up when Larken stepped out into the hall. Though, Levi was probably more upset over the antics of her brother than with Braves. Even Soren had wanted to hide Larken away from it all. She had continually proven herself over and over again the past month, and now she was back at the beginning. No one would see the girl who was capable of taking down her opponent in one move; they would only see Captain Dominic Braves's scorned lover.

Larken was punched in the stomach by one of the androids. She retaliated by screaming and cutting the thing's head off. She sliced another in half and tore the arms from the third with her bare hands. Soren was in motion before the last android hit the ground. If there hadn't been anyone watching her before, they were now. She was breathing heavily when he reached her, and he could smell the floral deodorant she wore. He grabbed her elbow and murmured, "That's enough."

Larken didn't move. She just stood there, staring at the dismembered head and the various wires sticking from its neck.

"Let's head back to the dorm. You've had enough training for today."

She still didn't respond, but she let him lead her away from the small gym. He didn't know what her schedule for the day looked like, but he would override it if he had to. The dark bags under her eyes told him that she hadn't slept well the night before, and the black mood that rolled off her felt so different from her usual demeanor that he found himself not knowing how to act around her.

"What do you have next?" Soren asked, wanting to focus on something other than her wilting emotions.

"I have to go to the medic."

"Are you ill?" he asked.

"No. I go every other Friday."

"Your adjustments." He remembered then.

Larken didn't say anything, but she rolled her right shoulder as if the mere mention of it pained her.

"We can go there first."

She pulled out her communicator. "I'll see if Jodi can see me early."

Her communicator went off a few times, but since Larken didn't say anything as they continued on their way, he figured that Jodi could see them. A team of soldiers rushed past them, and Captain Andrews gave him a quick nod, which he returned.

Soren would be lying if he said he wasn't a little curious about what had happened to Larken that the fancy Hale medic couldn't fix. He knew that General Maxwell had sent her a custom mattress and that she had to get adjusted, whatever that meant, but what happened? Loxly had only said that she had done something stupid, but when he had pressed the sharpshooter, he claimed that that was all she had said about it. Soren had gone through every file on Larken Hale that was available to him, but the only thing he could find was the recurring phrase, *SUSTAINED MINOR SHOULDER INJURY*. Something was definitely being withheld from him, and Soren didn't like it one bit.

When they reached the medic area that Jodi had been assigned to for the day, they went in. The girl from the first time they had brought Larken there sat in the waiting room with her feet propped up on the chair next to her. Her hair had been dark green at the time, but now it was a mess of pale blue and steel grey that had been pulled back into a giant bun. She still wore dark makeup, but this time in shades of blue instead of green. The emerald stud in her nose had also been exchanged for a sapphire. She didn't look up from her communicator when they walked in. Blowing a bubble, she let it grow until it popped over her bottom lip and then mused, "You brought a friend."

"He sort of followed me."

"That makes two. You need to tell me your secret."

"If I did," Larken said, making her way to the back, "you would get bored."

Jodi sighed and got to her feet, smoothing the wrinkles from her coat. "I suppose you're right."

Soren had no idea what they were talking about, but he felt like he should feel a little insulted. Jodi caught the door before it could swing shut and looked over her shoulder. She raised a thin eyebrow, asking silently if he was coming. He followed, unable to suppress his curiosity. Larken was already disappearing into a room at the end of the hall, and Jodi looked up at him, her eyes dancing mischievously. "Hope you have a strong stomach, Captain."

"What's that supposed to mean?" he grunted.

"Oh, I'd hate to ruin the surprise," she said, and then quickened her steps.

They entered the room that Larken had, and Soren found her sitting on a tall bench with stiff black leather cushions on the surface. Her hands gripped the edge and she slumped forward slightly. She looked up at them and her eyes fell on Soren. They narrowed and he felt her unspoken challenge.

I dare you to stay.

Jodi, getting her first real look at Larken, frowned. "You look like crap."

Larken only asked, "Blue today, huh?"

"It reminds me of the sky."

"It suits you."

"Thanks," Jodi said and then walked to the cabinets.

Soren didn't know if Jodi was purposely ignoring what had happened to Larken, or if she honestly didn't know. He couldn't get a good read on her and felt like she knew a lot more than what she was letting on.

Jodi pulled on some gloves, letting the left one snap against her wrist. "Shall we?"

Larken rolled her shoulder again.

Jodi opened a drawer and pulled a syringe from it with an impossibly long needle. Soren felt his eyes narrow to the point and wondered if it hurt. He had never liked needles or medics for that matter. It's the reason he let his nose heal on its own after he broke it when he was thirteen.

Jodi just marched forward and dropped the syringe on a portable silver table next to the bench Larken was on. Larken twisted to the side, kicking her legs up onto the bench. She grabbed her left shoulder and laid back. Jodi loomed over her, grabbing her elbow and moving Larken's arm exactly where she wanted it. Jodi looked up at Soren, her eyes dancing, before leaning onto Larken fully and pushing. A horrible series of pops filled the air and Larken sighed in relief. Soren watched in horror as Jodi did the same thing to Larken's hips, back, and neck. His skin crawled at the sounds, and he wanted to scratch it.

Larken sat up and moved her feet back to the floor. She put her arms over her head and grabbed her right elbow. Leaning first to the left, and then to the right, she stretched out her back and rolled her shoulders as she let her arms fall. She rolled her neck too, sighing contentedly. Soren couldn't understand how she could feel so rejuvenated when those pops had sounded so painful.

Jodi grabbed the syringe again and asked, "Ready?"

Without waiting for an answer, Jodi stuck Larken at the base of the neck and injected the contents of the vial into Larken's muscle. "Um, *ow*!"

"Stop whining."

"I swear, you like that part too much."

Jodi smirked. "Can you blame me?"

She pulled the needle free, and Larken brought her hand up to the spot, kneading it. Jodi cleared everything away and finished by tossing her gloves into a hazardous waste bin. "Don't—"

"Push myself too hard, and if I feel any swelling or discomfort, come right back. Got it."

Larken hopped off the table, and Jodi sneered, "You've got a smart mouth."

Larken rolled her right shoulder a few times. "So I've been told."

"Get out of here," Jodi said, smirking.

"Still on for tomorrow?"

"You bet."

"What's tomorrow?" Soren asked, speaking for the first time since walking into that exam room.

"Larken is taking me out for waffles and bringing me a new book."

Larken waved and started out of the room, leaving Soren to follow. He was still trying to settle his stomach and get that sound out of his ears. He had so many questions, but at the same time, he wasn't sure he wanted to know the answers.

They were halfway back to the dorm when Larken broke the silence. "It doesn't hurt."

Soren looked down at her. The bags under her eyes were still dark, but she had perked up a great deal. "What doesn't?"

"The popping. It's just a build-up of gas in my joints being released. I don't feel a thing."

"I didn't ask."

"You look like you still might be sick."

"Okay, then what did she do?"

"She pushed my spine back into place."

A new wave of nausea rolled over him and he had to force himself to breathe through his nose.

"It's no different from setting a broken leg. I don't understand why you're acting like this."

He said nothing.

Larken stopped and looked up at him. Her lips twitched and she asked, "Wait, that's why Levi was the one carrying the medical pack when you rescued Vallen and me, wasn't it?"

Soren kept walking and muttered, "I don't know what you're talking about."

"My first day, you were bragging about how good Levi was at first-aid. But, you have to be just as good as a Captain. So, why is Levi always the one to take the role of field-medic in our group training?"

Soren didn't meet her eyes as he plowed down the hall to their dorm.

"You don't have the stomach for it."

"I can handle myself just fine on the field."

"Then tell me what the label on the vial you kept staring at said."

Soren let go of the knob he had just grabbed and turned to Larken. The spark that had been missing from her teal eyes all day was starting to come back, and he didn't have the heart to be the one to make it disappear again. Taking a deep breath, he grunted, "It said, *chemically altered poison that you don't need.*"

The spark fully ignited, and Larken's eyes danced. "It was a muscle relaxer. It's how I can manage to go two weeks instead of every day."

Soren's stomach soured again. "You used to do that every day?"

"Yeah, for only about a year." She pushed past him and opened the door, revealing the common room. Looking over her shoulder, Larken whispered, "Vallen always felt sick afterward too."

Soren followed Larken into the common room, feeling a little bit better about himself. If General Vallen Maxwell, the fiercest man alive, felt sick after watching Larken's *adjustments*, then he couldn't be considered weak. Right?

Brecker appeared before Larken could drop onto one of the couches. "You're early."

"I was kidnapped," she said, indicating Soren with a nod of her head.

"Oh, well, I was told to send you to your room when you got here."

"But, *Dad!*"

"Just go look," Brecker huffed, rolling his eyes.

The little color she had drained from her face, and she asked, "What did you do to my room?"

Brecker dropped onto the couch across from the one Larken was about to fall onto. "It wasn't me."

Larked nearly tripped on the leg of the coffee table in her haste to get to her room. Soren, fearing that maybe Braves did something weird to it, was close behind her. When they got there, there didn't seem to be anything wrong. There were no flowers, no gift baskets, nothing. Only a piece of folded paper on her pillow. Larken rushed to her bed and unfolded the note. Soren followed and read what it said over her shoulder.

For when you need to block out the voices.

. . .

Larken looked up and made a weird choking sound. Following her gaze, Soren looked up and saw little speakers in the corners of her room. She dropped the note onto her bed and went back out to the common room. She popped her hip and crossed her arms. "Brecker, when did they install that?"

"First thing this morning. You also got a box I was told to stick in the fridge."

Larken was moving before Brecker finished speaking. Soren watched as she wrenched the fridge open and then pulled a box out. She placed it on the counter and opened the lid. Her head dropped and her shoulders heaved like she took a deep breath to gain control over her emotions. He could barely hear her trying to sniff back her tears, but he saw her wipe at her face. After a moment, she exhaled deeply. Then, she pulled a drawer open and took out a knife. She didn't turn around, but she called, "Anyone want pie?"

"Pie?" Brecker asked, looking up from his communicator, no doubt messaging Hinlee.

"Chocolate cream," she answered.

"Sure."

"Soren?" she asked.

He grunted, taking a seat on the couch adjacent to Brecker's. There was a clinking in the kitchen and Larken appeared with three plates. Both Brecker and him were handed small plates with a single slice, while Larken had a full-sized dinner plate with three. Whipped cream completely covered the top of all the slices, making him think that the whole pie had to be covered with it. Brecker gave his thanks and dug in. Soren had instead scraped off all of the white fluff. He had barely gotten the sickly-sweet mess off his fork when Larken leaned over and scooped it off his plate and stuffed it into her mouth.

Soren ignored her antics and Brecker asked, "So what's with the pie?"

"Whenever I got into a fight with Liam, or any other members of my family, Vallen would get one. We would skip training for the day and just eat pie." She looked at Soren. "He doesn't like whipped cream either."

"And the top-secret delivery?" Brecker continued.

"Sound system. I used to have one in my old room."

Brecker tried to get more out of Larken, but that was all she said about it. And, judging by the way she had tried to hide her tears in her room all those nights ago, Soren could imagine why she didn't want to share why she had them at the Military Manor.

The three sat and talked some, but Brecker had to leave soon for flight training. Soren pulled out his communicator and cleared the rest of Larken's schedule. She could go to the gym or whatever she wanted, but he wouldn't force her to leave if she didn't want to. He had promised himself that he wouldn't give her any special treatment, but he had also planned on her being able to leave her old life behind.

Soren stood, ready to leave for the shooting range. But one look at Larken had him pausing. "You gonna be okay?"

She nodded, staring at her empty plate.

"You sure?"

Another nod.

"Message me if you need something."

She nodded again, looking like the full weight of the day was finally hitting her. Larken stood and turned away, eyes glossy. Soren let her go and she left the common room. She had always been on her own, but she had also always had General Maxwell. Soren wasn't sure if the pie had helped things or made them worse. He could only hope that all of this would blow over soon.

CHAPTER 17

L arken sighed and rolled her neck. Her shoulder felt a little stiff, but she could wait until dinner was over to knead out the muscle. Music blared from her communicator that rested on the counter next to the stove. Soren had complained about it at first, finding the melodies annoying and wondering why some of the songs were in a different language altogether, but he quieted some when the smell of her dinner started filling the air.

A week had gone by and she was ready to fall into bed like she had been every night. The talk about Liam's interview was starting to die down around base, and that morning she finally decided to message Dominic back. He had kept his promise, only messaging her once every morning to let her know how sorry he was and that he was thinking of her. Needless to say, he was ecstatic at her message, but the last message she got from him was when he wished her a good day after she told him that she had medic training. Even now that the day was almost over, he still hadn't messaged her. The two of them had finally reached an understanding that she felt good about, and she wondered if they might actually be able to be friends someday.

The chicken breasts were a bright gold, and the sauce they were sitting in bubbled around them. The skillet she used was bigger than the one she was used to, but then again, she was making food for a lot more people as well. She hoped that she measured everything out correctly, having to do the math in her mind since she didn't have a recipe she could follow. The slices of lemon that were on top of the chicken, as well as in the sauce, seemed to be all she could smell, and she hoped that it wasn't too much. She and Vallen both liked a little more of the lemon flavor, but she didn't know what everyone else liked. Larken could only guess.

She started second-guessing her meal choice again, and the raspberry cheesecake that she had made to go with it. It was the beginning of summer, and everything was in season, but would it be too tart? Should she have picked something sweeter? Would everyone like it? Larken sighed and turned off the stovetop; there was only one way to find out.

No sooner had she opened a cupboard, than she sensed someone nearby. Her arms were still in the air, reaching for the plates, when she looked over and found Soren watching her with a frown. His hip rested against a section of counter, and his arms were crossed. The black T-shirt he had on stretched across his chest and biceps. His brown hair was damp, and Larken figured out why he had stopped complaining about her music. She could smell the soap that he used, the cool scent of it penetrating through the smell of the chicken. His eyes looked green just then, and they had an unreadable hardness to them. Larken tried to look away, to hide the slight blush that touched her cheeks, but she couldn't.

"Need help?"

"Ye-yeah," she stuttered, throat dry. Pulling her eyes away from his arms and chiding herself, she forced out, "Since you're a giant, you can get the plates down and start setting the table."

He walked up behind her and reached over her to grab the plates. She could feel his warmth through her shirt, heating her back. Goosebumps instantly covered her arms and she sidestepped out from under him. "Do you mind?"

"Oh, sorry, I didn't notice you there. Me being a giant and all, I didn't see you."

"*Whatever*," she huffed out with a laugh.

The two of them went back and forth like that for a good five minutes before Loxly and Levi walked into the dorm. Larken didn't bother trying to hide the smile that was on her face, even when she met Loxly's eyes. He gave her a grin of his own, as if silently telling her that her happiness, and her being able to smile, meant something to him.

"Somethin' smells great!"

"Glad you think so!" Larken called back, spearing the chicken and putting the breasts onto a serving dish. "It's one of my favorites."

"Then I guess it's my new favorite too," Loxly said with a wink.

"Aren't you ever gonna give up?" Levi asked, walking up and peering over her shoulder at the chicken.

"Not until I die, or she chooses someone else!" Loxly said cheerily.

"Please choose someone else," Levi muttered in her ear.

Larken laughed and handed him the dish. Soren reappeared in the kitchen, and she said, "There is a spinach and strawberry salad in the fridge."

Without a word, he pulled the fridge open and took out the salad. He also pulled out a bottle of dressing and held it up for her to see. Larken nodded and moved to the microwave. She took out the white corn that she had heated up and made her way to the fridge as well. Sticking a whole spoonful of butter on top, she passed it off to Levi's open hands.

The dorm door opened, and Hinlee and Brecker walked in, hand in hand. Hinlee took a deep breath and exclaimed, "Wow, Larken, that smells amazing!"

"Thanks!" she said around Hinlee, who had dropped Brecker's hand and come over to hug her. "I'm kinda nervous for you guys to try it."

"Don't be, it's great. I can tell." She winked.

Larken smiled and opened the fridge, pulling out the large bowl she had dumped the diced-up watermelon into. She turned to find Soren standing there. Larken stared at his chest for a moment, wide-eyed, and then looked up to meet his eyes. Very slowly, he reached up and grabbed the glass pitcher that sat on top of the fridge. Larken swallowed thickly, and Soren smirked at her. "Sorry, didn't see you."

"You already used that joke," she huffed, annoyed at her quickly heating cheeks.

"Is it a joke if it's still true?" He raised an eyebrow at her. "Move before you hit your head."

She ducked just in time for him to open the freezer and dump ice into the pitcher. Snarling under her breath, she marched to the table and dropped off the watermelon. Hinlee disappeared into the kitchen and came back with a handful of silverware and a stack of glasses. Soon, everything was ready, and they all sat down. Larken prayed with a small voice, and then Loxly grabbed himself a chicken breast.

"All of this looks so good, Larken." Hinlee's eyes gleamed as she asked, "Is there any dessert?"

"Of course," Larken laughed. "It's in the fridge."

"What is it?" Brecker mumbled around a mouthful of food.

"Raspberry cheesecake with a graham cracker crust."

"Yummy!" Hinlee cooed.

"What's in this?" Levi asked, looking at the chicken as if he could see what ingredients she used.

"It's lemon, chicken stock, honey, and parsley."

"It's good," he said and Larken beamed.

Soren kept quiet as he ate, and Loxly was already on his second helping. The honey and lemon coated Larken's tongue, and she was reminded of all the times she had shared this meal with Vallen.

"You're awfully quiet over there, Decks," Hinlee said. "What do you think of this fine meal that Miss Hale has made for us?"

"It's fine," he answered.

"*Of all of the perfect adjectives out there, he says fine,*" Hinlee muttered to Brecker.

"Leave him alone, Hin. It's not his fault that the food is so good it made him stupid."

Loxly choked on his water and Levi smirked. Soren just shook his head and said, "I think that was the meanest thing I've ever heard you say."

"You obviously haven't trained with him," Larken muttered, causing Hinlee to laugh.

"He *is* a bit intense, isn't he?"

The six of them fell into comfortable conversation, and Larken couldn't remember ever feeling this happy. Yes, she had loved her time with Vallen, and she still wished that he was with her, but this was what a family was supposed to be like. Larken couldn't focus on that feeling for long though; whenever she did, it became harder to swallow and her eyes got misty. But the way she was able to laugh, she never knew that a family she was a part of could be like this, and she thanked Maxim every second of every day for giving this to her.

When Larken brought out the dessert, there was excited squealing from Hinlee, and Loxly said, "There it is!"

Larken set it down and started dishing out slices. Soren got up, and Larken tried to watch what he was doing with the back of her mind. He rummaged for something in the kitchen, but she couldn't know what for unless she turned her head and looked. Larken, forcing herself to pay attention to what she was doing, placed Soren's serving on his plate and then sat down.

Pulling her piece close, she picked up her fork and was about to stab the cheesecake when she said, "Shoot! I forgot the—"

Soren dropped the tub of whipped cream onto the table, chasing it with a spoon. The spoon clattered against the wood, and Soren sat unceremoniously. Larken didn't say anything, but she smiled softly. Soren wouldn't look at her as he loaded up his fork with about half of his piece and stuffed it into his mouth.

Larken opened the tub and Hinlee chastised, "You're supposed to savor it, Decks."

He grunted and took another too large bite. Larken was still smiling when she took a bite as well. She closed her eyes, relishing in the tartness of the raspberry. Hinlee, despite giving Soren a hard time about savoring the cheesecake, had finished hers and was stealing bites of Brecker's. He let her, smiling each time she did so. It eventually got to the point where he just pushed his plate to her and she was able to have the rest of it.

Larken stood, grabbing empty dishes, but Loxly yelled at her to sit back down. "You cooked, we clean, Little Bird."

"I don't mind," she said, but Soren stood and grabbed the dishes out of her hands before disappearing into the kitchen without a word.

Huffing, Larken sat down and looked over at Hinlee, who had a sly smile and was still watching the spot where Soren disappeared. Her eyes moved to Larken and her smile turned wicked.

"What?" Larken asked, a blush creeping up her neck.

"Oh, nothing."

"*Hin,*" Brecker warned.

It was now her turn to ask, "*What?*"

"I know that look."

"You mind your own business, Brecker Wilton."

Brecker sighed and then gathered up the dishes around him and joined Soren in the kitchen.

<hr>

An hour later, they were all sitting in the common room, and Levi challenged Larken to another game of cards. He claimed that he had only won the previous game by default when she stopped playing to visit with General Maxwell. The Second obviously didn't like that there might be someone better than him in the squad.

Levi was all business as he sat forward and refused to take his eyes off Larken's hands. Soren's hand wasn't terrible, but he wouldn't win the round either. The goal was to get a run of five, all in one suit, the higher the number, the better. With spades being the best and diamonds the lowest suit, a rank system was set in place in case two or more people had the same five cards. Each person started a round by drawing one card at a time and discarding one to the person on their left, giving everyone ample opportunity to get what they needed. When the deck had been depleted, the round was over, and the one with the highest run, or the one closest to a complete run, won the round and took the most points. Since there were six of them playing, the winner got six points, the person in second place would get five, all the way to the person in last place taking a single point.

They were a few rounds in, and Larken and Levi were trading between the five and six-point takeaway, keeping them relatively tied. Soren sat comfortably in third place, while Brecker and Hinlee were fighting for fourth. Loxly grumbled, sitting at the bottom with only three points so far.

"Who even came up with this game? It's rigged," Loxly complained.

"For someone who works with numbers every second of their day, you're really bad at counting," Hinlee taunted.

"Well, what am I supposed to do when Larken and Levi have all the aces and kings up their sleeves?"

"Are you calling me a cheater?" Larken asked, daring him to say yes.

"Look, all I'm sayin' is, I think it's borin' losin' all the time." A sly smile pulled at his lips. "So, who thinks we should make this a little more interestin'?"

"What are you talking about, Lox?" Hinlee asked, looking at a card and then passing it off to Brecker.

"I'm sayin', how about instead of points, the loser of the round has to offer up a secret?"

Brecker laughed. "We already know everything about each other. What secrets could we possibly have?"

"So we don't make it loser's choice. The winner gets to ask a question that the loser has to answer honestly."

"There's a lot of ways that that could go wrong, Lox," Hinlee warned.

"But it'll make things a little more excitin', dontcha think?" he asked, bumping his shoulder into Larken's.

Soren crumpled his cards.

"I still don't know," Hinlee murmured. "What do you think, Larken?"

"As long as we have a *no questions about family* rule, I'm fine with it."

Loxly grinned. "Great," he said as he laid down a four, five, six, seven, and eight of diamonds, "I'll go first then."

Larken took the round and thought for a moment before asking, "Did you have any pets growing up?"

Both Brecker and Hinlee booed her, and Levi grunted, "What a waste."

Soren had to fight his smile; it was such a Larken thing to ask.

Laughing, Loxly asked, "Are we countin' the livestock?"

"I don't think we have enough time to, but if you had a favorite cow, you could count it."

"Then yes, I've had seven. Four dogs, two barn cats, and a favorite pig. His name was Hamm."

Larken looked horrified, and everyone else laughed, including Soren.

"Why would you name your pig Hamm?"

"Why not?" he asked shuffling the cards. "You can't tell me all the names you picked out for your mutts were gems."

"I never named one of them Wolf, if that's what you're implying," she retorted as Levi shuffled the deck and divvied out the cards.

They blew through the next round, talking about old pets and their names. Larken and Loxly were really the only ones who had any, but Hinlee used to feed a duck that hung around a pond by her childhood home.

Then, before they knew it, Levi was asking Loxly what kind of guns he was going to work with if he had been able to finish school. Loxly went on about old shotguns and revolvers as Soren shuffled. Brecker and Hinlee asked a few more questions about Loxly's schooling as well, but Larken remained quiet and listened politely. They must have already talked about it together.

The next few hours went on like that, each one trying to get the highest hand because of the new incentive. Most of Larken's questions had answers that he already knew, like how Hinlee's favorite dessert was brownies, and that Brecker had a secret library on his communicator that held well over two hundred mysteries. But he also learned a lot about his squad that he hadn't known before, like the fact that Brecker was the first boy that Hinlee kissed, but Hinlee wasn't the first girl he had kissed. Even Levi had been forced by Hinlee to reveal that he had a secret relationship after he first got here that lasted just over a year. He also had to answer Larken's question about how he became so good at cooking, and Soren was surprised to learn that his orphanage didn't have a caretaker, just a man who came to see how many kids were there each week and ship them out when they turned fourteen. And, being the oldest there, it fell on Levi to make sure the other kids were fed.

Soren had retained his hold on third place and hadn't been forced to answer any of the questions. Larken was the only other player who hadn't answered any either, not that she hadn't shared when she was able. Soren now knew the names of her favorite hybrids she had growing up, when she started cooking for General Maxwell and what her favorite things to make were, that she unsurprisingly had never been in a relationship, her favorite books were centered around old fairy stories, that her favorite desserts either had tart fruit or chocolate in them, and that she preferred sorbet to ice cream.

But, as everyone laid their hands down for this round, he watched as her face fell. Loxly was hooting and hollering, thinking he had the highest hand, and he was teasing her by wondering aloud what he should ask. He didn't stop talking until Hinlee interrupted with, "What did you get, Decks?"

Loxly watched in horror as Soren laid down the Ten, Jack, Queen, King, and Ace of spades; the perfect hand. The sharpshooter dropped his face in his hands and moaned as if all his dreams had been destroyed.

Soren crossed his arms and leaned back into the couch; he wanted to get this question right. There were so many things he wondered about her, but he wanted to ask the right thing. She looked at him as he stared at her. Her cheeks tinted pink, and she swallowed slowly as her teal eyes deepened to a shade of blue that reminded him of the ocean. She started biting her bottom lip, and her blush deepened ever so slightly.

Is she nervous?

Soren had no idea what he was going to ask her, but he opened his mouth anyway, deciding to go with whatever came out, but then his alarm that signaled Lights Out started going off. Hinlee jumped and grabbed her heart, and Brecker chuckled and looked at her with so much love in his eyes.

"It's just Lights Out, Hin, it's okay."

Laughing herself, she said, "I know, it's just been so long since we were all still up to hear it." Pulling out her own communicator, she gasped and then groaned. *"Oh no!* It can't be this late. I have to be up so early tomorrow."

"Let's get you to bed then," Brecker murmured, standing and holding his hand out for her.

Loxly stretched his arms and yawned, then stood as well. "This was fun; we *definitely* need to do this again."

Soon they were all up and wishing each other good night and then making their way to their rooms. Larken hung back to tidy the common room up a little, and Soren stayed to help her. Once all the pillows were straightened and the glasses were put into the dishwasher, the two headed to their rooms. Soren stopped outside his and looked to find Larken standing outside hers and looking at him as well.

"So…"

"So," he repeated.

"Looks like I owe you an answer."

"Looks like it."

She smiled softly and said, "Better not waste it then. Goodnight."

Then she opened her door and shut herself in her room, leaving Soren much more confused than he thought he should have been.

CHAPTER 18

When Larken woke up, she wanted nothing more than to shut her alarm off and go back to sleep. She had stayed up way too late the night before, and now she was regretting it. But she was glad that she got to know everyone a little better, and she already had plans to make a batch of brownies for Hinlee. Pushing out of bed, Larken felt a twinge in her shoulder. She hissed and groaned.

No, not today.

Larken tried to roll her shoulder, to push through the tightness, but she only got up to her ear before she had to drop her shoulder and realized that moving it was a bad choice. Forcing herself to stand, Larken got dressed as fast as she was able, pushing through the burning pain, and rushed out of her room. Stopping at the table, she found only Brecker and Loxly. Brecker was waiting for Hinlee to finish getting ready, and Loxly had been waiting for her. It wasn't unusual for the four of them to walk to the cafeteria together, but this morning, she ignored Loxly as she turned and ran out the door.

Soren was already at the end of the hall, and she rushed for him. Catching up, she winced as an awkward breath forced her to move her shoulder. Turning, the disagreeable Captain raised a dark eyebrow at her.

"Can you clear my schedule for the morning?" she blurted out quickly.

"And why would I do that?"

"I slept on my shoulder wrong or something. I need to—" She stopped when his face went slightly pale. He was obviously remembering her last adjustment.

"Whatever," he said, trying to cover up. "I'll clear you until lunch. Let me know if you need more time."

She opened her mouth to thank him, but Soren turned and disappeared into the masses heading to breakfast. Rolling her eyes, Larken pulled out her communicator and typed out a message to Jodi with her left hand.

"Little Bird! Where you off to in such a rush?"

Larken turned to see Loxly slowly jogging towards her. Concern was written all over his face, and she felt bad for ignoring him just now. "Sorry, I had to catch up with Soren."

He stopped in front of her, and his eyes dropped to her shoulder. "Everythin' okay?"

"Just slept wrong is all, nothing to worry about."

Her communicator buzzed in her hand, and Larken opened the message.

East wing 15 mins.

Larken tapped out a quick reply and then stuffed the device into her pocket. "I have to go. See you later?"

"Do you want me to come with ya?"

"No, I should be fine. Besides, you have med-training. You can't skip that."

"I don't mind."

"Believe me, it would be better for all of us if you went. Especially since—" Larken clamped her mouth shut. She almost let slip that Soren would be more likely to pass out than be able to help them if something happened to either her or Levi.

"Since what?"

"Since you're the one most likely to cause an air embolism."

"You sure that's what you were gonna say?" His eyes twinkled, and she narrowed hers in return. He knew her too well.

"*Yes.*"

"Fine, fine, I'll drop it," he said, holding up his hands in surrender.

"See you tonight."

"I'll count the seconds." He winked and headed down the hall and took a left, making his way to the cafeteria.

Sighing, Larken rolled her eyes at the sharpshooter's back and made her way down the hall as well but took a right instead. Her shoulder throbbed, and she pulled at the muscle. The fatigue and the tightness in her shoulder were starting to sour her mood, and she glared at anyone she passed that looked at her for too long. By the time she reached the area where Jodi had been stationed, Larken was practically spitting fire.

She stomped through the door and plopped down into a chair. Her fingers found their way to her shoulder again, and she dug into the muscle. Wincing, she pushed past the pain and tried to loosen the knots. Jodi appeared almost instantly and crossed her arms as she popped her hip. Plumb and lavender hair had been pulled into two braids, and the amethyst stud in her nose was the same color as her lipstick. Sighing, she asked, "Did the Princess not sleep well? Find a pea in your bed?"

Larken glared.

Jodi raised a fine eyebrow. "Or perhaps a *Prince*?"

Larken couldn't hold on to her irritation and melted into a tired laugh. "You caught me."

Smirking, she asked, "Was it the pretty one or the grumpy one?"

"Shadric Barlow, if you must know. He snuck onto base last night because he couldn't ignore his feelings for me any longer."

"If your goal was to make me jealous, you succeeded." Jodi uncrossed her arms and motioned to the door behind her with her head. "Come on back."

Standing up, Larken followed her friend into the back, and then into an exam room. Jodi quickly corrected her spine, and Larken could breathe normally again. The relief that flooded through her shoulder was so great that she didn't even notice Jodi injecting the muscle relaxer.

"Try not to do anything too crazy," Jodi warned.

"I won't, don't worry."

"On a separate note, how much do you think I can make for leaking the info about you and Barlow?"

"Depends on the reporter."

"Thanks for the tip."

"Don't mention it," Larken sighed, standing up. She rolled her shoulders and stretched.

Good as new.

"Tell that Prince of yours to keep his hands to himself; it's bad for your health."

"I'll mention it if he gives me enough time to think about it."

Jodi laughed as Larken left the room. Making her way back to the dorm to get a little bit more sleep before lunch, Larken was in a much better mood. She ignored all the looks she got walking back and was surprised when her communicator buzzed in her pocket. Dominic and Vallen were the only ones who ever messaged her, but it was too late in the day for Dominic to wish her a good morning, and Vallen only messaged her after his shift. Unless it was an emergency…

Pulling it out so fast that she almost dropped it, she jumped as an alarm went off overhead. Her stomach immediately fell to her feet as panic settled in. Was she being shipped out? Was Squad 19 needed before she could get her certifications? Larken's heart pounded as she looked at the screen, finding Soren's name.

We decided to take an early lunch. Need more time?

Looking at the top right corner of her screen as her heartbeat returned to normal, she saw that it was nearing 10:00, and she only now realized that she had been in with Jodi for over an hour.

No, I'm finished. When's lunch?

It wasn't even two seconds before she got a reply.

11:00

Sounds good, I'll see you guys there.

Larken was torn between going and getting some extra sleep and going to the cafeteria and getting a good seat. She had made up her mind to sleep in her spot at the cafeteria and turned that way when someone behind her cleared their throat. Turning again, Larken came face to face with a wisp of a girl who had a pair of glasses that were too big for her. She had on an oversized sweater, despite the warm weather, and she nervously pushed her frames up her nose.

"M-Miss Hale?"

Larken crossed her arms and raised an eyebrow. "Yes?"

"Could you please come with me?"

Larken didn't want to, but judging from the girl's lack of uniform, it was safe to assume that she worked for someone a lot higher up than her. Unfolding her arms, Larken motioned for her to lead the way. The whole time, the girl fidgeted, going back and forth between pushing her glasses up her nose and tucking her drab brown hair behind her ears. Larken should have said something, but she couldn't bring herself to care. Her only concern was where she was going, and what would happen when she got there. The sinking feeling in her stomach told her that whatever it was, it wouldn't be good.

When they finally stopped, they were away from the hustle and bustle of the base and, instead, in a more secluded hallway. The girl pulled open a door that had ADMINISTRATION written across the glass in white letters and waited for Larken to walk in before letting it close softly behind them.

Tucking her hair behind her ears again, the girl looked to the floor and murmured, "Down the hall, fourth door on the right." Then she sat behind a desk that made her look even smaller and pulled at her sweater, like she was hoping to get lost in it.

Sighing, Larken made her way to the right door and knocked. She spotted a little plaque on the wall to the right of the door that read DAYTON. Her stomach was in knots, and Larken wanted nothing more than to turn and leave. If she was in an administrative office, then it couldn't be good. And since she hadn't been stopped, she could only assume that neither Soren nor Vallen knew about this visit.

It wasn't long after her hand fell back to her side that a haughty voice on the other side of the door called, "Come in!"

Slowly, Larken turned the knob and walked in. The room was freezing, and goosebumps instantly broke out across her arms. Chafing her left one, Larken took in the room. It looked like any generic office, complete with a little potted tree in the corner by the door. The smell of aloe clung to the air, and Larken quickly spotted an air freshener on top of one of the filing cabinets.

"Cadet Larken Hale, it's so nice to finally meet you."

Larken's gaze snapped to a woman behind the desk, who looked to be in her late thirties. Her smile seemed forced, and she looked incredibly stiff. Her brown hair hung around her face in classic-looking waves, like the style that was all the rage in Stars. Deep red lipstick colored her lips, and her black eyeliner was thick. Her black blazer looked about a size too small, and the white shirt she wore under it was impossibly low cut and didn't look the least bit professional. The style reminded Larken of her mother, and she wondered if she was whom the woman modeled her look after. She unclasped her perfectly manicured hands and gestured to one of the two chairs that were facing the desk. "Please."

Not relaxing the least bit, Larken took a seat.

"You're probably wondering why I called you here." The smile she gave Larken was poisonous, and she reminded her of a snake. "My name is Connie Dayton. I am the Chief Administrator here at Base 14. I apologize for not introducing myself earlier."

"No problem," Larken muttered skeptically.

Connie's smile deepened. "Well, it would seem that you really are as pretty as what they say."

Larken kept her mouth shut. She didn't know what Connie was looking for, but she wasn't going to make it easy.

Connie only laughed coyly. "Surely you can take a compliment?"

"I'm not really sure what they say about me." Then Larken added, "Or why I'm here."

Connie's eyes glinted. "And there is no convincing you that this is just a friendly introduction?"

"Seeing as no one in my squad told me to watch my schedule for a meeting with you, and the fact that I've been here for over a month, no, not really."

She smiled wide enough that Larken could see her teeth, and they glinted like fangs. "Smart and pretty; no wonder all my Captains are fighting over you."

"Excuse me?"

"Listen here, Larken, this is a place of business. You are expected to behave the way a proper soldier would, and so far, you have not. Not only has there been fighting over you, but you were in a fight not so long ago."

"How is it my fault that the men you employ are pigs?"

"That is enough. I will not tolerate insubordination on my base." She bared her teeth again. "*And* I will not tolerate a little whore coming in from the Manor and using her previous status as a Luminary's daughter to her advantage. Is that clear?"

Larken almost leaped over Connie's desk and punched her. Instead, she balled her fists and gritted out, "I have not *once* used my ties to my family to get what I wanted."

"So you didn't redecorate the Squad 19 dorm to make it more to your taste? You haven't been skipping out on training to see to personal matters? You didn't get a member of Squad 15 discharged?"

"No! I—"

Connie put up a hand, and Larken clamped her mouth shut before she said something stupid. This wasn't some idiot soldier that she needed to prove her worth to; this was the Chief Administrator, and what she said was law. "If I see you in my office again, I will have you dishonorably discharged. Is that understood?"

Larken's eyes burned, but she didn't know if it was from fear or rage. Not daring to open her mouth, Larken nodded stiffly. She would just have to ask Vallen if she was the reason that jerk was discharged. It wasn't likely; Vallen never handed anything to her, and if it was that guy's first offense he would probably still be here. But she knew for a fact that he had harassed Hinlee as well a few years ago. And how was it her fault that other people wanted to sponsor her and her squad? It wasn't like she was asking them to. But still, she said nothing.

"Very good. You may leave now."

Larken nodded again and then stood quickly. She turned and rushed to the door only to be stopped again.

"Oh, Larken."

She paused with her hand on the doorknob, waiting for Connie to deal whatever final blow she had planned.

"Try going up a size in your uniform. You look like you're asking for it."

The words *you're one to talk* were on the tip of her tongue like a bad taste she needed to spit out, but she clamped her jaw shut and pushed through the door. Red colored her vision, and she actually snarled at the secretary wishing her a pleasant rest of her day.

Barely watching where she was going, she stormed back to the dorm in a fouler mood than the one she woke up with. Larken was just glad that Loxly didn't randomly show up because she wasn't sure what would come out of her mouth when she decided to unlock her jaw. Hushed whispers and blatant stares followed her all the way back to the dorm, and to give them even more to talk about, Larken slammed the door to the common room shut behind her.

All of her aggression fled in that one action, and she felt as if all the anger and rebellion drained from her. Instead, the words that had been thrown at her danced in her head. Was she being stupid? Was she throwing the Hale name around? Shoulders dropping, Larken hugged her waist and slowly walked to her room. She quietly shut the door behind her and slumped against it. Sliding to the floor, she fished her communicator out of her pocket. She needed to know.

Larken sent the video call out and waited. The screen darkened except for the three blue dots that appeared in the middle, signaling the call. First, the one on the bottom expanded, then the middle one, then the one on the top. The top one was still enlarged when the screen changed and she could see Vallen's face. The fierce look he wore that he used to mask his concern had her heart shuddering.

"What happened?"

Her lower lip trembled.

His frown deepened. "Larken."

"Why was that guy discharged? Was it because of me? Because of my relationship with you?"

"You know it's not. That weasel was written up for seven other incidents, one of which involved the Groves girl."

Larken nodded, trying to still her bottom lip. "And the tokens? You didn't ask people to sponsor me, did you?"

"The only sponsor I had control over was myself."

Larken nodded again.

"What's this about, Larken?"

A tear escaped her left eye, and she brushed it away. "I was called to Chief Administrator Connie Dayton's office today."

She could hear his soft growl through the video, and another tear slipped out. Soon, words were spilling out of her mouth faster than she could think. Tears rolled down her cheeks, and she sniffed back her emotions the best she could. Vallen glared at her the whole time, but she knew that he wasn't upset with her. He started shouting and snarling when she told him that Connie had called her a whore and that her uniform made her look like she was asking for it.

Vallen frowned for a long time before saying, "Larken, look at me."

Larken rubbed at her eyes, hating that she was crying.

"Look at me," he said again, softly. She looked up, and his frown deepened into a scowl, although the harsh lines of his face were softer now. "You are the last person that would brag about your heritage. You never had anything handed to you, and you have worked hard your whole life. Harder than any soldier I've trained.

You don't need to answer to anyone, least of all to a woman who has no business being Chief Administrator. Do you understand me?"

She nodded and rubbed at her eyes again, feeling more like a lost child than a grown woman.

"Tell me what you understand."

"That you didn't ask anyone to sponsor me and that guy was discharged for dishonorable conduct."

"Very good. Now," he was all business and over the high emotions of the conversation, "I will inform Captain Deckard of what transpired today, and I will report what happened to the Superintendent and the other heads in charge of administration."

"But she'll know—"

"All she will know is that she was accused of harassment, and when the video feed in her office is examined, she will be found guilty."

"But everyone will—"

"No, they won't, Larken. Trust me when I say you aren't the only one that she's bullied. Once they find your altercation with her, they will start looking into every single complaint that they brushed off in favor of keeping her around."

"So, she's going to get in trouble because of me."

"No, Larken, she'll get in trouble because I am now aware of her poor attitude. This, combined with her letting Braves talk her into suspending your file, tells me that she might not be the best person for the job. It's only a coincidence that you were involved both times."

"If you say so."

"Hey!" Larken looked up to find him glaring. "When have I ever lied to you?"

She sighed. "You're right. Sorry, I guess I'm just being paranoid."

"I'll take care of it. This is no longer your problem. When do you have to check in for personal training?"

"3:00."

"And it's," he straightened his left arm so his shirt sleeve rode up and looked at his watch, "12:30. Eat some lunch and use your dorm shift to pull yourself together."

"Yes, sir!" she said with mock enthusiasm.

"That's my girl." He didn't even say goodbye before he disconnected the call.

Larken sighed, dropping her communicator on the rug and pulling her knees tight against her. How had her life gotten so messy? She was supposed to be starting over, and each time she thought it might finally be happening, something would once again remind her that she was Larken Hale, and that she would never get a second chance. Groaning, Larken fell to her side and gathered up her communicator. She put on some music with heavy bass chords and pushed herself up from the floor. Felling a little sluggish after her waves of emotion, she stripped her clothes and pulled on something a little more comfortable. Clad in shorts and a wispy tank top, she ventured out of her room and fixed herself some lunch.

Once she finished, Larken meandered back to her room. She let herself fall to the blue rug Vallen had gotten for her and sprawled out. Moving the device somewhere above her head, she listened for a minute. Her fingers tapped her stomach to the beat of the song. Sighing, Larken stilled her fingers, then stuffed her hands behind her head. She started doing sit-ups, wishing she could go for a run instead, just like she had at the Manor whenever she would have a fight with her family. It wasn't uncommon to find her late at night, running away from the words that chased her. The ones she had said, and the ones she wished she could have spoken.

Stopping, Larken rolled over onto her stomach. She fiddled with the device, and soon the same husky voice that was blaring from her communicator spilled from the speakers. The familiar words surrounded her, and she rolled back over. Larken closed her eyes, letting the melody that she had memorized wash over her. She knew that she needed to get up soon, that she would be stuck on the ground if she didn't, but she didn't want to move. Larken got lost in the song, letting the lyrics and heavy guitar wash over her. Soon, it was the only thing she knew. Nothing mattered anymore other than the next phrase, the next word.

Pulling herself up, Larken lifted an arm. Then she extended a leg, brushing her toes against the floor as she arced her leg out around her. When her heels touched again, the bridge hit, and her hips swayed with it. The drumbeat sounded in her heart, and she opened her eyes as she grinned to herself.

After Soren had left Larken standing outside the dorm, he had plowed his way to the cafeteria. He had a feeling that it wasn't going to be a good day, and he was hardly ever wrong about that. Going through the motions of breakfast, his mind kept wandering back to Larken, wondering if she was okay. In all the time she had been there, she never talked about her shoulder, or if she was ever in any pain. He had assumed that she didn't like bringing attention to it or, more accurately, to herself. She seemed like the type of person who would keep a gunshot wound a secret if it meant that she could escape the attention of others.

After breakfast was personal training, and Soren pushed a lot harder than he needed to. The murmurs of the nineteen other Captains in the gym could be heard over his heavy breathing and the impact of his glaive connecting with the practice droids. He wasn't stupid, Soren knew that they were all talking about him. About how his once-coveted squad was now being dragged down by the Military Heiress, and how she took whatever special treatment she could get in this place. They were wrong, of course, but that didn't mean it didn't annoy him. Soren's mere presence used to command respect; now he was forced to listen to the gossip about his newest recruit giving him *special favors*.

More irritated than he should be, Soren gripped the rod of his glaive tightly, spun, and took off the head of the android that he was sparring with in one stroke. The gym finally fell silent, his peers suddenly remembering who it was that they were talking about. Soren ignored the startled looks shot his way as his communicator chimed. Pulling it out, he looked to find a message from Loxly.

Instructor ill, got out of med-training early. Lunch?

Soren typed back a quick reply.

Ill? Or kicked you out for your incompetence?

His communicator chimed again, and instead of the reply he was expecting, it was a different message from Brecker.

Levi and I are done. Hinlee proctored an exam today and is finished for the morning as well. Able to take an early lunch?

Soren sighed, the air spilling out of him and carrying with it his irritation.

Loxly and I are free. Have you messaged —

Soren stopped, and then deleted the last three words. He grabbed his glaive and started heading for the door, leaving the broken android behind him. His device chimed again with Loxly's reply, but he ignored it as he started a new message.

We decided to take an early lunch. Need more time?

It didn't take long for Larken to reply.

No, I'm finished. When's lunch?

Having already anticipated her question, he sent out the message that was waiting on his screen.

11:00

Soren opened the message from Loxly he had ignored.

Ha Ha, very funny, Cap.

He cleared the message away when Larken's reply came in.

Sounds good, I'll see you guys there.

Soren messaged Brecker and Loxly, telling them the new plan. Then he made his way to the cafeteria, only stopping at his personal gym to drop off his weapon and take a quick shower. Hair still wet, Soren walked into the cafeteria and looked for his squad members. He could hear Loxly's laugh before he spotted them at a table by the window. They were all there except for Larken, and Soren wondered where she was. She should have gotten there before him unless Jodi was stationed at the med-building. Pushing the thought from his mind, Soren grabbed some food and took the empty seat to Hinlee's left.

Both Levi and Brecker had damp hair as well, and Hinlee and Loxly were talking about how they wasted their last hour. Loxly, unsurprisingly, went for a quick joyride, and Hinlee had gone back to the dorm and taken a nap.

"You happen to see Larken while you were there?" Loxly asked Hinlee, trying to sound less interested than he really was.

"*No,*" she drew out around a mouthful of food. "Why are you asking? I thought you put a tracker in her shoe."

Brecker choked on his drink, and Levi snorted.

Loxly rolled his eyes, unable to keep himself from smiling. "It's malfunctionin'." He took a drink and then added, "No, her shoulder was botherin' her this mornin' and I was wonderin' how she was feelin' now. I thought about messagin' her, but I didn't think..." he trailed off.

"That she would want you worrying about her?" Hinlee offered.

"Somethin' like that," he agreed.

A silence settled over them, and Soren was surprised when Levi broke it.

"She's just not used to other people caring about her. Give it some time."

It was true, and if anyone would know, it would be the Second. After being transferred to the military, Levi had more than likely felt the same way. It took him a long time to open up to any of them, and even now, he still didn't share what he didn't think was necessary.

"Speaking of Larken," Brecker said, "did anyone tell her that we were taking an early lunch?"

Everyone was quiet and then looked to Loxly.

"I just told you that I hadn't messaged her today."

"Nice, Lox," Hinlee scoffed, pulling her communicator out of her pocket. Her glass was still in the air, halfway to her mouth.

"I did." Four sets of eyes landed on Soren, and he continued, "I let her know when I asked if she needed more time off for her shoulder after lunch."

"And you didn't feel the need to share that bit of information?" Loxly asked.

Soren only shrugged and stuffed a slice of cucumber from his salad into his mouth. Hinlee harassed Loxly some more, teasing him about his unrequited feelings. Brecker added his thoughts every now and then, but Loxly gave it as good as he got. When he started going after Hinlee's hair again, Brecker immediately pulled himself from the conversation, regretting opening his mouth in the first place. He took up conversation with Levi instead, and Soren was surprised how easily they fell back into their old habits without Larken there. She had been such a steady presence, bringing her own personality and opinions to the group, and it was like she had never been there. But, at the same time, Soren felt like they were missing a vital piece of the group that he never knew they needed.

He would be lying if he said that he didn't keep an eye on the time, counting every minute that she was late. Thoughts of her getting lost in the base, all the way to her lying about being finished and laying in an exam room somewhere assaulted him. No one said anything, but he knew they were all wondering where she was as well. Soren noticed Loxly pull out his communicator, then stuff it back in his pocket, shaking his head. Deciding to message her himself, Soren pulled out his own communicator, only to find the screen light up with an incoming call from General Maxwell.

"Is everything okay?" Hinlee asked, worry evident in her voice. Soren looked up to find her looking over his bicep at his screen.

"Gonna find out." Accepting the call, Soren held the device to his ear and said, "Captain Deckard."

"Deckard, it's Maxwell. We have a situation."

"What can I do to help?" Everyone stared at him.

"Dayton pulled Larken into her office just now and had a rather," he paused as if he was trying to find the right word, "*unpleasant* conversation with her."

Soren's stomach tightened. "Was she transferred?"

Brecker's mouth fell open, while both Loxly and Hinlee gasped. Levi set his jaw the same way he did just before he was about to get punched.

"No, not transferred. Look, I'm just going to be honest with you. She called Larken into her office to throw her weight around and accused her of using her name to get special treatment," his voice turned to a growl, "among other things."

Soren could only imagine what that could mean, but knowing what he did of Connie, he wouldn't be surprised if the *other things* were derogatory comments towards Larken's appearance.

General Maxwell continued, "As of two minutes ago, a lock has been put over Larken and the rest of Squad 19. None of you will be able to transfer out or have any one-on-one meetings with any of the Administration staff. Dayton has been reported for harassment, and it was done anonymously. Is that understood?"

"Yes, sir."

"I understand that you also had a recent altercation with her, so you and anyone else who have been involved with Dayton and Larken could be contacted, as well as anyone whom she had any suspicious interactions with."

"I will keep an eye out. Is there any paperwork—"

"No, this is all for the higher-ups to take care of. Just watch for the calls and answer honestly. But they will also have whatever video was taken in her office, so they might not even reach out to you. I just wanted to warn you."

"I appreciate it."

"There is *one* more thing." Soren didn't like the way General Maxwell's voice dipped, but he listened to what the man had to say. He went into more detail about what it was that Connie had said, making Soren clench his fist so tight that his knuckles popped. Soren remained silent the whole time, not knowing how to process what his superior told him. General Maxwell finally sighed and said, "I thought you should know. Larken will probably be sensitive to those types of comments for the next few days, and she needs someone on her side there. Make sure the rest of the squad doesn't push her if she isn't willing to talk, but I thought she should have someone there who knows the whole story."

"Understood." Soren's voice sounded thicker than he wanted it to.

"Good. I'll keep in touch." With that, the General disconnected the call.

Sighing, Soren met the worried eyes of his squad, not really knowing how to tell them what happened. They all cared for Larken, she was a part of them now, and every time something like this happened to her, it was like a personal offense. A headache started at the base of Soren's skull, and he wanted to crawl back into bed.

When he said nothing, Loxly blurted out the question they were all thinking: "Is Larken gettin' transferred?"

"No." There were sighs of relief. "But Connie went after her."

"What for?" Hinlee practically shouted, making the people around their table look.

"For using the Hale name to benefit her and her squad." He swallowed. "And for acting in a certain way that would make the other Captains fight to get her on their squads."

"Acting a certain way? What does that even—" Hinlee's jaw dropped and her eyes burned. *"She didn't!"*

"Unfortunately, she did." Soren was unable to keep himself from reacting to the sudden strain anymore and rubbed his eyes. "Just do whatever girly talk you do to make her feel better. I'm going back to the dorm."

Brecker leaned into Hinlee, asking something, but she waved him away with a, *"Later."* She looked after Soren and asked, "Are you okay?"

Soren stood and grunted out an, "I'm fine."

She looked like she didn't believe him. He wouldn't have believed him either, but he was done talking about it. Soren didn't want to think about it anymore for the rest of the day. It was getting to be too much, all the stress that Larken had brought to the squad, but it was Larken. He couldn't hate her; she didn't ask for any of it.

She couldn't help that people obsessed over her, or that the rich military families thought of her as a favorite charity case. Larken could no more help the associations her parents had than she could the color of her eyes.

Making his way back to the dorm, Soren scowled at anyone who met his eye. He was not in the mood to deal with people or their impossible stupidity. Soren knew that the people he worked with weren't always the sharpest blades, but he didn't think that they were capable of this level of ignorance. Larken had indeed turned the base upside down, and he didn't like what he was finding.

Pushing into the dorm, Soren stomped into the common room and made his way to his bedroom. The day wasn't even close to being finished, but he already wished it was over. Kicking his door shut behind him, Soren fell onto his bed. He set an alarm for ten minutes before his rec time ended. Normally he would be using this time to get another workout in, but he felt drained. Sighing, Soren stuffed his face into his pillow and closed his eyes.

His eyes snapped open suddenly, a noise causing him to jolt up in bed. What he had thought was gunfire in his sleep turned out to be nothing more than the pounding of a drum. The deep thud of the bass seemed to shake the wall, and a loud guitar competed to be heard against the rest of the band. A man with a raspy and whiny voice was singing about bedroom eyes, long legs, and not going home alone.

Soren groaned in annoyance, wondering how long he had been asleep. His alarm hadn't gone off yet, and he felt worse than he had when he stumbled into bed. Muttering, Soren pushed himself out of bed. There was only one person he knew that could make such a ruckus. Not even bothering to run his fingers through his hair, Soren left his room and made his way to Larken's. The music was louder in the hall, and it was a far cry from the music they played at the tabernacle.

Without thinking, Soren pushed his way into her room, his mind still wrapped up in the horrible day, and he wanted nothing more than to make the noise stop. But what he found instead had his blood heating and turning to ice at the same time.

Larken was dancing, in nothing more than a wisp of a shirt and a pair of shorts that revealed a very generous amount of thigh. His mind turned to mush, and instead of yelling at her to turn the music down like he had planned, he asked, *"Where are your clothes!?"*

Larken screamed and turned, managing to trip on a blanket that was half on the bed, half on the floor. She crashed to the ground with a painful sounding thud. He should have gone and helped her, picked her up off the ground, anything, but he could only ask again, "Where are your clothes?"

She looked over at him, face redder than a tomato, and stuttered, "I-I was getting ready to g-go to the gym."

Soren just looked at her, mind still lagging. He was suddenly angry and snapped, "Clean up this room."

Turning, Soren slammed her door behind him. He could have sworn he heard an embarrassed mewl under the music, but his brain was too fried to process it. The image of her milky skin, the way her hips had moved—he would never forget it. It was seared into his mind forever. Shaking his head, Soren did the only thing he could think of and made his way to his personal gym. He decided he would run until he couldn't think of anything other than his aching muscles.

CHAPTER 19

Service ended, and Larken practically shook with excitement. She had done her hair nice and even used a little bit of Hinlee's makeup. Loxly had told her that she looked more stunning than usual, and Hinlee was quick to agree. Even Brecker and Levi both had said that she cleaned up well. Soren had been just as tight-lipped as ever, and for some reason, that disappointed her a little. Not that she could blame him; they hadn't spoken since Friday. Her cheeks still felt hot whenever she thought about what had happened, which was a lot.

Her knee had bounced eagerly all through the service, and she jumped off the pew the moment they were dismissed. It was finally visitor's day, and she couldn't wait to see Vallen. She barely had any time to talk to him since his last visit, let alone video call him, but none of that mattered because she would be able to wrap her arms around him in only an hour or so.

Filing out of the pew, Larken didn't hear her name being called over the thoughts running through her mind. She kept walking, only paying attention to where she stepped so she wouldn't trip on one of the pew legs. But when a warm hand gently wrapped around her elbow, she knew who it was by the feel of it alone and turned to find

Dominic smiling down at her. Three warm bodies moved to stand behind her, and she knew without looking that Soren, Brecker, and Loxly had on their best glares, daring the Captain to try anything.

It was the first time she had seen him since the incident the week before, and she wasn't sure how she felt about it. He looked like he had after their last argument—hair mussed, dark bags under his eyes, and just as handsome as ever. He had forgone his uniform and instead wore a soft blue shirt that made his brown eyes look like melted chocolate. Again, Larken was drawn in by his eyelashes, and she had to shake her head when she realized that she was staring stupidly.

"D-Dominic," she stuttered. "What are you doing here?"

"Enjoying the service, the same as you, I'm assuming." His thumb brushed back and forth over her skin before he let go. "How have you been?"

"Fine." Soren cleared his throat behind her. "Listen, Dominic, I'm sorry but I can't stay to talk. It's—"

"Yes, I suppose you're anxious to see General Maxwell. I just wanted to see how you were doing."

She smiled warmly, her joy at seeing Vallen making her more forgiving than she probably should be. "That's very kind of you. Thank you, Dominic."

"I'll message you about lunch?"

"Sure," she said, waving to him and turning to leave with her squad.

When they were off a little ways, Soren leaned toward her slightly and muttered, "You shouldn't trust him."

"I know."

"Then, why do you keep agreeing to see him?"

Larken couldn't answer him; she didn't know how. She could say that he kept track of Wardell for her and that he told her how her little brother was doing, but that would have been a lie. Vallen could—*did*—do that for her. There were no logical reasons that she kept agreeing to see him, kept talking to him. Larken chanced a glance up at Soren, who stared straight ahead with his jaw set and his lips twisted down in a grimace.

Why is he so upset?

Larken looked forward as well, suddenly feeling guilty, but not quite sure what she did wrong. What did it matter to him who she spoke to, or who took her out to lunch?

Wait, he can't be—

Larken glanced at him again. His eyes were hard, like flash-frozen gold, and his jaw ticked.

Is Soren…jealous?

No, that was impossible, she was just imagining things. Loxly had told her about how Dominic had tried to get him for his squad. It was when he had first joined and became friends with the whole of Squad 19, although they were all only Cadets at the time. Dominic had tried to take Levi as well. That had to be why he was so upset.

Wanting to ease some of his tension, Larken looked back up at him and said, "I'm not planning on transferring if that's what you're worried about."

"And why would I be worried about that?" he asked, and then pushed his way to the front of the group before she had time to answer.

Larken faltered in her steps; it had been a long time since he had been that cold towards her. Her stomach knotted, and all of her excitement over seeing Vallen dissipated. A warm, calloused hand slipped into hers, and Larken looked up to find Loxly looking at her with eyes that said, *Just ignore him.*

Eyes burning slightly, Larken looked ahead just in time to see Hinlee smacking Soren in the back of the head. She hoped that the tension between them wouldn't last for the rest of the day; she didn't know how she would be able to enjoy her time with Vallen when Soren was upset with her. Larken wished she knew what was bothering him so she could fix it and they could move on, but she didn't. And she didn't know what to do about the wall of ice slowly rebuilding between them.

Soren could punch a wall and thought he would be the one still standing. Seeing Larken with Braves always did something to him. A very *bad* something. He knew he shouldn't have lashed out the way he did, but he couldn't help it. Soren couldn't look back at her, couldn't listen to the whispers that Hinlee hissed in his ear about what he had said. He was very aware that she struggled with feeling like she belonged, like she was wanted, but he hadn't been able to keep the venomous words behind his teeth. Soren knew that he would have to apologize later, but right now, all he could see when he closed his eyes was Braves's thumb brushing across her skin.

He stomped all the way back to the dorm and thought about locking himself in his room so he wouldn't ruin everyone else's good time. He had no visiting family, never had, but he also knew that Rich would be disappointed if he didn't at least stay and say hello before giving in to his black mood. So, instead of storming to his room, Soren dropped himself in his usual spot on the couch and crossed his arms.

Everyone walked in at the same time a few minutes after that; he hadn't realized that he had gone so far ahead. Soren didn't even have to turn his head to look up and watch them all. His eyes narrowed in on Larken's hand clasped tightly in Loxly's, and it added fuel to the fire as well as soothed it some. Breathing hard through his nose, he had to remind himself that it wasn't like that. That they were just friends and that the sharpshooter was probably only comforting her because of his insensitive comment. Soren wanted to pull out his hair.

Why do I even care?

Larken let go of Loxly's hand and went to the kitchen with Levi. The two got to work, pulling dishes out of the fridge and warming up the ones that needed it. It had been just over a week since Larken had made that chicken, and it had been decided that the squad would eat more meals in the dorm because what she and Levi could make tasted better than anything in the cafeteria. Levi seemed indifferent about it, but Larken had taken up that job seriously, asking about what everyone liked, and if there were any allergies she should be mindful of.

Larken had just dropped a pot roast off at the table, when Loxly grabbed her arms gently from behind and murmured, "Don't worry, you'll be great. He's gonna love you."

She dropped her head and said almost too quietly for Soren to hear, "I have a hard time believing that. Parents don't—"

But she was cut off by a knock at the door that Hinlee rushed to open. Rich stood there, holding six parcels instead of the usual five he had with him in the past. His wind-weathered face split into a grin, and with a rich and raspy accent that was even thicker than Loxly's, asked, "Hey sweetie, how you doin'?"

"I'm good, Rich. Yourself?" Hinlee sidestepped, holding the door and letting him in.

"Fine, fine," he answered, walking in. "Happy to be off that aircraft."

"How you share the same DNA with Loxly, I will never understand."

"I heard that," Loxly grumbled, walking up and taking the packages from his father.

Rich pulled Hinlee into a hug as the others crowded around him. Well, everyone except for Larken, who was hiding in the kitchen and pretending to look for something in the fridge. Levi and Brecker each shook Rich's hand, and he asked Brecker, "You still treatin' my girl right?"

"Yes, sir!" Brecker said, beaming at Hinlee. She grinned up at him as well, and that tightness pulled at Soren's chest again.

There was a small commotion in the kitchen with a soft, "*No, Loxly, I—*"

Loxly had both his hands on Larken's shoulders and pushed her out into the fray. They stopped right in front of Rich, and she looked up at him with those big eyes of hers. Her throat bobbed and she looked ready to run. Rich just stuffed his hands into his pockets and asked, "You the one that's been keepin' my boy fed?"

Larken opened her mouth, but no words came out. She was a frazzled mess, and the sight of her had Soren's lips twitching against their will. Rich was a stand-up guy, but being taller than even Soren and built like an ox, he was also extremely intimidating. Soren could remember the first time he had met Richmond Beau, and he would be lying if he said that he hadn't felt a little uneasy. Rich was like a wild bull, and you were left wondering if he was going to buck you off or not. Of course, the man was more bark than bite, but Larken didn't know that, and the sight of her was almost adorable.

"Dad, this is Larken," Loxly said, grinning ear to ear.

Rich's eyes went back and forth between his son and Larken, obviously trying to figure out the true nature of their relationship.

"N-nice to meet you, Mr. Beau," Larken stuttered out. Loxly let go of her shoulders and went to go finish setting the table.

Rich's slight scowl melted into a warm smile that made him look like Loxly. "No need for that, darlin', Rich is fine." He placed his hand on her shoulder and said, "I hear that my son plans on marryin' you someday." Larken choked and Loxly laughed. "But if your cookin' is half as good as what Lox says, then I might just have to marry you myself," Rich said with a wink, leaving Larken standing where she was, bright pink and opened-mouthed.

He made his way over to where Soren sat, and he stood to greet him. Reaching his hand out, Rich clasped it, but then pulled him into a hug instead. Clapping Soren on the back, he asked, "How you doin', son? She drivin' you crazy too?"

Soren just grunted and Rich chuckled at his expense. There was a whispered argument between Larken and Loxly over by the dining table. Both men pretended they couldn't hear it, even though Rich smiled and made small talk instead. Soren told him about the chaotic weeks that he had been having to push through, and Rich told Soren about the farm and the new livestock he had just purchased.

There was another knock at the door and Soren saw Larken perk up out of the corner of his eye. She always seemed to be there lately, and it annoyed Soren that he couldn't just ignore her.

Levi opened the door, and there was a boy who couldn't be older than fifteen that stuck out a white box and said, "Please give this to Miss Hale."

Levi accepted the box and shut the door in the kid's face. He didn't even move before the box was out of his hand, Larken already wearing the mask she put on so she wouldn't look too emotional. Soren's stomach soured and he watched her unfold a note stuck to the top of the box, and Larken's shoulders fell just the tiniest bit. She had been looking so forward to today, and now…

"What does it say?" Hinlee asked, her eyes colored with concern.

Larken straightened her back and said, "Vallen can't make it today. My mother wouldn't approve time off for him. Will you put this in the fridge so it stays cold? I have to use the bathroom."

Without waiting for an answer, Larken pushed the box into Hinlee's hands and disappeared down the hall. Soren watched her go, only half-listening to Rich finish his story about the calf that he didn't know he was expecting until the cow he purchased got to the farm. Apparently, she was pregnant, and that bit of information wasn't included in the sale agreement. Soren nodded and looked back at Rich, only to find that the man had stopped talking and stared at him in a way that made him want to squirm.

"Go talk to her," Rich murmured.

"What?"

"*Go talk to her.*"

"Why?"

Rich just gave him a knowing smile and whispered, "If you wanted me to think that you didn't care about her, you shouldn't have made it a point to *not* talk about her just now."

Soren just scowled but left Rich and made his way down the hall anyway. He bypassed the bathroom, knowing that she had shut herself in her room instead. Soren grabbed her doorknob and took a deep breath. Giving himself to the count of three, he twisted the knob quietly and opened the door.

Larken stood by her bed, her face buried in that black jacket. Soren wanted to turn around and go back to the common room, but he couldn't just leave her like this. He shut the door loud enough behind him to let her know that she wasn't alone. Her face shot up, and her eyes were red.

She snarled at him. "What are you doing in here? Get out."

"Not until we talk," Soren said gently.

"*Get out,*" she said more forcefully.

Soren took a step towards her, his hands up like he was approaching a spooked animal instead of her. Eyes narrowing, she followed his progress, scowling as he got closer. When he stood in front of her, and she didn't punch him in the throat, Soren reached out for the jacket. Reluctantly, Larken let him take it, and her arms wrapped around her middle. Soren held the jacket for only a moment before draping it around her shoulders. He straightened the lapels, making sure she was covered well, when he felt her eyes move up to his face. He finished what he was doing before he met her gaze. The words *I'm sorry* were on his lips, but his jaw was set and he couldn't move it. He swallowed, and his hands drifted from the lapels to her arms.

They were so close, and he was just now realizing it. The smell of grapefruit flooded his mind, and he felt like he was stuck in a fog of it. The thumb of his right hand started brushing the jacket of its own accord, and he felt the warmth of her skin seep through the fabric. Larken's lower lip trembled slightly, and she sucked it in between her teeth. Reaching up with his left hand, he cupped her cheek, and she released her lip as her eyes glossed over. She sniffed, and her eyes looked blue against her unshed tears. Soren felt a little lost, like he was drowning in a sea of grapefruit-scented ocean, but he couldn't bring himself to swim towards the surface.

A single tear slipped out of her eye, and he brushed it away with his thumb. Another quickly replaced it, and then a tear slipped from her other eye. His heart went cold as he realized that he had no idea how to comfort her. He pleaded her with his eyes, asking her to tell him what to do, but she only croaked, *"Why does she hate me so much?"*

Soren didn't even think as the hand cupping her face slid to the back of her neck and then pulled her close. She sobbed silently into his shirt, soaking the fabric and making it stick to his skin. Soren just held her, feeling like he was failing her. He had told her that she could lean on him, trust him to look out for her. But what was he supposed to do about this? He had no answers for her; his mother hadn't wanted him either. If she had, she wouldn't have traded him to the army for arii.

The two of them just stood there, holding each other, pushing through the worst of it. When Larken got a hold of her emotions, she pulled free and turned away from him. Soren took that as his cue to leave, so he did. He stopped at his room and put on a clean shirt, but the smell of grapefruit still danced under his nose.

Soren walked out to the common room; everyone was sitting on the couches waiting for him and Larken. Taking the only free seat, he slipped easily into conversation. Loxly talked about his shotgun, and both Hinlee and his father gave him a hard time about it. A few minutes later, Larken slipped onto the couch next to him. He made as much room for her as he could, but with Levi already sitting on his other side, he ended up having to drape his arm over the back of the couch and ignore her as she settled against him. The jacket had been left in the room, and she didn't look like she had just been crying. It made him wonder how often she had to pretend like everything was fine at the Manor, but Rich announcing how famished he was turned Soren's thoughts to the food as well.

The group stood and made their way to the table that had an extra mismatched chair squeezed onto one end. Soren watched out of the corner of his eye as Loxly walked up behind Larken and pulled her into a hug. She reached her hands up and patted his arms as he whispered something in her ear. She shook her head, and he dipped his head to kiss her temple. She scoffed and elbowed him in the gut, causing him to chuckle and her to crack a smile. A feeling a bit like jealousy stabbed at Soren, and he resented Loxly a little for being able to do what he couldn't.

When they were all seated, Rich grabbed Loxly's and Hinlee's hands. Forcing Soren to grab Levi's on his left and Larken's on his right. Her hand was soft and warm, and it distracted him through the entirety of Rich's prayer. It wasn't like Soren had never held a girl's hand before, it was just something about *hers*. He was only aware of where his skin touched hers, and he couldn't drop her hand soon enough.

Soren felt her look at him, and he pretended that the reason he let go so quickly was because he was hungry. Grabbing the closest dish to him, he started loading up his plate, not even paying attention to what he dished out. When he had three steamed carrots, which he didn't like, on his plate, Levi coughed next to him. It took all Soren had not to kick his Second under the table.

Rich started asking Larken about herself. She was polite and answered all of his questions, but Soren knew that her mind was somewhere else. She didn't help matters by accidentally grabbing his water glass instead of hers and taking a sip. Realizing her mistake as she set the glass down, she looked up at him, wide-eyed and cheeks pink. No one else noticed her blunder, so Soren just grabbed his glass and took a swig, pretending that nothing had happened.

Once the pot roast was gone and the strawberry pie that Larken had made was finished, Rich started passing out the packages he had brought. Hinlee wasted no time tearing into hers, and then threw her head back and laughed. Reaching into the box, she set a little figurine of a chicken on the table, making everyone, except Larken, laugh as well. "Where did you find that?"

"Junk sale," Rich said with the same crooked smile that Loxly wore too often.

Larken leaned into Soren and whispered, "I don't get it."

He leaned into her as well. "When they first met, he thought Loxly said Hen-lee. It's been a running joke since."

Larken smiled sadly, no doubt remembering all the jokes she had with General Maxwell, and pulled back to her seat. Soren then reached for his own package with prompting from Rich and opened up a pocket knife, suspecting that Loxly had told Rich that his other one had just rusted out. He nodded to Rich, and he beamed at him. Then he moved his gaze over to Larken. "Go ahead, darlin'."

"You didn't have to—"

"And leave you the only one not to open anythin'? Go on and open it already."

Larken opened her box slowly, apprehension in her every movement. He wondered what had happened to make her so wary of gifts, but from what he knew of her brother, he wouldn't be surprised if she had opened a snake or two in her youth. Instead of a snake, she pulled out a fair-sized black box as long as her forearm, and about as thick. Larken set it on the table and smiled sweetly before saying, "Thanks...what is it?"

"Hit the button in the middle"

She did, and a grinding sound filled the room as the box disassembled and morphed into a shape only it knew. Eventually, though, they were all looking at an android that resembled a puppy with floppy ears and a scrunched snout. Larken swallowed loudly and the whites of her eyes went pink.

"The man at the shop said that there was a panel in its chest to customize markings and that you could even order skins to make it more realistic, all hypoaller-whatever of course. Perfect for anyone who wants a pet but doesn't want to sneeze or clean."

Larken nodded, and only Soren could see her wrap her arms around her stomach under the table. Her fists were balled so tightly that her knuckles were white, and he thought she might be digging her nails into her palms to keep herself from getting too emotional. In that moment, he wanted to be more like Loxly, to know the right thing to do or say. But he wasn't, and Soren didn't have the answers. She was so different from the others, so closed off and abrasive, and yet...

That moment they had just had in her bedroom, he hadn't

thought then or worried about doing the wrong thing. Taking a breath, he forced all of the thoughts out of his mind and slowly reached out his hand. Her skin was cold, and he caressed her knuckles until she loosened her grip, all the while looking at the android. When her fingers were loose enough, he grabbed her hand and she squeezed his tightly.

"Lox said that you were missin' your mutts back home, and a friend of mine just got one for his boy. Figured they couldn't force you to get rid of it since it's technically a machine."

Larken nodded again, her throat bobbing as she swallowed. Soren shifted his gaze over to Rich to find him already looking his way, that same gleam from earlier in his eyes. Soren fought to keep his hand where it was; his squad member needed him more than his pride needed to be saved.

"Well," Rich clapped his hands and then stood up, "as nice as it is to see y'all again, I do have an aircraft to catch. Mornin' comes early on the farm, and I still have my ride back."

They all stood to wish him goodbye, and Larken made her way into the group after taking a moment to collect herself. Rich grinned at her before pulling her into a big hug, just as he had done with Hinlee. He bent his head and whispered something in Larken's ear, making her smile. Then, when they broke apart, Larken surprised Soren by getting up on her tiptoes and kissing Rich on the cheek.

As Loxly saw his father out, Larken moved to the table and started grabbing plates. Hinlee took the plates out of her hand, saying, "You look exhausted. Go get some rest, we'll take care of this."

"You sure?"

"Absolutely!"

Larken looked at her, giving her a moment to change her mind. When Hinlee didn't, Larken gathered up the android and headed to her room. It wasn't long after that a muffled, steady bass could be heard.

Hinlee set the plates on the table and sighed. She didn't have to say anything, because Soren understood. They *all* understood. Larken was one of them now, and her raw emotions clung to them like a heavy humidity. Silently, they all got to work clearing the table and cleaning the kitchen. About the time they finished and were dropping onto the couches, Loxly returned. His eyes were rimmed red and his smile a little too forced. He was always like that after his dad left, but none of them had anything to relate it to. If they had, they would all probably be locked away in their rooms as well.

Loxly dropped onto the couch he usually shared with Larken and sighed deeply, letting his smile fall away. Sinking back into the couch, he asked, "What are we gonna do?"

"We could petition that General Maxwell comes and oversees some basic training lessons. It's not ideal, but at least they would be able to see each other and work out together again," Hinlee suggested.

"And how isn't that ideal?" Loxly wondered.

"Because then *we* would have to work out with him too," Brecker answered for her.

"*Right…*" Loxly stretched the word out, comprehension tainting the idea for him. "We already have you. I'd hate to see what General Maxwell put us through."

Brecker threw something too small for Soren to make out at Loxly, who chuckled and tossed it back.

"Oh! Maybe you could put her in for a leave of absence?" Hinlee asked Soren.

But it was Levi who said, "If her mother wouldn't approve his time off to come visit her, what makes you think she'll let Larken onto the Manor grounds?"

They were all silent for a while, and then Soren pulled out his communicator. No one asked him what he was doing, but they would all find out soon enough. He tapped out a few messages and shuffled a few things around, but then everyone's communicator went off, alerting them all to the change in their schedule for the following day.

Levi, who was the first to pull his out and see his now empty day, asked, "What, are we going to go kidnap him?"

"No," Soren answered. "But I do think Loxly needs to make good on the promises he made to me and to Larken."

CHAPTER 20

Larken rolled an apple between her palms, feeling an awful mix of excitement and nervousness. She had been embarrassed that morning to learn that she was the reason everyone's schedule had been cleared, but she felt better knowing that gunning was also classified as a team-building exercise. The arena sat on the other side of the base, and they had just finished breakfast. Levi had made a hearty meal of meat and starch, but Larken could only manage a little bit of egg and some fruit. She had brought the apple only to get Loxly to leave her alone, but her stomach still felt too tight to eat it.

Soren had booked the whole day for them and only carved an hour out for lunch and for the crew to reset the arena and do any repairs that might be needed. The night before, everyone had determined teams, Loxly and Soren pitted against each other as captains. Loxly had dug his grave when he promised to get Soren back the week before and to add insult to injury, Larken had been Soren's first pick as a teammate.

Loxly comically moaned all morning of the injustice of it all, and how it wasn't right to force soulmates to fight each other. Soren's jaw had been locked and ticking from the moment Loxly had first opened his mouth. Hinlee and Brecker had explained the rules to her, what was considered fair and what was considered cheating.

Like, offering to kiss Loxly to get him out into the open, as Brecker suggested, would be considered cheating. Any hits against him in that situation wouldn't count and would instead go to her. If Loxly were to get shot in the leg, for example, it would be her gear that would lock up. When she had asked how her gear would know, Levi interrupted to tell her that the surveillance drones had been equipped with a good sportsman software and to stop fraternizing with the enemy.

Larken was pulled from her thoughts of all the ways she could mess up or cause her team to lose by Soren saying, "You better hurry up and eat that. You won't be able to take it in with you."

Larken only looked at the apple and picked at the stem.

"Token for your thoughts?" he sighed, sounding only mildly annoyed.

"What if I mess up and we lose?"

"Then we regroup and try again."

"What if I *only* mess up, and we lose?"

"Then I'll kick you out of Squad 19."

Larken smiled, despite herself.

"If you cost us every round, then you will treat Levi and me to a meal at the Dining Hall. But I doubt it will get to that."

"Because you didn't pick me for your team to get a rise out of Loxly."

"You were trained by General Maxwell; annoying Loxly was just a bonus. So don't worry about it, just try to have some fun today."

Soren was ahead of the group before Larken could even look up from her apple. She had to settle for watching the back of his head, and she couldn't help the small smile that turned at her lips. Larken wasn't sure what it was about him, but he was so different from anyone she knew. He was uncomfortable with a lot of things, like Vallen, but that was where the similarities ended. She was reminded yet again of that conversation she had with Loxly when she had first come here. She had compared Soren to one of the hybrids at the Manor, and she was slowly learning that the comparison wasn't that big of a leap. He was big and scary to anyone who didn't know him, but to her...

She never *ever* cried in front of anyone who wasn't Vallen if she could help it, and somehow, she had found herself in Soren's arms the day before. The memory of how warm he had been made goosebumps break out on her arms, and the way he had smelled, it was like leather and freshly tilled earth. It was like how a perfect summer's day smelled, and she was now aware of it whenever they were close. Soren was so different from Dominic, and Larken wasn't quite sure how she felt about it.

By the time they reached the building that separated the arena from the rest of the base, Larken had managed a full two bites of her apple, but with one look from Soren, she started chomping it down. The tart juice flooded her mouth, and the sensitive skin at her jaw hurt from it. Loxly walked up behind her and muttered, "You finally find your appetite?"

"No," she said around a mouthful of fruit. "Soren just doesn't want me to pass out in the arena."

"You should throw it out then."

Larken took another large bite. "Why?"

"Because, Little Bird, if you pass out, then I can wake you up with a kiss."

Larken laughed, then her cheeks started hurting again. She reached up and cupped her right one, glaring at Loxly. His eyes only danced, like he had accomplished what he was hoping to. When the pain subsided, Larken punched him in the arm, and he cried, "Interference! That's my shootin' arm!"

"You don't hear me complaining about punching you with my shooting hand."

"That's because you don't need to be coddled and actually have talent," Levi said to her left.

Larken laughed again, and Loxly's jaw dropped in faux astonishment. With his accent thicker than she had ever heard it, he said, "Well, I never..."

"Never what?" Soren asked, joining her and Levi. "Hit your target on the first try?"

"Oh, just you wait," Loxly purred through a big grin. "Just you wait, Deckard. I'm gonna be aimin' for you the rest of the day."

"Aim all you want," Soren said. "The goal is to hit me."

Loxly didn't get a chance to give his retort because Soren and Levi pulled Larken to the door on the left side of the desk that Soren had used to check them in at. Larken dropped her apple core into the trash bin just inside the locker room and then chafed her arms as the cool air hit her. The contrast between the air outside and the locker room was drastic, and she wanted to turn around and go back outside.

"Skies above," Levi muttered. "Why is it always so cold in here?"

"So you can complain about it," Soren retorted.

Trying to make herself as small as possible to conserve heat, Larken asked, "So, what do I do?"

Soren opened a locker and pulled out a black jumpsuit that looked to be covered in shiny obsidian scales. He tossed it to her, and she only just caught it. Unzipping the back, Larken got into it as fast as she could, wanting to warm up. Soren and Levi were both pulling theirs on as well, although their scales were a lot less shiny than hers. She wondered how long they had had theirs and was about to ask when Soren walked over to her.

Looking down at her, he murmured, "Turn around."

She was captivated by his eyes that looked more green than gold in that moment and swallowed thickly. It felt like there was a piece of apple stuck in her throat, so she swallowed again, but it didn't help. Soren raised a thick eyebrow at her, and she turned, but probably not fast enough for him to miss the blush that heated her face. She could feel the heat of his hands as he placed one on her waist to hold the jumpsuit, and the other that slowly pulled up her zipper. Soren paused when the zipper reached the top, and she felt his breath on her neck as he leaned into her and murmured, "How's the fit?"

"Good," she breathed, slowly losing the battle to *not* be affected by him.

"We'll rub some dirt on you outside so you don't shine so much."

Larken stepped away quickly, nodding. She looked up in time to see Levi watching her with a raised eyebrow, and she blushed hotly. Thankfully, he didn't say anything, but he didn't need to. Larken could read what he was thinking on his face.

"Alright, team," Soren said, all business, his arms crossed. "We're up against a sharpshooter who will probably hide in the trees, a mechanic who will be hanging around Loxly's hiding place to alert him of our movements, and a scouter who will probably waste no time rushing our side of the arena to take out as many of us as he can. So, any ideas?"

"You can use me as bait," Larken offered. "Loxly will probably make a joke of some kind when he sees me, giving away his position. If one of you follows me—"

"Loxly takes this too seriously to make a mistake like that," Levi interrupted. "I say you pit us against each other. You and Brecker, me and Hinlee, and Larken and Loxly."

"Works for me." Soren uncrossed his arms. "We can regroup after round one and discuss the strategy they went with and use it to anticipate the next one."

"That's it?" Larken asked, feeling like she was missing something.

"The important thing to remember here is that this is a game," Levi said as he made his way to the door Soren was already scanning a wristband at. "Don't take it too seriously, but don't be the reason we lose either. Simple as that."

Larken just shrugged and agreed with a sighed, "Simple as that."

The three soldiers made their way out of the locker room, and the warm air outside sent a new wave of goosebumps up Larken's arms. Soren grabbed a basic model tech-gun the same length as the one he usually wielded, but it looked much lighter. It didn't have any of the upgrades that his had, like the stun darts or the fog emitters, both of which would have been helpful today. He also grabbed a shotgun and tossed it to Levi, who caught it without even looking over at Soren. That left the handgun for her, causing her to roll her eyes.

"Really?"

Soren smirked. "You never know, maybe he'll try to get you face-to-face."

He reached into his pocket and pulled out what looked like a little black rubber ball and tossed one to her, which Larken almost dropped. Then he tossed one to Levi, who caught it and stuck it in his ear. Soren pulled out another one and stuck it in his ear as well. Larken looked at it, shrugged, and held it to her own ear. As soon as the rubber touched her skin, it morphed and pushed into her canal.

Soren made his way to the door, opened it, and went back into the locker room. He pulled the door behind him, leaving his foot wedged in-between the door and the frame. He was so quiet that Larken couldn't hear him say anything, but a whispered, *"Can you hear me?"* came through her earpiece.

Levi answered first. "Loud and clear, Black Hawk."

To which, Larken replied, "Black Hawk?"

"It's my codename," Soren said coming back out. "Levi's is Pretty Boy, and yours," he smirked, "is Songbird."

"How original," Larken deadpanned, fighting not to roll her eyes.

"If you would rather it be Princess—"

"I'm good," she interrupted.

"That's what I thought. Now, everyone clear on the plan?"

Levi gave a single nod before cocking his weapon and disappearing into the trees.

"I guess," Larken agreed.

"Good. Meet back here when round one is over." Soren didn't give her a second glance as he dashed into the trees as well, in the opposite direction from Levi.

"I guess I'm taking the middle then," she muttered. She gave their small clearing one last look over before slowly moving forward.

The earth around her was wild and unchecked, and bugs buzzed happily in places Larken couldn't see. There were no birds, but the sound of the mock weapons was most likely the reason that they didn't nest here. Every stick that she didn't see and snapped as she walked had her heart thudding as she looked every which way to see if anyone on the other team had heard it as well. None of her teammates said anything, and the earpiece served as nothing more than a way to block outside noise.

As she walked, she occasionally bent down and felt the earth. Everything was hard and packed, and there was nothing to tarnish the shine to her scales. Not only that, but when she tried to count the number of bullets she had, she found that the magazine had been fused to the weapon. Larken was left to assume that either she had no limit, or the gun would stop working after she fired the max number of shots. Unfortunately for her, she had no idea how many that was. All the weapons that Vallen had provided for her had upgrades, most of which were larger mags.

Larken had no way to tell what time it was, or how long they had all been wandering. Each second that passed with no noise only made her more on-edge. Right when she thought she was going to snap from the tension in her body, there were four successive shots that had Larken diving behind the nearest tree for cover.

"What happened?" she hissed.

"Loxly used Hinlee and Brecker as bait. We didn't realize it until it was too late. It's all on you now," Soren said.

"Wait, what?"

"Don't worry, Songbird," Levi grumbled wryly, "we eliminated our targets. Go eliminate yours."

"Sure, okay. Let me just find him first," she snapped, making Levi chuckle.

Larken crept out from behind the tree and got as close to the ground as she could without crawling. She knew that the shine to her scales and her blonde hair would give her away no matter what she did, but if Loxly was up in a tree like Soren had thought, then maybe she could use a bush to block her, or something.

Everything was still and so quiet that she could hear each beat of her heart. The sun sat high in the sky, and sweat collected at her brow. Larken didn't bother wiping it away and kept moving.

She entered a little clearing and debated back-stepping into the trees. Looking around, she noticed that the little bit of grass that was there had been mussed, and the dirt was kicked up. Taking a tentative step forward, she waited. When nothing happened, she took another. Slowly, she made her way in and then crouched down to examine the area. Reaching out, she lifted a few blades of grass to get a good look at a gouge in the ground that resembled a boot heel. She leaned in, and then there was a gunshot that had her pulling her hand back and screaming.

Her jumpsuit stiffened at the wrist, and she couldn't move it no matter how hard she tried. She could still bend her elbow, but her left hand was completely useless. There was a rustle of leaves, and then a thud as Loxly landed on the ground in front of her. He held his shotgun close to his chest and had a wicked smile as he crooned, "Hello, Little Bird."

Larken was up on her feet and running back through the trees faster than Loxly could grasp what was happening. Her throat went dry as she gasped in air to try and oxygenate her adrenaline-spiked limbs. She kept her left hand close to her chest, trying in vain to move her fingers. They were stuck, as if she was still reaching out for the blades of grass. She could wiggle her fingertips, but that was just because they were the only parts uncovered. That, and most of her thumb.

"Don't fly away, Little Bird!" Loxly called after her. "The party's just gettin' started!"

Think, Larken, think! What can you do? What do you have that will work in your favor?

She ran through everything that Vallen had taught her about being in situations like this. It wasn't the first time she had been cornered; Vallen had seen to it that she was able to live out the scenarios he had thought up, no matter how insane.

I need to get behind him somehow. It would be easier if he was still searching for me and didn't know that I had become the predator instead.

Looking around, she only saw trees and bushes. There was also a drone or two, and she wondered suddenly if the others were watching her. That would make everything so much worse if her team had watched her walk into the same trap that they had and then lose. No, there had to be something. Larken looked around again. She still had one working hand and the use of her elbow.

"Where'd you go, Larken?"

She shivered. Loxly was having *way* too much fun. Larken dropped her gun into a bush as quietly as she could and grabbed a thick stick. Angling it, she slipped it through her fingers on her left hand and then ran for a low-hanging branch. She jumped, catching it with her hand and left forearm. Kicking her legs, Larken pulled herself up as quickly as she could, and then reached for the next branch up. She made it to the third one before Loxly appeared under her.

She watched him as he looked around, his finger resting on the trigger of his gun. Holding her breath, Larken pulled the stick from her hand and whipped it behind her. The grin that crossed his face as Loxly headed in that direction made her shiver. Larken waited until she could barely hear him before dropping out of the tree. The drop was more than what she expected, and she had to roll so she didn't twist her ankles. Getting up, Larken hobbled to the bush, her right ankle not quite making it, and then fished her gun out. She pushed through the discomfort until the joint righted itself and quickly caught up to Loxly.

Larken decided not to wait this out and crept up behind him. Slipping her left arm around his neck, she pulled him down to her before he realized what was happening. Raising her gun to his temple, she pulled the trigger and felt as his gear locked up and he fell to the ground. The little drones that were around her opened their tops, and little blue flags popped out and spun. A robotic voice announced, "Team Feather wins."

"Team Feather?" she laughed.

"Yeah," Loxly said from the ground. "They randomize names for us based on who's playing."

It was only after the announcement that Larken regained the use of her left hand, and she clenched and relaxed it, sighing as she did. She would need to be more careful about getting shot, and what position her limbs were in. It would have been impossible to get away if he had hit her bent leg instead.

Loxly stood and pulled her into a hug. "Good game. Do you know the way back to your locker room?"

"Maybe?"

He laughed. "Come on, I'll show you really quick."

The two made their way back to where the rest of her team was waiting for her. Both Levi and Soren heckled Loxly about his dirty trick and then told him to get out of their locker room.

The rest of the day went on like that, and more often than not, Loxly and Larken were the final two. Every so often, she was the first one killed, but it was usually Hinlee that was taken out first. She had a great attitude about it though, joking about spending most of her time under aircraft, not charging in front of them.

They had stopped for lunch, like Soren promised, and Larken had eaten everything she could get her hands on. It was nothing fancy, just sandwiches, but they tasted wonderful and did their job. But, at the end of the day, Team Feather had beaten Team Gun 8 to 4. And, as great as Larken felt, she was just as sore. She couldn't wait to get back to the dorm and take a hot shower.

Larken still sat on the couch and had pulled her legs up under her, slouching and letting her head fall to the side. She reached up with her left hand and pulled at the muscle in her shoulder. Soren, who was the only one in the common room left with her, was transfixed.

Having gotten up to get a drink of water, he had come back to find her like that. He didn't know if he should stare at the blonde curl that rested against her neck, having fallen from her bun, or the elegant slope of her throat. Her milky skin looked so soft, and he started when he realized that he was wondering what it felt like. Was it soft like her hands? Or her elbows, that he found himself grabbing more and more lately?

Needing to do something to release the tension that had settled between his shoulder blades, he sarcastically asked, "What? Need a massage?"

"Yeah, if you wouldn't—" She looked over her shoulder at him and her cheeks turned pink at the sight of his dropped jaw. "Oh, you weren't being serious."

"N-no, I can help," he said, thoroughly embarrassed.

The shy smile on her face did something weird to his stomach, and he knew that he would see this task through, no matter what. She let go of her shoulder and said, "I have some lotion that Jodi gave me sitting on my case, if you want to use that."

"Whatever," he grunted as he made his way to her room.

The sweet smell of grapefruit that always clung to her greeted him as he walked into her room. Soren looked to the weapons case and found the bottle sitting next to a photograph that he couldn't help but pick up and look at. The smile that turned his lips was genuine as he took in her crossed eyes and the pink tongue that stuck out of her mouth. General Maxwell had her in a headlock, and she was pretending to die. It was that side of her, the silly one who dreamed of sunny days and sang about dandelion fluff and kisses, that he found himself needing to be closer to with each passing day.

Setting the picture down, he grabbed the lotion and left. Soren unceremoniously plopped onto the couch behind her, and she pulled the straps off her right shoulder. Heat crept up his neck at the flesh she exposed, but she didn't seem fazed by it. But, then again, she was probably used to exposing her shoulder like this.

"You took your sweet time," she teased. "You find anything interesting?"

"Just that picture of you and General Maxwell."

He could hear the smile in her voice when she said, "That one's my favorite."

Soren uncapped the bottle and squeezed some of the lotion onto her shoulder. She shuddered and complained, "You're supposed to warm it up with your hands first."

"Don't be such a baby," he grunted, the smell of eucalyptus filling his mind and clearing his sinuses.

Tentatively, he reached to her and smeared the lotion across the top of her shoulder and the curve of her neck. She tilted her head to give him a better angle, and he applied a little more pressure. His hand slipped too easily against her skin, so he pushed into the muscle more. She sighed, almost too quiet for him to hear, but the sound made it difficult for him to swallow.

In an attempt to focus on something else, Soren asked, "Does it bother you a lot?"

"Honestly…" she murmured, "yes."

Gripping her shoulder, he started working his thumb into the muscle, moving it in little circles, back and forth over the knot. His fingers tingled coolly as the lotion soaked into his skin as well as hers. Soren didn't know what to say; he wasn't expecting her to be so honest with him. Not that Larken was a liar, but she didn't like feeling exposed. Something that he easily related to.

They were silent for a long time, and Larken said, "It was the day after my sixteenth birthday. Vallen was the only one who had remembered, and that was when he gave me my sword. The next morning, I had to do an obstacle course to show how much I improved over the year. I planned on doing the one that Vallen had selected for me." She sighed. "*Then* my mother showed up."

Soren was still, apart from his fingers that pushed into her shoulder. She never talked about her home life, let alone her mother. He didn't want to say the wrong thing and have her stop talking. Partly because he wanted to know what had happened, partly because he wanted to be the one that she opened up to.

"Vallen told me not to run it, that I wasn't ready. But I used to do anything to try and get her approval. And completing the highest-level course four years early would have done that."

Soren knew that one. It was the final test for anyone hoping to achieve the title of General. There were impossible jumps, an unending supply of androids that would be released onto the course at any moment, and cages that fell on you that you could only escape by solving a puzzle in the given time limit. It was a course that he wouldn't be able to do without serious training. And it was always televised. But he couldn't remember ever seeing or hearing about Larken doing it.

"What happened?" he asked.

"I almost finished. I made it to the final jump, and that's where I messed up. I don't really remember what happened after I jumped. I know that I jumped wrong, trying to avoid a cage, but other than that..." Her face fell. "I remember my fingers grazing the handle and falling. I can remember the pain and Vallen punching someone to try and get to me. But the thing I remember the most was looking at the box where my mother was sitting and seeing her turn and walk away. Then...nothing."

No wonder she hated talking about it. This was the most vulnerable, most exposed, Soren had ever seen her, and he had held her while she cried the day before. How was it that someone so talented, so concerned for others, was so neglected? Soren had a new understanding of her relationship with General Maxwell and how close they really were. The memory of seeing him labeled as her father surfaced in Soren's mind.

"Larken..."

She grabbed her straps, and he pulled his hand away so she could cover herself. "It's fine. I just don't talk about it because I'm not proud of it. I was really reckless and let my emotions get the better of me. Vallen always tells me that it's going to get me in trouble. But I guess I don't learn because he has to keep reminding me."

That wasn't the only reason she didn't talk about it, but he didn't push it. Soren lifted his hand again and then closed it into a fist before he touched her. He couldn't see her eyes; he didn't know what would be too much.

"Do me a favor though? Don't tell the others, I don't want them to…"

Larken didn't finish, but she didn't have to. "I won't."

She turned to face him, her teal eyes so blue that he felt like he was suffocating. This sensation was new and terrifying, and he was startled to realize that this must be what drowning felt like. He needed to get up, to leave. But when he tried to stand, his legs wouldn't move. Instead, his hand reached up and cupped her cheek. A soft smile tugged her lips, and she leaned into his hand.

"Thank you."

His throat was dry, and he couldn't swallow the strange lump that was there. Nodding, he could only sit there and stare at her. Larken's little smile warmed, and that melted something in him that he didn't know was frozen. He really needed to get up and leave. But it was Larken that pulled away.

Yawning into the back of her hand, she exhaled, "*Sorry.*" Dropping her hand, she shook herself and stood. "I need to get to bed, I'm exhausted. See you in the morning?"

Another nod.

"Alright then." She made her way to the hall, but then stopped and turned. "And thank you. Not for listening, but for being someone I can trust and talk to."

She turned and rushed away before he could say anything, but what he would have said, he didn't know. Soren realized that his lips were parted, and he closed them. His legs were working again, so he pushed up off the couch and stood. He reached for the lotion that Larken had left behind on the coffee table and felt his lips twist into a small smile. She would get it back in the morning. Soren turned the lights off before he made his way to his own room and then set the lotion on his desk. They were all turning in early; the day had been exhausting, but worth it. He had heard the way Larken had laughed in the arena as she chased down a screaming Hinlee and a flirtatious Loxly.

Soren turned off his light, stripped down, and then fell into bed. He groaned as he sunk into the mattress and got comfortable. Closing his eyes, he waited for sleep to take him, but instead, he could only see Larken leaning into his hand, looking up, and smiling at him. His eyes shot open.

What is wrong with me?

Soren shook his head and tried again. Still, she was there. This time, thanking him and making him melt.

Opening his eyes, Soren instead stared at the black ceiling, deciding that was better than the alternative. He didn't know why he kept seeing her, and he didn't care. At least, he told himself that he didn't. If Soren was honest, he would admit that she was all he could think about anymore and that it frustrated him that he couldn't get her out of his mind. She was everywhere. Training with him, laughing with him and Loxly, eating in the seat next to him; she was always there. Just like how the smell of grapefruit was always under his nose. So, if it frustrated him so much, why did he reach up and touch her tonight? Why did he reach out for her? It couldn't be because...

Was I...

Soren raised his hand up in front of his face, and then balled it in a fist and let it fall to the bed.

If she hadn't pulled away, would I have kissed her?

The realization of what had really happened that night settled into his gut and made him want to get up and go to the gym. He couldn't be falling for her, he couldn't have *feelings* for her, he couldn't...

Soren rolled onto his side, promising himself that he would be more distant with her. He could still be a good Captain to her, a good friend, but he couldn't keep going down this road, because there was no saying what would happen to him if he did.

CHAPTER 21

L arken jolted out of bed, only this time, instead of it being a nightmare that woke her up, it was a disagreeable Captain leaning into her very, *very*, closely. Her face was hot, and she could feel the embarrassment swamping her as if it were sweat. She raised her hands to her head and started hitting it softly with her open palms.

"What is wrong with you?" she hissed at herself.

A knock sounded at her door, and Hinlee's voice called, "You okay in there, Larken?"

"Totally fine!" she answered too quickly. Another wave of heat rolled over her, and she worried that everyone would pick up on how weird she felt.

Larken jumped out of bed and slapped her cheeks, giving herself a mental chastising. Soren wasn't like Dominic, *at all*. So, more likely than not, he hadn't meant anything about last night and probably wasn't even thinking about it. He had comforted her, that was it, and she was making a bigger deal about it than she needed to. She would go out there, and he would be just as cold as ever. Yes, he had been kind to take her gunning the day before, and about the whole incident on Sunday, but she was willing to bet that he was back to his old, grumpy self that wouldn't talk to her unless she spoke to him first.

Larken looked at her communicator, cleared away a message from Dominic, and pulled up her schedule. Her whole morning had been blocked off for medical training, and after lunch she had rec time, which was followed by her dorm shift. Thinking that she was getting off a little easy for the day, she pulled up her schedule for the rest of the week. She winced as she saw gym hour after gym hour, and there was even a shortened lunch on Thursday. Larken decided that she would make plans with Dominic that day. The less time she had to spend with him, the better, but he was starting to get pushy again. He had kept his promise about giving her space; it was her turn to actually act like she had forgiven him and not just say she had.

Larken got ready quickly, making sure to slip on her sword belt before she left her room, and then ran bodily into Soren.

He grunted a, *"Watch it,"* and then ignored her.

Annoyed, she didn't even bother to apologize as she sat in Loxly's spot at the table instead of her own. Loxly took hers with a raised eyebrow, and she glared at him, daring him to bring it up. Making the right decision for a change, he just smiled and shook his head, pulling the eggs that Levi just dropped off towards him. After a groggy prayer was said, everyone quietly took a helping, and Hinlee could be heard whispering with Brecker about their days.

Larken stabbed at a bit of scrambled egg, not sure what about Hinlee and Brecker bothered her, and tried not to let her annoyance show. Loxly knew her too well though, and he leaned in and asked, "Want me to whisper sweet nothin's to you too?"

She smiled as sweetly as she could. "Would you like to wear your coffee instead of drinking it today?"

Laughing, Loxly stuffed an entire piece of bacon in his mouth. He chewed, and then before swallowing, said, "Oh, before I forget, Dad wants that pot roast recipe."

"I can write it down for you tonight."

"What does your day look like?"

"Med-training this morning, then dorm shift and rec time. You?"

"Rec and gun range this mornin', then flyin' until my dorm shift, which I think is during your rec time."

"Sounds good. You up for some *Bad Love, Good Enemy* later?"

"You'll just watch it in the common room even if I say no."

Larken winked. "That's because I know you secretly like it."

"Secretly like what?" Hinlee asked.

"A net drama I hooked him on," Larken answered.

"*Oooh*, what about?"

"An ex-con who wants to own a restaurant, but the guy who put him in jail keeps trying to get in his way. When Chad, the ex-con, gets the restaurant, he ends up falling for one of the waitresses he hires, who happens to be the jerk's ex."

"That sounds really good; why didn't you tell me you were watching net dramas with Lox? I would have asked to watch too."

Larken's face warmed a little. "Oh, sorry. I didn't plan it, it just sort of happened. I would be watching during my dorm shift, and then Loxly would show up for his rec time or something. And since our dorm shifts and rec times are usually scheduled together, it just sort of happened. We can wait if you want."

"No, we'd never be able to watch it all together," Hinlee huffed. But she perked up and added, "But I can watch it on my own, and we can talk about it. Brecker isn't super into those kinds of things."

The rest of breakfast was a hurried blur, like normal. They spent too much time talking and then had to scarf down their food before leaving. The only one who could take his time was Loxly. Larken snagged the last three pieces of bacon before standing up, and Loxly's hand slapped the plate, trying to get to them first.

"Better luck next time!" she called, munching on a piece.

"You're the only one I would willin'ly share with, Little Bird."

She blew him a kiss and scampered into the hall. Larken had spent much more time talking to Hinlee than she should have, and now she was running late. Dodging other soldiers, as well as drones making whatever deliveries throughout the base, she ran until she reached the med-building. It still had that overly clean smell that she just couldn't get used to, and even though there were people everywhere, it was unnaturally quiet. Sucking in as much air as she could, she punched in her code at the nearest Vendor and checked in. It told her where her station for the morning was, and she headed that way. When she got there, Larken learned she was to perform a surprise oral exam and show what she had learned using one of the more advanced practice droids.

She got to work right away, setting up her station and looking over her shoulder every now and then for Levi. He never showed up; instead, while Larken bent over to pull some gloves out of her pack, she heard a honey-sweet tenor voice say, "Too bad they couldn't give you a medic outfit for the exam. It would have made things a little more fun, don't you think?"

Without bothering to look back, Larken straightened and retorted, "They thought about it, but then I told them I didn't want to be held responsible for any brain damage."

A warm body sidled up behind her, and the smell of blueberries surrounded her. "You think waltzing around in a little outfit would give me brain damage?" the voice murmured in her ear.

"No, I think beating any Captain senseless for staring at me too long would give you brain damage."

Dominic took a step back and laughed. Larken looked at him, her lips twitching into a small smile. It had been a long time since she'd seen him, and he looked just as handsome as ever in his navy uniform. His hair had been styled in its usual fashion, and his warm brown eyes threatened her knees.

"*Lark*," he breathed, "I've missed you. I—"

"Quit flirting, Braves, Hale isn't our only examinee today." Jodi appeared at Dominic's elbow. Blowing a bubble, she let the gum pop against her blood-red lips. Her hair, now dyed in shades of red and orange, reminded Larken of lava as it spilled down her back in loose waves. The ruby stud in her nose glinted in the sunlight pouring through the windows.

Larken grinned at her friend, and Jodi offered her a wink in return. "I'm guessing you two are my proctors?"

"Smart *and* pretty. No wonder you managed to flip this base upside-down," Jodi mused.

Larken laughed, and Dominic smiled awkwardly, obviously not understanding that Jodi was making a joke.

"Should we get started then?" he asked.

"Just tell me what to do."

"Braves is going to handle the—" Jodi looked at the Captain, "*spoken* exam." Dominic grinned unabashedly and shrugged. "I'll be listening in and then watch as you bring back your android from the brink of death."

"Sounds exciting. What's my android suffering from?"

"Unfortunately, just a boring gunshot wound. I suggested an infarction, but, you know," Jodi rolled her eyes, "*what's the likelihood of that happening?*"

Smiling, Larken decided not to feed the fire. She loved spending time with Jodi, but she also had other soldiers she needed to give an exam to, and Larken didn't want to use up all of her time.

"I wish I could have had a little warning," she admitted.

"You won't have a warning in the field, so let's hope you've been paying attention." Jodi winked.

Larken swallowed her nerves and took a deep breath. "Ready when you are."

Dominic started the oral exam, and Jodi had to reprimand him a few times for trying to flirt with her. He wasn't so bad that Larken couldn't get through the answers; it was mostly just having enough time to answer the questions before he showered her with compliments. The questions were hard, meant to challenge her, but both Vallen and Levi were excellent teachers, and she breezed through them. Even Jodi seemed impressed with how far along she was and admitted that she was looking forward to seeing what Larken would do with the android.

The demonstration was a little harder; the android had been stuffed into full tactical gear, so Larken had to work around it. Although, someone had scattered a streak of red paint across its chest so Larken could visualize the wound and how the blood was flowing. Jodi would interject new problems every now and then to keep Larken on her toes, but she was able to tackle those easily as well. When Jodi said the patient was afraid and that its pulse was reaching dangerous limits, Larken regaled them all with a funny story of Loxly trying to help her in the kitchen a few nights ago. When Jodi claimed that the patient was cold, Larken took a blanket out of the pack and threw it over the android's legs. It went on like that for a good two hours before Jodi relented and said that Larken's exam was finished. She had passed, and Dominic pulled her into a celebratory hug.

Larken felt mentally drained. Jodi promised that this was the last *hard* exam that Larken would have and that all of them from then on out would only be to reinstate her certifications, now that Larken was a fully-fledged field-medic.

Grinning, Larken thanked the two of them. Jodi hummed, already lost in her communicator and heading to her next appointment. Dominic, however, tried to get Larken to hang back and talk with him some more before he left as well.

"I feel like I never get to see you anymore, Lark," he complained. "You know, with that whole news story and then my schedule being so full."

It's now or never, I guess.

"Well, I'm free for lunch on Thursday, if you want—"

"Yes!" Dominic beamed. "Absolutely, just tell me when and where. I'll be there."

Larken's stomach flipped, and she didn't know if it was a good flip or a bad one. But looking at his smile and sparkling eyes, she decided it was a good one. "I'll message you once I can think straight again. I'm feeling a little foggy after that exam."

Laughing, he pulled her into him and said, "Of course." He kissed her temple and murmured, "Go get some rest. I'll check in on you later."

"Okay." Larken looked away from him but knew that she couldn't do anything about her pink cheeks.

She walked back to the dorm, planning on just sleeping until she had to cook dinner. Her brain felt like mush, and somehow, she knew that some of the things Jodi had her do weren't part of the exam. When she walked in, though, it was empty. Pulling out her communicator, she saw that she had missed lunch with everyone by fifteen minutes and messages from Hinlee and Loxly, both wishing her luck with the rest of her exam. It figured that Soren would give everyone a heads-up but her.

Larken moved slowly to the kitchen and made herself something to eat. There was just enough of Levi's lasagna left to pair it with a salad and fill her up. Larken didn't even make it to her bedroom; instead, she flopped down on the couch and turned the television on. She flipped through the stations until she found a movie that she had seen two or three times with Vallen and turned the volume low.

It didn't take Larken very long to fall asleep, but she jolted upright after what felt like just a few seconds. Looking at the television, she realized that she had to have been asleep for a couple of hours because she was halfway through the third installment of the movie series. Larken rubbed her eyes and slouched back into the couch. A frantic knocking at the door startled her and had her up and across the room in seconds.

Pulling the door open, Larken was greeted by a very frazzled-looking Mr. Chin and an overly excited Jing, who blew past Larken and into the common room. Mr. Chin had his communicator in his hand and Loxly's voice could be heard from it, saying, "Just keep knockin', she'll answer. Probably just fell asleep after her exam this morn—"

"Miss Hale!" Mr. Chin interrupted Loxly. "Loxly said that you wouldn't mind keeping an eye on Jing until he got here. My mother has fallen ill, and I have to run home to care for her. It is alright, isn't it?"

"O-of course!" Larken stuttered, her still sleep-addled brain trying to catch up with what was happening. "It's no problem at all."

A look of pure relief washed over his face, and Larken didn't try to hide her smile. "Thank you so much. Here are her things." He handed Larken a bright pink pack that had been covered in rhinestones. "I should be back in the morning. Thank you again."

"It's really no problem," she assured as he dropped his communicator into her hands and walked into the common room.

"Little Bird, ya there?"

"I'm here." Larken watched as Mr. Chin dropped down to one knee and opened his arms. Jing ran into them, and he held her tightly, whispering something in her ear. Jing nodded, and her father hugged her tighter. "When are you getting back?"

"I'm on my way there right now. I got a call about seven minutes ago while I was still in the air. Sorry to drop this on you, but—"

"Loxly, it's fine. I like kids, and Jing is sweet. Take your time."

"How long were you asleep?"

"For however long it is between the second half of *Espionage and Intrigue* and the first half of *Espionage and Valor*."

"They're havin' a marathon? Oh man, I love those movies. Too bad they aren't Jing appropriate."

"Definitely not," Larken agreed as Mr. Chin walked over to her with Jing in his arms.

"No allergies, not allowed to leave the table until her plate is clean, and her bedtime is 9:00. Loxly has my information if you need to contact me."

"Can I please stay up late tonight, Papa?"

"You know the rule when Loxly watches you. He has to get up early."

"But he isn't watching me, Papa, *Larken Hale* is."

Mr. Chin sighed. "9:30, no later."

Jing squealed and wrapped her arms around her father's neck. It broke something in Larken, and she had to look away.

Mr. Chin set his daughter down, saying, "Be good."

"I will!" she said, already running back to the couch and jumping on top of it.

"Seriously, thank you."

"Don't worry about it." Larken walked him to the door, hanging up on Loxly and handing the communicator back. "I hope your mother feels better."

"It sounds like pneumonia, but she's all alone and needs someone to take her to a medic."

"Take as long as you need. Jing can borrow clothes, and we can stagger our schedules if you need more time."

Mr. Chin gave her a small bow of his head, and he looked like he wanted to thank her again, but instead, he told his daughter goodbye once more and left.

Larken joined Jing on the couches, sitting in her usual spot on the couch to the right of the little girl. Her head was tilted as she stared at the almost silent television. The woman just slapped the villain, and he, in turn, pulled her in for a kiss. Larken quickly grabbed the remote and turned the movie off. Jing asked, "What movie was that?"

"It was a grown-up movie. Super boring."

"Really? Are you just saying that?"

"Nope, I fell asleep watching it."

"Oh." She thought for a moment and said, "Papa says I'm not allowed to kiss boys until I'm married."

"That sounds like a good plan to me," Larken agreed.

"Have you ever kissed anybody?"

"*Me?*" Larken drew out the word to give herself time to think. The answer was no—she had never had any time for romance in her life being the Daughter of the Military—but her cheeks felt hot as she remembered her dream the night before. She opened her mouth to reply, but Loxly saved her by running into the common room and diving onto the same couch as Jing.

She giggled as he tickled her, asking, "How are you doin' squirt?"

"*Good,*" she said through her laughter.

"So, what were you two beautiful ladies talkin' about?"

"I asked Larken if she's ever kissed anyone, like the people on the television." Jing perked back up, remembering what she had asked Larken.

Larken felt her face rewarm, but Loxly answered, "Of course she has, she's kissed me."

Larken threw a pillow at him, and Jing exclaimed, "She has not!"

Loxly laughed and tossed the pillow back at her. "And how do you know? We're plannin' on gettin' married next week. Aren't we, Little Bird?"

"She can't marry you! Larken Hale is like a Princess. She has to marry a Prince!"

"Am I not princely?" Loxly asked, astonished, like the idea had never crossed his mind before.

"No!"

"Okay, Jing, who do you think I should marry then?" Larken asked, trying not to laugh at the face Loxly was making.

She thought a moment before exclaiming, "Shadric Barlow!"

Loxly groaned and let his head fall back onto the couch. Larken barked a laugh and said, "I have no problems with that."

"Jing, sweetheart, I thought we were friends."

"We are, but she should marry—"

"*Don't say his name,*" he groaned.

Larken laughed, and somewhere in the cushions under her, her communicator started buzzing. Fishing around for it, she watched out of the corner of her eye as Jing repeated *Shadric Barlow* over and over again between gasps of breaths as Loxly tickled her mercilessly. Larken's hand brushed against something cold, and she grabbed the device, pulling it from the crimson cushions. It was her alarm to start dinner, so she stood up and said, "Jing, you have two options. You can either find something to watch on the television, or you can come help me in the kitchen."

"I wanna help! I help Papa all the time. I think I'm good at it."

Larken smiled. "I bet you are. Do you like pasta?"

"I think so. Is it like beef and noodles?"

"Kinda, but I'm going to use a red sauce instead of the brown sauce your dad uses."

"I like red. It's my fourth favorite color."

Jing hopped off the couch and Loxly got to his feet as well. They followed Larken to the kitchen and she asked, "What are your first three?"

"Pink, then yellow, then orange."

"Do you like sunsets then?"

"They're my favorite! That's my favorite Shadric Barlow song too!"

"I like that one a lot," Larken agreed, pulling out the ingredients. "Loxly, will you—yeah, thanks."

Loxly pulled a large pot down off of the top of the fridge. He stuck it in the sink and started filling it up with water while Jing looked at the giant coffee maker. "What does this do?"

"It makes Loxly be nice to people in the morning."

"That's not even…okay, fine, it's true." He shut off the water and set it on the stove. "It's a coffee maker, and you're too young to drink it. But I bet if you ask real nice, Larken will let you have some tea with your dinner."

She perked up. "What kind do you have?"

Larken opened up a drawer that Levi said that she could use, and Jing gasped at the sight of all the boxes. She ran up to it and then grinned. "There are so many!"

"Is there any that you think you might like?"

She reached for the pink box in the corner. "What kind is that?"

Larken smiled. "It's hibiscus and pomegranate. It turns your hot water pink."

"Can I have that one?" she asked excitedly.

"You can, but it's a little bitter. We'll put some honey on the table too, okay?"

"Okay." Jing carried the box to the table and set it where Larken usually sat. She assumed that that was Jing's usual seat when she visited. Larken would have to remember to add an extra chair to the table. Where though, she hadn't decided yet, and she wasn't sure if she was still mad at Soren for ignoring her all morning.

Larken went through the motions of cooking. This was one of Vallen's favorite meals, so she barely even thought about what she was doing, her hands moving from memory. Jing was helpful and often asked if she could do some of the smaller things, like adding the chopped vegetables to the salad or stirring the pasta before the water boiled over. Loxly bounced around, anticipating her every move without her even having to ask for anything.

Soon, the table was set, and the food was ready. Larken put a lid on the pot with the pasta, and it fogged up immediately. Sighing, she fell back against the countertop and crossed her arms. There was still another ten minutes before anyone would get back, and that meant ten minutes she had to distract a hungry child from the food sitting right in front of her.

Loxly leaned against the counter next to her, mimicking her pose, and breathed deeply. "Smells good, not that I had any doubts."

"Did you or did you not accuse me of trying to poison you all a few weeks ago?"

"I was young and stupid then."

"Uh-huh."

Larken was still thinking about how to occupy Jing, but the girl seemed to have her own plans for the wait. She marched over to the stereo, and Larken watched as the little holographic screen popped up and Jing made her selection. Shadric Barlow's *Sunset Dreams* blared from it, making Larken smile. The acoustic guitar made the hair on her arms stand up like it did every time she heard the song, and she was reminded of the smell of sweat and roses. For a moment, she was back at the Manor, training with Vallen in the courtyard, her mother's roses in full bloom and barely able to hold themselves up to the sun.

Loxly looked down at her and she returned his gaze. He raised a single eyebrow in a silent question, and Larken grinned.

The music could be heard from the hall, and Soren was already gritting his jaw. It was that Shadric Barlow, *again*. Soren had been on edge all day, and he told himself it was because he hadn't slept well, despite being in bed two hours before he normally turned in, but he knew it wasn't true. Then, because he couldn't help but make things worse, he had been cold to Larken that morning, and she had noticed.

Stop being stupid. You're making more of this than it needs to be.

Releasing a hot breath, Soren forced himself to relax. Pushing his way into the dorm, his stomach tightened when he caught sight of her. Jing laughed and clapped as she jumped up and down on the couch Hinlee and Brecker usually occupied. Loxly was all limbs as he twirled a laughing Larken around where the coffee table was supposed to be. Her steps were easy and she had Soren transfixed, unable to look away as her hair swished around her and how her smile brightened her whole face. Loxly twirled her around again, and Jing's high-pitched voice matched Barlow's word for word. She had no problem remaining on the couch, watching Loxly and Larken dance. In fact, she seemed to be enjoying it and laughed as Loxly dipped Larken.

Loxly held Larken still for a moment, and her hair hung there, reaching for the floor. It exposed her whole neck, and Soren found himself staring at it again. Loxly pulled her up and spun her once more. Only, this time Larken caught sight of him and stopped mid-turn. Her hair didn't stop though, and it continued around and hit her in the mouth and neck. Pulling away the few hairs that remained stuck to her lips, Larken's eyes widened, and a pink tinge made its way up from her chest to her cheeks. She was no doubt remembering the last time he had caught her dancing, just like he was.

Loxly wrapped his arms around her stomach and pulled her back into him. Resting his head on her shoulder, he said, "Hey, Cap!"

The pink on Larken's cheeks deepened, and she tried to get out of his arms. Soren was torn between laughing at how frazzled she suddenly looked and wanting to punch his friend in the face. Jing, however, didn't seem to pick up on the sudden tension in the air, because she chimed, "My turn! My turn!"

Jumping off the couch, she landed with a *thud*. Jing rushed up to Loxly and pulled his hands from Larken. He went willingly, taking the child up in his arms and spinning around quickly. Peals of laughter spilled from her, and Loxly joined her. Larken made to leave, but Loxly stopped spinning and asked, "What's up with you?"

"Oh, I have to, umm…"

Loxly waited all of three seconds before asking, "Is this about that thing this mornin'?"

The warm pink turned to red, and she said too quickly, "Of course not!"

Soren felt his own ears warm up, but his stomach did a weird flip at the slight hitch in her voice. Had she realized what he had almost done last night? If she had, how did she feel about it?

"What's happening?" Jing asked, not liking that she couldn't understand the unspoken words between the three of them.

"It would seem, squirt, that Larken is too shy to ask the Captain to dance with her, and he's too borin' to offer."

"But Larken is a Princess. Why wouldn't he want to dance with her?"

Loxly grinned at Jing, obviously understanding what she was talking about, unlike Soren. Larken clapped her hands behind her back and dropped her gaze to the floor. Just looking at her, Soren could see how mortified she was. Not only that, but his own embarrassment threatened to pull him to his room until the others arrived for dinner. Instead, Soren walked across the room, hopped over the couch, and had Larken in his arms in seconds.

Soren didn't miss how Loxly rolled his eyes before he dropped Jing and started dancing with her, but he couldn't bring himself to care. Larken looked up at him, eyes wide and lips parted. She still blushed hotly, but her feet moved when he started leading her around the little scrap of rug that Loxly and Jing left them. His hand formed to the curve of her hip, and he could feel the heat of her skin through her clothes. Her hand was just as soft as it had been the last time he had held it, and it gripped his firmly. He was lost in a fog of grapefruit, but somehow, he managed to say, "No one calls Captain Soren Deckard boring."

Something passed behind her eyes that were deepening from green to blue, and he didn't know what it meant. Her lips quirked, and soon she was smiling as she said, "I wouldn't dream of it."

It wasn't long before everyone was back, but by that time, he and Loxly had traded partners and Soren was leading around a very bouncy Jing. They all settled at the table, and Larken sat in her normal spot. That eased something in him that he didn't know had gone rigid during breakfast. Cheery conversation filled the room as the smell of warm garlic encased them. The food tasted delicious like always, and Soren knew that the cafeteria was ruined for him forever. Jing often laughed and didn't put up a fuss when Larken or Loxly had to remind her to eat her food.

Soon dinner was finished, the table was cleaned, and Soren was in bed, listening to the soft sounds of Jing's, Loxly's, and Larken's laughter seeping in from under his door. The three were sleeping on the couches, and Soren hoped that Larken's shoulder wouldn't trouble her in the morning because of it. It wasn't lost on him that thinking about Larken before he fell asleep was quickly becoming the norm for him. He thought about his other squad members, just not quite as often. But instead of getting annoyed, the muffled lullaby that Larken was singing for Jing had his lips twitching.

Before Soren knew it, he had drifted off into a deep sleep and then bolted upright as his alarm gave him a small heart attack. There was perspiration on his brow, and he couldn't remember what he had been dreaming about, but he felt like he had just gotten done running six miles. Soren stayed there in bed, waiting for his heart rate to drop back to normal, and breathed deeply. The smell of bacon wafted under his door, and he could hear the clanging of pots and pans in the kitchen.

Pushing himself out of bed, Soren shut off his alarm and got dressed. He let his mind wander and instantly regretted it as the memory of Larken in his arms surfaced. Soren lifted his left hand and stared at his open palm. He could still feel the curve of her hip;

he could still see her blush and hear her laughter; he could still smell her hair. Closing his fist, he clamped his eyes shut and punched his wall.

What is wrong with me? Put your head on straight and get it together. You're better than this.

Taking two deep breaths, Soren composed himself and walked out into the hall. Hinlee had her head poking out of her room and asked, "Was that sound from your room?"

"Accidentally kicked my desk."

Her mouth opened in an *O* and she ducked back into her room, the door bouncing slightly instead of closing behind her. Soft music could be heard as Soren passed Hinlee's room, and he didn't recognize it. Larken must have shared a playlist with her or something. It sounded *exactly* like the kind of music that Larken would listen to, and even though it was a girl whose voice he heard, it sounded like it was in a different language. He couldn't understand how she knew so many different songs and could remember all the words to them on top of everything that General Maxwell taught her and all the recipes she had memorized.

Loxly and Levi were setting the table, and Jing sat on the countertop next to the stove, where Larken was scrambling eggs and flipping bacon and pancakes. He already knew that she wouldn't eat any of the latter, though. Larken wasn't a fan of sweet things in the morning. She would help herself to either the eggs or the bacon, and then whatever fruit she had stored in the fridge.

Loxly finished divvying out the plates and made his way to the cupboard behind Larken. He fished out three mugs and set two on the counter. The third went under the spout of his coffee maker, and he messed around with it until the dark liquid started streaming into the large red mug. It wasn't long before the whole common room smelled like coffee and hazelnut, and Larken gave him a hard time about the flavor he had chosen. She did that a lot, and Soren had noticed that Loxly was the one who she teased the most. He still wasn't quite sure how he felt about it.

Walking over to the table to see what he could help with, Soren saw two extra places instead of just one. Levi was still setting the silverware, so Soren asked, "Loxly's ego get so big that he needs an extra chair?"

"*Hey!*" Loxly called over Larken's bark of laughter.

"Larken invited Mr. Chin to breakfast," Levi answered, a mirthful smirk on his lips.

"Is that why we're getting pancakes?"

"Yup."

"Hey, if you want pancakes, all you have to do is ask," Larken said.

"I asked for pancakes last week and you told me to make them myself," Loxly huffed.

"That's because I was already almost done making breakfast and running late."

"You should have asked her the night before," Jing chimed in.

"That's right," Larken agreed.

"Why are all women out to get me?" Loxly grumbled.

"Why do you make it so easy?" Levi asked.

Hinlee's laugh and Brecker's chuckle told Soren that the two of them were now in the common room as well. Larken moved the pancakes from the griddle to a large plate and started pouring more batter. It sizzled as it hit the hot cast iron, and she passed the now-empty bowl to Jing, who set it in the sink. Her little feet kicked the cupboard door under her softly, and she started asking Larken questions about Shadric Barlow that ranged from favorite songs to if Larken had ever met him in person.

Everyone flooded into the kitchen and began bringing the hot plates of food to the table. There were enough eggs to fill up two salad bowls and enough bacon to feed a family of twelve. They all moved silently past each other, filling glasses and fetching napkins. Hinlee filled up the teapot and handed it off to Brecker, who set it on the stove. Larken lit the flame under it, and it soon whistled. Loxly took it off the stove as Larken added the last of the pancakes to the plate and filled the two mugs with the boiling water. Soren was by the drawer where Larken kept her tea and fished out the periwinkle box that she favored most mornings. A jasmine and green tea blend that smelled strong, despite the tea not getting very dark. Soren opened the fridge and grabbed a bowl of mixed berries and carefully brought it, and the hot mug of tea, out to her spot. She wasn't far behind him with the plate of pancakes.

Without looking at her, he asked softly, "How's your shoulder?"

Her hands stilled as she set the pancakes down, fingertips barely touching the plate. "Good, actually. Thank you."

A knock sounded at the door, and Soren looked over just in time to see Loxly help Jing off the countertop. She ran to the door and opened it. Her father immediately fell to one knee and gathered her up in his arms. Larken stiffened next to him and then disappeared into the kitchen. He couldn't blame her; not only did she miss General Maxwell, but now that he knew more about her family, he understood her pain a little better.

Jing pulled her father into the dorm, already telling him all about her night with *Larken Hale*, how they had a dance party and stayed up late talking about different kinds of dogs. Soren assumed that Larken had asked the girl what temperament she thought she should install on her new friend.

Larken rummaged around in the kitchen, and at first, Soren thought she was trying to avoid watching the small reunion, but she asked Loxly where her mug went and then asked about her bowl of fruit that was now missing from the fridge. When he said he thought he saw them on the table already, she looked out and scanned the table with a confused look on her face. Once she spotted the pale blue mug, her eyes darted to Soren, but he was already leaving the scene of the crime. He wasted no time asking Mr. Chin how his mother was, aware that Larken was still watching him.

"She's fine now," he answered. "Was able to get her to a medic quickly, and they gave her a shot that cleared everything up. I should really thank Loxly; if he didn't order so much food, I would have had a hard time paying for it."

Soren chuckled. They made their way to the table, Jing's arms around her father's leg. She stayed over often enough that she was used to everyone, but not often enough that she didn't cling to her father whenever he picked her up again. This was the first time the two were staying for breakfast though, and that was just another example of how generous Larken was. Mr. Chin had to go care for his mother about once a month, either cleaning her house top to bottom for her or for medical reasons like last night, but not once had any of them thought to invite him to breakfast. To be fair though, they used to all eat in the cafeteria. It was only after Larken cooked her first meal here that they started eating at the dorm.

Settling around the table, Soren prayed, and then they all started serving themselves. Jing dictated most of the conversation, teaching everyone everything that Larken had taught her about dogs the night before. She told them which breeds were more rambunctious and which ones were more docile. Then she told everyone what *rambunctious* and *docile* meant. The smile on Mr. Chin's face was one of pure joy and love as he listened to his daughter explain things that he no doubt already knew.

It was then that Soren wondered what it would be like to be a father. The thought had never crossed his mind before, and he didn't know how to answer it. He knew that Hinlee and Brecker talked about children and that Loxly wanted a big family one day. Levi wasn't opposed to children, but he would have to be sure it was what his future wife wanted. He wouldn't risk sending a child to an orphanage, like he had been. But Soren? What did he want? He hadn't really given marriage, or children, or a future beyond the military much thought, and now he wondered if he even should.

Larken congratulated Jing on remembering how to correctly pronounce a long word that she had taught her the night before. Soren had missed the word, but he didn't miss the way Larken's eyes sparkled. She was fully engaged in her conversation with Jing, and she had only been kind and patient with her during her stay. Then Soren couldn't help but wonder if Larken wanted children someday.

She wasn't the eldest Hale, so she wasn't required to like her brother, but Soren wondered what it was Larken wanted in life. He remembered the conversation he had with Levi all those weeks ago, and he knew that Larken hadn't chosen the military for herself. But he also knew that she wasn't happy at the Manor either. Would she have spent the remainder of her days training with General Maxwell, or would she have tried to find a way out?

Dangerous thoughts swam around in Soren's mind, and he tried to drown them with bacon and eggs. He shoveled food into his mouth, and he was momentarily distracted by Larken putting a strawberry on his plate. He raised an eyebrow at her, and she added a second one, saying, "You just ate twelve pieces of bacon. I'm worried your heart might stop from all the salt and fat."

Soren choked on the food in his mouth, and Levi chuckled on his other side. All conversation stopped as they looked at him, and he reached for his water. Gulping it down, Levi smacked his back a few times. Larken hummed contentedly as she continued on with her meal, acting as if she hadn't just almost killed him.

Stabbing one of the strawberries with his fork, he stuffed it in his mouth. It was quickly followed by the other, and then, just to get a rise out of her, he reached over and snagged another right out of Larken's bowl. She looked up at him, no doubt about to say something about him stealing the last one, but he schooled his features and asked, "What? I thought you said you were worried about me?"

The corners of her lips twitched, and she had to look away so she wouldn't lose her scowl. Soren smirked and his gaze met Hinlee's before dropping back to his plate. She was smirking too, but he didn't know why.

CHAPTER 22

The Arsene bounced slightly, and Larken stiffened. She trusted Loxly enough that she hadn't reached out for anything, but it still took her a couple breaths to relax. Hinlee was snuggled up to Brecker, her eyes droopy. He had his arm around her contentedly, and he spoke with Levi quietly. Larken had been left to entertain herself, with Loxly and Soren in the cockpit, but she didn't mind. She had synced her communicator with her earpiece, so she just stared out the window, listening to music as the world zoomed by underneath them.

She was chilly, and she thought about asking Loxly for the jacket he had hanging over the back of his seat, but that would involve her being near Soren. Larken had tried to get things back to normal that morning at breakfast, but now she worried that she had made them worse. Larken didn't know what it was, but there was something different about their relationship now. It was always hot or cold with him, and she never knew which one it was going to be. Either he would snap at her for something stupid, or he would prepare her morning tea for her. It was all so confusing. She honestly didn't know which thoughts she preferred—the mess with Soren or the nerves bubbling up inside her. If this practice run was successful, they would be free to be shipped out to the frontlines.

The Arsene jolted again, and this time it was severe enough for her to reach down and grip the edge of her seat. Loxly hollered, "Turbulence!"

"*Ya think?*" Hinlee grumbled, settling back against Brecker.

They were on their way to Field E for squad training, and she couldn't wait. It was the first field that they had gone to with Larken, and they had only used it twice since then. Larken liked this one the best; it was the only one that opened up to a forest, and she liked the layout of the land. It was almost like stepping into a different world, with the tall grass and giant pines. The air there smelled different than anywhere else on the base, and it was the only place that collected mist at twilight.

Levi and Brecker once again slipped into soft conversation, and Larken's eyes drifted back out the window. Not only was the land beautiful, but there was a split moment right before they started their descent where a line of deep blue separating the trees and the sky could be seen. It was the closest Larken had ever been to the sea, and she looked forward to that small glimpse every time they ventured out to Field E. Larken counted the seconds, afraid to blink in case she might miss it, and before she knew it, Loxly called, "Buckle up, we're goin' in."

And there it was, just a thin line, only an inch or so thick, but it was there. Larken reached a hand up to the window, pressing her fingers to the cold glass without thinking. She wondered if the water was cold like the glass or warm like a sun-soaked pond. Larken also wondered how salty it would be. Was it a subtle thing, or was it strong enough that the air would taste like it too?

The Arsene tilted towards the ground, and then the sea was gone as if it had never been there to begin with. Larken let her hand fall to her lap and sighed. Facing forward in her seat, she buckled herself in and let her head rest against the window. Looking once again at that jacket she was too stubborn to ask for, she caught a glimpse of Soren. He faced forward, but she met his eyes in the mirror he had been using to look at her reflection, and she wondered how long he had been watching her.

The descent was smooth, but Larken still felt the bounce of the land. Sounds of the Arsene powering down filled the cabin as they all unbuckled themselves and stood. Larken rolled her shoulder; she hadn't lied to Soren that morning about it not hurting, but now it was starting to feel a little stiff. Hinlee grumbled about her nap being ruined because of Loxly's jerky flying, and he insisted that he only flew that way because he knew she was sleeping on the job. The two bickered as they made their way out of the Arsene. Brecker was the first out, and Hinlee leaped out and into his arms. He caught her easily and spun her around, causing her to throw her head back and laugh. The others jumped out soon after, and Levi made a comment about their blatant display of affection.

Larken waited for Loxly to turn back and help her out of the cabin, but he rushed ahead to sign them in. Sighing, Larken crouched and turned. Laying on her stomach, she dropped her legs over the side and let them dangle as she moved further over the edge. She figured that if she dropped as close to the ground as possible, there was less of a chance of her hurting herself. A malicious chuckle sounded behind her, and she stiffened. Looking over her shoulder, Larken found Soren standing there, hazel eyes dancing.

Frustrated that he was laughing at her, she huffed, "Enjoying the view?"

Soren's ears went pink, and it was her turn to take pleasure in his discomfort. His jaw ticked and he asked, "Are you going to turn around, or am I going to have to help you like that?"

It was once again her turn to blush, and just like that, Soren was back in control of the situation. Pulling herself back up into the Arsene, Larken sat on the lip and held out her arms as if she were a small child. Soren walked up to her and grabbed her thighs loosely. She slid down and his grip tightened on her waist, ensuring he wouldn't drop her, as he gently lowered her. Soren held her gaze as he did so, and suddenly, Larken was unable to do anything other than breathe. Her mind went blank, and all she could focus on were his eyes that shone green in the afternoon sunlight. His lashes were long, much longer than Dominic's, and Larken wondered what made her think that.

This was the closest they had been since that night on the couch, and Larken felt like she was drowning a little. Her boots gently hit the ground, but Soren didn't pull his hands away. His jaw ticked again, and then she watched as his throat bobbed. Her own mouth felt dry, and she was suddenly dying of thirst. His attention felt more nerve-wracking than any camera crew, and she couldn't help it as she sucked her bottom lip between her teeth. His eyes fell from hers and landed on her mouth. Soren's throat bobbed again, and Larken let her own eyes fall to his lips. Memories of that dream assaulted her, and even though she was sure her face was an unflattering shade of red, she couldn't look away.

Loxly broke the spell by hollering, "Y'all comin'?"

Soren let go of her, and the summer air felt cold against the spots he had been touching. Without a word, he turned and walked to the area where he would be given his tactical gear. Larken thought that her legs would buckle if she tried to take a step, so instead, she closed her eyes and mentally ran through the maneuver she thought of whenever she needed to control her breathing. Speeding through the steps in her mind, she worked herself up and jogged to where everyone waited for her.

Hinlee wasted no time sidling up to her and whispering, "What was that about?"

"The turbulence had me feeling a little uneasy. I just needed a moment." It wasn't a complete lie, but Larken knew that if she were any more honest, Hinlee would weasel words out of her that she had no intention of sharing.

Hinlee looked at her for a moment, giving Larken the chance to change her answer, but eventually gave up when she remained tight-lipped. Together they all got ready, and Larken threw her hair back into a quick braid, her nerves starting to flutter again for another reason. Hinlee watched her, fascinated, but looked away to punch Loxly when he made a comment about short hair. Then, they were all pulling their helmets on and checking to see if they could hear each other. Everyone spoke their name, and Larken finished off with hers. It was then decided that they would retry their failed strategy, with Brecker scouting, Levi hanging back behind the group in case one of them were injured, Soren in the middle with Loxly and Hinlee flanking him, and Larken pushing forward once Brecker gave the all-clear and made his way back to Levi to help defend any wounded.

Soren gave the signal, and Brecker was off. His urgent whispers of *all clear* echoed in Larken's ear. Adrenaline started to pump through her heart, and she bounced from foot to foot like she did before a spar with Vallen. He taught her to be ready for anything, and this time there would be no slipping or getting overtaken. She was ready for whatever Maxim decided to throw her way.

Before she knew it, Brecker gave the all-clear, and she was off. Everyone kept up steady communication, moving through the plan like a well-oiled machine. Larken was thirty paces ahead of the others, and Brecker should be running into her any second. She pushed further and further into the field, and no androids appeared. Larken asked what to do and was told to push for more ground. She broke through the tree line just as Brecker did, and he gave her a small salute.

The forest was beautiful, and she could have sat in the cool shade for hours. If it wasn't for the pressure of her helmet, Larken would have never known that she had a black vizor covering her face. She could see everything clearly, and she only wished that she could breathe in the smell of the earth around her. Instead, she was left taking in the smell of recycled air as she jumped over and dodged roots. Every now and then, Larken would ask again if she should keep going, and each time she was told yes. But each step she took without spotting an android made her a little more uneasy.

The chatter in her ear was constant, and she was thankful for that at least, even if it was a repeated, *"Clear on my end."*

Eventually, Larken had to stop. She wasn't tired, but she felt like she was running out of air. She wanted to open her vizor but knew that she would get a stern talking-to if she did. Something about *the enemy knowing her face.* Not that everyone didn't already know what she looked like, but she knew that it was a silly disagreement that she could avoid.

So, instead, she just said, "I'm taking a small break. Still not used to breathing with this thing on."

Soren's voice sounded over the murmuring of the others, "Don't take too—"

The audio cut out, and then came back in as Hinlee finished, "—don't see anything."

"What was that? You cut out for a second."

Larken waited, but Soren's response was just as choppy as before.

"Soren?"

"Lark—" His voice cut out completely and replacing it was a small, barely-there humming.

"*Soren?*" Larken tried again, but she was only answered by the sound of gunshots behind her.

She turned around so forcefully that she almost tripped over her own legs, and then started back. How far away were they? Why was she able to get through but not them? What was wrong with the—

The earpiece.

No. No, no, no, no, no!

It was just like with her communicator, only this time, she didn't notice it right away because she wasn't falling out of the sky. Larken ran in a full out sprint, but she didn't run into the others after the thirty steps where they were supposed to be. Instead, something shot out and tangled around her legs. Larken hit the ground with a force that had her helmet bouncing off the dirt. Scrambling, she reached for her feet, only to find a three-stranded rope with a crystal ball on the end of each strand wrapped firmly around her calves. Freeing her pocketknife, she began hacking at the binds. Her breath was so fast and shallow that a warning sign showed in the lower left-hand corner of her vizor. She wasn't pushing enough air out, which meant the recycler wasn't filling up like it was supposed to.

Freeing herself, Larken jumped to her feet and took a few steps. If she had been any slower, she would have gotten tangled up again by the second rope thing that had been shot at her. Before she could turn and run, a figure broke through the trees and headed straight for her. Larken had less than a second to decide what she was going to do, but Vallen had turned her into a fighter, so she stood her ground and pulled the handgun at her left thigh free.

Firing off a shot, she hit him in the left shoulder. Purple sparks danced across his shoulder and part of his chest, making him shout out in pain. While he was distracted, Larken holstered her gun and charged him. Her lack of breath was forgotten as she calmed her racing heart. She could do this; this was what she had been raised to do. Whoever this guy was, he wasn't Vallen Maxwell, and he would be easy to overtake. Which was good, because she had a lot of questions. Especially since he was dressed *exactly* like the men who had shot her hover out of the sky and tried to kill her all those weeks ago.

By the time he realized that Larken was using his discomfort to her advantage, it was already too late, and she was aiming a kick at his head. He caught her foot with his forearm and sent out a punch of his own. They sparred like that for a while, no weapons, no relenting. Larken's muscles felt alive, and they were singing with her exertion. She should have been worried, she should have been afraid, but all she could do was grin wickedly behind her vizor.

This idiot has no idea what he's gotten himself into.

Over roots they stumbled, occasionally pulling free a weapon, only to have it deflected and tossed away. After a while, Larken was forced to admit that this guy knew what he was doing and that maybe this wouldn't be as easy as she had originally thought. Back and forth they moved over the forest floor, each one gaining an upper hand, only to lose it a split-second later. Larken's chest heaved, the helmet taking its toll on her. She needed to end this fast so she could get the thing off and get some fresh air.

A jab to her side had her wincing, and the assailant used his momentary advantage to push her back. She stepped on a tree root instead of over it, slipped, and fell to the ground. The guy was on her faster than she had time to react. One of his hands went to her neck, the other to her hip. Larken grabbed the edge of his helmet and kicked at him, but winced and gritted her teeth as her foot came into contact with him. She wasn't sure if it was a sprain or what, but that fall had definitely done something to it. Thinking fast through the pain, Larken yanked at his helmet, throwing off his balance. In one swift movement, she straddled his waist, pushing his shoulder down into the earth with her right hand, and had her sword out. She snarled as she pointed it at his now very exposed neck.

His helmet was lying an inch or two above him, having fallen off in their scuffle. Taking in his face, her scowl turned into open-mouthed disbelief. The man looked almost as shocked as she felt, but she couldn't compose herself. That light blond hair, his scruffy jaw, *that face*. She would know that face anywhere, and those sky blue eyes. They looked the same as the day she fell in love with them.

"Y-you—you're...*Shadric Barlow!*"

"And you," he said quietly, "you're stunning."

Larken blushed hotly and realized that he must have opened her vizor while her eyes were shut in pain. Then it hit her; he had said stunning, not *Larken Hale*. Whether it was the helmet, the tactical gear, or a combination of both, he didn't recognize her.

Her sword faltered slightly. Trying her best to get herself together, she asked, "What do you want?"

Despite having a sword pointed straight at his throat, Shadric never took his eyes off her. Larken was more confused than she had ever been in her whole life. She asked again, *"What do you want?"*

"To know your name."

"What?" Larken jerked back in surprise.

"What?" Her sudden movement seemed to remind him of where he was. He shook his head, and his eyes still seemed a little lost, but he corrected himself. "Where is Larken Hale?"

Larken tried her best not to flinch. "What do you want with her?"

"We need to talk to her."

"Who's *we*?"

"I can't tell you. But we need to talk to her. Please."

There were more gunshots, and Larken's hand tightened on her hilt. "Why did you shoot her out of the sky?"

"We didn't! They were—look, I have strict orders to only speak with her."

Give them two sentences instead of one before deciding if they are an enemy or an ally.

Vallen's words rang loud and clear in her mind, and Larken had to make a choice. Tell the man she had loved for the last seven years who she was or keep up the front and get out of there. She was torn between curiosity and fear. What if he really did have all the answers? What if he really was a Faithful and was just trying to kill her?

Maxim, what do I do?

The only answer was the rapid beating of her heart. So, she wondered instead what Vallen would do. The Faithfuls had murdered his squad, *his friends,* and left him alive only to deliver a message. Vallen would knock him out and then drag his unconscious body back to base for questioning. But was that the right thing?

Taking a chance, she asked, "How do I know you won't kill her?"

"Because she holds the key to a better tomorrow."

Larken stilled, her body rigid, and Shadric used that to get free. Still dazed, Larken tried not to wince as she scrambled to her feet, while he grabbed his helmet and jumped to his. Strengthening her stance, she chided herself for letting him distract her, but his eyes looked so sincere. Worry etched his features, and he pleaded again, "Please, we need to talk to her, to explain."

Someone stomped behind her in the bushes, and Shadric jammed his helmet on his head. A second man dressed all in black jumped out of the trees, and then a third from behind Shadric. His body relaxed, but Larken's tensed, and she snarled, "You tricked me."

"No, I didn't."

"You *lied* and set me up."

"No, I—"

Larken raised her sword; she wasn't going down without a fight. The men raised their tech guns, and Shadric put up his hands, holding them off. More crashing sounded, and a fourth man burst into their area. His vizor was up, revealing a handsome face with a strong jaw. Blood ran down his face from a gash at his temple. The injury screamed the butt of Brecker's gun, and Larken smirked in satisfaction.

"Something went wrong. We need to get out of here." His voice was deep, and his brogue was so thick that Larken almost missed what he said. Turning his eyes on her, he asked, "Who's the girl?"

There was no doubt about it; these guys were Faithfuls. There was no way that anyone who grew up in any of the Districts wouldn't recognize her. However, she had to wonder at Shadric. Was she right that he couldn't see past her tactical gear, or did he just not keep up with celebrity gossip?

Thinking quickly on her feet, Larken tried to figure out a way to get out of this situation. More gunfire sounded in the distance, and their voices grew more urgent as they discussed what to do with her.

"We could take her with us," Shadric offered.

"And explain to Blade how we brought back the wrong one? Come on, Fret, I thought you were smarter than that," the man with the accent accused.

"It was just a suggestion."

"We're running out of time," the one behind Shadric said, voice muffled by his helmet.

And so am I.

There was more crashing in the foliage to Larken's right, and the men all looked. She didn't care who it was, or what they wanted;

she wouldn't waste this distraction. Charging for the man closest to her, Larken raised her sword with her left hand. Feinting, Larken instead raised her leg and stomped on his knee. She didn't break it, but he crumpled all the same, as she turned to meet her next victim. Raising her sword, she expected to find someone behind her, but instead, one of the men fired their tech gun.

The bullet hit the flesh in the gap of her gear that showed as her arm was raised. Her sword fell, her arm burning and unable to remain up in the air. Dropping to the ground, she reclaimed her sword with her right hand, but the men were already running off. Shadric chanced one last glance back at her, but one of the guys forced him back around.

Then they were gone, and she was all alone again.

Someone shouted something, had been shouting for a while, but Larken couldn't understand what was being said. Her arm was on fire, and her whole shoulder felt wet and hot. Larken used her sword to try and get up, but the blade only sunk into the dirt, and she fell.

"Larken! *Larken!*"

That shouting, it was still crying out, but she couldn't make sense of the muffled words. The pain was all-encompassing, and Larken wondered how Vallen was able to run so far after getting shot twice. Though, now she understood why he hated it so much. Larken fought to keep her eyes open, and she wondered if the bullet had been enhanced with something. Everything looked hazy, and the only thing she knew was the smell of the earth that she was laying on. The sunbeams that were shining through the trees put a yellow glow on everything.

Her eyelids dropped and then opened again when someone shook her right shoulder. A face blocked out the rays of sun, a face she recognized. His mouth was moving, but she couldn't understand him. She was so tired, and she wanted to let go. The pain couldn't find her in sleep. Her eyelids fell closed again.

Larken was sat up, and someone slid her helmet off. Roughly, she was pulled up into the air, and her face was pressed into the crook of a warm neck. She breathed in the scent of leather and freshly tilled earth, and she realized that she could do that forever. She was addicted to this scent, and she snuggled in closer to it. A hand brushed at her forehead, and something warm pressed against it, and then there was only darkness.

CHAPTER 23

Larken opened her eyes, her lids feeling like they were a million pounds. Blinking a few times, she was able to make out her surroundings instead of just blurred colors. Brightness assaulted her, and a monitor beeped softly close by. Larken turned her head ever so slightly and found Jodi scribbling something down on a tablet with a black stylus. Her hair had been piled up in a messy bun at the back of her head; the shades of dandelion yellow and dark honey complemented her skin beautifully, and Larken was reminded of a sunflower with her dark brown makeup. Jodi had traded the ruby stud that she had worn the last time Larken saw her for a topaz one, and it gleamed in the bright white of the room.

Jodi didn't even look up as she said, "You weren't supposed to come see me until Friday." Larken wasn't sure how Jodi knew she was awake but wasn't really surprised.

"What happened?" Larken winced, her voice nothing more than a harsh rasp that grated against her ears.

"You were shot."

"I remember that part," Larken scoffed. "I meant, what happened *after*?"

Smirking, Jodi crossed her arms while still holding the tablet and said, "You lost a lot of blood. The bullet nicked your brachial artery, and it was coated in a dissolvable casing mostly comprised of valerian root extract. So, that's probably why you're having trouble remembering things, and why you passed out so quickly."

Jodi walked forward and set the tablet down. She motioned for Larken to sit up while she stuck her stylus in her bun, and Larken awkwardly pushed herself upright. Her shoulder throbbed, sore, but not unbearable. Not like the pain of being shot had been. Jodi pulled Larken's gown from her shoulder, and she could see the new, pink skin.

"The bullet went through, but you still needed a transfusion. You can thank tall and skinny for the blood; you're lucky you have another type O on your squad."

"Doubt it." Larken winced as Jodi prodded her new flesh. "Vallen probably did that on purpose."

"That doesn't surprise me."

A soft knock sounded at the door, and Hinlee tentatively poked her head in. "I heard voices."

Her eyes landed on Larken, and they went wide. Larken wasn't sure if it was from the amount of pink skin, or if it was because of something else. Either way, Larken covered her shoulder and snuggled back into the bed. Jodi helped Larken raise it so she could sit more comfortably and then fluffed her pillows.

Hinlee watched Jodi for a moment before asking, "You up for some visitors?"

"Sure," Larken lied. She wasn't, but she knew how worried she would be if it was one of them in this bed instead of her. Plus, with all of them there to back her up, maybe Jodi wouldn't make her stay the night.

Hinlee backed out and then reappeared with Loxly hot on her heels, the rest following as well. Loxly walked straight up to the bed and, gingerly, wrapped his arms around Larken. Hinlee joined him, standing on the opposite side of the bed. Brecker, Levi, and Soren stood at the foot of the bed, looking grim. Larken couldn't help her small chuckle. "It's okay, I'm fine. Just a little sore."

"You don't get to complain," Loxly mumbled in her ear. "You didn't have to watch you bleed everywhere and *not* wake up."

Larken sobered and took in all their faces again. She paused on Hinlee, and now that she was close enough, Larken could see the red of her eyes and dried tear streaks on her cheeks. Loxly's eyes were red-rimmed as well, but he would have held it together for his friend. Brecker gave her a soft smile, and Levi frowned at her, though it wasn't unfriendly. Soren scowled like usual, his eyes looking more gold as he did.

Shifting her gaze back to Brecker, Larken said, "I saw your handiwork."

His smile widened. "Busted his helmet up too, but I didn't get a good look at his face before he took off."

"I did, but I don't think it'll be much help. They were Faithfuls."

"How do you know?" Levi asked.

"They were looking for me, and even though I got into a scuffle and my vizor was opened, none of them recognized me."

"Did you recognize any of them?" Loxly asked.

"I—" Larken's voice caught. "I don't remember."

She dropped her gaze to the paper-stiff sheets, afraid that if anyone looked into her eyes, they would know that she was lying. But, as much as she hated lying to them, she didn't feel uneasy about it. Instead, she felt a calm peace, and she wondered if it was Maxim telling her that she made the right choice. She decided that she would keep Shadric Barlow's secret...for now.

Mentally shaking herself as she realized that she had *actually* shot Shadric Barlow, Larken forced herself to look up. "What happened? You know, after I got hit."

"Decks was the one that found you," Hinlee said. "He brought you back to the hover."

Larken suddenly remembered being held by a pair of strong, warm arms. She couldn't help the subtle blush that heated her cheeks, and she couldn't stop the pull to look at him. Soren was already staring at her, eyes hard with unspoken rage. They were somehow glowing gold and soft green at the same time, and Larken wondered if she was the one that he was upset with.

"We got you onto the hover, and Loxly booked it here. Not much more to tell."

"Unless you want to include Little Miss over here tracking me down and forcing me to check on you for them," Jodi added.

Hinlee didn't look the least bit sorry. "It's not like you didn't drop everything the moment I told you about what happened."

Jodi didn't answer, but her frown seemed a little forced. Everyone was quiet, and Larken had to fight not to squirm.

"*So,*" Larken mused, trying to lighten the mood, "when can I leave?"

Loxly, Hinlee, and Brecker all started their protests at the same time, but it was Levi who asked, "Was there any more serious damage than a nicked artery?"

"Nope," Jodi answered. She crossed her arms again and glared at Larken. "You can only leave if you promise not to leave your dorm for the rest of the day or tomorrow."

"If I don't?" Larken wondered.

"I'll keep you here like we kept General Maxwell. I'll cuff you to the bed too."

"You had to cuff Vallen?"

"Almost." Jodi's smirk was slightly malicious, and Larken laughed. The mental image of her teacher being so restless that he was threatened like that was almost too much. She was sure that he had made plenty of threats of his own as well.

"I promise I won't do anything crazy."

"Fine, I'll start the paperwork."

Jodi left, taking the tablet with her, and Loxly pulled Larken closer to him. He nuzzled her hair and ordered, "You are *never* allowed to scare us like that again. You understand me?"

"I'll do my best," Larken said softly, remembering another promise she had just broken. How was she going to tell him? What would she say?

Jodi was back after only a few minutes, asking about Larken's pain, and had her move her arm to check motor function. Soon, she stuffed her hands in her coat pockets, saying, "You're all clear to go back to the dorm, but you're going to have to be reevaluated in two months to see if you, and now your squad, are fit to return to active duty. Don't scrub too hard in the shower."

"Yes ma'am."

Jodi nodded and turned to the others. "Alright, everyone out."

"What, why?" Loxly asked.

"You can ask the Military Sweetheart if you can stay and watch her change, but my gut is telling me the answer would be no."

Loxly coughed, and Hinlee laughed at his expense. They all filed out of the door Jodi held open for them. Loxly was the last one out, the evidence of his embarrassment still visible on the back of his neck. Jodi stepped in line behind him, and Larken just realized that she hadn't been chewing gum. She really must have dropped everything to come see her. Jodi was tough and snarky, but she really was a good friend. Not getting overly emotional was probably why they got along so well.

Pushing herself out of the bed, Larken winced as she put pressure on her left hand. She remembered Jodi telling Vallen that he would be sore for a few days, and she wasn't looking forward to having issues with *both* shoulders. Maybe Larken could ask about something for it. She tested her twisted foot and found that there was no pain, so at least she didn't have to deal with that as well.

Larken shucked off the gown and started pulling on her bloodied, dirt-covered clothes. They reeked of stale iron, and her shirt in particular was incredibly stiff. It also housed two holes where she had been shot. A sick feeling gripped her stomach. What if it had been lower? What if she had died? What would happen to Vallen?

Her eyes burned, and she thought she might be ill. She was all he had left; what would happen if he had to tell someone else goodbye? A single tear slipped out of her eye, and there was a soft knock on the door. Harshly rubbing her emotion away, Larken turned to see Hinlee peeking through the crack.

"You okay?"

"Did someone tell—"

"Decks did."

Larken nodded and looked away. Instead of ignoring her and giving her space, Hinlee walked into the room and pulled Larken into a hug. Larken's heart broke for the only person she had let into the darkest parts of her, and she couldn't help the few tears that broke free.

"He'll be here as soon as he can. It's okay, you're safe now," Hinlee consoled, not understanding the reason Larken was truly upset.

Larken felt suddenly heavy, like it was all she could do to remain standing. Loxly peeked into the room just as she wobbled. Pushing his way in, he helped Hinlee steady her. "Easy, now. You sure you want to go back to the dorm?"

Larken nodded quickly. Loxly looked like he wanted to argue the point, but Larken looked up at him and whispered, "Please don't make me stay here."

He reached out and cupped her face, the look on his face twisting her heart. Then he pulled her close to him and murmured, "Of course not, Little Bird. Let's go."

His arm remained around her, keeping her steady, and Hinlee interlocked her fingers with Larken's. Together, the three of them made their way out to the waiting room and then into the hall after saying goodbye to Jodi. Brecker had made a comment about Larken staying a little longer, but she brushed him off. She was just tired and sore; she could sleep in her own bed and use her own shower, and she would still feel the same. But at least she would have the comfort of home.

Home.

Larken was surprised at how easily the word had come to her. She hadn't expected this place to be warmer than the Manor or be filled with people who cared for her the way her squad did, the way Vallen did. It was surreal, and Larken was suddenly afraid that she was opening her heart too much to the idea of it all. What would happen to her if something happened to Squad 19? What would have happened if she hadn't been the one that the Faithfuls were after, and it was one of the others that had been taken? What if something had happened to them? She had been afraid for Vallen, hearing stories of his days in the military, and he wasn't even there anymore. But these people, her squad, her new family, what would happen to her if one of them…

Larken shook the dark thoughts from her head, blaming the whatever it was Jodi had said was still in her system. They were fine. They were all fine, and Larken was safe. She could hear Brecker talking softly behind them with Levi, who had told him that Larken would make a full recovery. Levi had agreed that Larken would get just as well at the dorm as she would have in the exam room. She also heard him mention the meds Jodi had given him to give to Larken for the pain. There was nothing more Larken could do than sleep.

The group slowly made their way to the dorm, mostly because Larken kept tripping over her own feet. Her eyes felt just as heavy as the rest of her, but she was determined to get back to the dorm and shower before falling into bed. The smell of stale blood made her head swim, and Larken needed to wash it off. She needed to wash this whole day off. The smell of iodine that clung to her skin, the soreness of her new flesh, and the memory of Shadric Barlow looking like he found the sun under her vizor instead of her.

Larken shivered.

"You okay? You don't have a fever, do you?" Loxly asked, worry twisting his voice.

"No." Larken laughed tiredly. "Seriously, I'm *fine*. You can stop looking at me like I'm going to die any second now."

"I don't think you're gonna die! But I do think you might pass out," he shot back.

"Okay, I guess that's fair."

Hinlee let go of Larken's hand and jogged ahead a few steps to open the dorm door for them. Brecker pushed ahead as well, making sure that Loxly and Larken crossed the threshold without incident. Unable to help herself, Larken teased, "All this fuss over walking through a door; you'd think I was a new bride, not a patient."

That had Loxly finally laughing, and his worry seemed to roll off of him as he did. "Well, if you're offerin', then I accept. Can't wait to see the look on Jing's face when we tell her the good news."

Larken poked him in the side, but she didn't bother to try and hide her grin. Hinlee butted in, reminding him that they were all making a fuss over her and that her proposal could have been for any one of them. Loxly threw back another comment that Larken didn't catch over the relief of everyone acting like themselves again.

Larken shook Loxly off and disappeared into her room. She had wanted to shower right away, but the walk had taken a lot out of her, and she still felt drugged up. Sighing, she let herself fall onto her bed. She would rest for just a moment to get her strength back. A few seconds was all she needed, then she could shower and get on with the rest of her day. Slowly, her body started to relax and her eyelids grew heavy once more. She hadn't felt this awful since she was sixteen, but even though she had been shot, she wasn't as scared as she should have been. However, that could have something to do with the drugs that were still holding her body under. Larken mentally repeated, *"Just a few more minutes,"* and couldn't stop her eyes from completely closing. She reminded herself that she still needed to take off her boots, but sleep claimed her before she could untie the laces.

The five of them had given her four minutes to herself before they sent Hinlee in to check on her. She had come back to the common room and told them all that Larken was fast asleep. Levi had insisted that she would be fine and that the best thing for Larken was to let her get her rest. With nothing else to do other than sit and worry, the squad broke up and went to finish the rest of their days. Soren had changed their rec time so they could sit in the waiting room, but now they all had things to do. Except for Soren, who had just started his dorm shift, that way someone was there if Larken needed help.

He didn't know how long he sat on his bed with his elbows resting on his knees and his hands stuck in his hair. The memory of what had happened, how he had found her, was still fresh in his mind. He could still feel her in his arms, feel the way she shook. Soren could still smell the faint scent of the woods that clung to her hair, despite her overpowering shampoo. Jodi had said it hadn't been serious, and she was right of course; it had been a simple gunshot wound. Larken had barely been in the room for an hour before Hinlee heard her talking to Jodi. But the amount of blood…

Soren jumped to his feet, needing to do something else besides sit there and think of how much worse the morning could have been. He left his room and was immediately greeted by the sight of General Maxwell leaning against the wall next to the open bathroom door. Soren walked up to him, the sound of running water and music filling the hall. Larken must have woken up. He was about to say something—what, Soren didn't know, but he felt like he should —when General Maxwell put a finger to his lips.

General Maxwell leaned his head back against the wall and closed his eyes, seeming to be lost in the moment. Soren stood there, not quite sure what to do, when the music blaring in the bathroom changed. A beautiful voice flooded out of the bathroom, clashing against the tiles. It took a moment, but Soren realized that it wasn't just some random Star singing in the foreign language that spilled out of the bathroom; it was Larken. Soren looked wide-eyed at General Maxwell only to find him smiling. It was a smile that seemed to say, *I know.*

Larken's voice rose and fell in clear crescendos, carrying with it the sound of heartbreak and lost hope. It made something inside him squirm, and Soren was once again holding her in his arms as she bled everywhere. General Maxwell sighed, pulling Soren from his dark thoughts, and murmured, "This one is my favorite." General Maxwell shifted his gaze, a far-off look in his eyes. "She used to sing in the showers after we trained together. I could always hear her all the way in my room. I could sit and listen to her for hours."

"Did you teach her how to do that as well?" Soren asked, more interested than he was letting on. In all his years, he never thought he would be having this kind of conversation with General Vallen Maxwell.

"No." He looked at Soren and sighed. "No, she's always known how to do that. Always had her head in the clouds, lost in her music. It was never quiet. Larken was always humming, singing, or listening to that *Shadric Barlow*."

"Not much has changed," Soren said.

"Tell me, Captain Deckard," General Maxwell raised a skeptical brow, "have you caught her dancing yet?"

Soren's face went hot and he coughed, looking away. Memories of the first time he had caught her dancing flooded his mind. Then his hands heated at the thought of dancing with her, the way those swaying hips had felt under them.

The General chuckled, saying, "I'll take that as a *yes*." He sighed again. "That's good. She only does that when she's really happy. If she's dancing, then I have nothing to be worried about."

The two soldiers stood there, listening to the depressing opera that still poured from the bathroom. Soren could feel the anguish of Larken's voice even though he couldn't understand the words. His heart skipped a beat every now and then, somehow understanding the pain, even though he didn't know how. Not wanting to think about what his heart might be trying to tell him, Soren asked, "Do you know what she's saying?"

"No, I never asked. But I don't think I need to. I understand enough."

"How do you mean?"

General Maxwell looked him dead in the eye. "Can you tell me that you don't feel that?"

Soren only looked away, not willing to answer. He didn't know what to make of his roiling emotions; he only knew that he didn't want to think about it. He didn't want to think what it meant for him, and Soren most definitely didn't want to think what Larken was thinking while she sounded like she was breaking apart.

When someone cleared their throat, Soren realized too late that, even though the music still played, the water had been shut off and Larken had stopped singing. She stood in the doorway of the bathroom now, wrapped up in a towel that was a little too small, had her arms crossed, and glared at the two of them. "Should I be charging admission?"

General Maxwell pushed off of the wall and gave a long-suffering sigh. Soren could only choke and stammer, but managed to get out, *"What are you doing?"*

His eyes were at war, wanting to look their fill, but also wanting to look at anything but her. Her wet hair was snarled like she had taken a towel to it, and the ends dripped onto her shoulder. Her legs were shimmery, and the smell of something floral amidst the scent of grapefruit told him that they were coated in lotion. Soren was losing the battle of not looking.

"I thought I was *alone*. Otherwise, I would have brought my clothes to the bathroom." She turned in the direction of her room and, not bothering to look back, said, "And yet *I'm* the weird one for being naked in the shower, *not* the fully grown men waiting outside of the bathroom."

"Still abrasive, I see," General Maxwell grunted.

But Soren wasn't listening, his eyes locked on the pink skin on her shoulder where it had just been replaced. He felt sick, but he couldn't break his eyes away. Even after she slammed her door shut behind her, Soren still stared. Not daring to look at General Maxwell, he said, "I'm sorry, I should have—"

"Should have *what*?" he asked, much closer than Soren expected. "Should have known that they hacked the system, defused all of the practice droids, and decided to ambush you during a training session?" Soren looked over at his superior, but the man just said, "I don't blame you." Then he quietly added, *"I blame myself."*

General Maxwell left before Soren could say anything, making his way to Larken's room and knocking on her door. He waited, but when Larken didn't say she was still getting dressed, like she always did, he pushed his way into her room. Soren felt dazed like his body was slowly going numb. It didn't matter what General Maxwell said, Soren knew he was the one to blame. He shouldn't have let Larken get so far ahead; he should have told her to hang back when he first started thinking that something was up. But Soren had just assumed that the androids had a pre-programmed ambush waiting for them and continued on like nothing was wrong. She was the one who paid for it in the end, and he knew that he would never send her out as point again. Because, honestly, Soren didn't know what would happen to him if something happened to her.

CHAPTER 24

Larken didn't bother holding back her annoyance as she yelled at the waiter. She hadn't even wanted to have lunch with Dominic that day, not when she was still too raw from Vallen's last visit. Her temper had been quick to spike over the last week, and thankfully, Squad 19 just let her rage and often invited her to spar in the gym to help get out her aggravations. It was like they knew what she needed without having to ask, and she wouldn't have been surprised to learn if Vallen had told them how to handle her. But now, that ugly monster thrashed around full force in her chest.

"I'm sorry," the youth pleaded. He wasn't the same one that usually waited on them when they went to the Dining Hall, and Larken didn't think he would be quick to volunteer again.

The cloth napkins were soaked through, not doing much to soak up the wine that drenched her lap. She pulled another one from his hands, dabbing at her thighs, and seethed, "Well, if you had been paying more attention to how full the glass was instead of looking down my shirt, we wouldn't even be in this mess."

Dominic was no help, hiding his face behind his hands and laughing at the expense of the poor boy. He was a far cry from the man that had rushed and checked her over when he first saw her.

Word about her getting shot had somehow reached him, and Dominic had kept looking at her like she would start bleeding again at any moment. Now he was struggling to breathe as he watched her, the jealousy he had never bothered to hide nowhere in sight.

Larken had enough; she threw the napkin onto her plate with the others and stood. She was sticky and reeked of fermented grapes, and if Dominic had even bothered to notice that she never drank any of the fancy wines or champagnes that he ordered, she would be a lot dryer. Storming off, Larken heard his chuckles behind her and a hasty, "Don't worry about it, she has that effect on everyone. Keep the tip."

Everyone she passed stared at her openly, and Larken forced herself to ignore all of them. Right now, she didn't care if she was the crazy woman who had made a scene at the fanciest eatery on base; she just wanted to take a shower and get this smell off of her. Her head started to hurt as thoughts of her father spilling his drinks on her at dinner parties surfaced in her mind. All the nights she had to excuse herself to change, all the times he had smelled of booze as he clapped her on the shoulder and told her that she was *his special girl.* Those were not proud moments for her, and she hated remembering them. The last time she had been special to him was long before Wardell had been born, and before the rumors about her parentage had started.

Dominic caught up with her outside the Dining Hall. Still laughing, he slipped his hand into hers and pulled her to his side. Larken immediately pulled back and glared at him. He met her gaze, and even though he still grinned, the laughter faded from his eyes. He stared at her for a moment and then swore. Stuffing a hand into his hair, he swore again and said, "I'm an idiot. I'm sorry, Lark, I completely forgot. This probably isn't very funny to you."

She rolled her eyes and started walking back to the dorm. "Forgot what?"

Dominic fell into step with her. "Your eighteenth birthday party."

Larken faltered and almost tripped. She had forgotten too. She had done everything she could to forget that night. Vallen had taken her dress shopping, and she picked out a stunning white lace dress. Larken could still remember the way she felt in it when she first tried it on, how she had felt beautiful for the first time in her life. Cam did her hair and makeup personally, wanting her to look her best, and he even kept all of his snide comments to himself.

She had been so excited to dance the night away with Vallen and a two-year-old Wardell that she didn't care that they were probably the only ones that would dance with her anyway. It was her night, and she had planned to make the most of it. That was, until Liam had poured a very full glass of red wine down the front of her dress in front of everyone. Ignoring the gasps and camera flashes, she disappeared into a bathroom and fought to keep the stain from setting. That had been when a very drunk Dominic had stumbled in with some girl who had her lips plastered to his neck and pulled at his tie. He had slurred out an apology and then asked if she was okay. At the time, Larken had only sniffed back her tears and nodded, mortified that he had seen her, and had bitterly assumed that he would tell Liam about her crying.

Dominic raised an eyebrow at her. "Or, maybe that wasn't what you were thinking about."

Bristling, Larken shook herself, trying to bring her anger back. "I was sober and forgot about that. How do you remember when you could barely stand up?"

Instead of laughing like she thought he would, Dominic went quiet. Larken looked at him, and he very actively tried not to meet her eyes. He also tried to hide a blush. She raised an eyebrow of her own.

Combing his fingers through his hair again, his brown eyes met hers. Sighing, he said, "Well, I guess there's no use lying about it."

She stopped. "Lying about *what?*"

Larken had never seen him frazzled before, and she couldn't say that she didn't like the look on him. "Before that night, you had always been Liam's little sister. I didn't even know you were at the party yet. I was..."

"Indisposed?" she offered.

He gave her a warm smile. "When I finally did see you," the smile faded and his eyes heated, "you were all woman, and I wondered why I hadn't ever noticed you before."

It was Larken's turn to blush. She started walking again. "No." She shook her head, not wanting to believe him, and laughed. "No, you were with that other girl."

His hand shot out and grabbed her elbow. Pulling her back to face him, she couldn't help but get sucked into his warm brown eyes. "I gave her the slip. I left her by the bar and then tried to sober up, but I couldn't find you again."

Larken's tongue felt too fat for her mouth, and she swallowed thickly. Still unable to look away from him, she said, "I was at the east training field."

Dominic's serious expression cracked and he laughed. "What were you doing at the training field? And during *your* party, no less?"

"No one missed me, and I figured you rushed off to tell Liam about how pathetic I looked, so I didn't really see the point of hanging around." She shook her head. "Not to mention that I no longer had a dress."

Dominic cupped her cheek and softly assured her, "I never told him what I saw. I didn't even know he was the one that did it until I found him laughing about it later."

Larken finally let her eyes drop, and she slowly backed out of his grasp. Dominic let her go, and he was quiet for the rest of the walk. She had never seen him act so serious before, and she had never seen him look that sincere. This whole time she had thought that he had something more sinister in mind when it came to his relationship with her, but her party had been two years ago. Larken risked a look at him; he was smiling at the ground with his hands in his pockets, looking perfectly content just to be near her.

Have I been wrong about him?

They made it to the dorm just as Levi was leaving. He grabbed her elbow and gave her hurried instructions to put the covered dish in the fridge in the oven in an hour and then take it out in four. Then he set off, too late to stay and ask why Dominic was now making himself at home in their common room. Larken set the reminder on her communicator and awkwardly stood next to the couch that Dominic sat on.

"Please, feel free to clean up."

She hadn't planned on him staying, but as he pulled out his communicator, it didn't seem like he had plans to leave any time soon. Shrugging, Larken went to her room, grabbed some clothes, and then locked herself in the bathroom. She peeled the pants off of her thighs, and they itched like mad. Larken couldn't jump into the stall and turn the water on fast enough. The warm water soothed her, and she was soon in a fog of her peach and honey-scented body wash. Words started spilling from her mouth, and before she knew it, she was singing. She stuck her head under the spray, the lyrics to her favorite song in the opera *Libri E Beaus* pouring from her as she soaped up her hair. The haunting melody surrounded her, and she lost herself in it. Even without the music to accompany her, she lost herself in a world of lights and costumes. Like the ocean, Larken had resigned herself to only watching snippets of the opera on her communicator, and she knew that she would probably never see the real thing.

Shutting off the water, Larken grabbed a soft towel that was a little too small for her. It was the same grey color as all the others their dorm had been issued, and she used it to quickly dry off. She hurriedly pulled on her clean clothes and was annoyed when they stuck to her damp skin. Throwing the towel and her dirty clothes down the chute, she left the bathroom, combing her fingers through her hair. It was getting a little long now, ending at her collarbone instead of resting atop her shoulders. Maybe Hinlee would be able to cut it for her later.

Dominic sat, waiting for her, arms crossed with a smirk on his face. He looked so at ease, like he was exactly where he wanted to be, and it make Larken feel a little embarrassed. She wasn't sure why; this was her home, her safe place, but Dominic had that sort of confidence that told everyone that he belonged wherever he wanted to belong.

Dropping her gaze, she hugged her middle and asked, *"What?"*

He stood and crossed over to her. Reaching out, he gently grabbed her arms and simply answered, *"You."*

Looking up, she met his gaze. "What about me?"

"Every time I think I have you figured out, you always surprise me with something new."

"I hope that's supposed to be a compliment and not a complaint."

His hand moved from her left arm to her cheek. The way he looked at her made her breath catch, and she could only stare at him as he said, "It is."

Larken's heartbeat sounded in her ears, and she melted a little as he brushed his thumb over her cheek. They were so close, and she could smell the faint scent of blueberries that always clung to him. Something in his eyes changed, and then they dropped to her lips.

Larken started to panic as he leaned in, not knowing if she was ready for this, not knowing if this was even a good idea. He may have been different from the man she thought he was, but he was still Dominic Braves. The flirt who smiled easily and always had a beautiful woman on his arm, and she was just the shy girl, the black sheep who was always overlooked unless someone needed something that the Hale family could offer them.

His lips had just barely touched hers, when she put her hands on his chest, stopping him. Letting out a breath of annoyance, Dominic pulled back a little and looked at her. Larken couldn't meet his gaze as she said, "I don't...I don't know if I'm ready."

He sounded frustrated when he asked, "And when do you think you will be? Haven't I given you enough proof that I've changed?"

His tone had her hackles rising. Snapping her eyes up to him, she asked, "When did I say that you were the one to blame? I said *I* wasn't ready; it has nothing to do with you."

"Nothing to do—" Dominic let go of her and took a step back, stuffing his fingers into his hair. "Larken, it has *everything* to do with me. I'm the one that you keep stringing along, only to change your mind."

"I do not! I have been honest with you this whole time. And even if I did keep changing my mind, who cares? You should respect my decisions!"

Larken's communicator went off with the reminder to stick Levi's dinner into the oven. She left Dominic standing in the middle of the common room, and he groaned as he scrubbed at his face. Ignoring him, Larken smashed the buttons to preheat the oven. Not finished with their conversation, Dominic appeared behind her.

He breathed heavily as he accused, "When will I be good enough for you, Larken?"

She scoffed. "And what is that supposed to mean?"

"I mean that every time I mess up or make a mistake, I always have to beg you for forgiveness, and you ignore me for days at a time."

"That is not—"

"It *is* true! I am *always* the one that has to reach out to you. I'm always the one that has to apologize. When will it be enough?"

"Dominic—"

"When will *I* be enough for you?"

Larken felt like she was drowning; this wasn't about him. This was about her inability to trust another human being outside of her makeshift family. It had nothing to do with her playing with his emotions, or whatever else he seemed to think she was doing. This was about her not being ready for the same thing he was, and now he was getting upset about it.

She tried again. "Dominic, this isn't—what does me not being ready have to do with this?"

"It has everything to do with this!" The oven dinged, signaling that it was hot enough. Larken brushed past him and pulled the dish out of the fridge and stuck it in the oven as Dominic accused,

"Every time I think we've moved past this, you come up with some excuse to turn me into the bad guy."

Larken slammed the oven shut and turned on him. "I never said that you were the bad guy. It's your own fault that you decided to only start acting like an adult a few months ago, not mine. And then you have the audacity to tell me that I'm stringing you along when *you know* the kind of family that I grew up with!" She crossed her arms, watching as the fight left him, as the realization of what she was really upset about softened his features. Larken didn't care though; she was too worked up, and before she knew it, she was shouting at him. "I never got to decide anything for myself, and now that I finally found where I think I belong, you come along and remind me of all of my insecurities and why I am so afraid to let myself trust anyone who isn't Vallen! But I don't get to be nervous, or shy, or scared, because then I'm just playing with your emotions and leading you on!"

She marched over to the door, and Dominic rushed to her. With pleading eyes, he said, "Lark, I'm sorry. Let's talk about this!"

"No, I'm done talking. I'm done being vulnerable, and I'm done second-guessing myself." She yanked the door open and turned to him expectantly. "Please leave."

Dominic looked like he was breaking in front of her, but she pushed her sympathy away. She didn't let any of the other soldiers at base walk all over her; she didn't know why she kept letting him.

"Lark, please, I was wrong. I shouldn't have pressured—"

"No, you shouldn't have. *Leave.*"

Dominic stuffed both hands into his hair, messing it up. He looked panicked like he knew he had made a mistake that he wouldn't be able to fix. "Lark..."

She only stood quietly by the door.

He reached out to touch her but let his hand fall before he could. The way he looked at her made her feel more exposed than she had ever let herself be in front of him. She barely heard him ask, "Please don't give up on me, Larken. Not yet. Please don't give up on me yet."

Larken said nothing, and she slammed the door as soon as he was out of the way. She grabbed fistfuls of her hair and snarled at the floor like it was the reason for her problems. Running to her room, she tore off her clothes and pulled on some shorts and a breathable top. Marching back out to the common room, she turned the stereo on to something that reflected her black mood and turned the television to an intense exercise program. Pushing the couches and coffee table out of the way, Larken took up her spot in the middle of the room. Crouching, Larken kicked out her legs behind her and started doing push-ups. She had a dorm shift followed by her rec time, and she was determined not to think about what just happened, or how she had just admitted how afraid she really was to Dominic Braves.

Soren could smell the smoke the moment he turned down the hall. He rushed to the dorm door, praying that nothing was wrong, that it wasn't his common room that was burning to the ground. Without thinking twice, he grabbed the doorknob, only realizing how stupid that was after he felt the coolness of it. Throwing open the door, he peered inside. White smoke blinded him for a moment, making his eyes burn. Blinking, Soren could make out two figures huddled next to the oven.

Levi fanned the smoke with a dishtowel, his shirt missing and his pants hanging low on his hips. Even through the smoke, Soren could still see the droplets of water that clung to his back. Then there was Larken, who coughed and apologized over and over again, only stopping when Levi told her to shut up. She had on those shorts that had haunted his dreams since the first time he had seen her in them and a white tank top almost the same color as the smoke that choked her.

Three heartbeats later, Larken opened her mouth again, saying, "Levi, I really am so sorry. I—"

"Just go open a window or something," he interrupted, his voice nowhere as irritated as it would have been if it had been anyone else.

Jumping to her feet, Larken rushed to the door, only to blindly collide with Soren. Without thinking, his hands grabbed her elbows, holding her to him. She looked up at him, her eyes red. Tears streaked down her pink cheeks, but they were probably from the smoke. Soren meant to ask her if she was okay, but catching Levi fanning the oven again out of the corner of his eye and seeing how frazzled Larken looked, he ended up laughing instead. This whole day, *this whole week*, had been more stressful than his whole career as a Captain, and he just couldn't keep it in any longer.

Larken narrowed her eyes at him, and Soren tried to stop, he really did, but he just ended up laughing harder. She yanked her arms from his grasp, and he let her go willingly. He had left the door open in his haste to get in, so Larken stormed off to the single window that was in the common room. Throwing it open, she huffed as Soren continued to laugh at her expense.

Levi tossed the dishtowel into the sink and turned, looking completely ridiculous standing shirtless in the midst of the smoke, like he was at a photo shoot instead of a dorm kitchen. Shaking his head, Levi frowned and said, "I think you broke our Captain."

"Are you sure that he didn't have faulty wiring, to begin with?' she asked, still upset.

Levi only shook his head again, chuckling as well. Larken crossed her arms and took in the two men before her. Sinking to the floor, she covered her face, and soon her shoulders were shaking with the laughter she was trying to suppress. It was like a breath of fresh air, like whatever had been suffocating the two of them had been yanked off, and they were allowed to be Soren and Larken again.

Still grinning, Soren walked over and helped Larken back to her feet just as the three remaining members of their squad rushed into the common room. Questions of what happened and if everyone was okay were hurled at them, but Soren was lost in a teal sea.

Larken's eyes sparkled as she grinned at him, and he couldn't help but grin back.

When the questions didn't stop, Larken broke her gaze away and said, "Yes, we're all fine. I forgot to set a timer, so I ruined dinner."

"I'm not making another one," Levi grumbled. Soren didn't miss the wink he sent Larken's way.

"I'm taking everyone to The Grill tonight," Larken announced. Then, looking down at herself, she laughed and said, "Although, I should probably change first."

Protesting, Loxly said, "Those shorts ain't hurtin' no one." He smiled his crooked smile, and Soren took a moment to seriously consider if they needed a pilot.

"Great idea," Hinlee agreed, ignoring Loxly. Pushing forward, she grabbed Larken's hand. "I'll help you."

"I'm just going to wear a uniform," Larken muttered, but Hinlee shushed her.

Together, the two girls disappeared down the hall and into Larken's room. Soren shook his head, trying to remember the last dinner they had as a squad when nothing crazy happened. It had been before Larken joined up, that was for sure. Walking down the hall to the Vendor, Soren ordered a smoke vacuum to be delivered to their dorm immediately. They would leave the thing running while they were out and, hopefully, all of the smoke would be gone by the time they got back.

Soren was on his way back to the common room when he heard Hinlee's muffled voice say, "Okay, girl, spill it."

Soren stopped and looked at Larken's door. It wasn't all the way closed, cracked just enough that he could see Hinlee sprawled out on Larken's bed. Knowing he shouldn't be listening, Soren made to keep moving.

"Spill what?"

"You and I both know that you are the most anal person there is when it comes to cooking. Why didn't you set the timer?"

"No reason." Larken sounded more unsure than Soren thought she meant to.

"Does it have anything to do with a rumor I heard about a certain Captain following you into the dorm?"

Soren stopped trying to fight his curiosity and walked back to the door. The lingering feeling of laughter left him, and Soren's mood turned black.

Larken sighed, dropping onto the bed next to Hinlee, already dressed and ready to go. "Do you think Soren heard about that?"

"Soren doesn't listen to gossip. Are you gonna answer the question?"

The whole story came out, like Larken couldn't have held it in any longer if she wanted to, and Soren had to actively fight not to punch a hole in the wall next to her door. His stomach soured and he balled his fists. Soren didn't know that he was about to burst into Larken's room until he felt a firm hand grip his bicep. He glared, hauling his fist back to punch whoever had grabbed him, but stopped when he saw the cold fury in Levi's green eyes.

Levi snarled and whispered, "If you go in there, she will never forgive you."

Soren said nothing, knowing that his Second was right, but not liking it. Levi let go of him and made his way out to the common room where Loxly and Brecker were messing with the vacuum that had been delivered. Soren looked back at Larken's door just in time to see her pull it open. She squeaked in surprise, and then the color drained from her face. He could see the question she wanted to ask in her eyes, but he only grumbled that it was time to go.

Together, the six of them made their way to The Grill, no one daring to break the tense silence. Loxly had tried to get Larken talking by pulling her close to him and raising an eyebrow at her, but she only shook her head, looking like she might be sick. Soren knew that the kind thing to do would be to pull her aside and tell her that he had no immediate plans to track Braves down and murder him, but he wasn't quite sure if he could say that honestly yet. He had been forced to accept the fact that she tolerated him, got along with him even, but he had made no such promises, and he planned to dislike Braves until the day he died. But this, this was too much, even for that sleaze bag.

Once they were all seated, Hinlee decided to break the tension by asking Levi if it was by chance that he was shirtless when the dorm was burning down, or if he thought his abs would charm the smoke into submission. Grasping at any chance to lighten the mood, both Loxly and Brecker began heckling the Second as well. Levi took it in stride, keeping everyone's attention off of Larken, and Soren was surprised to realize how much the grumbly field-medic had come to care for her. He was even more protective over her than he was of Hinlee, and Soren thought it was probably because they both knew what it was like to not be wanted. He began to wonder if this was how Levi treated the other kids he grew up with before he had been sent away.

With everyone's attention elsewhere, Larken leaned over and parted her lips. Soren glared at her, and she looked like she might change her mind and go back to her menu, but then she asked so softly that he almost didn't hear, "How long were you standing there?"

The mortified look on her face told him that she thought she already knew the answer, and the hard glare that he gave her told her his. Her eyes fell, and she nodded. Then, steeling herself, she looked back up to him and said, "I took care of it. Nothing is going to happen between—"

"I don't care," he lied, pulling out his communicator.

Larken sucked in a breath and turned back to her menu, mindlessly scrolling through it. He could feel the shift in her mood, the quick change from hurt to furious. Soren didn't know what she wanted, and he was determined to ignore her for the rest of the night. That was his plan anyway, until she looked back at him and announced loud enough for everyone to hear, "I think I'm going to sleep with Dominic."

No one said anything as they all gaped at her, everyone except Soren.

She continued, "I'm not sure what it is about him. Maybe it's the way that he thinks he doesn't have to work for anything."

Soren kept staring at his communicator, his hand shaking.

"Or maybe it's the way that he's always undressing me with his eyes."

Loxly choked, but Soren still ignored her.

"Or maybe it's because he just has one of those faces. You know, the handsome kind that you can't help but want to—" Soren slammed his communicator onto the table as he turned on her, but she only grinned and said, "*punch.*"

That was it—that one word and the devious look on her face had all his anger melting away. Loxly leaned over and whispered to Hinlee, "What's goin' on?"

She just waved him away, saying, "Shhh, you're ruining it."

"Ruinin' what?"

Hinlee just rolled her eyes and asked what the sharpshooter planned to order, taking his attention off Soren and Larken.

Larken shot a grateful glance to her friend before meeting Soren's eyes again. She gave him a sad smile and said low enough that only he could hear, "I'm a tough girl, I can handle myself."

"I know you can. The last time I doubted you, you knocked me on my backside, just like you promised you would."

"*Pompous* backside," she corrected, her smile turning a little less sad. "What makes you think I would treat Dominic any differently?"

"I don't think that you will treat him differently. I think that Braves is willing to do whatever it takes to get what he wants."

"I don't think that's what's happening," she disagreed, her eyes dropping to a gouge in the wooden table. She ran her finger over it, like the damaged wood could give her the right words. "I think that he's confused. I'm not like the other girls he chases after, and I don't think he knows what to do about that. He really seems to be trying, but then he does stupid stuff like this, and I just get so mad." She met Soren's eyes again. "I'm not saying what he did was right, and

I'm not saying that I'm considering dating him, but I do know what it's like to be confused."

Soren swallowed hard, not wanting her words to make sense. He wanted to be angry and break things, and he really wanted to mess up the Star's perfectly manicured face. Instead, he understood Larken's confusion all too well, and that kept him from saying anything else as she turned back to her menu. Soren couldn't give her any advice because, if he was being honest with himself, he was just as confused as she was. Only, it wasn't his feelings for Braves that had him at his wit's end.

CHAPTER 25

I t was a little over a week before Dominic reached out to Larken again. He had sent a message apologizing and claiming that he knew he didn't deserve a second chance, but he was asking for one anyway. It was the most Dominic message he could have sent, and Larken seriously considered ignoring it. But he had asked for her to meet him at the table in the cafeteria where Squad 19 used to sit before they started eating at the dorm. He also said that, if he couldn't convince her to give him one last chance, she wouldn't have to speak to him again.

"When will he get here? I still have to replace the fuel pump on the Arsene before I can head back and shower." Hinlee rubbed at her oil-stained cheek, making it worse.

"He said 3:00, that's all I know." Larken looked at her communicator, seeing that he was now eleven minutes late. Feeling like she was imposing, Larken looked at her friend and said, "Thanks again for coming with me. I'm sorry that—"

Hinlee cut her off by grabbing her hand and forcing Larken to look her in the eyes. "Never *ever* apologize about asking me to come with you when you don't feel comfortable going alone. I would rather be mildly inconvenienced than have you get into trouble because you went somewhere by yourself."

Larken nodded, compulsively checking the time again.

Finally, Larken felt a set of eyes on her and stiffened as a silver box was placed on the table in front of her. Dominic sat across from her unceremoniously, and Larken chanced a glance at him. He looked worse than the last time they fought, and a twinge of pity twisted Larken's gut. She had gone on like nothing had happened, but Dominic obviously hadn't.

Dropping her eyes to the box instead, she asked, "What's this?"

Hinlee leaned in close to get a good look at the small box, and if Dominic was annoyed that she was there, he didn't show it. "Open it, then I'll explain."

Larken looked over at Hinlee, who only shrugged. Picking the box up, Larken took the top off. It took her a moment to realize what she was looking at. There were two pieces of stiff-looking paper with the words *Libri E Beaus* written across the top in sprawling silver letters. Underneath that were the words *Admittance 1* and the seat numbers F11 and F12.

Larken's hands shook as she held the box. Looking up, she asked, "Dominic?"

"I wanted to make things right, and I wanted to prove that you weren't just some passing fancy." His eyes flicked to Hinlee, who looked very confused. "I meant it when I said that you were—*are*—special to me."

"But," her eyes dropped to the tickets again, "how did you know?"

"I heard you singing."

Larken suddenly remembered that she had been singing in the shower just before they had fought. She touched the top ticket gently like it would disintegrate under her finger.

"I had ordered the tickets, thinking it would be a nice surprise for you, but now I'm hoping that you understand that I'm trying. I'm making more of an effort with you than I have with any other girl because that's what you deserve. I'm so, so sorry that I keep messing things up, but I want you to know that I really am trying."

Larken could only nod, still not believing that she was holding tickets to an impossible dream in her hands.

Hinlee nudged her and asked, "What are they?"

"They're tickets to *Libri E Beaus.*"

"What's that?"

"An opera," Dominic answered.

"Is that the one with the song you're always singing?"

Larken nodded again.

"And they're using paper tickets? Classy."

Ignoring her, Larken instead rounded on Dominic. "How did you get these?"

Dominic shrugged sheepishly. "My mom is friends with the director."

Even though it killed her, Larken set the box on the table and pushed it back to Dominic. "I can't, it's too much."

His face fell. "You don't like it."

"No! It's not that, I just," her eyes dropped to the tickets again, "I'm not worth it."

Dominic placed his hands on top of hers and pushed the tickets back her way. "You are."

Larken grabbed the top one and tried to give it to him. "At least take yours. I would never forgive myself if I lost it."

"I already have mine." He smiled. "That other one is for Vallen."

Tears pricked Larken's eyes; no one other than Vallen had ever done anything like this for her. Yes, Squad 19 had taken her in and adopted her into their family, but this was different. This was more than a fun trip to cheer her up—it was a sincere apology from someone who was truly sorry for hurting her.

Larken met Dominic's eyes again, and her heart squeezed at the hope in them. "I want to make one thing clear."

"Whatever it is, I'll do it," Dominic promised.

"If I accept these, I don't want you to think that you can buy my forgiveness the next time we have a fight."

"Of course."

Larken took a deep breath. "Then, I guess we're going to the opera next week."

Dominic let loose a breath, and he sagged as if a weight was dropped from his shoulders.

Not wanting to hang around long enough for Dominic to mess up their new understanding, Larken put the lid back on the box and said, "Well, we have to get going. I need to call Vallen, and Hinlee has to change the fuel on our squad aircraft."

"Fuel pump," Hinlee corrected softly.

"Right, that."

Dominic smiled. "I'm just glad that you agreed to meet me. I really am sorry about what happened, Lark."

Larken nodded, not knowing what else to say, and then stood the same moment Hinlee did. Together, the two girls made their way out of the cafeteria, Larken clutching the box to her like it might slip away at any moment. When they were out the door and could no longer feel Dominic's eyes, Hinlee sighed and muttered, "That wasn't what I was expecting."

"Me either," Larken agreed.

"I think I understand a little better, though, why you keep talking to him."

Hinlee was fishing, and Larken wasn't sure she was ready to voice her confused thoughts on the matter, so she just said, "He doesn't act like the same person who used to hang around my brother."

Hinlee stopped her and gave her an encouraging smile. "Would your brother know what those tickets meant to you?"

Larken thought for a moment and then shook her head. Liam thought that everything she liked was stupid and not worth his time. He would much rather slum it in a bar than go anywhere with her, let alone the opera. It was also safe to assume that Dominic felt the same way, only, he would rather be at the races than in a stuffy theater.

Seeing the look on her face, Hinlee's smile deepened. "Just because Decks doesn't like him doesn't mean you can't. From where

I was sitting, it really looked like he was trying to make up for what he did."

"So, you don't think it was wrong of me to take the tickets?"

"How likely is it that you would get this opportunity again?"

Larken's hands tightened on the box. "Not very."

"There you go." Hinlee winked. "I'll see you at dinner."

Larken waved to her friend and then headed back to the dorm for the remainder of her rec time. It was Hinlee's turn to come up with a dinner plan for the night, and Larken was excited about the break. Since she cooked all the time now, she was glad that it wasn't up to her to come up with something. Her mind felt foggy suddenly, and she knew that there was a lot that she needed to think about.

Reaching the dorm, Larken let herself in and crept past a dozing Loxly. She shut herself away in her room, only to have her heart melt at the sight that greeted her. Estelle smiled broadly, her pink tongue lolling as she did so. Her tail whacked Larken's bed, and it wasn't long before she rolled onto her back, begging for belly scratches. Larken complied, falling onto her bed next to the terrier and nuzzling her close. Estelle had been programmed the night of the small fire, when Larken thought she might go insane from all the stress she was under. She had ordered an all-white skin for her, complete with pink silicone toes, and adjusted her eyes to a soft cornflower blue. The small dog yipped in excitement, and nudged Larken's face with her stout muzzle, before licking her with a dry tongue. It wasn't the same as the hybrids she was used to that were living, warm, and at times, extra slobbery, but Estelle had filled a large hole in Larken's heart that she didn't know had been slowly eating away at her.

Rolling onto her back, Larken called Vallen, and Estelle basically fell on top of her chest in an attempt to be as close to her as possible. Stretching out, Estelle rested her face in the crook of Larken's neck, and Larken could feel the little puffs of hot air that the android released every ten seconds to keep from overheating. It would have been easy to believe that Estelle was breathing if she took in air as well. Reaching up and scratching at a spot behind the android's ear, Vallen answered before the first ring could end.

"Are you okay?" Vallen asked as a hello.

"Yeah, I'm fine." Larken could hear the hesitation in her own voice, and she winced knowing that he would pick up on it.

"Tell me what happened," Vallen demanded, his voice stern but not unkind.

She did, starting with the argument, after which her former instructor had a few choice words regarding Dominic, and ending with their most recent encounter. Larken finished by saying, "Hinlee was there with me because I didn't think it was a good idea to go alone, and she thinks that he sounded sincere as well."

Vallen said nothing, and Larken was forced to wait as he thought about what he was going to say.

When he didn't, Larken added, "I should probably tell you that the gift was two tickets to *Libri E Beaus*."

A long sigh sounded from the other end of the call that made Estelle's ear twitch, and Vallen was forced to ask, "And how did he manage to think up that grand gesture on his own?"

"I'm not sure," she answered. "But Hinlee thinks I should go, even if I don't plan on pursuing a relationship with him, just because I probably won't get another chance."

Vallen apparently couldn't disagree. "Who is the other ticket for?"

"*You?*" Larken asked hopefully.

Vallen grumbled in that way that he did whenever Larken asked him to do something that he really didn't want to. Finally, he gave the answer that he always did in those situations. "We'll see."

Larken beamed, and she kept a firm hold on her tongue, not wanting to tease him and have him back out. There was what sounded like an explosion on Vallen's end, and Larken pulled her communicator away from her ear for a second. Estelle jumped and growled low in her throat. "What was that?!"

Vallen yelled at someone, the sound muffled; he probably had his communicator pressed against his chest so he wouldn't be shouting in her ear. When she could hear him clearly again, he said, "I have to go. They're trying out new weapon upgrades today, and some idiot just set himself on fire."

"Stay safe," she said as he ended the call.

Squealing, Larken jumped off her bed and did a weird little dance, stomping her feet on the ground and punching the air a few times with her fists. Estelle was once again beating her tail against the bed, and she barked a time or two, sensing the excitement from her owner. A knock on her door pulled her from any further silliness, and Larken opened the door to reveal a bleary-eyed Loxly. Estelle hopped off the bed and tried to get at him. He smiled warmly and asked, "Somethin' good happen?"

"You could say that."

Meet me at the garage.

It was all Hinlee's message had said. So, when Soren had finished up at the shooting range for the day, he made his way to the garage to find an oil-stained Hinlee waiting for him. He couldn't get a good read on her, and he wondered for a moment if he was in trouble for something. It wouldn't be the first time, and since Larken's arrival, he had been finding himself in trouble with the small mechanic a lot.

Seeing him, she pushed off of the wall and said, "I have to tell you something that you aren't going to like."

Already getting irritated at the prospect of where this conversation was going, Soren asked, "Is that so?"

Hinlee sighed and rubbed at her temples, smearing the oil that was there. "Look, I thought it would be better if you weren't blindsided, but if you're going to be a jerk about this, I'll let you rot in whatever hole you dig yourself in."

Soren's jaw ticked, but he swallowed back his comment.

Meeting his eyes, Hinlee didn't back down as she said, "Larken met with Braves today."

It took a moment for what she said to sink in, the ringing in his ears too loud. *"What?"*

"He asked for one last chance to prove that he wasn't a total jerk, and Larken, being the sweetheart that she is, gave him another one." Hinlee rubbed her cheek with the back of her wrist. "Lucky for you, I was there."

"Why were you there?" Soren was aware of the people that were looking at them and giving them a wide berth.

"She didn't want him to pull something, even though he asked to meet her in the cafeteria. Anyway, that's not the point." She looked him dead in the eye. "The *point* is that he got her tickets to some fancy opera so she and General Maxwell could go with him."

"And she took the tickets?"

"Would we be talking about this if she hadn't?"

"If you were there, why didn't you tell her not to go?" Soren's fists were shaking, and he was losing the battle of keeping his cool.

"Because he seemed sincere enough to me, and she said that she would probably never get another chance to go." Hinlee's eyes went soft. "This isn't a date, Decks. This is about Larken finally catching a break and getting to do something that she enjoys. Could you see the five of us dressed up at the opera with her?"

Soren didn't answer because he didn't want to give Hinlee the satisfaction of agreeing with her.

"She'll be there with General Maxwell, and everything will be fine. Just," she dropped her gaze, "just be happy for her, okay?"

Soren couldn't look at her anymore, so he turned and made his way to the dorm. He was going to tell Larken exactly what he thought, and where she should stuff those tickets that Braves gave her. This wasn't right, and he knew that there was no way that Dominic Braves was sincere about anything. Larken wasn't a stupid girl—she had made it clear that she understood what direction Braves wanted to take their relationship in, so why did she keep buying into his meaningless apologies?

I'm not saying what he did was right, and I'm not saying that I'm considering dating him, but I do know what it's like to be confused.

Soren sighed, releasing the anger he felt towards Larken as he remembered her words. He had reached the dorm, but instead of going in, he leaned against the wall and stared at the door. Somehow, he knew that she was on the other side, probably laughing and joking around with whoever was in there. It was her night off for dinner, and even though she was cooking most of their meals now, he knew that she would do whatever she could to make tonight perfect. Just like she always did.

Larken never complained about her work and was always quick to offer a smile or a compliment in the gym. She would pretend that her shoulder didn't hurt even when it did and that the things that were said about her on the base didn't bother her. Soren sighed again, sticking his fingers into his hair. She really did deserve a night off, even if it was with that jerk. A night where she could dress up, see General Maxwell, and listen to music that only she could possibly understand. And, really, what could happen with the General there playing chaperone?

The door flew open, and Soren stiffened. Larken jumped a little and she almost dropped Loxly's wristband when she saw him, but then her face split into the biggest smile he had ever seen on her. No, there was no way he could take this from her, even though he really wanted to.

"Soren, hey. I was just on my way to go rescue Loxly from med-training. He grabbed the wrong band and can't turn in his android." She held up the wristband as proof. "Hinlee just messaged me and said she was thinking about ordering in tonight; what do you think?"

He was lost in her eyes, in the excitement that he saw there. It was the same look she had when Loxly had promised to take her gunning, and when General Maxwell showed up for that surprise visit all those weeks ago. Their teal depths were sucking him in, and he was helpless against it, like being lost at sea and knowing that it was impossible to swim anymore. Soren was sinking, and for some reason, that didn't scare him as much as it should have.

"Whatever you want." The words tumbled out of his mouth before he could stop them, and he wondered if she knew he was talking about more than food.

CHAPTER 26

"What do you mean *you're sick*?!" Larken practically shouted into the communicator. Estelle whined at her feet, picking up on her frustration.

"It means that I'm sick, and I can't go on Saturday," Vallen answered, not sounding sick at all.

"Oh yeah? What are your symptoms?"

"It's the flu, Larken. I'll be quarantined for the next four days. *Meaning* I won't be released until the morning after the show."

Larken groaned. *"This can't be happening!"*

"As upset as I am to be missing your opera—"

"You don't sound very upset."

"—you're just going to have to take one of your squadmates instead," he continued as if she hadn't cut him off. "Look, they're saying they need to take my temperature again. I have to go."

"No, Vallen, I—" Larken was cut off as he hung up. She dropped her communicator onto the table and buried her face in her hands, her hair falling over them like a blonde curtain. "This sucks!"

"What happened?" Hinlee asked, selecting a card out of her hand and passing it to Brecker. He scoffed when he looked at it and muttered about how unhelpful it was. She only replied with a wink and a, "Sorry sweetie, the point isn't to help you."

Larken let her arms fall to the table, and she looked at Hinlee wide-eyed. "Vallen is sick! He can't come Saturday!"

"Well, there are three eligible bachelors living in this very dorm," Brecker mused as he drew a card and immediately tossed it to Hinlee. She giggled and then laid down three Queens in front of her. Hinlee blew him a kiss, and he muttered, "You're lucky I love you."

"Yes, I am." She turned to Larken and winked. "I'm sure someone would be willing to go with you."

Larken groaned. "I suppose I'll just have to ask Loxly. He likes music, right?"

"I wouldn't consider what he likes music," Hinlee said, scrunching up her nose and going back to the game.

"Well, either way, I can't go alone."

"I thought you liked that opera?" Brecker asked, looking at Hinlee like she had given him false information.

"I do!" Larken insisted. "I just don't trust Dominic in a dimly lit room."

Hinlee laughed while Brecker made a face. She drew a card and then added the fourth Queen to her pile. "Well, I'm sure you'll figure something out."

Larken's communicator buzzed again, and she scrambled for it, thinking that it might be Vallen. Her heart fell when she saw it was just an alarm reminding her that her rec time was almost over and that she needed to start making her way to the shooting range. Sighing, Larken turned it off and pulled herself up from the table, Estelle whining as she did. Hinlee watched her as Brecker drew a card and gave an excited chuckle. He laid down his whole hand and Hinlee threw her cards to the table.

"That was a cheap trick, Brecker Wilton!"

"Oh, come on, Hin," he laughed. "If you didn't keep giving me bad cards, I wouldn't have picked up this strategy."

She only rolled her eyes and turned to Larken. "Just don't make any rash decisions. You tend to not think clearly when you're upset."

It was Larken's turn to roll her eyes. "I have to get to the range."

"Hey, what are you planning for tomorrow night?" Brecker called after her.

"Not sure yet, why?"

"I don't want to get chicken wings tonight if you're making chicken too."

"Well, then I won't make chicken tomorrow. See you two at dinner."

Larken left the dorm, leaving a dejected-looking Estelle behind with Brecker and Hinlee, and headed for the shooting range. On her way, she passed the girl who had led her to Connie's office all those weeks ago talking to some burly guy who held a thin section of her hair between his finger and thumb, making her blush and giggle. Larken looked away, nauseated, and decided it would be better to look at the floor than the soldiers around her. She hadn't seen Connie since that day in her office, and last Larken had heard, she had been let go for bullying many of the young women at the base and for giving certain Captains favors for sleeping with her. Thankfully, Dominic's visit was revealed to be just a visit, but thinking about it still made Larken uneasy.

Entering the range, Larken waved to the freckly, curly-haired boy at check-in. Jake was only fifteen, and he was a sweet boy whom Larken had often caught looking at the guns she brought with her. She had offered to show him how to shoot the more advanced guns more than once, but he refused each time. He knew that it was different shooting in a range than out on the field, and he didn't really want to do anything to improve his skill. Jake was hoping for an administrative job, and Larken thought that suited the kind boy.

Grabbing some glasses and earplugs, Larken pulled her guns from the holsters on her belt and set them on a little table. She walked over to the Vendor and ordered some bullets, tapping her foot as she waited for her order to go through. She started to wonder what sort of upgrades Vallen had been playing with over the last week, and it stung that she wasn't there to help him.

Someone cleared their throat behind her, and Larken turned to find Jake holding the box that usually would have dropped out of the bottom of the Vendor. His dark hair looked messier than usual, and Larken thought it made him look younger than he was. "Miss Hale, the Vendor is on the fritz." He handed her the box. "Is it all there?"

Popping the lid open, Larken nodded and smiled. "Thanks, Jake."

"Would you—" his eyes dropped to his feet, "would you mind if I watched you fire those? I haven't seen the Ignitors in action before."

"Sure," she shrugged, "you can even shoot some if you'd like."

Jake smiled that same smile he always did and then quietly followed her to where she had left her guns.

Picking up the tech-advanced handgun that she favored since Vallen had given her that new arsenal, she loaded it and then took aim. Pulling her gun back, she adjusted the distance of the dummy, pushing it back about six feet. She aimed again and fired off three rounds.

Jake hesitantly took a step closer to her as she lowered the gun. "Nothing's happening," he whispered.

The words were barely out of his mouth when the bullets exploded in the chest cavity, and the dummy ignited. Jake jumped a little, and Larken laughed. She turned to him and asked, "Are you sure you don't want to give these ones a try?"

Jake looked at her and then down to the pristine handgun that fit perfectly in her hand, with a silver handle to match her sword. He met her eyes again, saying, "Maybe just once."

"What do you mean *I have to go*?"

"Okay, let me put it this way," Hinlee said, her arms crossed and her hip popped. "Do you want Larken to go to the thing with Braves *unchaperoned*?"

Soren's jaw ticked, and he just barely sidestepped the punch that Levi threw at him.

"That's what I thought."

"What about Loxly?"

"What about him?"

"Isn't he Larken's second choice?" Soren asked, dodging another blow from his Second. Levi had a dangerous smirk, knowing that Soren didn't have his full attention on the fight.

"Not if you tell him not to."

"I'm not going to do that." He threw a punch of his own, and Levi blocked it with his forearm and jabbed him in the ribs.

"What if *I* tell him not to?"

Soren didn't answer for a long while, trying to focus on the fight. Thoughts of Larken in a dark room with Braves while Loxly snored next to them blinded him temporarily, and Levi's fist connected with his cheekbone. He felt a bruise starting, and Soren turned on Hinlee. "What are you even doing here? Aren't you supposed to be under some hood or something?"

She rolled her eyes. "Larken won't go if she has to go alone, and we both know that Loxly sleeping through the whole thing would be just as bad."

"And Levi isn't an option because?"

"Because Levi would murder himself before putting on a tie and drinking champagne with pampered Stars," the field-medic answered, unscrewing the cap to his water bottle. "Although," he paused, the bottle halfway to his lips, "it might benefit the Military Princess if she was photographed with a sexy, bearded stranger."

Soren glared at his closest friend for a good while before grumbling, "Do whatever you want."

Hinlee's grin was pure feline, equal parts deviousness and calculated glee. Soren didn't like it one bit.

"Guess you better start looking for a suit then," she said in a sing-song voice and left the gym.

He growled, and Levi chuckled. Soren turned on him, and Levi challenged, "What? You gonna punch me now?"

He thought about it, he really did. But instead, he just pulled off his shirt and mopped his face with it. Tossing it aside, Soren said, "I'm going for a run."

"Dinner is in one hour, and Brecker will be absolutely heartbroken if you don't show up."

He purposely bumped into Levi, making him spill water down his front. Soren laughed at Levi's angry mutterings and started running. He lost count of how many times he ran around the gym after five laps. Much to his annoyance, Levi had hung around, doing sit-ups, push-ups, and whatever else he could think of. Soren just kept running circles around him, wondering where on earth he would find a suit. Was it something that he could order from the Vendor? Or would it be socially acceptable to wear his Captain's uniform? He thought, but he couldn't remember seeing any photos of General Maxwell in his uniform at social events.

Pushing his legs faster, Soren fumed. How was he always roped into situations that involved Larken? He missed the simpler times when he wasn't expected to play bodyguard, look out for creeps that might mess with his squad members, and when music wasn't blared at all hours of the day in their dorm. But Soren soon ran out of hot air, knowing that the music seemed to make their dorm homier, that he was usually scowling anyways, and that he would have jumped to the defense of any of his friends if they needed it. It was just Larken Hale that had him so frustrated, and he had no idea why.

The way he saw it, Soren had two options before him. Either he could tell Larken to suck it up and go alone and trust that her *friend* wouldn't try anything in a room full of people, or he could suck it up and wear the stupid suit for a few hours and ruin whatever plans Braves had with Larken. Soren knew what he would do immediately, and he didn't fight the smirk that twisted his lips.

"I hate it when you do that," Levi said, pulling Soren's attention to him.

"Do what?"

"Smile like you're planning a murder instead of enjoying a workout."

"Who says I'm not?"

"It would never work," Levi jabbed. "Everyone knows how you feel about Braves; they would know it was you."

"Innocent until proven guilty."

Soren picked up his pace again, but Levi stopped him, claiming that it was time to get back to the dorm.

He just shook his head and said, "You go on without me."

"The dinners were your dumb idea, to begin with."

Soren stopped, let his head fall back, and blew out a long breath. "Fine."

They showered and then made their way back to the dorm, where they were greeted with loud music, barking, and laughter. The song that was playing was a bouncier version of one that they sang frequently at the tabernacle, and the smell of spicy barbecue wafted over them as they walked in. Immediately, the little white monster that Larken had programmed bounced over to Levi, loving him almost as much as it loved her. Soren's eyes narrowed in on Larken of their own accord, and he couldn't help but chuckle as well. The poor girl's face was beet red, and she guzzled down water like there was no tomorrow. Brecker and Loxly were roaring with laughter, but Hinlee at least had the decency to cover her mouth as she laughed.

Loxly stopped laughing long enough to ask, "They never gave you hot sauce at that fancy house of yours?"

Larken set her glass down roughly, shook her head, and then grabbed the full one next to Soren's plate. She drained that glass as well, her face still red, and coughed. "*That was awful!*" she sputtered, making everyone laugh again.

Soren's voice must have caught her attention because she looked over his way. She offered a kind smile to Levi as he dropped to rub the mutt's exposed belly, but then her eyes narrowed at him, and she marched over. "What happened?"

Thinking she referred to the conversation he had with Hinlee not too long ago, he answered, "Well, Hinlee—"

Larken cut him off by reaching up to his face. Her fingers were light on his cheek, the one that Levi had hit, and she gasped. "Hinlee did this to you? What did you do?"

"That's my work," Levi interjected. "Looks nice, doesn't it?"

Larken smiled and rolled her eyes. She grabbed Soren's elbow and muttered, "Come on, Jodi gave me something for bruises the last time I was with her."

Soren followed willingly, ignoring the smug look on Hinlee's face as he did. The conversation started up again as they made their way down the hall, and Soren drowned it out. All his focus was on the spot where Larken touched him, and he was once again amazed at how soft her hand felt.

She pulled him into her room without ceremony and motioned for him to sit on her bed. He did, and he didn't sink into it like he had expected to. Her mattress was firm, and her sheets were even softer than his. Still staring at the midnight blue bedspread, he asked, "Why do you have a bruise treatment?"

Larken fished in a drawer and didn't turn as she answered, "Apparently I kick the wall in my sleep. I kept waking up with bruises and didn't know where they came from." Larken pulled out what looked like a bottle of lotion and moved in front of him. "Jodi gave me this so I wasn't so sore all the time." She uncapped the light pink bottle and squeezed a little dab onto her finger. She stood between his knees, and leaned in before asking, "So, what's your excuse?"

Soren could only think about how close Larken was, but he somehow managed, "Levi and I were sparring. He got in a hit." The lotion felt cold as she dabbed it on his cheek, and his lips twitched. "Aren't you supposed to warm that up with your hands first?"

Her eyes twinkled. "Don't be such a baby."

Soren huffed a laugh, his eyes falling to her lips, remembering the last time they were this close. Remembering what he had almost done.

Her smile faded, and her cheeks flushed. "What?"

"Nothing," he lied.

She licked her lips, and he followed the motion with his eyes. "It doesn't seem like nothing."

He looked up and met her gaze. Her eyes seemed clouded with something that he couldn't read but somehow understood. Lashes fluttering, her gaze dropped to his lips, and he would have given anything in that moment to know what she was thinking. He moved closer, just the tiniest bit, and her eyes fell shut as she held her breath. Not knowing what to do with the strain in his chest, Soren leaned even closer, getting lost in the smell of grapefruit.

Her breath hitched just as his lips were just about to touch hers, and then Loxly shouted down the hall, "Hurry it up in there! I'm starvin'!"

Soren had never considered murder so seriously before, but he did in that moment. Images of strangling the sharpshooter flooded his mind as Larken jumped back like he was an open flame that had just burned her. She turned, capping the lotion and hiding her red face behind her hair. Soren stood, not wanting to prolong her embarrassment any further, and left her room. Walking down the hall, Soren grabbed Loxly by the neck and led him to the table. Even over the music, he could hear the faucet in the bathroom being turned on and then Larken splashing what he could only assume was her face. The mutt disappeared down the hall and reappeared a few seconds later, trotting happily after Larken. Her blonde hair was now pulled back at the nape of her neck, her face less red than when he had left her.

When Hinlee asked what had taken so long, Larken claimed that Soren was acting like a baby, and he didn't offer up any contradictions. She refused to even look at him throughout dinner and then didn't even wish him a good night before turning in, leaving him to wonder the rest of the night if he had just ruined everything between them.

CHAPTER 27

L arken stood in a world made of pink, orange, and yellow glass. Everything was smooth surfaces and shimmering waves of sunset. She couldn't remember what she was doing, but she thought she had been looking for something. Or, was it someone? Taking a step, her heeled shoe clicked against the glass, and she looked down to find herself in the outfit that she had worn in the crash. No, not the crash; the Vixon wasn't anywhere in sight, only the swirling colors. She took another step, and then another, hearing only the clicking of her heels. Something felt wrong, and after she took another step, she realized that she wasn't tripping over herself.

Looking down at her feet again, she heard a snide voice say, "It's a shame I raised such a disappointment."

Larken's head shot up. "Mother?"

Cornella Hale stood before her, dressed all in black with her lips painted red. She looked like a spider, and Larken shivered as she took in the familiar frown. Her light brown hair was pulled back into its signature twist, and her nails were painted the same shade as her lips. Larken's mother narrowed her heavily painted eyes and sneered, "Why couldn't you be more like Liam?"

Larken's eyes burned. "Liam is lazy, why would you want me to be like him?"

"Liam has my eyes."

"I've done everything you've ever asked!" Larken cried, a tear slipping free.

"It's not enough!" her mother hissed. Her lips parted, and her teeth turned to fangs, as her nails grew to sharp points.

Larken screamed, and then her mother pushed her. She tied to catch herself, but she fell through the glass. Her hair whipped past her, and Larken flailed wildly, trying to find anything to hold onto. She lost one heel, then the other, and her feet burned as the bottoms split open and began to bleed. A voice echoed in her mind, asking what had happened to her shoes, but when she opened her mouth to answer, only screams came out.

She hit the floor hard, and the glass shattered under her, cracking the swirling sunset. The colors seeped out from beneath her, making the world around her hazy as the glass dug into her shoulder. Tears seeped from her closed eyes as she shrieked in pain, too afraid to look at the damage.

A hand cupped her cheek gently, and she stopped screaming. Larken opened her eyes and relief flooded her. Soren was there, eyes a heated green. "Don't be such a baby."

Leaning down, he pushed her shirt off her right shoulder and kissed the top of it, taking the pain away. Slowly, he moved up her shoulder to her neck, where he sucked at the skin just under her ear, making her sigh. Letting her eyes fall closed, she tangled her fingers in his hair, reveling in how soft it felt. He moved up to her jaw, kissing down to her lips. He pulled away just long enough to tell her how perfect she was, and then his lips finally touched hers.

Larken gasped and bolted upright in bed, startling Estelle awake. Sweat made Larken's nightshirt stick to her skin, and her hair was plastered to the back of her neck. Her heart beat rapidly in her throat, and she couldn't gulp down enough air. Feeling feverish, Larken stumbled out of bed, leaving the small dog to stretch out as much as she could across the sheets. Grabbing some clothes, Larken wobbled on her shaky legs all the way to the bathroom and into the shower. Not even bothering to strip out of her sweat-soaked clothes, Larken turned the knob to cold and stood under the spray until she shivered and no longer felt like she might melt.

Shucking off her wet clothes, Larken continued with her shower like nothing had happened, telling herself that everything was fine. She was the one who was making it weird; people had dreams about kissing their Squad Captains all the time. Especially if those Captains had eyes that couldn't decide if they wanted to be gold or green, and they smelled like leather and freshly tilled earth, and they had gravely voices that made any girl's knees weak…

Larken closed her lips tightly and screamed through her nose, putting her face under the jets. This couldn't be happening. What was wrong with her? What was wrong with him for confusing her like this? Larken groaned and started soaping up her hair, wondering what was happening to her life. Wasn't it bad enough that she had to deal with everything else? And now, some gorgeous Captain was threatening to turn her life into a living Shadric Barlow song, and she had no idea how to handle that.

Turning off the water, Larken quickly dressed and was on her way back to her room, when a loud knock shook the dorm door. Larken looked around, wondering what time it was and who would be knocking on their door on a Saturday morning. Eyes landing on the clock on the wall as Estelle's barks sounded throughout the dorm, she saw that it was already 11:00. The knock sounded again, causing her furry friend to come bounding out of her room, and Larken looked around. When it was clear that no one was going to answer it, she tentatively made her way to the door.

Nudging Estelle back with her foot, Larken opened the door to find a very frazzled-looking man with a peppermint pink suit, brown leather shoes, and deep navy-colored hair that still held a subtle wave even though it had been slicked over to the side. He held an armload of garment bags that Larken raised a skeptical brow at and the handle to a rolling luggage case that was almost as big as him. The man stared warily at an equally suspicious Mr. Chin.

Jing looked incredibly excited and asked, "Are we going to play dress-up?"

The man gasped, looking like he might faint, and in a very haughty Star accent exclaimed, "Absolutely not! Maxim only knows what disgusting and sticky residue is covering those fingers!"

Larken rolled her eyes as she opened the door wide enough to let them all in. Jing squealed as Estelle jumped on her and started licking her fat cheeks. "You turned it on!"

"I did." Larken grinned as Jing hugged the android and petted it.

"What's its name?"

"Her name is Estelle." Estelle tilted her head at the sound of Larken saying her name.

Hinlee then came out of her room and asked, "Larken, is someone here? Who is it?" Estelle left Jing to go get some attention from Hinlee.

"A pleasant surprise," she answered, and then glanced at the man before adding, "And a prissy Star, apparently."

He glowered as he drew himself up to his full height. "I am here as a *personal* favor to Captain Braves, and despite everything I have heard about how difficult Miss Hale was to work with, I promised I would give you the benefit of the doubt, especially since I know exactly how unpleasant Cameron Brady can be. But," he looked her up and down like she was a poor dog who couldn't help her ignorance, "it would seem that the rumors were correct."

Larken saw Jing pull her foot back the same moment her father did. He picked her up and she kicked nothing but the air in front of her. Larken was tempted to kick the man herself; only her foot would land a little higher than his shin.

"You might hate Cam, but you're just as snobbish," Larken retorted. "What do you want?"

"I have your dresses for the evening."

"She needs more than one?" Hinlee asked, stepping over Estelle and joining the conversation. The mechanic reached out and fingered a garment bag that housed loose bits of pink lace.

The man looked like he was trying to burn her with his eyes alone. Taking a step back so Hinlee was forced to let go, he muttered, "Captain Braves insisted that Miss Hale needed options, claiming that she would cause him bodily harm if he only provided one."

"At least he's learning," Hinlee murmured, bumping Larken's hip with hers.

"Bodily harm?" Mr. Chin inquired.

"Yes, I believe *castration* was the word he used."

Jing looked at her father, her face scrunched up. "What does *cast-mation* mean?"

"Nothing," her father answered, pushing her into the common room. "Go find something to watch on the television while I talk to Miss Hale." Jing obeyed, Estelle quickly joining her on the couch, and Mr. Chin dropped the bag he had slung over his shoulder. Sounds of some action flick flooded the room as Mr. Chin said, "Loxly said that she could stay overnight so I could go check in on my mother."

"Of course!" Larken smiled. "Although, I'm not really sure where the guys are." She looked to Hinlee, who only shook her head and shrugged, though the gleam in her eyes suggested she wasn't being completely honest. "But," Larken continued, "they're bound to show up eventually."

"Thank you." He gave her a small bow of his head and then called his daughter back to him. Jing bounded over, Estelle hot on her tail and the remote still in her hand, and fell into his arms. He squeezed her tightly, saying, "You listen to everything that Miss Hale and Loxly tell you."

"Yes, Papa."

"You are my whole world," he murmured, kissing her cheek and making Larken's stomach twist in jealousy. The two finished their goodbye, and then Mr. Chin left, calling over his shoulder a last reminder for Jing to behave herself.

As soon as the door closed, Jing wrapped her small arms around Larken's legs and looked up at her with pleading dark eyes. "Can we play dress-up now?"

"How about some lunch first?"

The small girl's face fell, but she nodded as she put her hand into Larken's and followed her to the kitchen. Larken picked Jing up, the remote still in the girl's hand, and set her on the counter before asking if she wanted a sandwich. Getting the bread out, Larken ignored the Star complaining about how they didn't have time for this and how children and animals ruined everything. Rolling her eyes, Larken made a face at Jing that had her covering her mouth to suppress her giggles.

"Do you want anything?" Larken called to Hinlee, who waited for them at the table and rubbed Estelle's rump with her bare foot.

"No, I already ate."

Larken helped Jing down after giving her two cups of water and then grabbed the two plates. Getting settled at the table, she prayed with Jing, and then took a large bite. The roast beef had Larken sighing in contentment, and with her mouth still full, she asked, "So, you don't have any idea where the guys went?" '

"Nope. All I know is that Brecker woke me up this morning and told me that they would be back before you had to leave."

Larken huffed and took another bite.

"Maybe they're playing dress-up too," Jing offered, a tomato seed stuck to her upper lip.

Larken smiled and used the girl's napkin to brush it away. "You're probably right. I don't think Loxly owns any clothing that isn't military-issued."

Hinlee's eyes sparkled and she opened her mouth to no doubt make a joke at Loxly's expense, but the Star cut her off by demanding, "I would appreciate it if you kept your creature away from me."

Larken looked over to see Estelle sniffing at the man's feet. Rolling her eyes, she said, "She's an android. Just tell her to leave you alone if you don't want her by you." Larken took a drink and muttered under her breath, "Although, how you can tell a face that cute to leave you alone, I have no idea."

The Star shooed the android away, and Estelle dejectedly found a space on the couch to curl up on. Larken wolfed down the rest of her sandwich, wanting to get this over with as soon as possible. Putting her dishes in the dishwasher, she walked up to the Star, who was now turning their common room into his own personal fitting room. He assembled a makeshift clothesline and began hanging up the dresses. When he looked up to see her, he sighed irritatedly and, as if he couldn't help himself any longer, asked, "Did you even bother to brush your hair today?"

Larken reached up and scratched her scalp, the hair there still damp. She could only shrug. "I was going to brush my hair, and then someone knocked on my door."

The man sighed, fetched the chair that Soren usually used from the table, and set it by his things. Motioning her to sit in it, he began pulling out electric baubles and turning them on. They started to float above his head, pouring out white light into the room. He looked at Larken's face as if she were a bacteria under a microscope, and he hoped to make a new discovery.

He shook his head. "When was the last time you had your eyebrows done?"

Larken balled her hands at her sides so she wouldn't reach up and touch her face. "The day before I shipped out."

"I suppose that's when you were last waxed too?"

Larken's face heated. "I know how to use a razor. I'm not a complete idiot."

The Star gave her a look that suggested otherwise. He started digging around in the drawers in the top of his luggage carrier, which turned out to be a giant caboodle. Pulling out what he would need to melt the wax, he simply said, "My name is Carl. We might as well use first names since we are about to become very close."

Larken groaned and stood, not missing this part of her pampering at all. "The bathroom is this way." She looked at Hinlee, asking her silently if she could keep her eye on Jing until this was all over.

Hinlee nodded and sent her off to be waxed, plucked, and whatever else Carl had in store for her before she re-entered society.

"I still don't understand why I can't be the one to go. She thinks I am anyways, so what's the problem?" Loxly adjusted his collar in the floor-length mirror and winked at himself. "Besides, I look fantastic in a suit."

The clerk that was helping them obviously agreed. She had dark brown hair that she had pulled back into a ponytail that curled at the ends and a pair of bright blue eyes that she couldn't take off of Loxly. Any of them, really. She had nearly choked as the four hardened military men walked into her little Star boutique and hadn't been able to decide who she liked looking at the most. She had been pushy, insisting that she take all their measurements, and fitted them out with suits, even though they all insisted Soren was the only one who needed it. A part of him was glad that Brecker and Levi seemed to be suffering just as much as him, but Loxly was yucking it all up like an attention-starved puppy.

Brecker, who sat in an uncomfortable-looking straight-back chair, said, "Because you wouldn't make it five minutes into the show without passing out."

"Says who?" Loxly demanded.

"Says the fact that anytime Larken watches something of culture, you're snoring on her shoulder before the opening credits are finished," Levi grumbled. He leaned against the wall, jacket discarded, sleeves rolled up, and hands stuffed into his pockets.

"*I'm cultured*," Loxly insisted.

"Knowing six different breeds of cows does not make you cultured, it makes you weird." Soren pulled at his collar, but the clerk slapped his hand away.

Loxly harrumphed, knowing that they were all right about the show, but not liking it. They had been having this same argument since they left base that morning. He didn't like that everyone had seemed to give the extra ticket to Soren, but there was nothing he could do about it. Soren knew that Loxly was aware there was nothing romantic between him and Larken, but that hadn't stopped him from teasing or flirting with her whenever he could. And even though he never said anything, Soren had caught the sharpshooter looking between him and Larken with more interest than Soren thought necessary.

Soren had been fully fitted in a white shirt, black slacks, shoes and a jacket to match, and a black satin tie. He wouldn't lie, he filled the suit out well, and he had seen more than one approving once-over from the clerk. But it wasn't her opinion that had his stomach in knots. Soren felt more stupid in that suit than he could ever remember feeling. He didn't look like himself; instead, he looked like someone from the Military District trying to pass for a Star. Which, he kind of was, but he pushed that thought from his mind.

"I still think I'm gonna get it," Loxly said, bringing the subject back to himself.

"It will get rumpled under your gear," Brecker mocked.

"Like Hinlee wouldn't love to see you in one," Loxly tossed back.

Brecker's cheeks heated and Loxly laughed. It looked like Soren wouldn't be the only one making a purchase after all.

"What about you, Levi?" Loxly asked.

"What about me?"

"You're gonna need a suit when you get your award for being the grumpiest field-medic."

Levi gave Loxly a dark look that had Brecker and Soren chuckling.

"*Suit yourself*," Loxly said with a grin, causing the rest of them to groan. Loxly laughed at his own joke like he was the funniest guy in the world, which to him, he probably was. Clapping his hands, Loxly was suddenly all business. "Right, now for the fun part."

"There's a fun part?" Brecker asked.

"Of course there is." Loxly gave him a very Hinlee-esque smile that said he had been planning something. "Time to look at the dresses."

"If you want to wear a dress, that's none of my business," Soren said with a smirk.

"Very funny, Cap." His face went serious. "It's not for me. It's for Larken."

The laughing stopped as they all looked to the only man who had been thinking of more than how much he didn't want to be there. Soren grumbled something, irritated with himself. Of course Larken wouldn't have a dress. He was here looking at suits, and she was back at the dorm, probably watching something stupid on the television. Soren had assumed that General Maxwell would bring her something from the Manor, but he wasn't going with her anymore. Soren was, and he hadn't even thought once about how her perfect night was falling apart. He had been so annoyed that it was him that had to go, he didn't even think of the reason why he was going in the first place.

The four men just looked at each other, not saying anything. The clerk, who had been blatantly eavesdropping, squealed, "This is so exciting! What size is the lucky girl?"

"Perfection." Loxly grinned and then threw his arms up as Brecker and Levi booed and threw their shoeboxes at him.

The girl only laughed and asked the four of them to follow her. She asked them a series of questions that none of them could answer. Soren grew frustrated at the sheer amount of information that the clerk needed to know, and that none of them had any answers. Loxly, just as fed up as him, pulled out his communicator and called General Maxwell, asking him for help.

The clerk took the communicator gratefully and began taking notes on a sketch pad that had a half-finished model wearing a large red hat with cropped pants to match. Once she finished jotting down what she needed to know, she disappeared into the mass of clothing racks and started pulling out dresses. When she returned, she handed the communicator back to Loxly and hung up three dresses on the hooks by the mirrors they had all just been standing in front of. Turning, she claimed, "These are the only ones I have that would fit her."

Loxly started laughing and walked up to the one on the left. It was frilly, magenta, and would have made Larken look more like a loofa than a woman going to the opera. "I'd suggest this one, but somehow, I don't think Larken would let me live if I brought it home."

"Maybe you should bring it then, just in case," Levi suggested.

Loxly tossed the dress to him. "I think it would look better with your figure, green-eyes."

Levi's response was cut off by the clerk shrieking. They all looked at her and she exclaimed, "Do you have any idea how much that dress costs?!"

"Uh…*no?*" Loxly answered.

"20,000 arii!"

Levi almost dropped the thing, not wanting to be responsible for ruining it. He quickly hung it up as Loxly asked, "*20,000?!*" Looking to Soren, he rubbed the back of his neck and asked, "What are we gonna do, Cap?"

Soren turned to the clerk, and she raised an eyebrow at him. He had quite a bit of arii saved up, with two arii to a token, but even he didn't have anywhere near enough for the suit *and* a dress. He just frowned and asked, "Do you have anything cheaper?"

She pursed her lips, thinking, and then gasped. "There is something, I just got it in last week, but I haven't put it out because it isn't designer. I honestly didn't know what I was going to do with it. Let me go see what size it is."

With that, she bounced off into a back room, and the four soldiers looked at each other. Brecker finally voiced the question that they were all thinking. "What are we going to do if it isn't the right size? Hinlee will kill me if we come back without a dress."

"I can spare 1,000 tokens," Levi offered.

Loxly rubbed at the back of his neck again. "1,100."

Brecker mentally added in how much he could spare, tapping

his fingers to his palm as he added. "Which means, Soren would need 7,100 tokens."

"Which, I don't have."

The clerk returned, breathless and carrying a scrap of black fabric. "I think it might work!"

Soren took the dress from her and held it up to the other two that she had brought out with the magenta one. It wasn't like the teal sequined dress that cut down to where Larken's belly button would be, or like the lavender one with a skirt made out of layered tulle. It was a simple, one-shoulder black dress made of breathable fabric. Soren knew immediately that this was the one, not because it was cheap, but because it was simple and wouldn't draw much attention.

He looked to the clerk and nodded. She beamed and took the dress. "I'll take this up front and bag it. Just bring me your suits when you're ready to check out."

Levi let out a sigh of relief and was the first one into a changing room. Soren changed, trying not to wrinkle the suit. He knotted his boots and was out of the changing room as fast as he could manage. It had made him feel cramped, and he smacked his elbow on the wall more than once.

Everyone already stood next to the clerk, scanning their communicators for their suits. Soren headed that way, and he was almost there when something caught his eye. Loxly hollered for him to hurry it up.

Looking over at the sharpshooter, he said, "I'll meet you at the aircraft."

Loxly shrugged. "You heard 'em, boys, let's go."

The three of them filed out of the boutique, and Soren waited until they were out of eyesight before leaning down and examining the necklace he had spotted. It hung on a little bracket that was shaped like a T, and the thin silver chain sparkled in the afternoon sunlight. It wasn't the chain that had caught his eye though; it was the milky pearl that hung from it.

Memories of flying to Field E, before Larken had almost died, danced in his mind. They had reached the point where they could just barely glimpse the sea, and she had reached up and touched the window. He didn't know if the sea had a special memory for her, or if it just represented something, but he had never seen someone look like that before. She had looked so hopeful and so defeated in that moment, like it caused her a pain that she couldn't help but love, and it had twisted something inside him.

Carefully, so he wouldn't snap the chain with his fingers, Soren lifted the necklace from its bracket and brought it to the clerk. He nodded at it and asked, "How much for that?"

The clerk smiled but kept what she was thinking to herself as she answered, "2,000 arii."

He nodded and noticed for the first time that she wasn't unpleasant to look at; it just wasn't the same as looking at Larken. Whereas this girl's eyes were a bright blue, Larken's constantly shifted between blue and green depending on what she was thinking. Shaking his head, Soren tried to get Larken out of his mind. He thought she was always on his mind before, but that was before he had almost kissed her, before she had closed her eyes and let him lean into her, and before he could almost feel the shape of her lips with his own.

The clerk told him what he owed, and Soren let her scan his communicator. Smiling again, she held up the black box she had placed the necklace in and asked, "What bag do you want this in?"

Not answering, he just took it from her and put it in his pocket. He nodded again at her, silently giving her his thanks.

"Have a nice weekend!" she called.

The warm air hit Soren's face as he opened the door and waved at her. It cleared his head a little, but he still felt like he was losing his mind.

Loxly was already in the pilot's seat, drumming his fingers on the steering wheel. They had requested a four-seater aircraft to take with them off base, and Soren would have to request another one for later when he got back. He just hoped that the evening would go as smoothly as his shopping trip had.

CHAPTER 28

Larken huffed and griped loudly as she tried to force the zipper in the back up over her ribcage. A strand of hair fell into her face, and she blew it away more forcefully than she needed to.

"Come out, and I can help you," Carl called.

Giving up, Larken stopped twisting her shoulders to reach the zipper and left her room. She stomped down the hall, crossing her arms as she reached the common room. Estelle snoozed contentedly with her head on Hinlee's thigh. The mechanic gently rubbed the android's belly and leaned against the chair that Jing had stolen from Larken to watch the show. Jing's black hair had been curled and pulled up to the top of her head, and she was garbed in a frilly orange dress that Larken had nixed without even trying on. Carl applied blush to her cheeks as she beamed at him.

Carl turned out to be a pretty okay guy. Larken had made a joke about him having to buy her dinner after waxing her while she applied the lotion to take away the sting, he had barked a laugh, and his snobbish exterior melted away. He had warmed up to Jing pretty quickly too, once he learned that her mom had died, and she had never been able to play dress-up or mess around with makeup before. Since then, he had been referring to her as Princess Jing and had been more than willing to give her a complete makeover. He was still wary of Estelle though, and Larken had a hard time getting over that.

The Star looked up as Larken cleared her throat, and his jaw dropped. "That's it! That's the one!"

"This is most definitely not the one!" Larken seethed. "This dress is embarrassing, and I feel like a piggy pouch!"

Hinlee sniggered as Jing asked what a piggy pouch was. Looking at the girl, Hinlee explained, "It's a sausage wrapped in a biscuit, so it looks like it's wearing a blanket."

Jing scrunched up her face as she looked at Larken. "That doesn't look like a blanket."

Carl laughed as he stood and crossed over behind Larken. She felt his warm fingers brush across her back as he messed with the zipper. Larken heard the zip more than she felt it, the dress already so tight. It was candy apple red and hugged her like a second skin. There were no straps, and it cut off just under her backside, making it look more like she squeezed into a cloth tube than a dress.

"I don't see what the problem is," Carl complained. "No one will be able to keep their eyes off of you."

"That *is* the problem!" Larken huffed.

She had already tried on a floor-length, shapeless emerald gown with incredibly thin straps she hadn't trusted and a slit that went all the way up to her left hip. Tried a pink lacy dress that had cut off above her knees and fell into a sort of train in the back. She had also tried on a dark navy dress made up of lace and tulle that had hugged her curves and flared at her calves. That one had been Jing's favorite because it had reminded the child of a mermaid. The rest Larken hadn't even been willing to try on since they were either cut low enough to show off the majority of her belly or a see-through mesh material that Larken had made a face at.

"Well, you are *Larken Hale*. There's going to be staring either way."

"You don't need to remind me, Carl."

"Just trying to help!" he chirped, his tone teasing.

The door opened, and Estelle woke up with a bark as Loxly

stumbled into the common room with an armload of gift bags. He dumped them all onto the table before even sparing them a glance, and then when he did, he frowned at Larken. His eyes moved down her body, landing on her bare feet, and he said, "I hope that's for makin' me sandwiches and not to go out in public."

"Doesn't she look amazing?" Carl asked, obviously still hoping he could talk Larken into choosing it.

"She'll turn heads, that's for sure." Loxly's tone sounded more irritated than she had ever heard it before.

"Relax, I'm not wearing it."

Loxly perked up, and he finally took in the mess Carl had made of the common room. "So, what's goin' on here then?"

"We're playing dress-up for the party tonight!" Jing answered excitedly.

Loxly's eyes fell on Jing, and then he feigned confusion. Looking around, he asked, "Little Bird, Hinlee, did you hear that? It sounded like my sweet Jing, but I can't find her anywhere. All I can find is a Princess."

Jing giggled and hopped off the chair. She rushed to Loxly, Estelle running alongside her, nipping at the hem of the dress. Loxly caught her and spun her in the air as she shouted, "It's me, Loxly!"

"Could this little angel possibly be my Jing?" He stopped spinning and took in her grinning face. "Hmm," he mused, "you look a lot like Jing, but I'm still not convinced. Tell me something that only Jing would know."

Jing placed her finger against her chin as she thought. Then she said, "You don't want Larken to marry Shadric Barlow!"

Loxly stumbled back, pretending to be physically hurt by her words. Jing laughed, but Larken's stomach knotted. The Shadric Barlow that Jing was talking about wasn't the same one that Larken now thought of. Before, he had been nothing more than a silly girlish fantasy that she could tease Loxly about; now he was a Faithful who she tried not to think about.

Loxly set Jing down, and she rushed to the stereo. *Sunset Dreams* could soon be heard blaring from the device, and Loxly just shook his head in defeat. Grabbing the gift bag closest to him, he walked over to Larken. Handing it to her, he smiled sheepishly and said, "We didn't know you had called a stylist, so we picked this out for you while we were gone."

Larken peered into the navy bag, but white tissue paper hid whatever was inside it. Looking back up at Loxly, Larken could only say, "I didn't call him."

Carl walked over and tried to get a good look at what was inside the bag as well. "Captain Braves sent me."

Loxly tried to hide his scoff, but he didn't do a good job.

"You better hurry up and try it on," Carl murmured. "We're running out of time, and I still have to do your hair and makeup."

Carl tugged the zipper at the back of her dress down a little without prompting and ushered her back to her room. She kicked the door closed as she pulled the zipper the rest of the way and then had to fight to get the dress past her hips. When the red satin pooled around her feet, Larken stepped out of it and pulled the tissue paper from the bag. Carefully, she took out the contents and gasped when she unfolded the black dress. Hot tears pricked her eyes as she took in the simple design. They did this for her because they thought she wouldn't have anything to wear. She was going to wear the pants she had when she came to base and a nice shirt she had ordered a while back, but they had wanted her to have a good time.

Larken sniffed back her emotions and pulled the dress on. It fit like a glove, and she thought she might burst from the love she felt from her friends. There was a knock on her door, and Larken sniffed again as Loxly called, "Does it fit? Do you need help with a zipper or somethin'?"

Shaking herself, she opened her door. "No, the zipper was on the side. Thanks though."

Loxly didn't appear to have heard her, he was too busy staring. His eyes flicked up to hers, and then his admiration faltered. Cupping her cheek, he said, "You don't like it."

Larken had to fight to keep her lip from wobbling. Covering his hand with hers, she stared him in the eye as she said, "This is the best dress I've ever owned."

Loxly beamed at her, and Carl ruined the moment by calling, "I'd like to see this best dress sometime today!"

Loxly glared down the hall, but Larken only laughed, insisting that he wasn't that bad.

"He works for Braves," Loxly insisted.

"He's better than Cam and Cindy, so I have no problem with him. Besides, he made Jing's whole week."

Loxly couldn't argue, and the two made their way down the hall. Upon seeing the dress, Carl smiled and Hinlee called, "Hottie comin' through!"

Estelle bounded up to Larken and put her little paws up on her leg. The small dog sniffed at the dress as her silicone pads slipped against Larken's lotion-slicked thigh.

Carl ushered Larken to Soren's chair and gently pushed her into it. He opened up a drawer in the bottom of the giant caboodle and pulled out a pair of black pumps. They weren't as tall as the ones Cam had made her wear on her initiation day, but they still made Larken's eyes widen. Grabbing her ankle, he slipped one shoe on, and then the other, saying, "*There.*"

Carl and Loxly helped Larken to her feet, and she wobbled once before finding her footing. Hinlee was over by the stereo with Jing, listening to the girl tell her about Shadric Barlow's new song. An acoustic guitar sounded, and the singer poured out his heart while Jing talked over him.

Larken thought it a pleasant enough melody but couldn't be sure if it really was his best one yet until she listened to it herself. Jing seemed to think it was though, so she turned it up even more as Larken started to follow Carl and his many baubles to the bathroom. The phrase, "*So much like the sea, your blue-green eyes stop the heart in me,*" had Larken stumbling and falling into Carl.

"Watch it! I just had this pressed," he grumbled, brushing away the wrinkles that Larken had caused.

"Sorry."

Hinlee and Loxly chuckled to themselves, not knowing that it hadn't been her own clumsiness that had tripped her that time.

It can't be...

Larken's heart pounded in her ears, and she couldn't get his words out of her head. He couldn't be talking about her, could he? No, there was no way. He wouldn't openly draw attention to the fact that they had somehow met while she was on base. She wasn't allowed to leave, and if he hadn't had an approved visit, that really only left two options. The public would be able to figure out that he was either one of the psychopaths that shot her out of the sky or one of the Faithfuls that had almost killed her in the woods.

Larken shook her head, trying to clear it. She needed answers, and she wouldn't be able to stop thinking about it until she had them. Larken left Carl at the bathroom door and grabbed her communicator from her room. She would simply look up the lyrics, and then she would know for sure that he was talking about someone else he thought was stunning that also had blue-green eyes.

Carl was tapping his foot and reminded her again that they didn't have all day when he followed her into the bathroom. Soren's chair had been moved in there, and Larken had been so distracted that she hadn't even realized that Loxly had brought it in. He gave her a warm smile as he left the bathroom, and Larken worried that he could see how panicked she was. This wasn't just about everyone learning that she had lied to them about not recognizing anyone in the woods; it was about Shadric Barlow announcing to the world that Larken had almost killed him while he attacked her with his buddies.

Carl started on Larken's hair, not burning her with the curling iron or stabbing her with a bobby pin once, as Larken searched furiously for the lyrics. When she found them, she saw that nothing pointed to her other than the lyrics about the eyes. Larken sighed, relief flooding her. He was talking about someone else. She tried to ignore the heartbreak of her inner thirteen-year-old and told herself that it was better this way. He had completely forgotten about her, and now she could forget about him as well.

"Those weren't your eyes Shadric Barlow was singing about just now, were they?" Carl asked, his tone dripping with curiosity.

"*Pffft*, no!" Larken scoffed, laughing.

"Just wondering…"

"Well don't, and if I hear a rumor that the two of us are secretly dating, I'll know who to go after."

"Just don't mess up my face too bad; my girlfriend wouldn't be very happy with you."

Larken met his gaze in the mirror. "You have a girlfriend?"

The smile he gave her melted his features, and he looked like a fool in love. "Candy. We grew up together, and she bullied me into asking her out four years ago. We've been together ever since."

"So…" Larken mused, turning the tables, "is she the one?"

"Most definitely." Carl came around in front of her and looked her dead in the eye, suddenly serious. "Now, stop talking so I can do your makeup."

Larken looked over the different cosmetics that he must have brought in while she had been trying on one of the dresses and found soft, simple shades that she preferred to the vibrant ones that Cam's team usually picked for her. He brushed a curl that had fallen from her updo out of her face and started dusting her eyes with a sandy gold. He contoured her lids with a pale olive color, teasing her about how her eyes really did look like the sea now.

After what felt like forever, Carl sat back, having just finished her lips. They felt odd—she wasn't used to anything being on them, but he insisted the pink-mauve color he had painted them with wouldn't come off, no matter how much she bit them. Not that she would purposely try to ruin his work. He made her feel better about herself than Cam ever did, and she was honestly a little excited to see what the others thought. She felt beautiful, and she didn't know how to thank Carl for what he had done for her. He was so different from the man that had barged into their dorm hours ago, and Larken was glad to have met him.

When she began to thank him, he brushed her words away, saying, "Prince Charming hasn't gotten a good look at his Cinderella, so don't thank me just yet."

Larken laughed and followed him out of the bathroom, communicator still in hand. She walked out into the common room, and Loxly greeted her with a loud whistle. He grinned and said, "Well don't you look purdy."

Larken looked him up and down, frowning when her eyes settled on his mud-caked military-issued boots. Meeting his eyes, she asked, "Where's your suit?"

"In my room."

"Well, go put it on." Larken could feel everyone's eyes on her. "We have to leave."

Loxly rubbed the back of his neck, looking sheepishly behind her. Larken looked at him for a moment longer before following his eyes with her own. She turned slowly, and her jaw dropped as she took in the sight before her. Soren stood there, hands in his pockets, and dressed like he was ready for a net drama award ceremony. His hair had been brushed out of his face, and his eyes sparked green as they bore into hers. He looked so deliciously handsome that her knees suddenly felt weak. The world had stopped moving for a minute, and Larken had to remind herself to breathe. It was just the two of them in that moment, and nothing else mattered.

Realizing that she was still gawking at him like an idiot, Larken clamped her mouth shut and dropped her eyes to her feet. Loxly walked up behind her and gently grabbed her arms. "Sorry, Little Bird, but I didn't think you'd enjoy yourself if I was snorin' in the seat next to you while you were tryin' to watch the show."

Larken couldn't say anything as her eyes found Soren's again. She felt herself blush, and she suddenly remembered the dream she had the night before. Larken waited for Soren to say something, anything, but instead of complimenting her, he scowled. Her heart fell, but she really wasn't surprised.

Sighing, she stepped out of Loxly's grip and asked, "Are you ready?"

Soren nodded and made for the door. Larken hung back long enough to say goodbye to Estelle and receive a hug from Jing. Hinlee hugged her too, telling her that she looked gorgeous, and Brecker and Levi complimented her as well. Carl waved goodbye as she reached the door Soren held open for her and called, "Don't do anything I wouldn't do!"

When Soren let the door close behind them, a heavy silence filled the air. It was so thick that Larken was finding it hard to breathe. Soren didn't help anything by putting his hand on her lower back and leading her to the hangar. The two of them received plenty of curious looks along the way, but no one dared to stop and ask them what they had planned. Larken tried to keep her head down, not liking all the attention, but she would be lying if she said she wasn't tempted to laugh at the way Soren scowled at everyone they passed.

Once they reached the hangar, Soren led her wordlessly to a two-seater black aircraft that looked to be a newer model than any of the others she had seen on base. He opened the door for her and didn't say anything as he helped her in, careful not to touch her updo as he did so. When he climbed in and fired up the engine, he let out a long sigh and grabbed the steering wheel. He frowned out the window and then used the little radio to request leave. His voice sounded husky like he hadn't spoken in hours, and Larken turned to look out her window. The words, *Don't be such a baby*, playing over and over again in her mind like a song she couldn't get out of her head.

Take-off was smooth and, for some reason, Larken didn't freak out when they shot out past the drop-off and into the sky. The sun had just started to set, bathing the world in pink and yellow clouds, and Larken was once again reminded of her dream. She closed her eyes, trying to forget, but finding it impossible. A hand grabbed hers and pulled her from her thoughts, and Larken looked over to find Soren staring straight ahead, jaw set.

Her eyes fell to the large, impossibly warm hand that clasped hers, and he asked, "You okay?"

"Yes," she whispered, still staring at their clasped hands. "I'm alright."

"Are you nervous?"

Looking back up at him, she asked, "Why would I be nervous?"

"I wasn't sure if this would be something that your family—"

Larken shook her head, cutting him off. "No, Wardell is too young, and my father is probably too drunk to know that the opera is even happening. As for my mother and Liam," Larken let her eyes drop and she squeezed his hand a little harder, "they think anything that I might like is a waste of their time."

Soren tightened his grip as well, and the rest of the ride was silent. They just sat there, quietly holding hands, him giving her the strength she would need to face society, and Larken giving him the strength he would no doubt need to put up with Dominic for the next four hours.

Once they had docked, the sun had fallen a little lower, creating shadows that danced in the sky and the world around them. Larken reached for the button to open her door, but a small tug on her hand had her turning back to the brooding Captain beside her. Soren's eyes were so green, and they seemed almost unsure as they looked at her.

"What?" she asked, dropping her communicator in her lap and reaching up to her face. "Is something wrong with—"

He grabbed her hand just before she could touch her cheek. "No, you look..."

She waited for him to finish, but he never did.

Instead, he let go of her hands and fished for something in his pocket. He took a deep breath and murmured, "I didn't want to give this to you in front of everyone."

He handed her a little black box that she took with shaking fingers. Opening it slowly, she gasped softly when she saw what was inside.

"It's—well, I saw the way you were looking at the sea, and well, I—" Soren grumbled something under his breath, frustrated with himself.

Larken shook her head, grabbing one of his hands again, and waited until he met her eyes. "I love it, thank you."

He frowned and nodded, the look so him that it warmed her heart.

"Will you help me put it on?"

He didn't say anything as he took the box from her and pulled out the pearl necklace. She leaned into him, and his cheek almost brushed against hers as he reached around her. He grumbled again, fumbling with the clasp, and she smiled into his neck. Once she felt it drop against her skin, her hand reached up to touch the pearl as she leaned back a little.

His face was so close to hers, just like it had been the night before when she had waited for him to kiss her. He reached up and cupped her cheek, looked like he wanted to say something, but didn't. Soren let go of her, nodded one last time, and got out of the aircraft. He walked around and opened her door, holding her hand as she got out. Larken looked up and smiled at him, thanking him softly for the help. That was when the first camera flashed, closely followed by a second.

Soren grunted, placed his hand against her lower back, and griped, "Here we go again."

CHAPTER 29

Soren tried his best to protect Larken from the cameras and the reporters that shouted questions at her. She seemed to be trying to melt into his side, and he had to fight the urge to turn them around and march back to the aircraft. The pearl at her chest reflected the camera flashes, making it shine and appear even more opalescent than before. Soren didn't bother trying to smother his pride; he had finally done something right. All those times he had been jealous of Loxly, and all those times he had worried about messing up, they were all forgotten each time she reached up and caressed the precious stone.

Voices called through the air, clashing with the quietness of the gardens the two of them had to walk through to get to the theater's entrance. The reporters cut through the zinnias and snapdragons, asking her about her dress and her new life on base. One question, in particular, had Soren smirking down at her, and she met his eye before scoffing, "Oh, get over yourself."

He raised an eyebrow at her. "What, you aren't going to tell them who your *handsome stranger* is?"

"I could," she teased, "but then they would know where to find us."

"Hmm," he grunted, "good point."

Larken smiled at him, and he was once again blown away by how beautiful she looked all done up like this. She was pretty before, but now she looked breathtaking. So much so that he almost couldn't see the sarcastic thorn in his side, who lazed around the common room in her free time. He knew he would never forget the way she looked in this moment. Her hair pinned up in curls, the way her new dress hugged her curves, and the makeup that made her eyes look like they could see into his very soul. And he would never forget how close he came to crashing his mouth against hers in the hover. Soren had thought he wanted to kiss her the night before, but that was nothing compared to how he felt as he helped her with the necklace.

They made their way through the gardens, ignoring the flashes around them. Larken's communicator buzzed in his jacket pocket next to the tickets, and he assumed it was Braves asking where she was. Larken had given him the device to hold on to shortly after they had entered the gardens. Instead of telling her it went off, he asked, "Any idea where he might be?"

Soren didn't elaborate, not that he needed to. Larken wrinkled her brow and shook her head. "No. By the entrance maybe?"

"Do you want to message him and—"

"No," she said again. "I would rather get inside before we start looking around." She looked up at him conspiratorially. "Fewer cameras in there."

"Good idea." Larken reached up and placed the back of her hand against his forehead. He moved his head out of her reach almost as soon as she touched him. "What?"

"You said I had a good idea; I was worried you might be delirious with fever."

Soren snorted, and she brought her hand up to cover a giggle. He couldn't help but smile at her, wondering how someone so small could wreak so much havoc in his life in such a short time. Another flash lit up the space around them, and Soren pushed her to walk a little faster. She didn't protest, just let him quietly guide her the rest of the way. Larken did well, only tripping twice, and Soren was there to catch her both times.

Her shoulders sagged when they got inside, and he barely heard her relieved sigh. The whole place looked to be made of white marble with red carpet covering the entirety of the floor and gold paint on all the walls. The carpet reminded Soren of blood, and he wondered why they decided red would the best choice. Gold chandeliers hung from the tall ceilings, casting everything in a warm yellow glow. Soren felt extremely out of place, and he had to force himself to relax as they walked through the foyer. If Larken picked up on his discomfort, she didn't say anything, and he was glad.

When they reached the center of the room, Soren almost tripped over Larken. He grabbed her waist, trying to steady himself and keep her upright, but she hadn't seemed to notice. Her eyes were on one of the chandeliers, and her lips were parted in awe. It appeared to be bigger than all the others, and it looked to be covered in diamonds instead of lights. The thing was so huge that Soren almost didn't trust standing underneath it, but with one look at her face, he knew that he would stand there for however long she wanted.

Soren was about to ask if this was her first time here when a voice that made his spine stiffen called Larken's name. She turned to the approaching Captain before her eyes were willing to let go of the chandelier, and she only pulled her eyes away when Braves stood before her.

"You made it," he said with a relieved smile. Braves looked smug in his grey suit and bright red tie, and it made Soren want to hit him. Then, as if the idiot couldn't help himself, he looked Larken up and down, his smile turning more devious. "You look perfect."

"You don't look so bad yourself," Larken said with a little awkward laugh that made Soren fight to keep his scowl.

Braves's smile never faltered as he asked, "Do you have your tickets?"

Larken turned to Soren, her hand disappearing into his jacket pocket. "Yes, they're right—"

"Captain Deckard," Braves sneered, cutting her off as he noticed

Soren for the first time. "What a pleasant surprise. I was under the impression that General Maxwell would be joining us this evening."

"Vallen is quarantined with the flu," Larken said, looking at Braves. "So, Soren offered to come along instead. Is that not okay?"

Face still pale with anger, he forced a smile for her benefit. "It was your ticket; you were free to give it to whomever you wanted. But," Braves grabbed her hand and pulled her from Soren's side to his, "I think it's about time we went and found our seats." He placed her hand in the crook of his elbow. "Shall we?"

Larken looked back at Soren, apologizing silently with her eyes. He gave her a nod and then caught the murderous glare that Braves shot him before Soren was forced to follow them to an overweight man collecting tickets. The portly fellow was almost as short as Larken, and he bowed as they filed into the theater with the other guests. The red carpet continued into the theater and down the aisles, covering the seats as well. Soren cleared his throat as a hushed muffle settled over everything, and he winced at how loud the sound was in the quiet room.

They quickly found their seats, Larken sitting between him and Braves, and she turned to him. "Are you okay?" she whispered.

"Fine."

"Are you sure? Back there it sounded like—"

"Strong perfume," he lied.

She looked at him like she didn't believe him, but he wasn't going to ruin her night by telling her how uncomfortable he felt. The boutique had seemed so long ago, and he wished he could still feel annoyed instead of on-edge.

Braves leaned into Larken's right, pulling her attention from him. Soren allowed it, not wanting her focus to be on him. Instead, Soren peered at the oily-looking wooden stage and a little pit where he saw chairs, a podium, and a pianoforte. Everything was so elegant and glossy, and Soren had to fight the urge to pull at his tie. People around them muttered in hushed tones, like there was a spell on the stage and speaking too loudly would break it.

Larken's communicator buzzed in his pocket again, and this

time Soren pulled it out. He found that the one earlier was indeed from Braves, but he ignored it as he pulled open the one from General Maxwell.

Have fun.

Soren nudged Larken and leaned into her, offering her the device. She took it, not pulling away from him as she typed out a reply. Handing it back, she asked softly, "Did you save the tickets?"

"Do we need them to leave?" he teased.

She rolled her eyes. "I'd like to save mine."

"To remember your date with Braves?"

Her eyes sparked as she teased back, "To remember my date with you."

Soren's voice lodged in his throat as Braves asked, "Was that the General?"

Larken, unable to resist harassing him even more, winked at Soren before she turned and jumped back into conversation with the Star. He could only watch her as she talked, occasionally getting death glares from Braves. Soren was half-tempted to pull Larken into his side just to get a rise out of the man, but he knew that Larken would be furious if he did.

Braves was mid-sentence, talking about all the actors he knew in the performance tonight, when the lights dimmed. He lowered his voice, but Larken hushed him and turned excitedly to the stage. Soon everyone found their seats, and the musicians Soren watched enter the pit not too long ago took up their instruments. A single trumpet sounded as the red curtains drew back, setting the tone for a jovial song that soon poured from the rest of the instruments. A single man stood on stage, dressed in a ridiculous purple and orange outfit, complete with puffy sleeves and a feathered hat. His booming voice cut through the theater, saying what, Soren didn't know. He looked at Larken, unable to help himself, and found her eyes glued to the stage, an awed smile turning her lips. Her hands were clasped in her lap, and a single finger tapped along with the melody.

Three hours later, Soren's eyes burned with the strain of keeping them open. He couldn't ever remember being so bored in his entire life. The seconds passed like hardening molasses, and not even imagining the actors tripping or messing up could keep him entertained anymore. Larken had been a little helpful, at least. Every time a new character appeared or something related to the plot happened, she would lean over and quietly whisper what was going on in his ear. Soren would be lying if he said that he didn't enjoy the look of pure jealousy on Braves's face whenever she did so.

The music wasn't terrible, but he didn't enjoy it either. At first, he had been mildly annoyed that it was all in a different language, but now it grated against his nerves. The instruments weren't enough to drown out the words, and it seemed like the worst singers had the most lines, if that's what they were even called. But he kept his complaints to himself for Larken's sake. Her eyes were still wide and shining like they had been when the curtains first opened.

Soren learned that the man at the beginning had been the narrator, setting up the story in a rural village in a long-forgotten kingdom. There was also a fat woman dressed in shades of orange and gold finery, who was supposedly an overbearing mother married to a man shaped like a stick. The father, who barely had time to squeak in lines between his wife's, was the comic relief, full of snide one-liners, and he often poked fun at his wife's weight. At least, that's what Larken said that's what he was saying. The man could be singing about monkeys and Soren would be none the wiser. Then there was their beautiful daughter, Estelle, who hadn't done any singing yet because her nose had been in a book the whole time. Her mother constantly demanded that she get her head out of the clouds and find a husband, but because she didn't conform to society, none of the other characters really seemed to like her. Except, of course, the two men who were fighting over her. Three, if Soren counted the stable boy who harbored secret affections for her.

The story played out, the two men wooing the girl and fighting for her affections. They had apparently made a bet at the beginning to see who could win over her unattainable heart first. Estelle would be showered with gifts and words of love, then seek advice from her only friend, the stable boy. Her lips remained sealed as the scenes jumped from the suitors' proclamations right to the stable boy's opinions. He would weigh the pros and cons for her, telling her what he thought she wanted to hear, and then saying what he really wanted to tell her after she had left and he was all alone.

Soren's eyes felt bleary, and he was forced to rub them. Larken hadn't explained anything new to him in a while, and the mother had just finished a solo that he thought would never end. When he looked back at the stage, the girl stood with one of the two men who had been fighting over her. But, instead of triumphant melodies of found love, sad strings played alongside the piano, creating a somber mood.

The man, the one that had wooed her with elaborate poetry and flowers, was grinning because he had won. Then, the whole story came out. Larken didn't explain what was happening, but the way the man looked down at Estelle, and the way she looked like she had been hit, told Soren all he needed to know. For the first time in the three hours he had been sitting there, the woman opened her mouth and began to sing. Her voice was clear, loud, and beautiful. After a moment, Soren realized that he recognized the music. Sniffing to his right told him that Larken was trying to gain control of her emotions.

Soren looked at her, and she looked so heartbroken for the character, lost in the words that poured from her. Keeping her eyes on the stage and without any prompting, she whispered, "Why do you grin, foolish man? Know you not that I am more than a possession to be won?"

The man started singing again, his voice drenched in oily pride, and Larken translated, "If you would but look up, you would see that no man wants you. You are lucky to have me."

Estelle started singing again. "Were you not fighting another for me?"

The man laughed. "I fought so that I may prove my own worth."

The words he had heard Larken sing in the shower that day, the melody that he often heard her humming distractedly, spilled out of Estelle. "How could you say such a thing when you have already professed your love? How could such a kind man hurt me so? The words that had once put color into my life are now drowning me, and I cannot reach the surface. How dare you make my heart feel for yours. How dare you force me to feel the emotions of bitter death."

Soren stared as a fat tear rolled down Larken's cheek, somehow knowing that to Braves she appeared stoic. The music seemed to fill Larken, and she looked so impossibly beautiful as the melody tore through her. Larken was so strong all the time, and it didn't seem possible that something as simple as a pretty song could move her like this. But it did...and Soren was there to see the perfect destruction. He thought about reaching up and brushing the tear away, but the music changed again.

A single violin painted the air with heartbreaking notes. Looking back to the stage, he saw the woman on her knees, sobbing into the skirts of her simple gown. Larken sniffed again, and Soren tentatively brushed his knuckles against hers. She didn't twine her fingers with his like he hoped she would, but her hand stayed by his, giving him gentle caresses of her own. The woman started singing again, her words flowing through a somber reprisal of an earlier song that had been bouncy and jovial. Estelle's emotions overtook her, and her voice cracked. Unable to keep singing, she gave in to her sorrow. Then, from somewhere offstage, the stable boy's voice rang out loud and clear, finishing the melody that Estelle couldn't. She looked up as her friend approached her, and they began a duet.

"What my eyes have always seen but never understood," Larken said in a cracked whisper. "What my heart had reached for without my knowing. It is you, my love, always you. And together we will rebuild our souls anew. Give our souls a place where they can live and love for the rest of our days."

They reiterated the last verse again, and Larken shuddered. She looked down and clasped her shaking hands, pulling hers away from his. Another tear slipped from her eye, and this time Soren didn't hold back. He leaned toward her, causing her to look at him. Reaching up, he cupped her cold cheek and used his thumb to brush the hot tear away. Her lips parted, and it looked like she stopped breathing. Larken's teal eyes glittered, and she looked more perfect than he had ever thought possible.

People around them began to stand and cheer, and he realized that the music and singing had stopped. Soren let his hand drop, and he stood as well. Flowers were thrown to the stage as the cast took their bows, but Larken remained seated. Soren would allow her a moment to collect herself, but then they were getting out of here. His tie was choking him with renewed vigor, and he had to fight not to rip it from his neck.

CHAPTER 30

"**D**id you enjoy yourself?" Dominic took up his seat again and looked at her as if he could see through her dress. He had been staring at her like that all night, even though his red tie told her what dress he had wanted her to choose, and Larken had to constantly fight the urge to disappear into Soren's side.

"It was everything I hoped it would be."

"Good, because I've arranged for you to meet the director."

"Dominic, that's not nes—"

"Sure it is. I told you that my mother is friends with him, and he's excited to meet you." He grabbed her hand and helped her to her feet.

Larken shot Soren a glance and found him still standing and tugging at his tie. He wanted to leave as much as she did, if not more. Dominic began pulling her down the row of seats, not giving her an option other than to follow. She hadn't passed two seats when she could feel Soren's warmth at her back, and she had to fight not to melt into it. She loved the dress that the guys had picked out for her, but she was starting to get a little cold.

Through masses of elegantly dressed guests and past the occasional photographer, Dominic led her to the back of the foyer where the entrances to the dressing rooms were. The theater was just the right amount of elegant and cozy, and even though she had never been to this exact one, Larken had always loved the sort of muffled atmosphere that each theater seemed to have. There was just something about the quiet respect for the stage that always made her feel giddy with excitement.

Larken received many looks from the people they passed. Some were snooty, and the old women they belonged to were quick to whisper to their partners behind fans or gloved fingers. Others were more appreciative and lingered a little too long on her thighs, making her tug at the hem of her dress. Larken was about to ask Dominic if she couldn't just leave when a rich laugh cut through the air. Something about it seemed almost familiar, and any thoughts of leaving disappeared as Dominic steered them towards it.

The man's back was to them when they reached him, kissing the actress who had played Estelle on both cheeks. He was tall and appeared to be well built, his dark brown suit fitting him well and showing off a fair amount of muscle. The actress whispered something to him, and he threw his blond head back and laughed again. Dominic pulled her closer to the director and cleared his throat to let him know they were there. The man turned just as Dominic said, "Larken, this is Fisher Fillmar."

The eyes that met hers were the same ones that she saw every time she looked into a mirror. Larken stopped breathing as those teal eyes melted, and a grin broke across the man's handsome face. It was all the same, their eyes, their noses, their cheekbones, even the color of their hair. She could feel Soren at her side instantly, as the people around them faded into the background. Larken felt suddenly dizzy, and the man's features, *Larken's features*, went from excited to worried. Even the way his brows crinkled together was the same.

He took a step towards her, and Larken took a step back, almost tripping over her feet. Soren caught her, and she stupidly said, "I have to use the restroom."

Turning, she stumbled again, and this time Soren had to hold her up to keep her from falling over herself. She didn't know who saw them, or what similarities they picked up on. Soren obviously noticed, but the way Dominic made excuses for her suggested that he hadn't.

Dominic appeared in front of her; she hadn't gotten more than three steps away when he gently pulled her from Soren's grasp. He softly asked, "Are you okay? You look like you might be sick."

Larken managed a weak, "I'm fine."

"Good." He smiled. "Mr. Fillmar was really excited when he heard I was bringing you and asked to meet you."

Larken looked back at the man, not sure what to do. Soren stood behind her, a steady rock, and Dominic in front, the current trying to take her to something she wasn't sure she was ready for. Thoughts of her father clouded her mind, of all the fights he had with her mother, the way he had pulled her close after he found her crying outside their room, the way he started drinking more and more as she grew up. But this man, this *Fisher Fillmar*, Larken didn't know him. She didn't know if she had been purposely kept from him, or if he only now had an interest in her, but Larken had never felt more confused in her life.

A panic started in her chest as Dominic won and dragged her back before the man. His eyes were still crinkled at the corners with concern, but the emotion in them kept her from looking away. She stood rigidly in front of him, and he breathed, "*Larken.*"

Her spine stiffened even more, and her feet tried to run again. Dominic held her there, more worried about disappointing this man than her comfort. When she didn't speak, Dominic moved to shake his hand, saying, "Mr. Fillmar, it's a pleasure. This is Miss Hale's favorite opera. She's a fantastic singer herself."

Soren was there in Dominic's absence before Larken could force herself to take a breath. He pulled her into his side, his hand on her waist to keep her from swaying. Dominic continued to schmooze Fisher, but the man's eyes never left Larken.

Soren gently put his lips to her ear. "Did you know?"

Larken shook her head, not knowing if he was asking if she knew that Dominic had this planned, or if the man before her was her real father. But it didn't matter, the answer to both was the same.

Fisher cut Dominic off and walked tentatively over to her. He slowly reached out and took one of her shaking hands. Offering her a kind smile, he asked, "Miss Hale, if I may?"

Larken could only swallow as he placed her hand in the crook of his elbow and led her through a door that had the word DIRECTOR in gold letters on it. Soren wasn't far behind her and was able to slide in before Fisher closed the door, shutting them in a room with vanities and costumes crammed against one wall and a desk pushed against another. Larken was shaking so badly now that Soren slipped off his suit jacket and wrapped it around her. She was momentarily lost in the comforting smell of leather and tilled earth before she was forced back to reality.

Fisher turned and had his arms wrapped around her in three steps. His suit smelled like spearmint, and he shuddered as he held her. He murmured, "Larken, my little songbird, I'm so sorry. This isn't how I planned this at all."

He pulled back enough to look at her. There were so many things that she wanted to ask, so many things that she didn't want to know the answers to. She felt like she was back in the Vixon, falling to the ground. Her voice was raw as she blurted, "What do you want?"

He offered her a kind smile and let go of her. "I wanted to meet you. That's all. I've spent the last twenty years watching you grow up, wishing that I could have been there."

"Why weren't you?" she accused, not sure what to do with the anger and hurt swirling in her heart.

"As much as I would have loved to hurt your mother by causing a scandal, I didn't want you to have to deal with that."

Larken shook her head, backing away from him into Soren.

"I'm sorry, but I couldn't pass up the chance of meeting you when I heard that Ophelia's son was bringing you tonight."

It was too much, too *unexpected*. She couldn't handle all of this tonight, not when she was already so confused about so many things. A small part of her was glad that she now knew the truth, but that didn't stop her stomach from jumping up to the back of her throat. Larken needed time to think, time to process. And tonight wasn't enough.

"I—I have to go."

Fisher looked hurt, but he didn't do anything to stop her from leaving. Larken knew that she should have been grateful that he was so understanding and willing to give her the space she needed, but she couldn't bring herself to feel anything other than hurt. What she had always suspected, the reason she thought that her father looked at her with so much hurt in his eyes, was true.

Her emotions choked her as she stumbled away from Soren to the door. Dominic was on her the moment she had it open, but she pushed past him, only half-hearing Soren's explanation of her falling suddenly ill. Larken didn't hang around to see if the Star believed the Captain's excuse, nor did she pay any attention to the not-so-hushed comments that started as she rushed past everyone in her attempt at escape.

Pushing past the doormen, Larken stumbled out into the gardens, the cool evening air choking her even more with the scent of snapdragons. Rushing down the steps, she wrapped Soren's jacket around her tighter and tried to lose herself in the garden. When she thought she was far enough away from any cameras, Larken sunk onto the closest bench and sobbed. Soren's jacket caught most of her tears as they fell hotly from her eyes.

A weight on the bench next to her and the warm hands that pulled her close told her that Soren had found her. Larken leaned into his chest, her heart breaking for the man that she had always loved, but no longer knew if he had ever loved her. Soren said nothing as he held her close and let her cry her fill. At some point, he had pulled her into his lap, mistaking her tremors for shivers, and that small act of kindness had her falling apart all over again. Her throat burned with the questions that she wanted to ask him, even though she knew Soren wouldn't have any of the answers.

Larken wanted to know why no one had ever told her, why they let her believe that Trogar Hale was her father her whole life. She was confused, and hurt, and *angry*. Larken wanted to hit something, but she felt too useless to move. She shouldn't be surprised; after all, it was something that she had often wondered herself, but still…

Larken took one last shuddering breath and chanced lifting her head from Soren's chest. She had soaked his dress shirt, but thankfully there were no black stains from her mascara. Her head felt heavy, and she was almost tempted to set it back down when Soren cupped her cheek. She met his eyes, almost afraid of what she would find in them. They shone a golden green in the moonlight, and he looked so hurt for her. Larken's heart squeezed, and she dropped her gaze, afraid of what she might do or say if she kept looking at him.

His voice sounded gruff as he muttered, "It doesn't matter. You're still Larken Hale of Squad 19. Who your parents are won't change that."

Her eyes snapped back up to him, but Soren was already looking away. Taking a shuddering breath, Larken let his words wash over her. He was right; who her family was didn't matter, it never had. How many times had Vallen, Loxly, and Hinlee reminded her of that? They were all her *real* family, and that was all that mattered.

Larken sniffed wetly, using Soren's jacket to wipe away some lingering tears from her jaw. Soren silently helped her to her feet and then kept her close as he led them out of the gardens. There were still a fair amount of aircraft and hovercrafts lingering in the lot, and Soren directed her to where they were docked. He didn't say a word as he helped her into the aircraft, and he was still silent as he climbed into the pilot's seat.

When the door latched, blocking out the outside world, Soren sighed deeply and leaned back into his seat. He didn't lift his head as he turned and looked at her, appearing as exhausted as she felt. The cab felt thick with Larken's raw emotions for a moment, when his lips twitched. His eyes narrowed ever so slightly and danced as he asked, "Estelle, huh?"

CHAPTER 31

From the moment they stepped out of the gardens, Soren had racked his brain for something to say that might make Larken feel better. He would never, as long as he lived, forget the look of complete shock and betrayal that crossed her face when she saw that *Fisher Fillmar*. It wasn't fair that things like this kept happening to her. Soren might not know what Larken wanted for the rest of her life, but he knew that the life she wanted now was a simple and quiet one. She wanted to train during the day and spend time with the ones she loved at night, only to wake up each day to do it all over again. After everything that she had been through, she deserved some happiness.

So, he had decided to bring up the connection between the heroine of the opera he had just been forced to sit through and the little white monster that she had waiting for her back at the dorm. He didn't miss the way her lips twitched as she realized that she had been found out. She thought for a moment before admitting, "Yes, I named my puppy after my favorite operatic character." Then her face fell again. "I suppose I'll have to reprogram another name though."

"Why?"

She curled up in the seat, fingering the button at the left cuff of his jacket. "I won't be able to think of the opera without remembering tonight."

His heart squeezed, not wanting this thing that she loved so much to be ruined for her too. Soren reached out for her hand, pulling her attention back to him. Even though he didn't want to, Soren forced himself to ask, "Tonight wasn't all bad, was it?"

Even in the dark, he could see the color that touched her cheeks as she whispered, "No, not all bad."

Satisfied, and done feeling so vulnerable himself, Soren let go of her hand and yanked off his tie. He wadded the accursed thing up and stuffed it in his pocket before he started unbuttoning his cuffs. He quickly rolled up his left sleeve, then noticed Larken's eyes on his forearms. He took his time rolling up the right one, smirking as he did.

He wordlessly fired up the hover, and they shot into the air. Larken didn't bother looking out the window at the theater fading into the distance, the place probably ruined for her forever. Soren didn't try to break the heavy silence, but her mood seemed to improve the further away they got, so he was content to sit in the quiet. It was like this unspoken agreement between them, one where they didn't force each other to talk if they didn't want to. But, even though they didn't say anything, they were somehow still communicating. Every time he raised an eyebrow at her and she rolled her eyes, or each smile she gave him that he grimaced at, it was that silence that drew them together. It was also that silence that Hinlee had noticed and asked him about more than once, much to his annoyance.

They were halfway into their hour-long trip back when Larken pulled her communicator out of his jacket. She messed with it for a second before it started ringing loudly. Soren glanced over and saw the white letters that spelled out VALLEN for the outgoing call before he answered.

"What?"

"How you feelin', faker?" Larken asked, her voice raw from

crying. Even with her eyes puffy and her face blotchy, she was still the most beautiful thing he had ever seen.

"Fine. How was the show?" Larken parted her lips to answer, but no sound came out. Soren's hand found its way back to hers as General Maxwell asked, "Larken? You there?"

"Yeah." She squeezed his hand. She took another second and then admitted, "I met Fisher Fillmar tonight."

This time, it was General Maxwell who didn't say anything for a long time.

"Vallen?"

"What did he say to you?" he asked, his voice more cautious than Soren had ever heard it.

"A lot, actually." Larken squeezed the life from his fingers, but he didn't dare pull away.

"Look, Larken, I hate to ask this, but did anyone—"

"Soren did. I don't know about anyone else. Not that it would be hard to tell with us standing right next to each other."

Muffled grumbling sounded from the device, too garbled for Soren to make out. There was more silence, and then General Maxwell asked, "Are you okay?"

Larken looked up at Soren with glossy eyes. He nodded, telling her that she could do it, she could say the truth, and no matter what it was, he would be right there. She took a deep breath and said "I'm—"

The aircraft jolted as whatever had been shot at them collided with the gravity booster under Larken's feet. She rammed into her harness as Soren tried to rectify the sudden loss of altitude. Larken screamed, and General Maxwell demanded to know what was happening. Soren pulled his hand from Larken's, hating himself as he did so, and started trying to correct the situation. They were falling, *fast*, and he couldn't see another aircraft for miles.

Larken panicked, shouting into her communicator, "The aircraft was shot at! We're falling!"

"Wha—you—I—cut—" General Maxwell's voice cut in and out as the screen on the device flickered.

Larken was in a full-blown panic and kept screaming into her communicator. Soren tried everything he could think of to slow the descent, but nothing worked. They were going to crash, they were going to crash *hard*, and there was nothing he could do about it.

General Maxwell shouted, "LARK—" before the device died altogether.

Soren unbuckled his harness, thinking fast, and pulled Larken as close as she could get. She shrieked into his shoulder, and he worried that he would never be able to get her into another aircraft again…if they lived.

He put his hand on the back of her head, murmuring into her hair, saying whatever he thought might help. Her panic didn't subside, and he chanced a glance out the windshield. They had split seconds before they crashed, and Soren closed his eyes. He wrapped his arms around her tighter and pressed his lips to her temple. He was probably going to die, and the smell of grapefruit, and her warmth, would be the last things he would ever know.

Maxim, let her live. Please, let her live…

The crash was a surreal mix of crunching metal and skidding across the earth. Larken still hadn't stopped screaming, and Soren thanked Maxim for every second she did. It didn't matter if he lost his hearing, as long as she *lived*. Every scream was another second she was breathing, and he would do whatever it took to keep it that way.

When the aircraft eventually stopped moving, Larken had been reduced to a mess of trembling sobs. Each breath she took was a wet-sounding wheeze, and she had a death grip on his shirt. Soren rubbed his hand up and down her arm, while simultaneously trying to unbuckle her harness. When it started to sound like Larken might be sick, he pressed his lips to her ear, saying, "Larken, we made it. We're alive. *It's over.*"

She shook her head, not willing to believe him.

"*Shhh,* it's over. It's over, Larken."

Larken shuddered again, her whole body convulsing like it was trying to purge her fear.

Soren lifted her face and made her look at him. Tears streaked down her cheeks, and her eyes darted around in a panicked frenzy. "Look at me."

She met his eyes, trying but failing to gulp down air.

"Look at me," he said again. "I'm not going anywhere." Soren waited a few seconds before adding, "Take a breath."

She tried but dissolved into a coughing fit.

"With me." Soren made sure she was watching him when he opened his mouth and took a slow, deep breath.

Larken still shook, her lungs hitching several times as she tried to breathe with him. Soren repeated the process until her severe tremors turned to mild shaking, and then asked, "Are you able to fight?"

"W-what?" she hiccupped.

"There wasn't an aircraft near us, so whoever shot us down is somewhere around here. *Can you fight?*"

Larken stiffened her spine the best she could and answered, "Yes."

Soren smiled at her. Yes, she could fight. It was the one thing that General Maxwell had ensured that she learned, to not die lying down. Soren stared at her for a moment, knowing that they very well could die tonight and that he should tell her *everything*. He should tell her that she drove him crazy, that he hated the music she listened to with a passion but could never get the melodies out of his head. He should tell her that whenever she was near him, he didn't know if he should pull out all his hair or pull her into his arms. Soren should tell her all the times he had come so close to kissing her, and how she made his heart feel like it was going to explode and stop all at once. He knew that if there was ever a time to be honest with her, this was it, but he couldn't.

Soren didn't want her to think that his confession was a good-bye, and being that honest was still too big a step for him to take. Angry with himself, he pulled open a hatch in the dashboard and took two handguns from it. He lifted his hips, sticking one in the waistband of his pants at his back, and held the other tightly with his hand. Larken had already taken what she wanted from the dashboard as well, cocking the handgun, and then nodded at him.

Soren threw his shoulder into the door, having to help force it open. He crept out of the aircraft, trying not to cough as he was assaulted with the smoke and fumes that the thing emitted. On the plus side, they would hopefully have a few seconds of cover while Soren helped Larken out. Turning, he reached for her, and she placed her hand in his, the jacket sleeve falling far enough to cover both of their hands. Soren reached for her with the hand his gun was in, trying to help her over the seat, when a shot was fired.

A burning pain exploded across his abdomen, as his right side screamed in agony. Soren grunted and fell to his right knee, trying to breathe past the fire in his lungs. Quieter than a mouse, Larken hopped from the aircraft and pushed him to the ground. She was practically on top of him when she put her lips to his ear and asked, "Can you move?"

Soren sucked in a breath through his teeth and grunted, *"Yeah."*

He tried to ignore the blood creeping across the white of his shirt and let Larken help maneuver him away from the direction where the bullet had come from. Gone was the terrified mess that Soren had held so close only moments ago, and in her place, a calculated soldier that had no intentions of dying.

"We can assume that Vallen called for help," Larken whispered. "He no doubt activated the tracking device in my communicator, so he would know the general area that we crashed in. Now, it's only a matter of staying alive until we're found."

"Easier said than done," Soren said with a wince. "You're not the one that was shot."

Larken's eyes danced as she looked at him. "Don't be such a baby."

"Oh, just you wait. When we get back, I'm going to—"

Larken gasped, cutting Soren off. She was pulled to her feet by a man about their age, dressed all in black with an open military-issued helmet. She winced as he held her upright by her hair. In the fading smoke, Soren could see he had grey eyes that glinted in the moonlight, and they danced as they looked at him bleeding on the ground. Larken whimpered and he yanked her even closer, making her drop her gun, a sick grin crossing his face as he did. Soren felt his blood boil, and he tried to get to his feet.

"Ah, ah, ah," the man chastised with a thick, smoky accent. "Not so fast." He took a step back, pulling Larken with him, and pointed a gun at her jaw. "One more move and the girl gets it."

Soren snarled, his bullet wound burning more than it should be. He welcomed the pain, thankful that it wasn't infused with valerian extract, like the one that had hit Larken. At least this way, he would be awake and get a chance to try and fight back.

A faint crackle could be heard, and then a murmured voice. The guy cocked his head to the left like it would help him hear whoever was talking better, and said, "Yeah, I got the girl." There were more staticky murmurs, and then the man asked, "What do you want me to do with the boyfriend?"

"Let him live!" Larken pleaded in a strangled cry. "Please, I'll go willingly, just let him live!"

He pulled Larken's hair again, making her yelp, and pressed his nose to her neck. Soren could see the twisted look on the man's face as he said, "I don't care if you're willing or not, love, you're coming either way. You'll have to do a lot more if you want him to keep his life."

"Don't even—"

Soren's snarl was cut short as Larken agreed, "Whatever it takes."

The man's grey eyes glinted. "Is that so?"

Soren glared daggers at the guy but had to force his eyes to stay on his face, as Larken moved her hand to the pocket of his jacket.

"*Yes,*" she whimpered, still playing the role of the scared, helpless girl. "I'll do whatever you want if it means he can live."

The man chuckled. "You always so willing, or does being held at gunpoint get your blood going?"

There was a click, and Soren let his eyes fall to the gun that now dug into the man's side.

"You tell me," Larken snarled. "Are you suddenly all hot and bothered?"

Soren gripped his gun once more and aimed it at the guy's head. The man pulled his gun away from Larken, lifting his finger from the trigger as a show of peace. Then he let go of her hair, and she stumbled away from him, losing a heel in the grass. The man scowled at them for only a moment, before he dropped and leaped behind the aircraft. More shots fired in their direction, and Larken tried to cover Soren with her small form.

Gritting his teeth, Soren tried to suppress his cry of pain as he rolled and threw himself over her. He seethed, *"Not a chance!"*

Soren stared down at Larken, her glare fierce enough to make General Maxwell proud. The urge to kiss her was so strong that he almost couldn't help himself as he smirked down at her. She only rolled her eyes and scoffed, *"You idiot."*

"What?" he rasped. "I thought girls liked grand romantic gestures?"

"Bleeding out and *dying* on top of a girl is *not* a grand romantic gesture. It just makes you stupid."

The chuckle that fell from his lips sent stabs of pain through his abdomen. He cupped her face as he asked, "Are you still okay?"

They could hear footsteps, and Larken sent a panicked look in their direction. The assailants were calling to each other, working out a plan as they approached. Larken's eyes shot back to his, and they were wide as she hurriedly said, "I have to tell you something."

"Wha—"

"These men aren't Faithfuls. I should have told you sooner, but I —" Larken swallowed hard. "That doesn't matter now. But, I know for a fact that these aren't—"

More gunfire cut Larken off, and she grunted as Soren let himself drop onto her, his stomach sinking as her words settled over him. He could hear her struggling to breathe under him, but she would thank him later when she wasn't shot. Thinking fast and pushing her admission to the back of his mind until this was over, he hissed, "Grab the gun in my waistband."

Soren had to lift off her a little so she could reach the gun. When her fingers closed around it, Soren rolled off of her. She took aim and hit one of the guys in the ankle, causing him to crumple to the ground as he screamed in agony. She fired again and had another guy dropping his gun as she hit his wrist. They didn't know how many enemies there were, but Larken could handle herself, and she had two other guns with her that Soren knew of. Determining that she had control of the situation, for now, Soren made his way around the aircraft in search of the guy that had man-handled Larken.

After stumbling a few times, Soren managed to get to his feet and rounded the aircraft. His stomach fell when he found that the guy was nowhere to be found. Knowing that there was no sense standing there and thinking about what he would do if he ever saw him again, Soren turned and made his way back to Larken.

She was gone too, having abandoned the spot where he had left her, along with her other shoe, and charged the men that shot at her. Larken looked like the living embodiment of a long-forgotten warrior goddess as she took her anger out on the men that had almost killed them. Soren hobbled out to her, wanting to help, holding his side as he did. Larken dodged bullets, fired her own, and was no doubt griping about not being better prepared.

There were three assailants left that Soren could see, and four moaning on the ground. He had no idea if there were any more, or where they might come from. Thoughts of hanging back and giving Larken cover or joining her in the fray warred in his mind. But one lucky shot that grazed Larken's exposed calf had him charging in, completely forgetting his own wound.

Larken cried out and stumbled, leaving her open for the man that rushed to her. She had just enough time to look up at her assailant before he lifted his rifle and knocked the butt of it against her temple. Larken collapsed to the ground without a sound, and Soren roared as he shot at the man. The first bullet hit him in the chest, the second in the gut. Soren was already onto the next one, knowing that he wouldn't need the remaining ten bullets in his gun.

He quickly took out the last two guys, not even bothering to watch them fall to the ground. Soren could only focus on Larken as he dropped to her side. She was still breathing, but it sounded ragged. He looked her over for any other wounds than the two he witnessed, and when he was satisfied that there weren't any, he reached for her face. A trail of blood trickled from her hairline down the side of her face, staining the blonde curls that were falling from the pins.

His fingers trembled as he touched her, reliving the last time he had found her like this. There had been so much blood, and he hadn't been able to wake her up then. Soren shook her slightly, whispering her name. Larken's eyelashes fluttered but didn't open. She looked so small and pale, laying there covered in his jacket in the dark grass. Sighing, Soren looked to the sky, praying that she had been right about help finding them soon.

Another shot was fired off, though it missed him. Soren raised his gun and took out the last few men. He didn't even bat an eye as the last one stopped breathing. If he were in better condition, he would have tried to question one, but his side protested any movement. And Larken... He shook his head, chasing away the thought.

Time passed slowly, and soon his wound throbbed and burned again. Larken started to shiver, and Soren knew that they couldn't wait around all night. Pulling her towards him, Soren took her in his arms and forced his feet to bear his weight. He staggered a few times as he willed his legs to cooperate, and whatever clotting his wound had managed was now gone. Pushing through the pain and the dizziness, Soren took a step, and then another. He had made it back to where Larken had left her shoes when he heard the engines. Soon floodlights chased the darkness from the field they were in, and Soren thought his knees might give out in relief.

Around twenty aircraft landed in the open field, some with the crossed swords insignia of the Military District, others he recognized from the base, and the rest he had to assume were from Base 13 since it was closest.

General Maxwell was the first one out, leaping from one of the aircraft from the Manor, and Soren knew that he, more likely than not, had probably knocked out a few medics before being allowed to leave. Levi and Loxly were out next, jumping from the Arsene, and were followed by more faces that faded into the background. General Maxwell reached Soren first, his eyes hard and lined with silver as he took in his adoptive daughter, who was still unconscious in his arms.

Something passed between the two men, and instead of trying to take Larken from him, General Maxwell called, "Out of the way, these two need a medic!"

Loxly and Levi were soon flanking Soren, but he refused their help as he carried Larken to the aircraft that General Maxwell indicated. People were rushing around, already preparing stretchers for them. Levi jumped into the fray, pulling supplies and filling syringes with unknown antibacterial substances that Soren didn't want to think about. There was another medic with dark caramel skin and wavy black hair that General Maxwell barked orders to, and Soren assumed that he would be caring for Larken.

Gently laying her across one of the stretchers, Larken's lashes fluttered again. Her eyes opened briefly, and she smiled at him after her gaze fell briefly to a soldier rushing past. Her lips parted, and Soren bent close so he could hear her. Shallow breaths puffed against his neck as she whispered, "Told you they'd come."

Soren pulled back just enough to cup her cheek. He noticed her necklace was still around her neck, and he smiled despite his pain. "Yes, you did."

Levi barged in, forcing Soren onto the stretcher reserved for him. Ripping his shirt, the blond looked at the wound and grunted. Looking up at him, Levi apologized, saying, "Sorry, friend." Then he stuck Soren with a needle, pushing the contents into his body.

Eyes growing heavy, Soren grunted, "That hurt, you no good pretty—"

Then the darkness swallowed him before he could finish.

CHAPTER 32

Larken stretched, her back popping as she did. Soren grimaced at her side, and she pushed him further by cracking her knuckles as well. He stood and loomed over her, glaring at her in the way only he could. His brown hair fell into his eyes, and he didn't bother to push it out of the way. It had gotten longer in the week that he had spent recuperating in the medic building, and it somehow managed to make him look even more handsome.

Larken raised her eyebrow in a challenge, daring him to say something and open himself up to a joke about squeamishness. His jaw ticked, and he took a step away. Larken beamed at him, rubbing in her victory as he went back to his own stretches. He lifted one arm behind his head and pulled at the elbow, making his biceps bulge. Soren sent Larken a challenging smirk of his own, and this time it was her turn to look away.

Face hot, Larken dared another peek over her shoulder. Soren was now on the ground, stretching his legs, making sure that he was ready for their workout. The week he had spent in the medic building had gone by in a blur of training and spending all of her free time there. Larken had done whatever she could think of to help make him more comfortable. Making playlists of songs that he sang in the tabernacle, purchasing books and sending them to his new communicator so he wouldn't be bored, even bringing him food so he wouldn't have to eat what was being served in the cafeteria. He often complained about the amount of soup that she brought him, but the hearty broth kept his weight up, and he always ate every single spoonful.

The bullet wound wasn't that big of a fix; it was the infused monkshood that kept Soren under constant surveillance. With the adrenaline pumping through his veins that night, it was a wonder that he didn't have a stroke then and there. But, he had somehow managed to pull through, with nothing but a scar to remind him that it had happened. Larken had heard Hinlee giving him a hard time about the thing one evening, but she didn't know about Soren's distrust of medics. Larken had kept her mouth shut through the whole of the conversation, making herself a promise that none of her squad members would ever receive another injury like that because of her.

Needing to pull herself from the dark turn her thoughts had taken, Larken synced up her communicator with the speakers in the gym, blaring Shadric Barlow just to get a rise out of Soren. She laughed as he grumbled behind her and then took off at a slow jog. Larken wasted no time catching up, and they fell into silence as they ran around the gym. They didn't talk about what had happened at the opera, or in the garden, or what was said before the crash. It was like a weight that had settled between them that they were both too stubborn to try and move.

There had been one night though, shortly after Soren had been admitted, when she had been forced to crawl into his bed and hide from the speculations that had started circulating after the excitement of their crash died down. Photographs had been taken, and every reporter on every major channel thought it was their duty to add their thoughts on why the Military Sweetheart would resemble a famous Star that had left the stage to direct what happened on it instead. She had buried her face into his chest as he pulled the covers up over her head, the silent promises he had made her in the aircraft still staying silent as he kept them.

But now that he was out of that room and back in the dorm, Larken was almost tempted to try and push that weight a little. She would never forget the way he had held her as they crashed to the earth or the things he had whispered in her ear. She had wanted so many times to ask if he had meant any of those things, or if he just thought that saying them would help calm her. She felt hollow whenever she told herself it was that latter, but her heart hoped that when he said that he would always be there and that he would never let her go, no matter what happened to him, that he really meant it.

They jogged for about three more songs before building up to a steady run. Soren was already sweating, and she wanted to remind him not to push himself too hard, but she knew he wouldn't listen even if she did. He was a soldier, and he would push himself until the day he died. It was something that Larken both loved and hated about him. Not that she could judge him for it when she was the exact same way.

Larken had to eventually stop, lying about a stitch in her side to get him to take a break. Soren grumbled about stopping, claiming that if she hadn't slacked off while he was at the medic building, she wouldn't be in such poor shape. She let him huff and puff about it, his eyes not able to hide his relief at finally stopping.

"*So*," Larken tentatively asked, already knowing the answer, "does this mean we can be done for today?"

"Did you turn senile as well as lazy while I was held up?"

Larken shrugged. "It was worth a shot."

Soren made his way over to his water bottle as the song changed again. A booming bass filled the room and threatened to shake the gym floor. Larken lost herself in the music for a moment, letting the sad lyrics paired with the upbeat tune twist her heart. Lost in the words, Larken walked over to her sword, which rested by her own water bottle, and gripped the cold hilt. Moving onto one of the mats, she started warming up her limbs with a basic maneuver that Vallen had taught her. It forced her muscles to flex and loosen as she stretched, reached, and arced the blade. She was one with her sword, and one with the music. It wasn't until her blade collided with a glaive that she realized how distracted she had become.

"I've been calling you. Get your head out of the clouds."

"Sorry," she apologized, dropping her sword and gripping the hilt with both hands behind her back

"What's with you today?" Soren gave her a once-over and asked, "Is it your shoulder? Or a headache?"

"No," she insisted. "It's been over a week, Soren. Give it a rest, my head is fine."

He looked at her like he didn't believe her, obviously not giving her the same courtesy of ignoring her problems as she gave him.

Sighing, Larken admitted, "It's the song, it always makes me sad."

"If it upsets you, then why do you have it?"

"That's why I have it, because it makes me feel something."

Soren grunted and rolled his eyes. "Whatever."

Larken just shrugged her shoulders and then restarted the set that Soren had interrupted. The music still played, and she tried to center herself again.

"Does upbeat music always bring you to tears?" Soren teased. She shot him a look, and he smirked, not willing to pass up the opportunity to harass her.

"*No*, it's the lyrics," Larken said, giving him an eye roll of her own. "*You are hot, but I am too, and now I'll never be lonely because of you.*" She shrugged. "It's sad."

Soren grunted again.

"It is!" she insisted.

"I don't care."

"Then why did you bring it up?" Larken suspected it was because he was already exhausted and had been looking for any excuse not to move, but she didn't say anything.

"Fine," he said, lowering his glaive and turning to her. He tried to hide a wince as he did, telling her that her assumption was probably right. "Why is it sad?"

"His heart was broken," she answered. "And instead of trying to heal, he's holding onto his hurt and looking for resolution in the arms of whoever's available." Soren looked at her long enough for her to squirm and ask, "What?"

"Have you ever considered," he leaned into his glaive to get a better look at her, "and this is a stretch here, that maybe it's just a song?"

Larken scoffed and turned away from him, unable to drown out his deep laughter. She also couldn't help the small smile that tugged at the corner of her lips at the sound. It was something that she would never grow tired of and thought it was cut off much too quickly by his wailing communicator. Hers went off too, and even though it barely made a sound, it moved on the gym floor by her things, the vibrations pushing it around.

The fake sirens were cut short as Soren checked the notification. He was all seriousness when he said, "We're needed back at the dorm."

"I hope everyone's okay." Larken's voice sounded small as she voiced her worry.

Soren gave her that same look that she had seen in the aircraft, the one that said he wouldn't let go of her. It gave her enough bravery to gather her things and make her way back to the dorm with him.

General Maxwell was waiting for them in the dorm when they arrived, along with all the other members of Squad 19. Soren knew that something was wrong just by the way the man's jaw was set, and he had to fight the urge to pull Larken to him to protect her from whatever it was the General had to say.

She noticed it, too, because she rushed up to him and willingly gave him her sword as she asked, "What's wrong? Is Wardell—"

"Everyone at home is fine."

Larken still looked at him skeptically, not believing him. "Vallen, what aren't you telling me?"

General Maxwell took a moment to look each of them in the eye. When his gaze met Soren's, it was almost like he knew what the man was going to say, and he readied himself for the blow.

"I want to personally thank you all for making Larken's time here enjoyable."

"What do you mean *time here*?" Hinlee asked, defensive, and tears already gathering in her eyes. "Larken is still here." Her voice cracked as she asked, "Isn't she?"

General Maxwell sighed deeply, and that was when they all knew. Larken started shaking her head as he said, "With the constant threats on Miss Hale's life since joining the military, the Luminary has determined that her presence is bringing unnecessary dangers to Base 14, as well as Squad 19." Larken choked as her mentor continued, "As of right now, Miss Hale has been honorably discharged and is being sent home where she can be monitored and help eradicate the threat that the Faithfuls are responsible for."

Hinlee covered a sob with her hand, not wanting to make it harder for Larken. Brecker tried to put his arm around her, but she pushed it away and rushed to Larken. Levi set his jaw, looking at the ground with hard eyes as Loxly pushed past him. Soon Larken was wrapped up in his arms as well, that emotionless mask that Soren had seen too often on her face now firmly back in place.

She took a slow, shuddering breath, and then said quietly, "I guess I'll go get my things."

General Maxwell shook his head. "Your necessities are already packed and waiting in the aircraft."

Soren knew that he had wanted to make things easier on Larken, but this was too soon. It was too soon and there wasn't enough time to say what needed to be said. Soren wasn't ready, and it could very well cost him everything.

Larken nodded and then turned to Hinlee. She wrapped her arms around her and whispered something in her ear. Then, after kissing her on the cheek, Larken turned and did the same to Loxly. Loxly made no jokes about finally getting his kiss, or Larken finally realizing that she loved him; he only stood there as serious as a soldier who learned that his squad member wouldn't be coming home again.

Larken moved on to Brecker, who picked her up as she hugged him. He whispered to her as much as she murmured to him, no doubt thanking her for giving Hinlee the one thing she had always wanted—a sister. Then it was Levi's turn, and he held her longer than any of the others had. Hinlee quietly sobbed into Brecker's chest as they watched Levi do the one thing he had never wanted to do again: say goodbye to someone he loved. He nodded as Larken spoke softly and then he pressed his forehead to hers, closing his eyes so his emotion wouldn't show.

Before Soren knew it, Larken stood in front of him, looking just as awkward and lost as ever. Her masked slipped a little now that she had her back to everyone, showing parts of her that only he had ever seen. She looked up at him, her teal eyes swimming with unshed tears. Soren couldn't bring himself to reach out to her, feeling like he was back in that aircraft, not willing to tell her goodbye yet. Little by little the mask slipped away until a single tear rolled down her cheek.

Larken took a shallow breath and asked, "Did you mean it?"

"Mean what?" His throat felt tight, and his voice came out as a rasp.

"What you said, when we were—" She looked down at her shaking hands. "Did you mean it?"

His stomach tightened as he realized that she had heard him over her terrified shrieks. Balling his fists, Soren frowned and gave a single nod. It was all he could offer her.

She nodded in return, then met his eyes again. Her lips parted and she said, "Ask me to stay."

Soren's heart stopped.

Larken took a small step forward. "Tell me that none of this matters and that you don't care about any of it. Ask me to stay, Soren."

Soren couldn't breathe as she stared up at him with those doe eyes of hers.

"Ask me to stay, and I will."

Soren willed his jaw to move, pleaded with his hands to grab onto her and never let her go, but nothing happened. He was as unmovable as stone as he stared at her. She had so much hope in her eyes, hope that he would be the man that she somehow always knew that he was. And with each second that passed where he did nothing but stare at her, Larken broke a little more, her arms wrapping around her middle as she tried not to crumple in on herself. Soren looked deep into her eyes, telling her everything that he couldn't, hoping that she would understand that he couldn't, that he was still too broken. He wasn't ready, and he didn't know if he would ever be. Then Soren thought that maybe she should leave, that maybe it would be better for her to find what she needed instead of staying here and hoping for something that he might never be able to give her.

Her teal eyes cracked as she took a step back and nodded. She turned and walked to Vallen, not looking back at him once, each step putting a nail in his heart that he knew could never be removed. He was damaged, and he knew he had just damaged Larken as well. She deserved so much better than him, and Soren hated himself for admitting it. The door shut quieter than it should have behind the two of them, taking Larken out of his life forever.

Everyone went their own separate ways after that. Hinlee dissolved into tears, and Brecker held her on the couch. Loxly left the dorm, needing to either shoot something or try and out-fly his hurt. Levi said nothing as he locked himself in his room, and Soren didn't know when the field-medic might come back out. Following his Second's lead, Soren shut himself in his room as well, then collapsed onto his bed. He closed his eyes and saw her sitting there, hair done up and a tear running down her cheek. Her voice was a soft rasp as what she said stabbed him in the gut.

The words that had once put color into my life are now drowning me and I cannot reach the surface. How dare you make my heart feel for yours. How dare you force me to feel the emotions of bitter death.

TO BE CONTINUED IN BOOK 2...

ABOUT THE AUTHOR

C.C. Urie is a Multi-Genre Christian Author who lives in Michigan. Her whole world revolves around her family, and her favorite time of year is when the leaves start to change. She's always had a love for reading, and enjoys sharing her stories with others. Her true calling in life is using her books to help spread the Good Word and show others how God has changed her life for the better.

OTHER BOOKS BY THIS AUTHOR

The Divine Courage Trilogy

Defender

Betrayer

Vanquisher

Hearts of Deadgrove

Southern Charm